COLLECTOR'S EDITION

CONTENTS

ADVENTURE 79
Airing Out Aerodactyl 13

ADVENTURE 80
Draggin' in Dragonair 29

ADVENTURE 81
Aerodactyl Redux.. 43

ADVENTURE 82
Eradicate Raticate!....................................... 57

ADVENTURE 83
Bang the Drum, Slowbro............................ 71

ADVENTURE 84
Clefabulous Clefable 85

ADVENTURE 85
Gimme Shellder.. 106

ADVENTURE 86
Double Dragonair.. 129

ADVENTURE 87
Rhyhorn Rising.. 143

ADVENTURE 88
The Beedrill All and End All 157

ADVENTURE 89
The Might of...Metapod?!........................... 171

ADVENTURE 90
The Legend.. 187

GOLD & SILVER

ADVENTURE 91
Murkrow Row 223

ADVENTURE 92
Who Gives a Hoothoot 237

ADVENTURE 93
Sneasel Sneak Attack 251

ADVENTURE 94
Elekid Incorporated.................................... 264

ADVENTURE 95
Stantler by Me... 281

ADVENTURE 96
Number One Donphan................................ 302

ADVENTURE 97
Bellsprout Rout 321

ADVENTURE 98
Totodile Rock.. 337

ADVENTURE 99
Sunkern Treasure 351

ADVENTURE 100
Into the Unown... 368

ADVENTURE 101
Teddiursa's Picnic 385

ADVENTURE 102
Ursaring Major.. 405

ADVENTURE 103
You Ain't Nothin' but a Houndour 421

ADVENTURE 104
The Ariados up There 439

ADVENTURE 105
Smeargle Smudge 455

ADVENTURE 106
How Do You Do, Sudowoodo? 472

ADVENTURE 107
Gligar Glide 486

ADVENTURE 108
Quilava Quandary 514

ADVENTURE 109
Ampharos Amore 527

ADVENTURE 110
Piloswine Whine 541

ADVENTURE 111
Tyranitar War.. 558

ADVENTURE 112
Raise the Red Gyarados.............................. 584

ADVENTURE 113
Delibird Delivery, Part 1 598

ADVENTURE 114
Delibird Delivery, Part 2 612

ADVENTURE 115
Forretress of Solitude................................. 626

ADVENTURE 116
Rock, Paper...Scizor 640

COLLECTOR'S EDITION

03

Story by HIDENORI KUSAKA Art by MATO

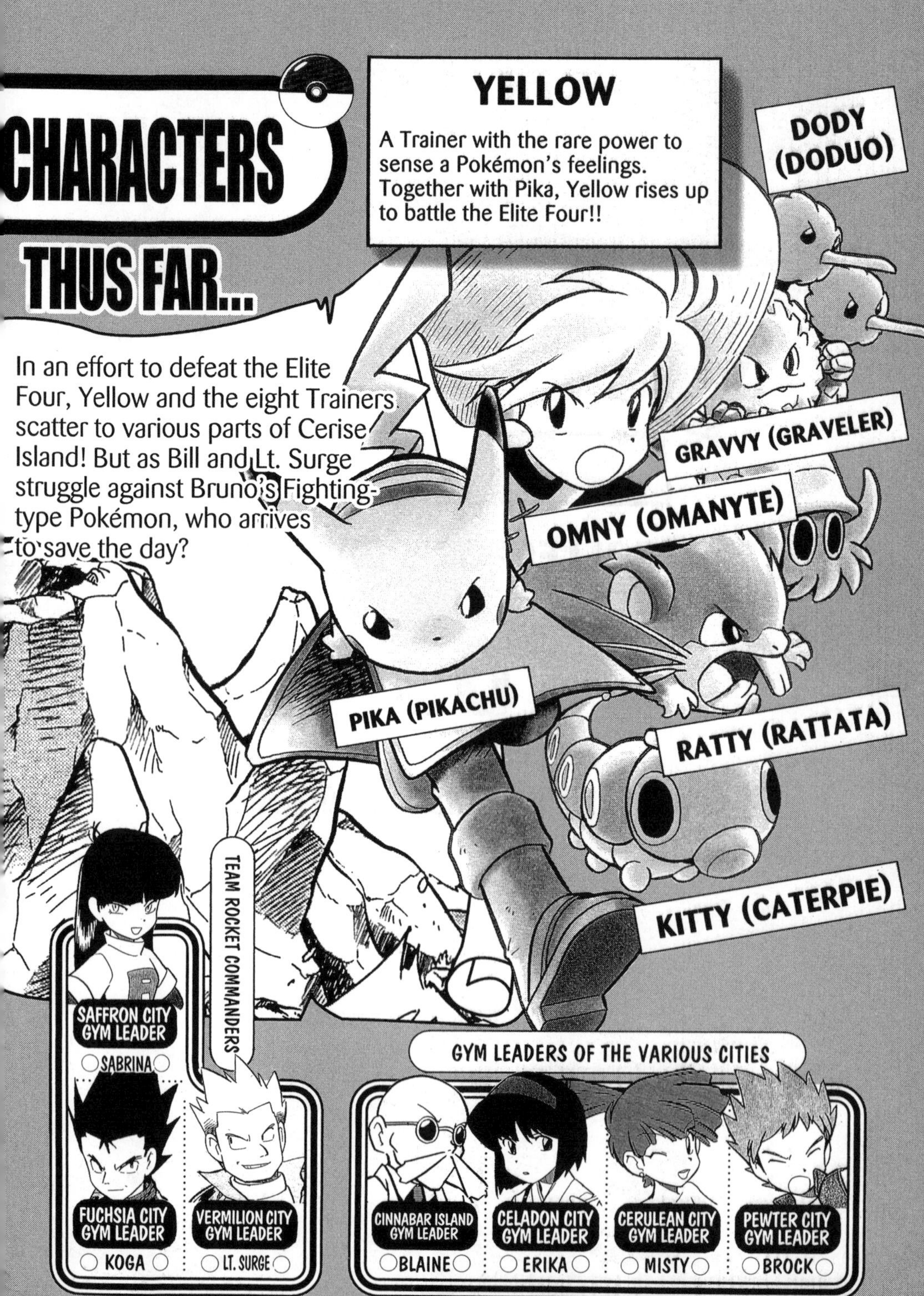
CHARACTERS
THUS FAR...
In an effort to defeat the Elite Four, Yellow and the eight Trainers scatter to various parts of Cerise Island! But as Bill and Lt. Surge struggle against Bruno's Fighting-type Pokémon, who arrives to save the day?
YELLOW
A Trainer with the rare power to sense a Pokémon's feelings. Together with Pika, Yellow rises up to battle the Elite Four!!
DODY (DODUO)
GRAVVY (GRAVELER)
OMNY (OMANYTE)
PIKA (PIKACHU)
RATTY (RATTATA)
KITTY (CATERPIE)
TEAM ROCKET COMMANDERS
SAFFRON CITY GYM LEADER
SABRINA
FUCHSIA CITY GYM LEADER
KOGA
VERMILION CITY GYM LEADER
LT. SURGE
GYM LEADERS OF THE VARIOUS CITIES
CINNABAR ISLAND GYM LEADER
BLAINE
CELADON CITY GYM LEADER
ERIKA
CERULEAN CITY GYM LEADER
MISTY
PEWTER CITY GYM LEADER
BROCK

GREEN
A Trainer who uses a Blastoise. Has an easygoing personality.
MAIN JOURNEY
None other than Red! Overjoyed by Red's safe return, Yellow's celebration is cut short when a torrent of underground rapids washes away both Yellow and Blaine. What will happen to Yellow?!
BLUE
Red's rival. Locked in a battle against his archenemy Agatha.
RED
Had previously been missing but returns in time to help his friends in danger!!
ELITE FOUR
A highly skilled group with abilities surpassing even those of the Gym Leaders. They are master Trainers who favor Dragon-, Ghost-, Fighting- and Ice-Type Pokémon, respectively.
LANCE
AGATHA
BRUNO
LORELEI

Message from
Hidenori Kusaka

Just like that, this manga is at volume 7, which will take us to the climax of the second chapter of this adventure! How will the final battle against the Elite Four end…?! For the Pokémon and their Trainers alike, this will be the final battle to test their grit! Keep a close eye on Yellow's team battles!

–2000

Message from
Mato

As I play the new *Pokémon Gold* and *Pokémon Silver*, I'm continually surprised at how rich the gameplay is! Daily and nightly events, mysterious packages and interconnectivity with printers–there are so many things I want to try out every time I play it. But thanks to the many side-quests, my Pokédex is far from complete…or is it? How is everyone's capture rate??

–2000

WHRRRRRR
CERU-LEAN CITY

VSH
THAT HAUNTER'S TRYING TO GET IN THE WAY OF MY STARMIE?! I DON'T THINK SO!!

VV
M
GNG

GUILLOTINE!
ZWOK
STARMIE'S SENDING A MESSAGE TO CERISE ISLAND RIGHT NOW, ERIKA.
THANK YOU, MISTY.
TUP
DONK

BUT WAIT A MOMENT.
THERE IS MORE.
?!

DO YOU NOTICE SOMETHING ABOUT THE NAMES OF THE CITIES THAT THE ELITE FOUR AND THEIR ARMIES HAVE DESCENDED UPON?

OH! OF COURSE... THE **GYMS** !!

VIRIDIAN CITY, SAFFRON CITY, VERMILION CITY, FUCHSIA CITY, CINNABAR ...
HM?

INDEED. THE CITIES UNDER ATTACK AT THIS MOMENT, INCLUDING MY OWN, PEWTER, CERULEAN AND CELADON, ARE ALL CITIES WITH POKÉMON GYMS!

79 Airing Out Aerodactyl

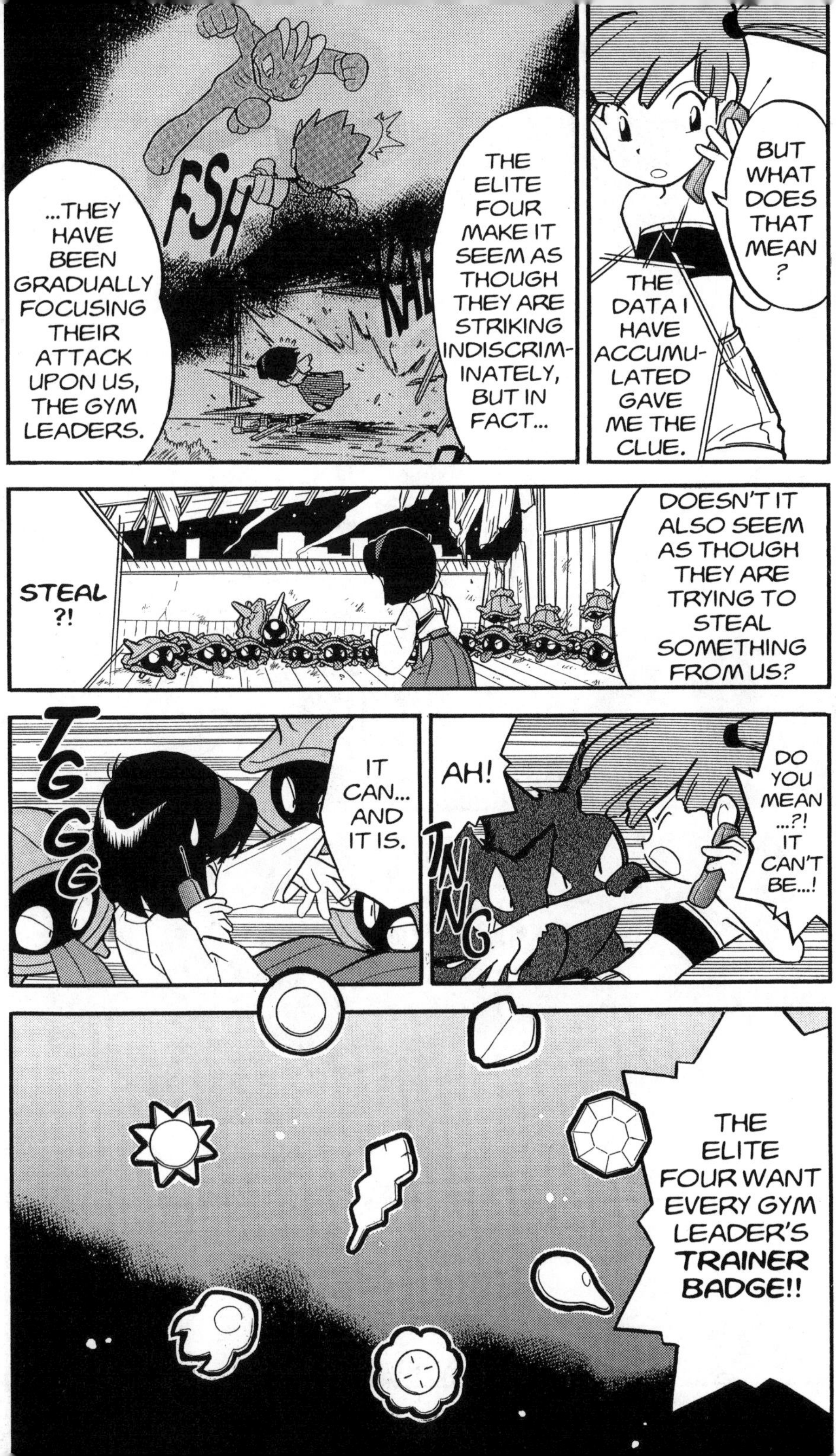

DOESN'T IT ALSO SEEM AS THOUGH THEY ARE TRYING TO STEAL SOMETHING FROM US?

STEAL?!

DO YOU MEAN...?! IT CAN'T BE...!

AH!

TNNG

IT CAN... AND IT IS.

TGGG

THE ELITE FOUR WANT EVERY GYM LEADER'S **TRAINER BADGE**!!

STAR-
MIE!
HURRY!!

SHP
AH!
SHP
NO! MY
BADGE!

ZIP
GLOW

PINNNG
!

COME ON...
GET THIS
MESSAGE
TO THE GUYS
ON CERISE
ISLAND!!

SSSHHH

NNH...

Y...
YELLOW!
YELLOW!
NN...
NNN
...

BLINK

OH...!
USH

YELLOW...? ARE...ARE YOU REALLY ...?
SSSHHH

...
PLEASE... DON'T ASK NOW.

LET'S JUST SAY... I DON'T FEEL LIKE MYSELF WITHOUT IT!
HUG

EH?

RED'S POKÉDEX... AND MY SKETCH-BOOK... THEY'RE GONE!

SSSHHH
I MUST HAVE DROPPED THEM WHEN WE GOT SWEPT AWAY!

RED!! WE GOT SO CLOSE!! AND YET...
BAM
BAM

SSSHHH
HWOOO
FLIPFLIP

ALL RIGHT, YELLOW.
I WON'T ASK ANY QUESTIONS NOW.
HM... LOOKS AS THOUGH WE'VE BEEN SWEPT DOWN PRETTY FAR...

THE ENEMY MAY BE GETTING CLOSE...
THIS REMINDS ME OF AN OLD RIDDLE. DO YOU KNOW THIS ONE, YELLOW—WHAT HAS ONLY ONE ENTRANCE BUT THREE EXITS?
...
!
HMMM
IS IT A SWEATER?
YOU'RE GOOD. BUT NOW...

...IF WE ASK...
TONG
WHAT HAS ONLY ONE EN-TRANCE...
...BUT NO EXITS, WOULD YOU SAY.... CERISE ISLAND?
!

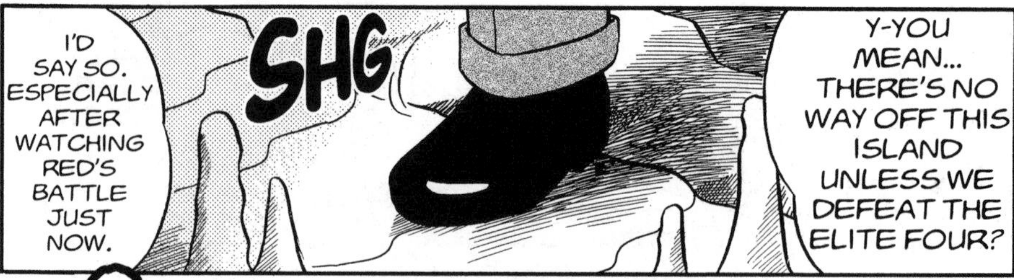
Y-YOU MEAN... THERE'S NO WAY OFF THIS ISLAND UNLESS WE DEFEAT THE ELITE FOUR?
SHG
I'D SAY SO. ESPECIALLY AFTER WATCHING RED'S BATTLE JUST NOW.

HMM. THE DEEPER WE GO, THE DARKER IT GETS. IF ONLY WE HAD A LIGHT...

OKAY, GROWLITHE!
BOOM

POOF
GRROW

PERFECT. NOW—HURRY! OR ELSE CERULEAN, PEWTER AND THE OTHER CITIES WILL BE DESTROYED!

HA HA HA HA HA HA HA!
THE FATES OF PEWTER, CERULEAN AND CELADON CITIES ARE ALREADY SEALED! CONSIDER THEM ALREADY GONE!

ALL OF HUMANITY—ALL ITS CITIES—WILL BE **LEVELED**! THEN THE WORLD WILL BE AS I WANT IT!

AND SOON SAFFRON, FUCHSIA, VERMILION AND VIRIDIAN CITIES WILL FALL TO OUR ARMIES!

KRAK

FLASH!

PIKAA!

OKAY! PIKA!

YELLOW!! SHINE A LIGHT THROUGHOUT THIS CAVERN!

NOD

SO YOU'RE ALIVE!

PIKAAA

LANCE
!!

HMPH

YOUR POWERS ARE IMPRESSIVE, YELLOW... BUT... WELL...
TO DEFEAT HIM, IT'LL BE NECESSARY TO MERGE OUR POWERS.

FSH
WHAT ?!
I'LL TAKE THIS.

BLAINE!
WATCH HIS BATTLE STYLE CARE-FULLY!
VSH
FWIP
LET'S RUN A TEST FIRST—SO WE'RE NOT BOTH WIPED OUT WITH THE FIRST BLOW!
OH? YOU'RE COMING AT ME ALONE?
FWIP
KLOP
IT DOESN'T MATTER TO ME IF THERE ARE TWO OF YOU...OR A HUNDRED!
AERO-DACTYL!
KRAK
HYPER BEAM—NOW!!
AAAAAAGH!!
WHOOOO
BLAINE!

SSSSSSS
WHAT?!
IT CAUGHT... THE BEAM?! THAT MUST BE...
YOINK
MEWTWO!

HAA A HA HA HA! I'VE HEARD OF YOU! THE GENETIC POKÉMON BORN OF ARROGANT HUMAN EXPERIMENTATION!
SHF
THIS WILL BE INTERESTING!
LET'S TEST OUT THAT POWER OF YOURS!
PNG
?
ZZZ ZZMMMMM
?
KRRM
YAA-AAGH!!
DMDMDM
YELLOW!
TTOOM

PLINK
HA HA HA HAA!!
SHOOH
I WAS FEELING A BIT CRAMPED... SO I THOUGHT I'D OPEN THINGS UP A LITTLE!
SUPER-SONIC!
ARROOOOOO
VUUN
MEWTWO! BARRIER!
KRAK

TNG TNG TNG TNG

TNG TNG

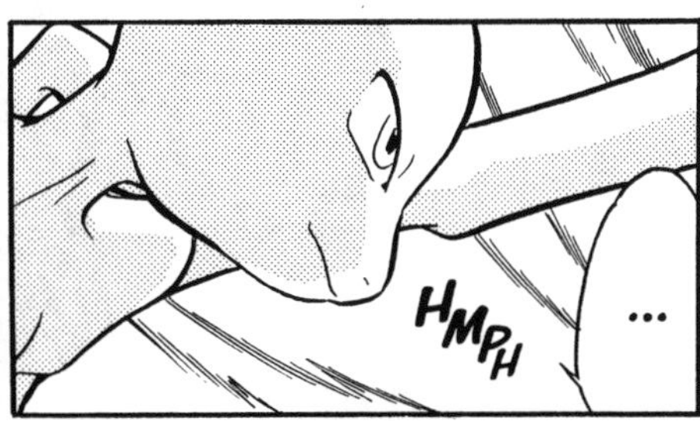

...

DING

TTTTTTTTTT

80 Draggin' in Dragonair

...!
WE'RE...
FLOATING!!
HMPH
MMM
...
HWOOO
HWRRRR
WHAT?!
BASH

BOM
DRAGON-AIR!
MWRLLLL
BLAST YOU—!!
TP

CALL UPON THE **WINDS!** CALL UPON THE **THUNDER-CLOUDS!**

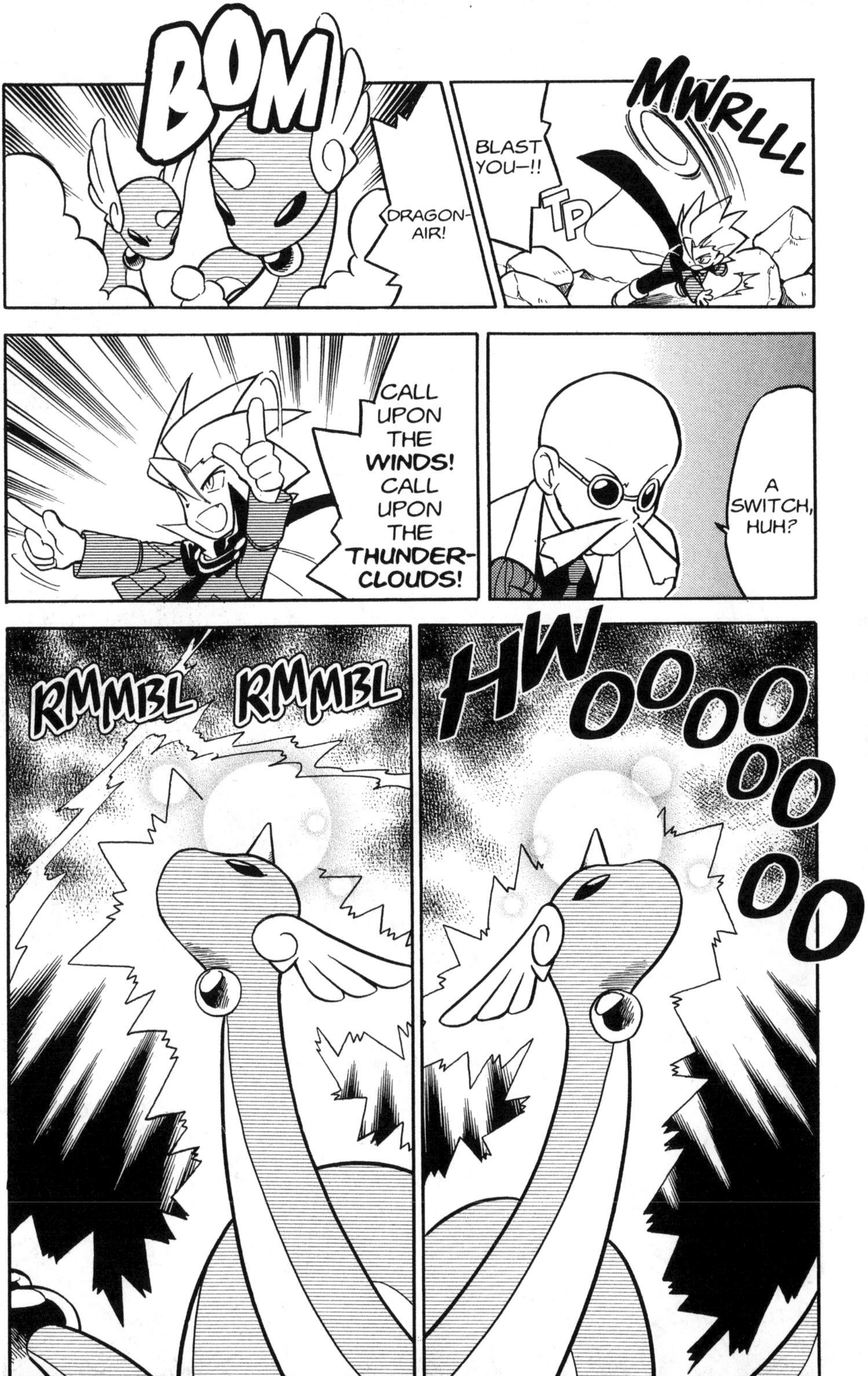

A SWITCH, HUH?

RMMBL RMMBL
HWOOOOOOOOOO

VSH
AGILITY!
KRAK
HHHOOOOOOO
IT'S... IT'S ALMOST AS IF... THEY ARE THE GODS OF THE STORM!
WOBBLE
AGH!

GWOOOG
TP
WE'RE SWITCHING TO ATTACK MODE! WE'LL HAVE TO DROP PART OF THE BARRIER TO DO IT—OKAY?
O... OKAY!
HHHHHH
THEY SAY DRAGONAIR HAVE THE POWER TO CONTROL THE WEATHER... BUT THESE TWO ARE HEIGHTENING THEIR POWERS BY COMBINING THE FORCES OF WIND AND LIGHTNING! ALL RIGHT, THEN...!
LET'S GO!
GWIP
PFFF

HOOOOOOOO
ARE YOU SURE YOU WANT TO LET DOWN YOUR PRECIOUS BARRIER?! ATTACK!
ZP
ZP
WAAAAAH!!
HAAA HA HA HA HA!
VNNN
HWRLL
PNG

...
SO... TORRENTIAL RAIN AND THUNDERCLOUDS ON OUR SIDE... AND A TORNADO ON YOURS! A WEATHER WAR?!
HWRLLLLL
NGGG
PSYWAVE !!
PSYYYYY
KRKL KRKL KRKL
TGGG

NOW—
THE VORTEX WILL SUCK YOU IN!!
I SEE A VERY CLEVER TRAP...
HOWEVER...
GNG
GLINT
IT WON'T DO YOU MUCH GOOD TO PULL US INTO THE CENTER...
GNNG
TINK
HWRRRRR
...IF IT ONLY GIVES US ANOTHER OPPORTUNITY TO ATTACK!
WHAT?!
VSH
VSH
VSH
VSH
AAAAAH!!
PING!

SSH
DROPPING BACK TO PROTECT YOUR TRAINER...? **COWARD!** WELL, I'LL FINISH YOU OFF IN CLOSE COMBAT!
HOOOSH
AERO-DACTYL!
FINISH OFF?!
AND NOT JUST ANY ATTACK!
MY AERO-DACTYL'S WINGS ARE AS SHARP AS SWORDS!
KLANG

RRRGGG
THAT'S—
MEWTWO'S PSYCHIC WEAPON— THE SPOON!!
KLANG
EH ?!
KLANG
KLANG
WOBBLE
!
KLANG
KLANG
...

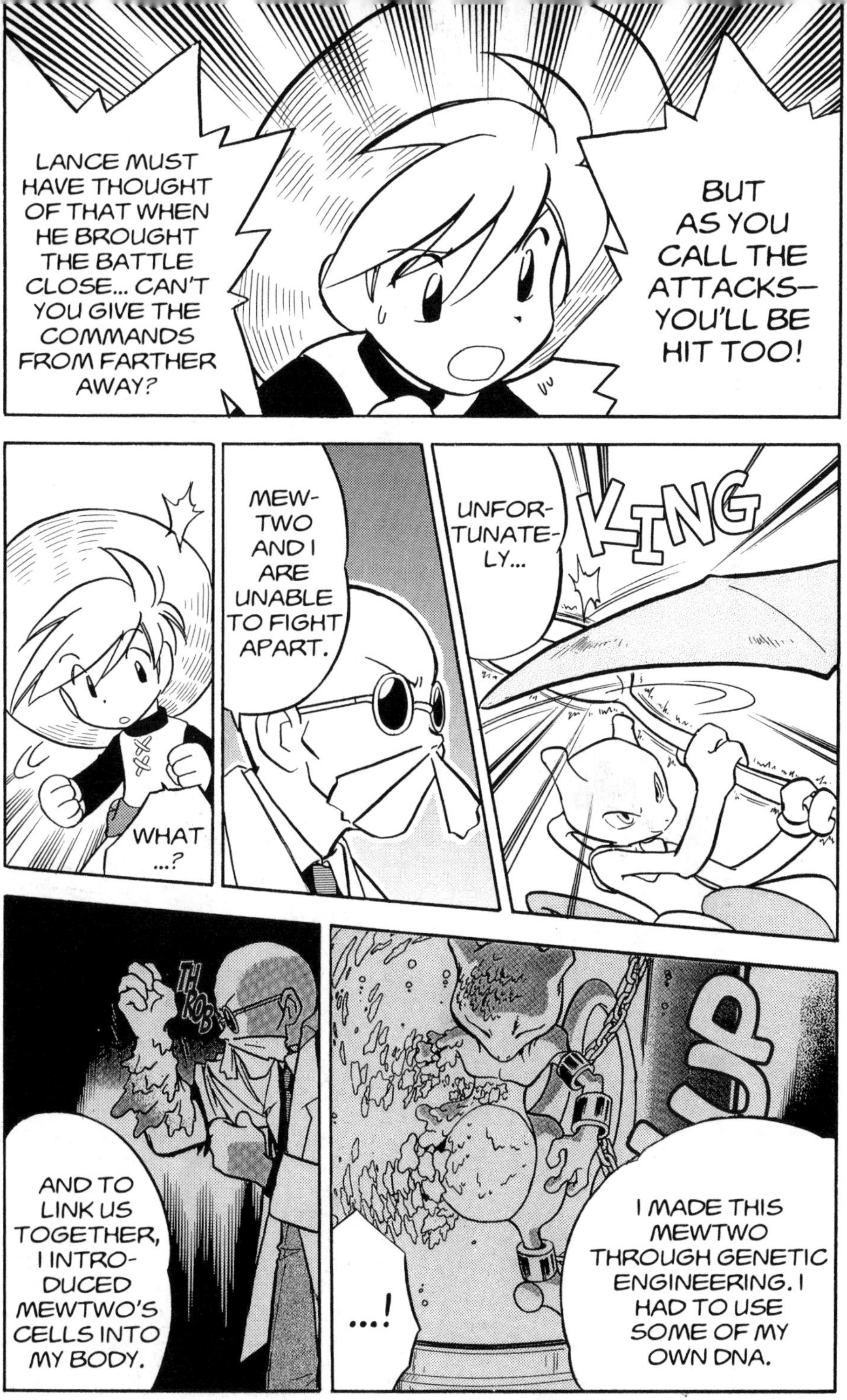

UNFOR-TUNATE-LY...

KING

MEW-TWO AND I ARE UNABLE TO FIGHT APART.

WHAT ...?

THROB

I MADE THIS MEWTWO THROUGH GENETIC ENGINEERING. I HAD TO USE SOME OF MY OWN DNA.

AND TO LINK US TOGETHER, I INTRO-DUCED MEWTWO'S CELLS INTO MY BODY.

...!

IF WE'RE BOTH TO SURVIVE, WE CAN'T FIGHT VERY LONG. WE ARE A STRANGE PAIR, EH?

ANY LONGER THAN THAT... AND MY BODY STARTS TO GO. HEH.

THREE MIN-UTES ?!

TREMBLE TREMBLE

NNNHHH

SO... LET'S END THIS **FAST!!**

THE DEGENER-ATION ONLY REACHED MY ELBOW TWO YEARS AGO... BUT NOW IT'S UP TO MY SHOULDER

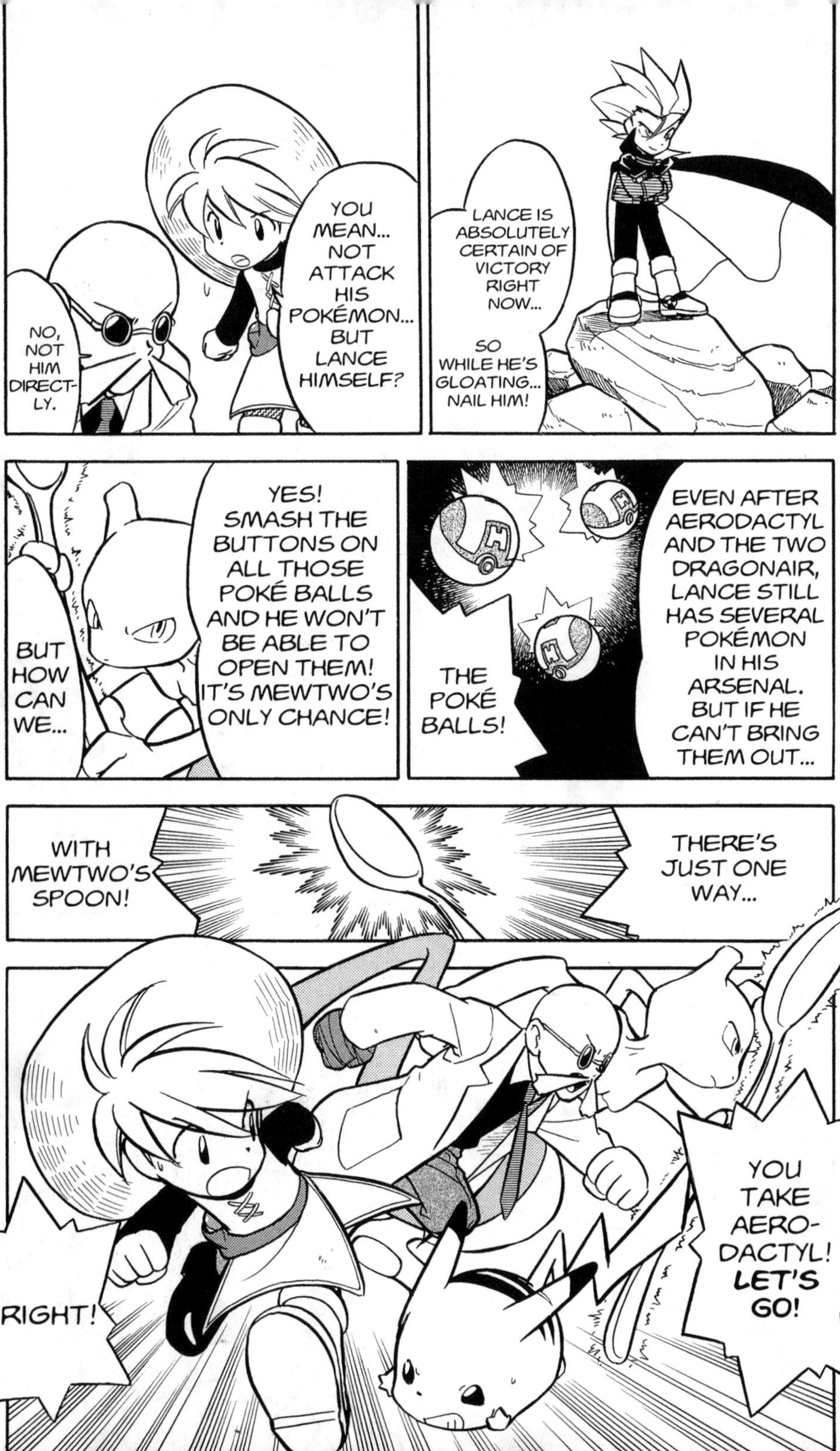

LANCE IS ABSOLUTELY CERTAIN OF VICTORY RIGHT NOW...
SO WHILE HE'S GLOATING... NAIL HIM!
YOU MEAN... NOT ATTACK HIS POKÉMON... BUT LANCE HIMSELF?
NO, NOT HIM DIRECTLY.

THERE'S JUST ONE WAY...
WITH MEWTWO'S SPOON!

YOU TAKE AERODACTYL! LET'S GO!
RIGHT!

FSH
PIKA!
VMMM
NOW!
GWOOP
WHAT ?!
THAT DID IT!

THE TRANSFORMED SPOON... ITS JAGGED POINTS ARE FLYING AT LANCE'S POKÉ BALLS...!

NO!!!!

IT'S BEEN MORE THAN TWO MINUTES SINCE MEWTWO BEGAN BATTLING! WILL THEY MAKE IT IN TIME?!

TNNNG

NNNNGAAHH!!

POW
81 Aerodactyl Redux
DUMPH
GONG

FUMP
BLAINE! MEWTWO!

WE... DID IT!

PFFFFF

THEY'VE FAINT-ED!

THREE... TWO... ONE... TIME... OVER!
3
2
1
!
IT MUST HAVE TAKEN MORE THAN THREE MINUTES!

HWOOOOO
BUT ...
...WE WON!

MEWTWO... YOU USED UP ALL YOUR POWER WITH YOUR PSYWAVE... AND THE ENERGY YOU NEEDED FOR THAT SPOON ATTACK...
WHEEZ! WHEEZ!
BUT YOU WERE ABLE TO DAMAGE LANCE'S POKÉ BALLS SO THAT HE CAN'T OPEN THEM...AND RELEASE HIS POKÉMON!

WE WON! WE BEAT LANCE OF THE ELITE FOUR!
PWIK!

HEH... HEH HEH HEH ...

WRA HA HA HA!
!

THAT MEW-TWO... HAS SOME AMAZING POWER!
TO DAMAGE NOT JUST POKÉ BALLS... BUT AN ULTRA BALL THIS BADLY...!
WOBBLE

VSH

RRRIP

THAT STILL WON'T BE ENOUGH TO WIN!!

IT'S JUST... TOO BAD...

FLAP

SNAP

THOSE MOVES HAVE CAUSED MY DRAGONAIR AND AERODACTYL TO USE UP A GREAT DEAL OF THEIR HEALTH. MY SITUATION WOULD BE HOPELESS IF I WEREN'T ABLE TO GET ANY MORE POKÉMON OUT OF THEIR POKÉ BALLS. LUCKILY...

WHAT—?!

RRRUMMBBLE

...ARE OVER HERE!

!!

MM-HM. **THESE** WERE THE FORCES THAT PUSHED YOU UP FROM WITHIN THE CAVES!!

UNDER-GROUND! THEN THAT RUMBLING IN THE EARTH...!!

SO THE POKÉ BALLS THAT YOU TWO RISKED LIFE AND LIMB TO TARGET... WERE ALL **EMPTY**!!

THESE TWO LEFT THEIR POKÉ BALLS LONG BEFORE TO HIDE UNDER-GROUND AND CAUSE TREMORS!

DRAG-ONAIR.
DRAG-ONITE.
GYARA-DOS.
AERO-DACTYL.
THIS... IS LANCE OF THE ELITE FOUR'S DRAGON FORCE!!
NOW... HOW WILL YOU FIGHT?!
!
LANCE'S ENTIRE FORCE!
WHAT AM I GOING TO DO?!

HWOO

UNNN

TING

GYARR

...BUT ARE YOU PREPARED TO HURT YOUR TRAINER TOO?
PWIK

DID YOU THINK THAT I WOULDN'T NOTICE THE CONNECTION BETWEEN YOU AND BLAINE??
YOU MIGHT BE ABLE TO INFLICT SOME DAMAGE ON ME...
...BUT AT WHAT COST?!
...
GNNG
BLAINE'S BODY IS BADLY INJURED... ISN'T IT?! HA HA!

NH... NN...
RRRRRRR

GGGG

FFFSSSH
TOM
KONG KONG KONG
MEW-TWO ...?
ARE YOU SAYING WE CAN'T AFFORD TO INJURE BLAINE ANY FURTHER...?!
GLEAM
SHP
NOD

...
HHSSSS
DRAGON-AIR AND AERODACTYL ARE PRETTY EXHAUSTED. BUT THE OTHER TWO STILL HAVE MAXIMUM HEALTH!
SWP
MEWTWO AND BLAINE BROUGHT IT THIS FAR...
CHK
CHK
THE REST IS UP TO ME!
OH?! STILL GOING TO TRY?!
HYAAAAAAAAH!!
VSH

B-B-BOM
BOM
?!
BUT... NOT ONE OF THEM HAS EVEN BEEN EVOLVED !!
I HAVEN'T LET THEM EVOLVE!
YOU'RE TO BATTLE ME WITH THAT TEAM?!
I AM!

WHOOPS.
HAA HA HA HA!! YOU'RE A STRANGE ONE! FINE THEN! BUT I WON'T PULL ANY PUNCHES!!
WAIT!
BLAINE... PLEASE WAIT THERE FOR JUST A LITTLE WHILE.
WHRL
SHOVE
WOOOSH
BZZT BZZT
OKAY!
PYOO
SWRLL
LET'S GO, GUYS!

VMM
HYAAAAAAAH!!
IT WON'T BE LIKE THAT TIME IN VER-MILION CITY!
HA!
AH, BUT FIRST... I SHOULD REJUVENATE AERODACTYL AND DRAGONAIR... HEH...
SWSH
MMMMMM
WHAT?! YOU'RE—

MMMMMM
82 Eradicate Raticate!
MMMZZZ
RATTLE RATTLE
MEW-TWO!
LANCE DOES HAVE THAT POWER!
THEN... THE STORIES WERE TRUE!

NOD
DID YOU SEE THAT, MEWTWO ?!

MMM
JUST LIKE ME... LANCE IS A TRAINER...
...WHO CAN READ POKÉMON'S MINDS AND HEAL THEIR WOUNDS!!

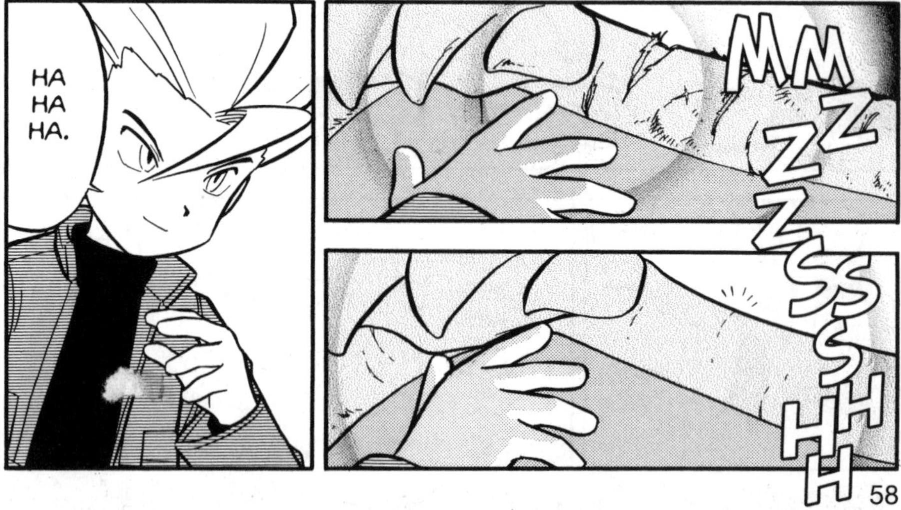
MMZZZZSSSHHHH
HA HA HA.

MEWTWO, DO YOU KNOW OF THE VIRIDIAN FOREST?

VIRIDIAN MEANS AN EMERALD HUE... DEEP AND RICH. IT'S A VAST AND LUSH FOREST.

IT IS SAID THAT ONCE EVERY FEW YEARS, A CHILD IS BORN POSSESSING THE MYSTERIOUS POWERS OF THE FOREST.

...JUST BECAUSE I HAIL FROM VIRIDIAN... CAN I TRULY GO UP AGAINST LANCE? CAN I TRULY OVERCOME SUCH INCREDIBLE POWER?
BUT ...
THANK YOU, MEW-TWO!
I KNOW! I'LL DO MY BEST!
RATTLE
RATTLE
RATTLE
HEH
EVERY-ONE...
LET'S GO!

FWAH
HA HA HA!
GLANCE
GLUP
GLUD
HHHSSSS
THIS PLACE!

HA HA HA. THIS IS THE VOLCANO AT THE HEART OF THE ISLAND! NOTHING LIKE THAT OLD, INACTIVE CRATER ON CINNABAR ISLAND!

HHHOOOSSS

ENG
HWOOOO
DRAGONITE!
STRENGTH!
BRAK BRAK
KRAK
BSHOOOOOO
!!
YEOW! HOT HOT HOT HOT HOT!!
PSSSHH
PSH
LAVA SPOUTS FROM THE CRUSHED BOULDERS!!

BLOOOG
HAVE YOU EVER SEEN SUCH POWER?!

DRAGON-TYPE POKÉMON ARE DIVINE, MYSTICAL BEINGS! THEY ARE DIFFICULT TO CAPTURE... BUT WITH GOOD CARE, THEIR STRENGTH BECOMES UNBEATABLE! HA HA HA HA!!

OF COURSE...

WHEN BLAINE AND MEWTWO WERE TRAINING, THEY WERE FLINGING AWAY BALLS OF FIRE. THEY MUST HAVE FORESEEN A BATTLE LIKE THIS!

COME TO THINK OF IT, BLUE WAS DOING THE SAME... THOSE TWO ARE ASTOUNDING! COMPARED TO THEM, I'M JUST...

NO! I CAN'T BE AFRAID!

DODY! PECK! RATTY! SUPER FANG!
TNG
TNG
TNG
GNASH
GNASH
SNORT
BAM
BASH
AAAH! DODY! RATTY!
BASH

SHLOOO
KITTY, STRING SHOT!!
OMMMMMM
OMNY! WATER GUN!!
HOOSH
NO! GRAVVY! TAKE DOWN!!

NOW! WILL YOU FLAIL ON—OR WILL YOU PUT YOUR TAIL BETWEEN YOUR LEGS AND RUN AWAY?!
I WILL... NOT... RUN!
IF I GIVE UP NOW... ALL THE CITIES WILL BE DE-STROYED!!
OH, BUT THEY WON'T SIMPLY BE DE-STROYED!!
I WILL REBUILD THEM!
I WILL CLEANSE THE LAND OF ARROGANT HUMANITY AND BUILD A WORLD WHERE ALL POKÉMON CAN LIVE IN FREEDOM!!

THAT'S WRONG!! IT'S **WRONG**!! I UNDERSTAND YOUR RAGE—
IT'S TRUE THAT HUMANS HAVE DONE SELFISH THINGS, TAKING AWAY POKÉMON HOMELANDS...
STRIPPING THEM OF THEIR FOOD SUPPLY... I'VE SEEN THE RESULTS OF THAT ON MY JOURNEY!

JUST NOW...YOU WERE HEALING BOTH OF YOUR DRAGONAIR AND YOUR AERODACTYL, RIGHT?
YOU HAVE INCREDIBLE POWER!! WHY DO YOU USE IT FOR DESTRUCTION?! WHY DO YOU USE IT FOR EVIL?!
YOU... ARROGANT LITTLE...
SSSS
THE PERSON WHO FIRST INTRODUCED ME TO POKÉMON ONCE TOLD ME...
"IF YOU CARE FOR THEM WITH A KIND AND GENTLE HEART, THEN THEY'LL ALWAYS BE YOUR FRIENDS."
AREN'T POKÉMON **YOUR** FRIENDS TOO?!

NOW VANISH IN A RIVER OF LAVA!!
GGGGRRRROOOO
AAAA-AAAA-AAGH!
GGRRROOOO

A WHOLE GROUP OF DRA-GONAIR!

MEAN-WHILE, AT THE CINNA-BAR ISLAND GYM...

DOOM
KRAK
AAAA-AAH!

THE... THE GYM!
FFFSSHH
I'M SURE IT WILL BE ALL RIGHT.
WE MUST TRUST THE **GOOD TRAINERS** WHO ARE BATTLING ON CERISE ISLAND!

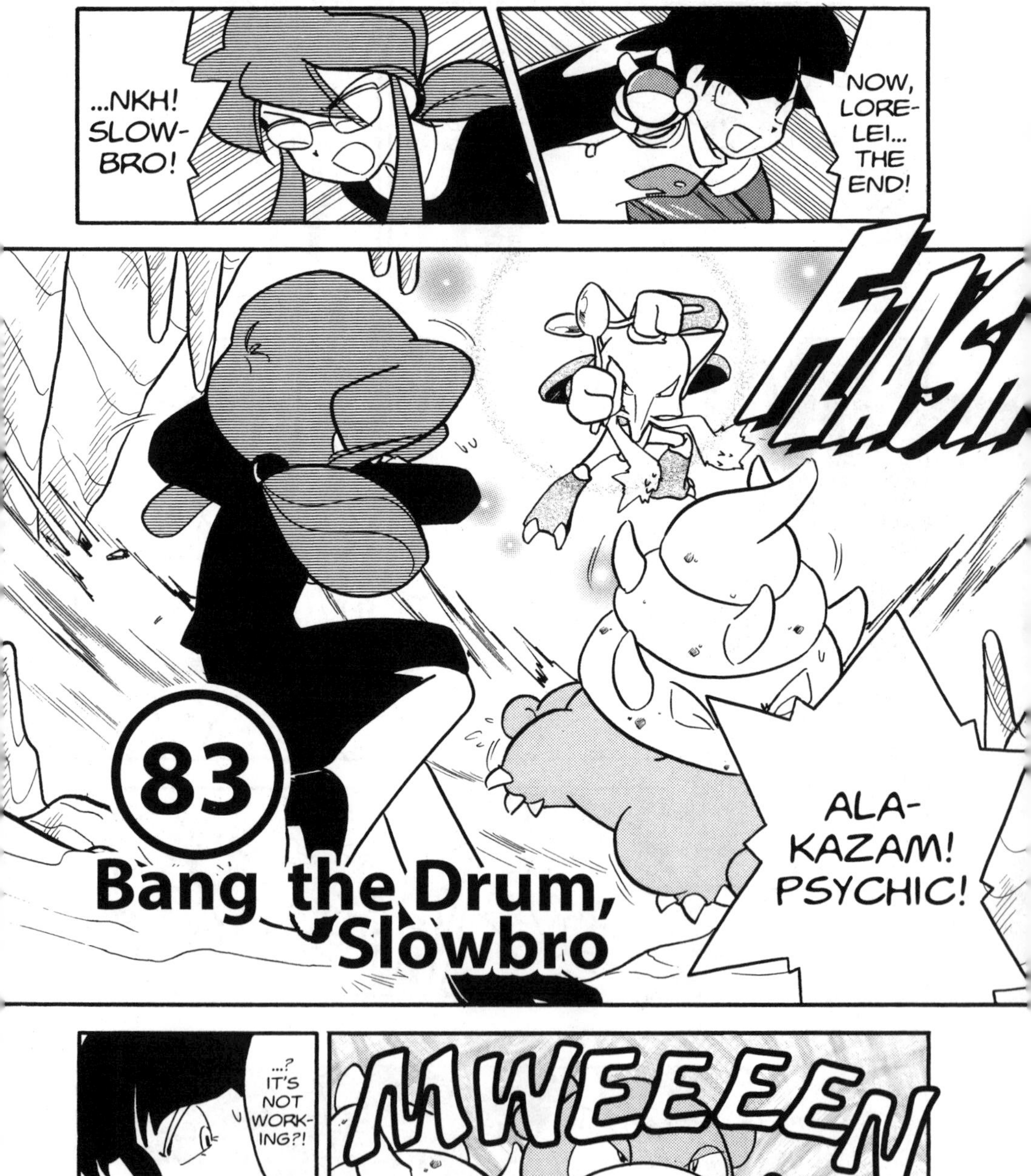

...NKH! SLOWBRO!

NOW, LORELEI... THE END!

FLASH

83 Bang the Drum, Slowbro

ALAKAZAM! PSYCHIC!

DUHHHHHH
ANTICI-
PATING
SOMETHING
LIKE THIS...
I HAD MY
SLOWBRO
USE
AMNESIA!!

UHH!

WITH AMNESIA IT "FORGETS" THE HIT IT'S JUST TAKEN... AND KEEPS FIGHTING! SOMETIMES THERE'S AN ADVANTAGE TO BEING SLOW!

AND SINCE THE SHELL BITING ITS TAIL IS PART OF ITS BODY—IT CAN WATCH ALL FOUR DIRECTIONS AT ONCE!

OF COURSE, ITS SLOWNESS ONLY EXTENDS TO ATTACKS. SLOWBRO CAN BE QUITE SHARP.
IT KNEW ABOUT HORSEA'S PLOY—AND BROUGHT IT TO ME!

BEING BITTEN ON THE TAIL MAKES IT A GREAT DEAL MORE ALERT...
SO CAN YOU IMAGINE WHAT MIGHT HAPPEN IF IT WERE BITTEN ON ITS HEAD? WOULD YOU LIKE TO FIND OUT?

SMOOOCH
LOVELY KISS!
DO YOU SEE NOW, SABRINA? NO MATTER WHAT YOU DO... THE ELITE FOUR WILL ALWAYS BE FAR AHEAD OF YOU MANYFOLD!
... JYNX!
OOHHH
WOBBLE
CURSE-YOU!
VENO-MOTH! ALAKA-ZAM!
NN... NNN... GH!
GNNSH
AGH!
SLIP
GGGG

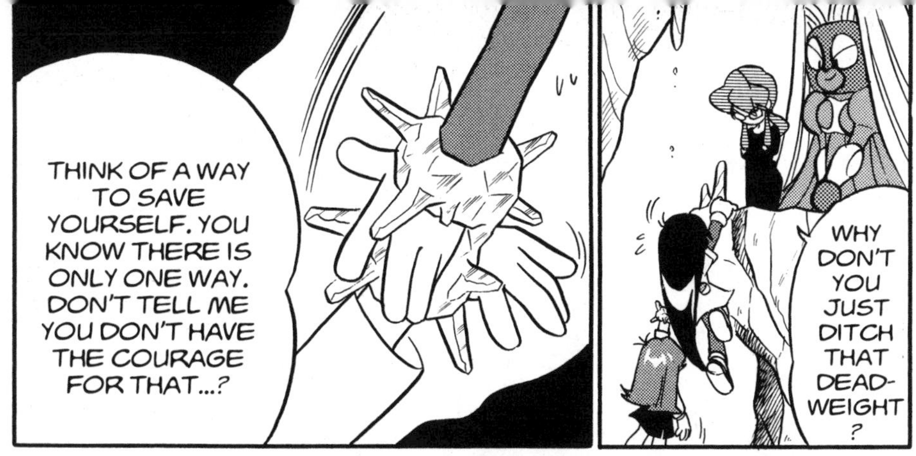

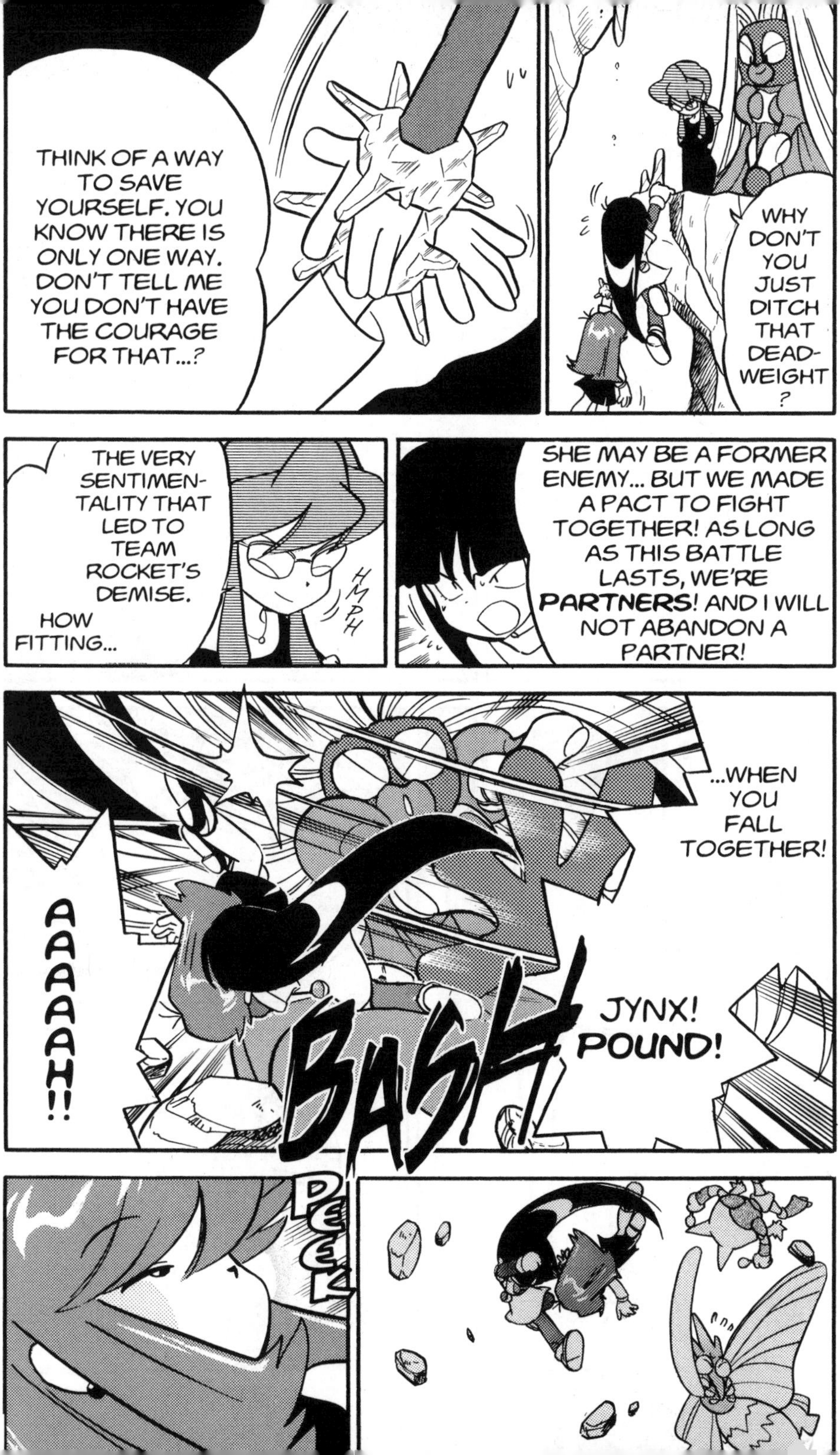

...WHEN YOU FALL TOGETHER!

AAAAAAH!!

BASH

JYNX! POUND!

PEEK

WHRL
...
SHF

BOOM
WHAT ?!

BBBBBBBB

BBB B

BLASTOISE'S WATER CANNON...! STILL ALIVE, EH? YOU'RE A STUBBORN ONE!

VERY GOOD.
I HAVE BEEN HUMILIATED ENOUGH.

BEFORE I DESTROY YOU THEN, I'D LIKE TO HEAR THE REASONS BEHIND YOUR... IRRATIONAL ACTS.

TP
ALL RIGHT ...

AFTER THE POKÉMON LEAGUE TOURNAMENT TWO YEARS AGO, I BEGAN A JOURNEY TO FIND THE POKÉMON THAT ABDUCTED ME AND TOOK ME TO THAT FAR-AWAY LAND...!

LANCE...?! WORKING ON TAKING CONTROL OF A GIANT FLYING POKÉMON ?!

NOT JUST THAT...
WAFT
WAFT

THEY SAY HE'S INCREDIBLY STRONG AND HAS SOME KIND OF SPECIAL POWER. TO COUNTER IT...

WHAT? HOW DO WE COUNTER IT?

THEY SAY YOU'D NEED A COMBINATION OF ANOTHER VIRIDIAN TRAINER WITH SIMILAR POWERS AND A POKÉMON BORN IN THE SAME FOREST ...

A VIRIDIAN TRAINER ...
PIP!
VSSSSSH
HUH?
SHPWING
SHPWING
VVVMMM
!!
THAT'S... RED'S PIKA?! WHY?!
OH!
I LOST IT!
IT LOOKED HURT...!
SOME-THING MUST HAVE HAPPENED TO RED!!

VIRIDIAN FOREST
FWAAAA
CHUP
THERE.
SKRITCH
SHHKK
THAT'S WEIRD... I COULD'VE SWORN IT WENT SOMEWHERE OVER HERE...
EXCUSE ME... DID YOU HAPPEN TO SEE A PIKACHU RUN BY HERE? IT'S HURT, AND...
NO, I HAVE NOT. BUT...A MOMENT PLEASE!
MMMMM
NO... RATTY HAS NOT SEEN IT EITHER.
YOU... YOU CAN TELL?! YOU UNDERSTAND WHAT POKÉMON ARE THINKING?!
VIRIDIAN FOREST... POSSESSING A SPECIAL POWER... CAN IT BE...??

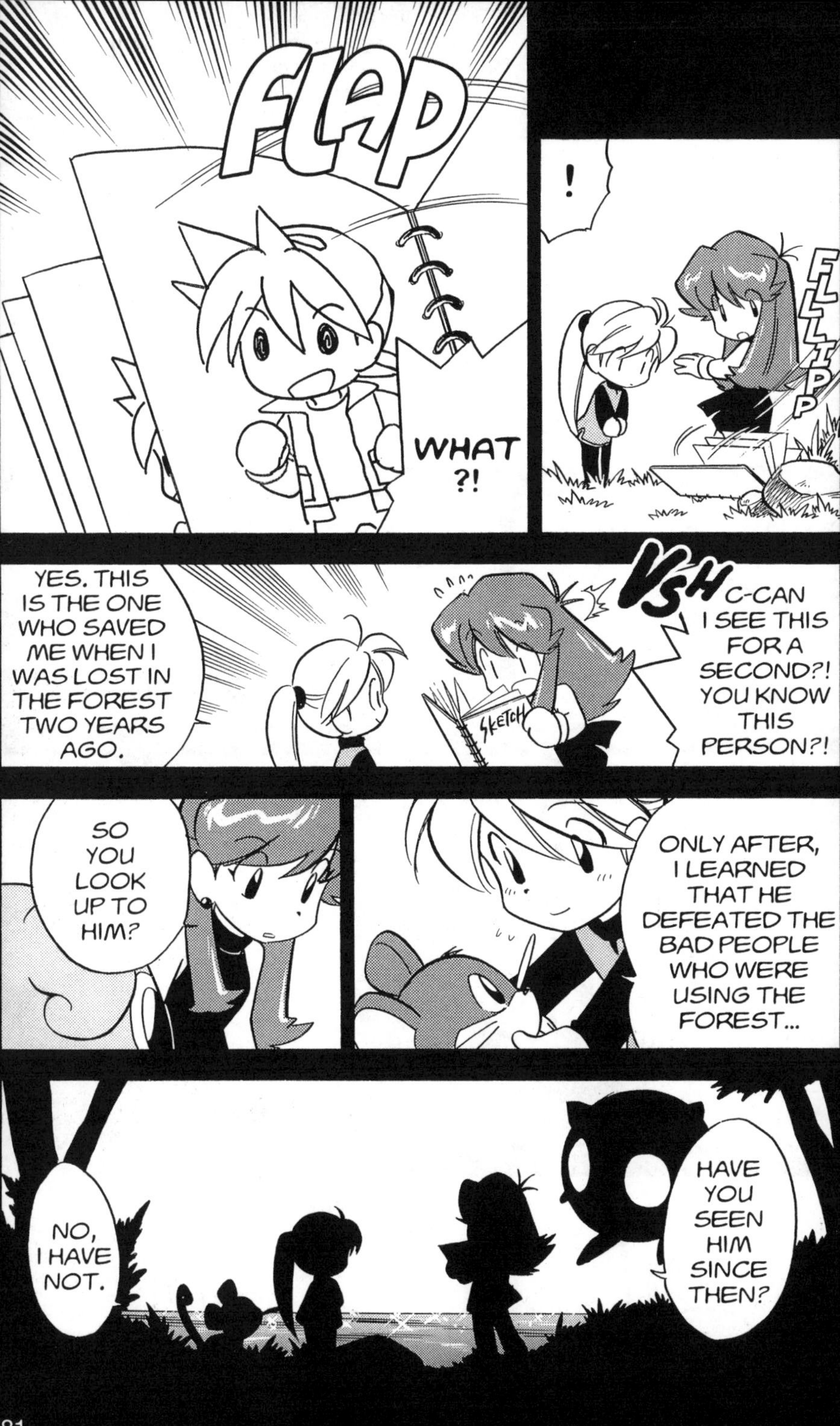
FLAP
WHAT ?!
!
FLLIPP
C-CAN I SEE THIS FOR A SECOND?! YOU KNOW THIS PERSON?!
VSH
YES. THIS IS THE ONE WHO SAVED ME WHEN I WAS LOST IN THE FOREST TWO YEARS AGO.
SKETCH
SO YOU LOOK UP TO HIM?
ONLY AFTER, I LEARNED THAT HE DEFEATED THE BAD PEOPLE WHO WERE USING THE FOREST...
HAVE YOU SEEN HIM SINCE THEN?
NO, I HAVE NOT.

HELP ...?!
LISTEN. I'M A FRIEND OF HIS. IF IT'S ALL RIGHT WITH YOU... WOULD YOU MIND HELPING ME A LITTLE BIT...?
...
HE HAPPENS TO BE IN TROUBLE RIGHT NOW.
WHAT ?!
THE BOY WHO SAVED ME...
...IS IN TROUBLE ...?!
SSSH
YOU MAY HAVE THE POWER TO SAVE HIM.
SO PLEASE... WILL YOU HELP?
...
NOD

SO I DEVISED A PLAN TO SEND THIS YOUNG GIRL OUT TO SEARCH FOR RED...AND TO ACT AS A SCOUT TO HELP ME DISSECT THE ELITE FOUR'S BATTLE STRENGTHS.
I TAUGHT HER A FEW BASIC POKÉMON BATTLE SKILLS, AND THE NEXT DAY...
NOW JUST REMEMBER... FIRST I WANT YOU TO LOOK FOR RED'S INJURED PIKA. SINCE IT PASSED THROUGH HERE, IT'S MOSTLY LIKELY HEADED TOWARD PALLET TOWN.
AFTER THAT, TRY TO TRACK DOWN LEADS TO RED.
RULE NUMBER ONE—NEVER TELL ANYONE ABOUT ME OR WHO MIGHT HAVE SENT YOU ON THIS MISSION.
RULE NUMBER TWO—NEVER GIVE OUT YOUR NAME.
OUR ENEMIES ARE LIKELY TO USE ANY INFORMATION AGAINST US!
I UNDER-STAND.
BOM
WELL... I AM OFF THEN!
...

KLOP
?!
?
WAIT A MIN- UTE!
THE HAT WILL HELP DISGUISE YOUR IDENTITY A LITTLE MORE BY HIDING YOUR HAIR.
YOUR IDENTITY WILL BE A LITTLE HARDER TO DISCOVER... IF THEY THINK YOU'RE A BOY.
I'M COUNTING ON YOU... AMARILLO DEL BOSQUE VERDE!!

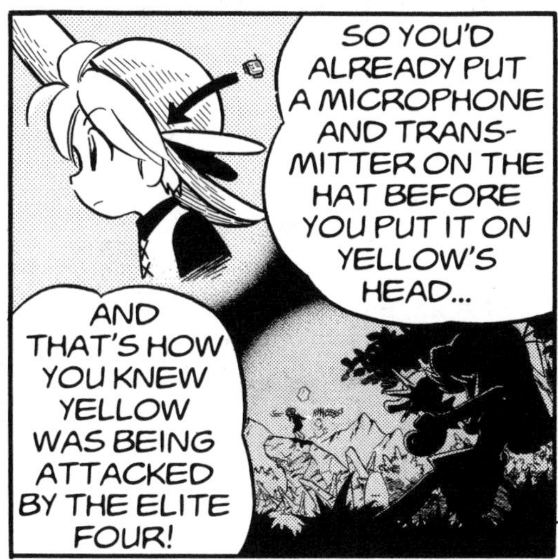
SO YOU'D ALREADY PUT A MICROPHONE AND TRANS-MITTER ON THE HAT BEFORE YOU PUT IT ON YELLOW'S HEAD...
AND THAT'S HOW YOU KNEW YELLOW WAS BEING ATTACKED BY THE ELITE FOUR!

I SEE...

AND IF YOU'RE WONDER-ING WHY I TOLD YOU ALL THIS...
SHF

UH-HUH! SUR-PRISED?

YES?

SHWA
CALL IT MY VICTORY STRUT!! CLEFABLE!!

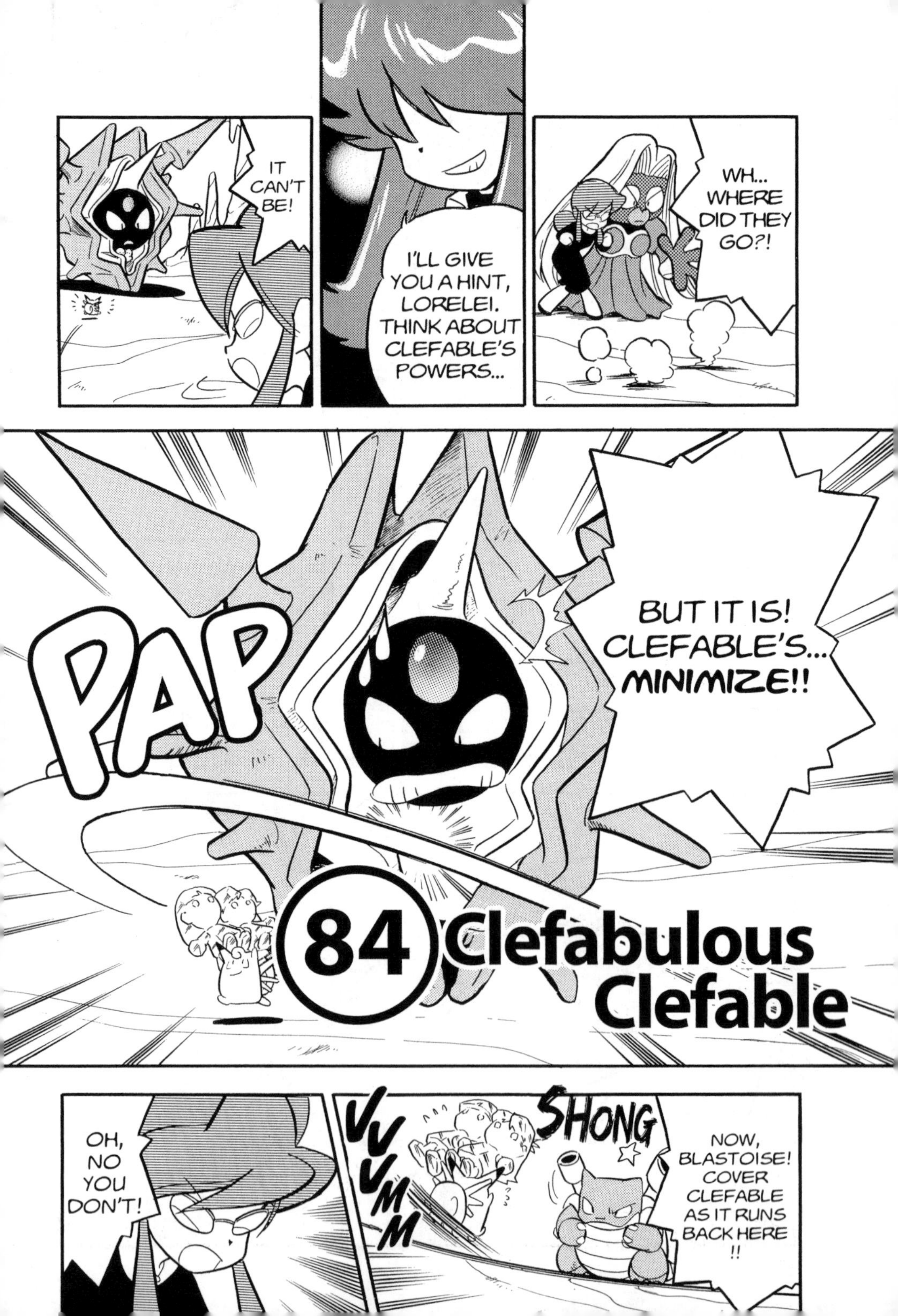

PAP

BUT IT IS! CLEFABLE'S... MINIMIZE!!

84 Clefabulous Clefable

BLASSST
THIS HAS GOT TO WORK...
MMGH !!
!
TRIP
VMMMM
BRAK

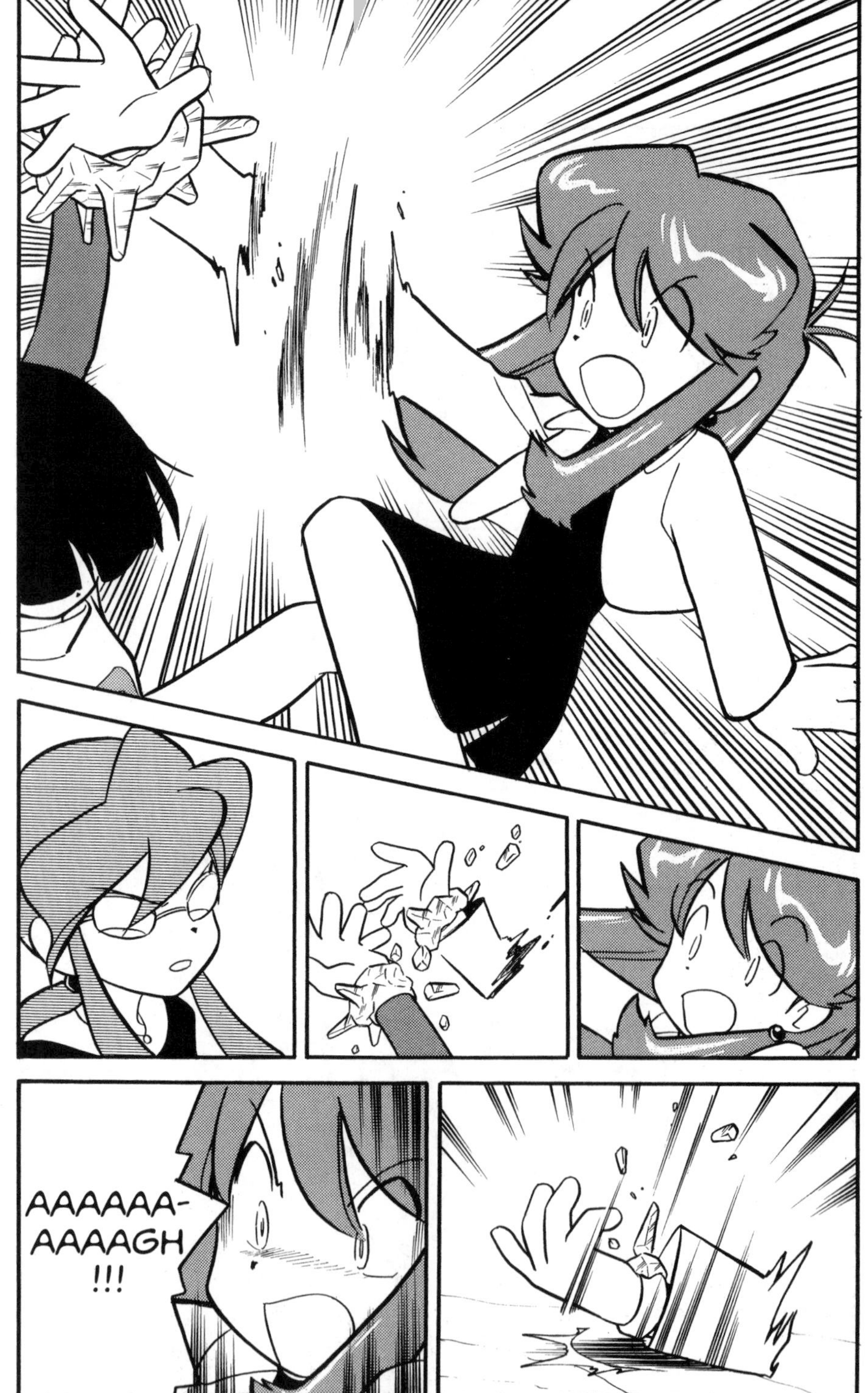
AAAAAA-
AAAAGH
!!!

ACTU-ALLY... I MEANT TO DO THAT...
FOOL!! THIS IS WHAT YOU GET FOR DEFYING... LORELEI!

BOMP
I... I CAN...
HUF
WOBBLE
HUF
DIDN'T YOU... TELL SABRINA... TO GET RID OF MY DEAD-WEIGHT... THE HARD WAY...?! WELL... NOW THAT THAT'S DONE...

YOU'RE A FOOL, GREEN !!

VWRR

IT'S OVER NOW! IT'S... ALL OVER.

MWEEEEEEEN
PWIK
GWONNG
!
KWEE KWEE
D-DITTO?!
GWONNG
MWUK
Y-YEAH... DITTO...!

I KNEW I WASN'T GOING TO BE ABLE TO BEAT ANY-ONE OF YOUR ABILITY... WITHOUT SOME TRICKERY!
THAT'S WHY I PUT ON THIS JACKET AS SOON AS I GOT TO THE ISLAND... HA HA HA!
There.

I TOLD YOU... THIS WAS MY VICTORY STRUT...
MY REAL ARM IS... RIGHT HERE!
HUF HUF
FLLLAP

HEH... VERY CLEVER... TO PULL THAT OFF AGAINST A MEMBER OF THE ELITE FOUR... AMAZING.

YOU WERE PRETTY AMAZING YOUR-SELF.

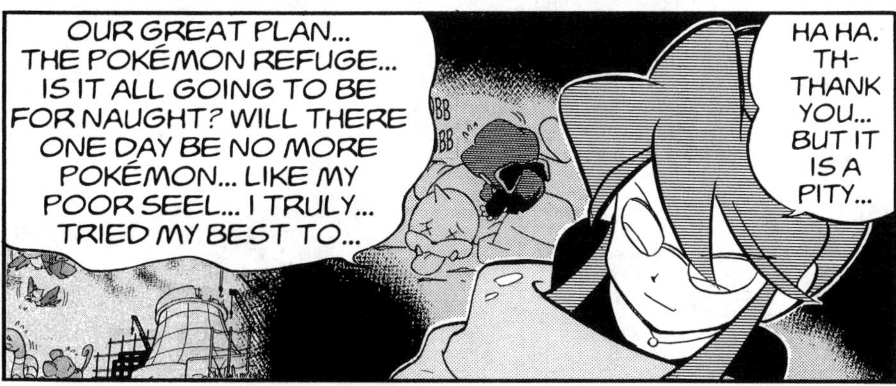
HA HA. TH-THANK YOU... BUT IT IS A PITY...
OUR GREAT PLAN... THE POKÉMON REFUGE... IS IT ALL GOING TO BE FOR NAUGHT? WILL THERE ONE DAY BE NO MORE POKÉMON... LIKE MY POOR SEEL... I TRULY... TRIED MY BEST TO...

OOOH
YOU TRIED YOUR BEST... BUT YOU WERE FIGHTING THE WRONG BATTLE ...
I WAS GUILTY OF THE SAME THING... ONCE...

ZLUB
ZLUB
THEY SHOULD WAKE UP AFTER A LITTLE WHILE... DITTO!

NOW TO WAKE SABRINA ...

I'M ALREADY AWAKE!

GAH!! S-SINCE WHEN?!

DITTO
K-TINK
SINCE YOUR "ARM" WAS TORN OFF! SO ALL THAT TIME I WAS REALLY CHAINED TO A DITTO?!

AND ALL THAT TIME...WE COULD HAVE GONE OUR SEPARATE WAYS WHENEVER I WANTED TO?! FROM THE VERY BEGINNING...YOU WERE TRICKING ME?!

HEH HEH HEH... *AHEM.* YOU KNOW WHAT THEY SAY... TO FOOL YOUR ENEMIES, FIRST FOOL YOUR FRIENDS!

UM... SO YOU DO FORGIVE ME... RIGHT?
DON'T HOLD YOUR BREATH !!

R... RED... HUF HUF...

IT HAPPENED... AGAIN... THE TERRIBLE HEADACHES... AND THEN THE BLACK-OUTS!

RED! WATCH OUT FOR THIS GUY! HE'S MIGHTY POWERFUL! AND HIS HITMONLEE'S ARMS STRETCH!! THEY'RE THE ONES THAT BUSTED UP MY HOUSE!!

THANKS, BILL. BUT I ALREADY KNOW HOW STRONG HE IS!

HEY, LT. SURGE! WOULD YOU MIND LEAVING THIS BATTLE TO ME?

I HAVE TO ADMIT THAT I'D USED UP MOST OF MY ENERGY BEFORE YOU GOT HERE. I DOUBT I'D BE ABLE TO FIGHT AT FULL POWER ANYWAY...
NO, IT'S NOT JUST THAT.

IT'S **HIM!**

I'VE GOT SOMETHING TO SETTLE WITH BRUNO OF THE ELITE FOUR!!

SSS
HA! YOU HAVEN'T CHANGED A BIT, RED.
SNAP
EVEN IF I TELL YOU NOT TO... WOULD YOU LISTEN?

SHAP

MY HITMON-LEE DE-STROYED HIS HOUSE ?!
I HAVE NO MEMORY OF THAT!

WAS MY HITMONLEE BEING USED WITHOUT MY KNOWLEDGE ?!
HA... HA HA HA HA HA HA!

WHAT ARE THESE HEAD-ACHES... AND THIS MEMORY LOSS...?!

AND WHY IS THE MEMORY OF MY BATTLE WITH RED IN PIECES?!

NONE OF THAT MATTERS NOW!

BAM

PRE-PARE FOR BATTLE, RED!
YOU'RE ON, BRUNO!
NOW... **NOTHING** MATTERS!
I STAND FACE-TO-FACE WITH THE ONE I DEEM THE PERFECT OPPONENT! AND THIS TIME...I SHALL BE ABLE TO FIGHT A PURE MATCH!

MWOO

HITMON-CHAN!!

FIRE PUNCH!!

BLAST IT ... A FIRE-TYPE MOVE AGAINST MY GRASS-TYPE VENUSAUR!! SHOULD I CHANGE POKÉMON? NO...

FLIP

PINK
BZZT
FWOO
HITMONCHAN'S FISTS CONTAIN THE POWERS OF FIRE, ELECTRICITY AND ICE! IN OTHER WORDS...

IT'S LIKE HAVING THREE POKÉMON IN ONE!

VSSH

GH!!
LUCKILY WE HAVE A POKÉMON LIKE THAT TOO!!

SSSHHHHH

SSOOOO

CHANGE INTO WHAT FIRST?!

TM
WHATEVER YOU MIGHT THROW THIS WAY, WE'LL KNOCK IT DOWN!! ICE PUNCH!!
KIIIIII IIIN
CHK
IF YOU'RE LEADING WITH ICE, WE'LL COUNTER WITH THE FIRE STONE !!
KRAK
FLAREON!

KRAK
NEXT... WATER STONE!!
HOOO
NKH! DON'T FLINCH, HITMON-CHAN!!

IT'S TRUE! MY EEVEE CAN CHANGE INTO VAPOREON, JOLTEON AND FLAREON AT WILL...AND THEN CHANGE BACK AGAIN!
WHAT ...?! I- IMPOS-SIBLE !!

AND THEY DON'T LOSE THEIR POWER NO MATTER HOW MANY TIMES THEY'RE USED!!
IT WOULD SUFFER FROM THIS POWER... SINCE IT CAN'T CONTROL IT BY ITSELF. BUT I HAVE POSSESSION OF THE EVOLUTION-ARY STONES ...

TEAM ROCKET WAS RESPON-SIBLE FOR THAT MUTA-TION...
BUT NOW EEVEE **WANTS** TO USE ITS POWERS FOR ME!

ARHHH! MACHAMP! HELP HITMON-CHAN!
SHA
THE ENERGY IN THE STONES HELPS BOOST EEVEE'S POWERS!!

GRRRN
THERE'S HELP ON THIS SIDE TOO!
POLI-WRATH!!

KLANG
WHAT?! SO THERE WAS A SECRET HIDDEN IN THAT BELT!!
UHHHH! GHH! MACHAMP... IT'S TIME... FOR YOU TO TAKE OFF THAT BELT!

GMMM
MWKWKWK

NGH!! HAH!! THIS BELT USUALLY FALLS OFF WHEN MACHOKE EVOLVES INTO MACHAMP...
BUT MY MACHAMP INSISTED ON KEEPING IT ON!

EEVEE!

IT ABSORBS EXCESS POWER... AND CONSERVES IT...
... AND THEN... ...WHEN IT'S TAKEN OFF, RELEASES IT ALL AT ONCE!!

BOOOSH
ARGH! WATER GUN!
NO EFFECT!

POLI-WRATH!!

BWASH

SORRY... BUT THIS MATCH IS OVER. YOUR ACE IN THE HOLE, EEVEE, IS OUT OF IT. YOU HAVE NO POKÉMON LEFT WHO CAN TAKE ON MY MACHAMP.

PLINK

GRRRRNNG

GNNG

WLLOB

BLASH

WHAT?! VAPOREON... INSIDE THE PUDDLE LEFT BY THAT WATER GUN...?!

YOU GOT IT! IT'S **ACID ARMOR**... A MELTING ATTACK! EEVEE MADE IT LOOK LIKE IT FELL... WHEN IT WAS ACTUALLY CLIMBING UP AS WATER!!

AND FINALLY... THE THUNDER STONE! JOLTEON'S...

THUD

THUD

PIN MISSILE !!!

THUD

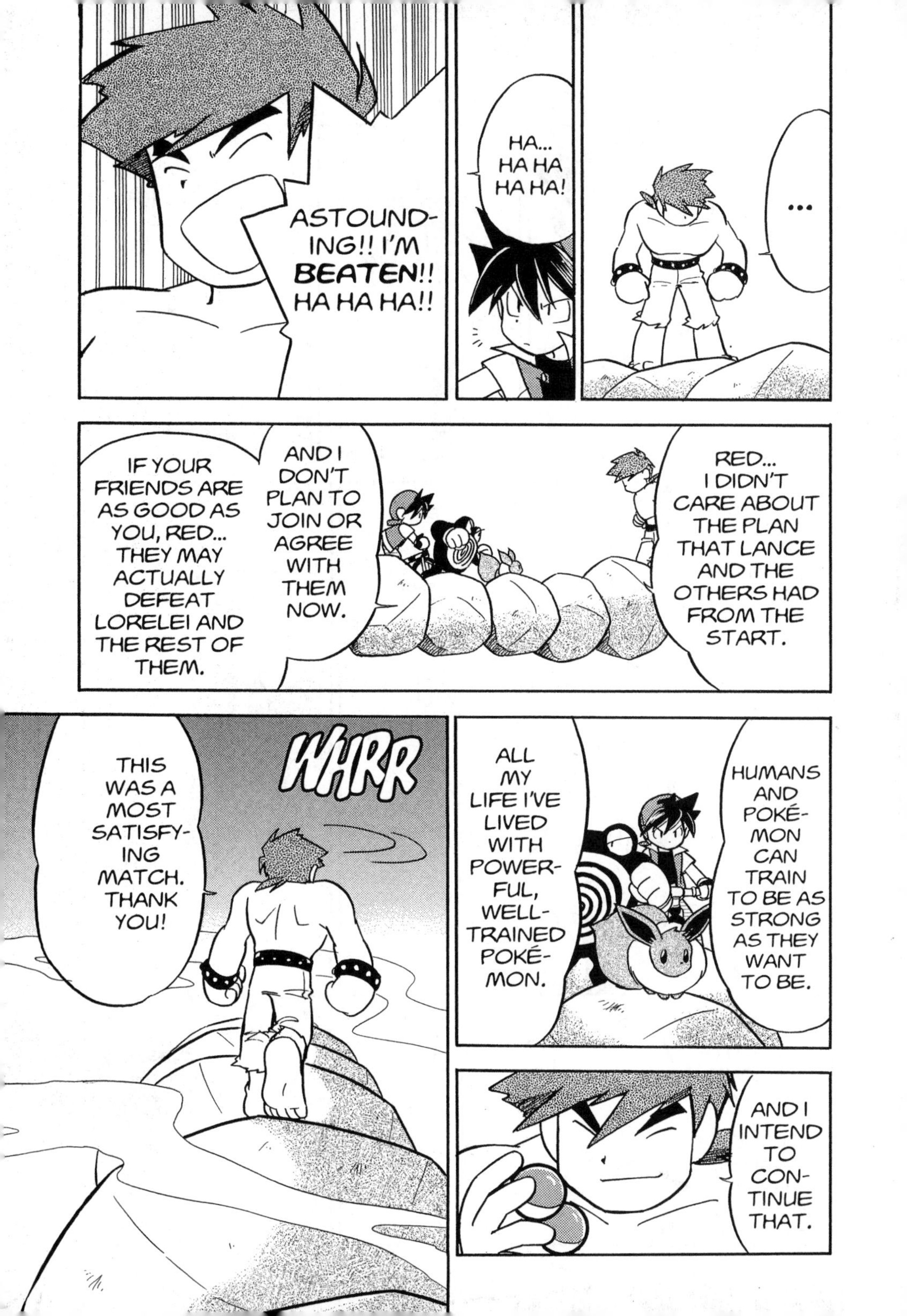

...
HA... HA HA HA HA!
ASTOUNDING!! I'M **BEATEN**!! HA HA HA!!

RED... I DIDN'T CARE ABOUT THE PLAN THAT LANCE AND THE OTHERS HAD FROM THE START.
AND I DON'T PLAN TO JOIN OR AGREE WITH THEM NOW.
IF YOUR FRIENDS ARE AS GOOD AS YOU, RED... THEY MAY ACTUALLY DEFEAT LORELEI AND THE REST OF THEM.

HUMANS AND POKÉMON CAN TRAIN TO BE AS STRONG AS THEY WANT TO BE.
ALL MY LIFE I'VE LIVED WITH POWERFUL, WELL-TRAINED POKÉMON.
AND I INTEND TO CONTINUE THAT.
WHRR
THIS WAS A MOST SATISFYING MATCH. THANK YOU!

DMMP
AGH!
HE'S GONE.
BRUNO ...

ONE ELITE FOUR MEMBER PER TEAM. THAT WAS THE AGREEMENT.

SO I'M GONNA GO MEET UP WITH SABRINA AND KOGA NOW. SEE YA!!

VOOON

W'LL HOW D'YA LIKE THAT?! TEAM ROCKET TO THE CORE!! WHAT MADE ME THINK HE COULDA EVER TURNED INTO A GOOD GUY?!

HUH ?!

LT. SURGE! WH... WHAT THE HECK?!

THERE'S A PATH BEYOND THE WALL THAT JOLTEON'S PIN MISSILE ATTACK BLASTED THROUGH...!

H- HEY, RED! LOOK !!

WHAT THE HECK?! THERE'S A PICTURE OF...ME?!
FLIP
M-MY POKÉDEX! AND A SKETCHBOOK?!!

!
SKETCH

THAT'S RIGHT! YOU DON'T KNOW!!
WHO'S YELLOW ...?
?
IT'S YELLOW! YELLOW WAS HERE!

SO IF THIS YELLOW'S HERE... DOES THAT MEAN PIKA IS HERE TOO?!

AND OUGHTTA BE WITH BLAINE... BATTLIN' ONE O' THE OTHER ELITE FOUR RIGHT NOW!!
YELLOW'S THE TRAINER THAT TOOK CARE O' PIKACHU WHILE YOU WERE MISSIN', RED...

TALK LATER!
H-HEY, RED...
FSSSHH

!!
WHAT ...?!
PIKA'S IN... SOME KIND OF DANGER ?!
CHANGE THE MODE TO CHECK ON PIKA'S CONDITION— IT'S A NEW THING THAT PROFESSOR OAK ADDED TO THE POKÉDEX!

RED... WHILE WE'RE RIDIN'... CAN YOU TELL ME SOMETHIN'?

THERE WAS AN ICE STATUE OF YOU AWAY UP ON MT. MOON THAT EVERY-BODY WAS FREAKIN' OUT ABOUT.
HOW'D YOU GET OUT OF THAT THING ?!

AND ON TOP OF THAT... THOSE EVOLUTIONARY STONES YOU WERE USIN' JUST NOW... AREN'T THEY THE LEGENDARY STONES OF VERMILION?!
I MEAN... WHAT'S GOIN' ON HERE?!

85
Gimme Shellder
I DIDN'T GET OUT OF THE BLOCK OF ICE ON MY OWN.
THERE WAS SOME-ONE THERE WHO HELPED ME.
I GOT THOSE STONES FROM THAT PERSON TOO.
WHAT ?!

RRRMMMMMMM

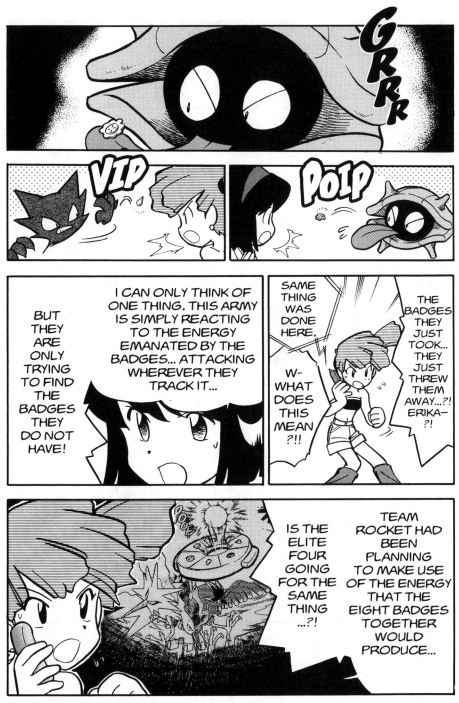

GRRR

POIP

VIP

THE BADGES THEY JUST TOOK... THEY JUST THREW THEM AWAY...?! ERIKA—?!
SAME THING WAS DONE HERE.
W-WHAT DOES THIS MEAN?!!

I CAN ONLY THINK OF ONE THING. THIS ARMY IS SIMPLY REACTING TO THE ENERGY EMANATED BY THE BADGES... ATTACKING WHEREVER THEY TRACK IT...

BUT THEY ARE ONLY TRYING TO FIND THE BADGES THEY DO NOT HAVE!

TEAM ROCKET HAD BEEN PLANNING TO MAKE USE OF THE ENERGY THAT THE EIGHT BADGES TOGETHER WOULD PRODUCE...
IS THE ELITE FOUR GOING FOR THE SAME THING ...?!

BASH

GAH !!

RRRGH... IF THIS CONTINUES, THEN MY POKÉMON AND I WILL HIT OUR PHYSICAL LIMITS! WE WON'T HAVE A CHANCE!

THERE ARE TWO THINGS TO CONSIDER IN ORDER TO CAPTURE GENGAR...

THE FIRST IS THAT THIS GENGAR HAS THE POWER TO MOVE FROM SHADOW TO SHADOW. THE SECOND IS THAT IT'S REACTING TO **SOMETHING** BEFORE SHIFTING SHADOWS...

I ALREADY KNOW **HOW** IT DOES...
IT JUMPS FROM SHADOW TO SHADOW WHENEVER THE SHADOW OF ONE CROSSES WITH ANOTHER.

RIGHT NOW, SINCE KOGA AND I HAVE PUT SO MUCH DISTANCE BETWEEN US, THERE'S NO LONGER ANY CHANCE...
...THAT IT MIGHT JUMP FROM MY OR PORYGON'S SHADOWS TO KOGA'S.

BUT I DON'T UNDERSTAND WHAT IT'S REACTING TO. IF MY GUT INSTINCT'S RIGHT...

...

ZZZH

HWA

NKH!

I WAS RIGHT! IT'S SOUND!!

IT'S REACTING TO ANY SOUND WE MAKE WHEN WE MOVE OR SPEAK!

THIS TRICK HAS AGATHA'S NASTY STYLE WRITTEN ALL OVER IT...!!
I FIGURED SINCE AGATHA WASN'T ON THE SCENE, THERE WAS SOMETHING GUIDING IT OTHER THAN A TRAINER'S COMMANDS...!
I CAN BUY SOME TIME BY BEING SILENT, BUT...
DRIP
BUT NOW THAT I KNOW... WHAT DO I DO...?
PLOP
!
BLINK
SNEER

SO IT WON'T EVEN LET ME SWEAT, HUH?!
WHAK
UGH !!

!
WHAT'S THIS SMOKE ...?

OOOOMMM

...
KOGA !!
CHK
...
NOD

PSSSS
PSSSS

SSSSSHHHH

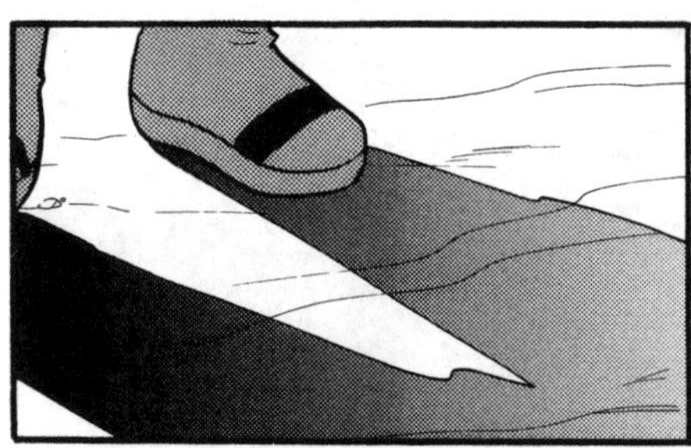

NOW!

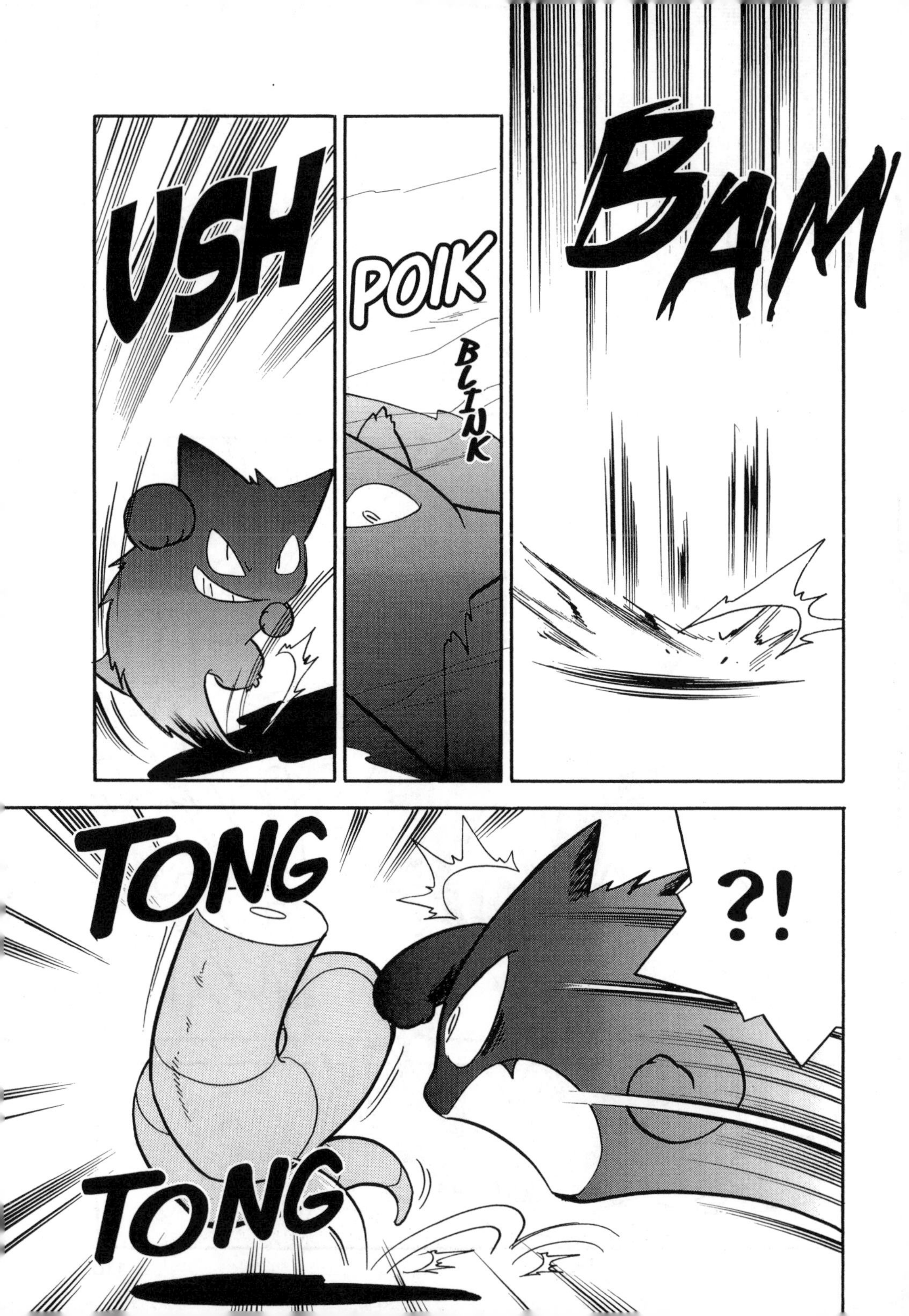

USH
POIK
BLINK
BAM
TONG
TONG
?!

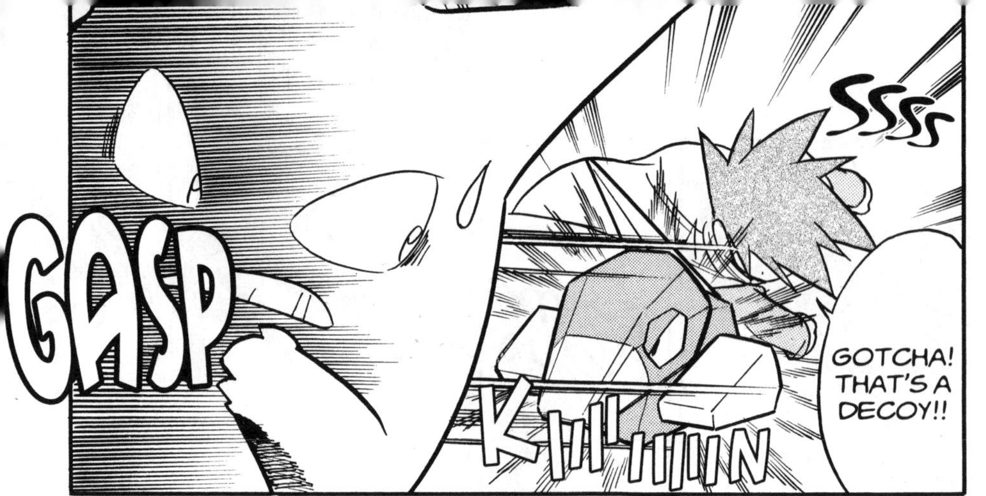
SSSS
GOTCHA! THAT'S A DECOY!!
KIIIIIIIN
GASP

MWAWAWAWA
PSYBEAM!!

DOM
HUF... HUF...

GASP
WE WON !!
SSSSSSSS

SSSSSS
THIS WAS THE ONLY WAY TO CONVEY THE IDEA OF THE TAIL TO YOU...GIVEN THAT WE COULDN'T MAKE A SOUND.
I'M IMPRESSED THAT YOU WERE ABLE TO DECIPHER THE MESSAGE IN MY KOFFING'S SMOKE.

TWITCH
TWITCH
I KNEW THAT AN ARBOK'S TAIL CAN CONTINUE TO MOVE ACCORDING TO THE CREATURE'S WILL... IN ORDER TO LURE THE ENEMY'S ATTENTION AWAY FROM THE BODY.

I REMEMBER THE CHARAC-TERISTICS OF ALL MY ENEMIES' POKÉMON... FOR CAPTURING PURPOSES.

THE SEVERED TAIL CAME IN UNEXPECTEDLY HANDY, DIDN'T IT?
AND THAT'S SOMETHING I CAN USE FOR THE NINJA ATTACK... THE SECRET BODY SWITCH.

MOST LIKELY ELSEWHERE, LT. SURGE AND SABRINA ARE ALSO BLASTING AWAY THE ELITE FOUR. OUR MISSION SHOULD BE NEARLY COMPLETED!
ZZIP

BY THE WAY, BLUE... THAT GENGAR'S ABILITY TO MOVE IN AND OUT OF SHADOWS... A MOST UNUSUAL ABILITY...
...WAS UNMISTAKABLY AGATHA'S CREATION. THAT MEANS WE'VE DEFEATED HER... AND THERE'S NO LONGER A NEED FOR US TO BE A TEAM.

NEXT TIME WE MEET AS ENEMIES... YOU WON'T BE ABLE TO USE THE SAME TRICKS!

...AND SEEING YOUR FIGHTING SKILLS FIRST-HAND!

...
I ENJOYED MAKING USE OF YOUR POWERS... HEH HEH...

MWIP

SAME HERE.

DON'T MOVE!!
SHP

WITH GOLBAT'S CONFUSE RAY, I'VE LIGHTED THE ENTIRE CAVE.
SHADOWS HAVE BEEN CUT TO A MINIMUM.
DID YOU REALLY THINK I'D LET YOU ESCAPE BACK INTO THE SHADOWS...

WOBBLE
AGATHA ?!!

YOU KNEW THAT I WAS LURKING CLOSE BY. VERY CLEVER.

AND A VERY CLEVER SOLUTION TOO...

RE-MARK-ABLE.
I COULDN'T USE GOLBAT DURING THE BATTLE BECAUSE OF THE NOISE ITS WINGS WOULD MAKE. IT WOULD ONLY HAVE DRAWN AN ATTACK.
BUT I COMMANDED IT TO DO THIS... IF GENGAR WAS DEFEATED.
YOUR GRANDFATHER, PROFESSOR OAK, USED TO BE SUCH A MAN...
THAT'S MY BLUE... JUST LIKE AT THE POWER PLANT...
SO HOW DOES IT FEEL, AGATHA? YOU LAUGHED WHEN I SAVED THE GOLBAT. BUT NOW THAT SAME GOLBAT IS PREVENTING YOU FROM MOVING.

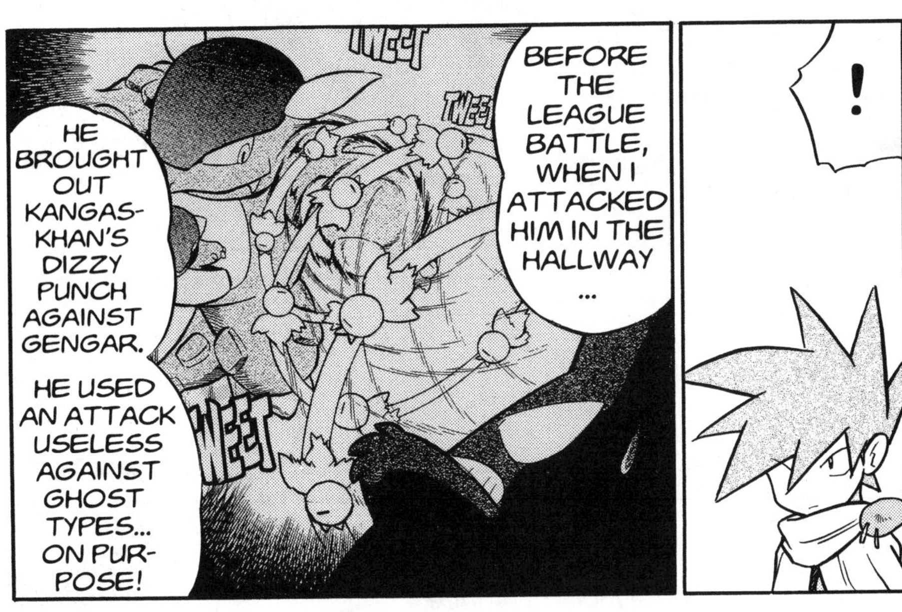
!
BEFORE THE LEAGUE BATTLE, WHEN I ATTACKED HIM IN THE HALLWAY ...
TWEET
TWEET
HE BROUGHT OUT KANGAS-KHAN'S DIZZY PUNCH AGAINST GENGAR.
HE USED AN ATTACK USELESS AGAINST GHOST TYPES... ON PUR-POSE!
TWEET

I SHOULDN'T HAVE LET IT GET TO ME, BUT... WELL... I'M SUCH A SOFTY... HEH HEH HEH...
...
HE WAS GOOD...AND BRAVE...AND STRONG, THEN! HE ISN'T EVEN A SHADOW OF HIS FORMER SELF NOW! MAKING SILLY LITTLE TOYS LIKE THE POKÉDEX! FEH!

OH, BY THE WAY, BLUE. BY LIGHTING THE PLACE FROM ABOVE... AREN'T YOU OVERLOOKING SOMETHING VERY IMPOR-TANT?
THAT BEING ...? GASP ...

STARMIE! IT'S GIVEN US A GUIDING LIGHT—A MESSAGE WRITTEN IN THE SKY!!

"THE ARMY OF DRAGONS HAS INVADED THE MAINLAND. SEARCHING FOR BADGES. ELITE FOUR'S GOAL IS BADGES' COLLECTIVE ENERGY..." WHAT...?!!

I ONLY HAVE JUST ENOUGH POWER...
...TO ESCAPE!
AND I'VE SUSTAINED MUCH DAMAGE FROM THE BATTLE WITH THAT NINJA THERE.
HUF HUF
EEE HEE HEE HEE!! THAT'S RIGHT! WITH MY LAST GENGAR DEFEATED, I NO LONGER HAVE THE POWER TO RETALIATE.

KRAK

RRRRRRMMMMMMM
EVEN IF WE'RE ALL DE-FEATED HERE.
THE ELITE FOUR'S MASTER PLAN IS ALREADY WELL ON ITS WAY TO COM-PLETION!!

RRRRMMM
BUT IT DOESN'T MATTER.
I MIGHT HAVE LOST THE BATTLE... BUT I WILL SEE THIS WAR WON!!

!
KOGA!
GRUMBLE

BOOM
FLAP
SHP
NNH!
THE OLDEST TRICK IN THE NINJA HANDBOOK—HIDING IN PLAIN SIGHT!!

SHRIII

HWOOOOO
LISTEN WELL, BLUE! WHEN ALL EIGHT BADGES COME TOGETHER ON THIS ISLAND, LANCE'S PLAN WILL BE COMPLETE!
AND NOW ONLY ONE REMAINS!!

FOR THAT ONE BADGE, I SENT THE ENTIRE FORCE TO THE MAINLAND...
AND KNOWING LANCE, HE'S PROBABLY TARGETED IT THROUGH A DIFFERENT MEANS AS WELL!

THE ENTIRE MAINLAND FORCE... WAS CONTROL-LED BY AGATHA ALONE!!

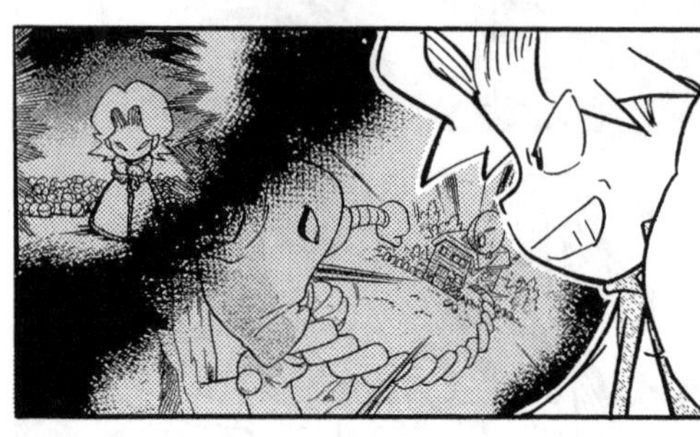
ORDINARILY... IT'S NOT POSSIBLE TO MIMIC ANOTHER'S POKÉ BALLS OR CONTROL ANOTHER'S POKÉMON... CORRECT?
BUT IN MY YOUTH, I STUDIED HOW TO DO JUST THAT!

WHEN I'M CONTROLLING A LARGE NUMBER OR MANIPULATING THEM FROM A DISTANCE, I CAN ONLY SEND OUT SIMPLE COMMANDS... SUCH AS "FIND THE BADGE"...
THAT'S WHY I NEED TO KEEP THE FORMATION OF TROOPS SIMPLE. FOR THE FIGHTING AND ICE TROOPS THAT I SENT TO THE MAINLAND, I GAVE MY COMMANDS TO ONE GROUP LEADER EACH, WHO IN TURN COMMANDED THE REST OF THE TROOPS. BUT I HAD AN ADVANTAGE WITH MY OWN GHOST TROOPS...
GROUP LEADER
TROOPS

THE BANDS ON HIS WRISTS ARE THE SAME AS THE ONES ON MY OWN POKÉMON!
I CONTROLLED BRUNO WITH IT TOO!
THE STAGGERING POWER THAT EMANATES FROM THE BADGES COMBINED!

KRAK
BATTLE FORMATION... ICE-FIGHTING-GHOST!!
BUT I DON'T SUPPOSE I NEED TO EXPLAIN THAT TO YOU, DO I, BLUE?
YOU SAW YOURSELF HOW TEAM ROCKET USED THAT POWER TO COMBINE THE THREE DIFFERENT TYPES...
AND, OF COURSE, THAT'S HOW WE CAPTURED YOUR DEAR FRIEND RED!! EEE HEE HEE!!!

SO YOU **WERE** INVOLVED IN RED'S DISAPPEARANCE!
ZZIP
CHARIZARD!!

!
NN?
HOOOSH
CHARRR

ALL OF THIS HAPPENED, REALLY, BECAUSE THAT PIKACHU ESCAPED DURING THE BATTLE WITH RED...
DOOOO
FSH
AND THE CREATURE SAW OUR ATTACK.
IT MOST LIKELY HATCHED ITS PLAN OF ATTACK AGAINST US AT THAT POINT.

IT MUST HAVE REALIZED THAT IT'S IMPOSSIBLE TO RETURN ENERGY ALREADY RELEASED. IN ORDER TO OVERCOME THAT ENERGY, ONE CAN ONLY COUNTER WITH AN EVEN STRONGER FORCE...!
NOT THAT IT COULD DO ANYTHING LIKE THAT...
UNLESS IT HAD SOME-THING MORE POWERFUL THAN **THUNDER-BOLT**!

I'VE TALKED... TOO LONG.
HWOOOO
BUT THEN... YOU ARE OAK'S GRAND-SON...
EEE HEE HEE HEE.

AGA-THA !!
KRAK
!

!
THAT SOUND ...!
PII PII PII

DAWN... THE DAY'S ABOUT TO BREAK. I CAN'T SEE THE MESSAGE ANYMORE.
BUT THANK YOU, GOOD TRAINERS! THANK YOU! BECAUSE OF YOU, I WAS ABLE TO GET SOME VALUABLE INFORMATION!

MY POKÉDEX...IT'S RESONATING. THAT MEANS THAT ALL THREE POKÉDEX ARE IN CLOSE PROXIMITY TO EACH OTHER.
PI PI PI PI PI
AND IT'S ALSO GIVING OFF THE SIGNAL THAT THE PROPER OWNERS ARE IN POSSESSION OF THEM!

THAT MEANS THAT RED IS ALIVE—AND HE'S HERE! IT MEANS THAT RED HAS HIS POKÉDEX AGAIN!

WOOSH

YOU'RE SAYIN' THAT NOT ONLY DID THIS PERSON SAVE YOU... BUT ALSO GAVE YOU THE STONES ?!

WHO THE HECK WAS IT?!!
WELL, I DIDN'T SEE HIS FACE. BEING FROZEN IN A BLOCK OF ICE WILL DO THAT TO YOU...

BUT AFTER WHO-EVER IT WAS GOT ME OUT OF THE ICE ...
HE GAVE ME THE STONES AND SAID, "TAKE THESE WITH YOU, RED. YOU'RE NOT GOING TO END HERE."

AND THEN... HE GAVE ME THIS.
HE SAID, "THIS WILL LEAD YOU TO YET ANOTHER DECISIVE BATTLE."
THE **SPOON OF DESTINY** !!
BY FOLLOW-ING THE BEND OF THIS SPOON, I'VE BEEN ABLE TO FIND MY WAY TO THIS ISLAND!

WHOA!! BLUE AND GREEN MUST BE NEAR-BY!!
PII PII PII

YOU SHOULD HURRY! YOU GO ON AHEAD WITHOUT ME! I'LL FOLLOW YA!
OKAY !!

RRROOOOO
86
Double Dragonair
WAAAAAAAAGH!!
HWOOH
!!!
GGGRRMM
KLATTER
KLATTER
YOU'RE FIN-ISHED!!

TNG
VSSSH
PIKAAAAA!
VMMMM
PIKA !!

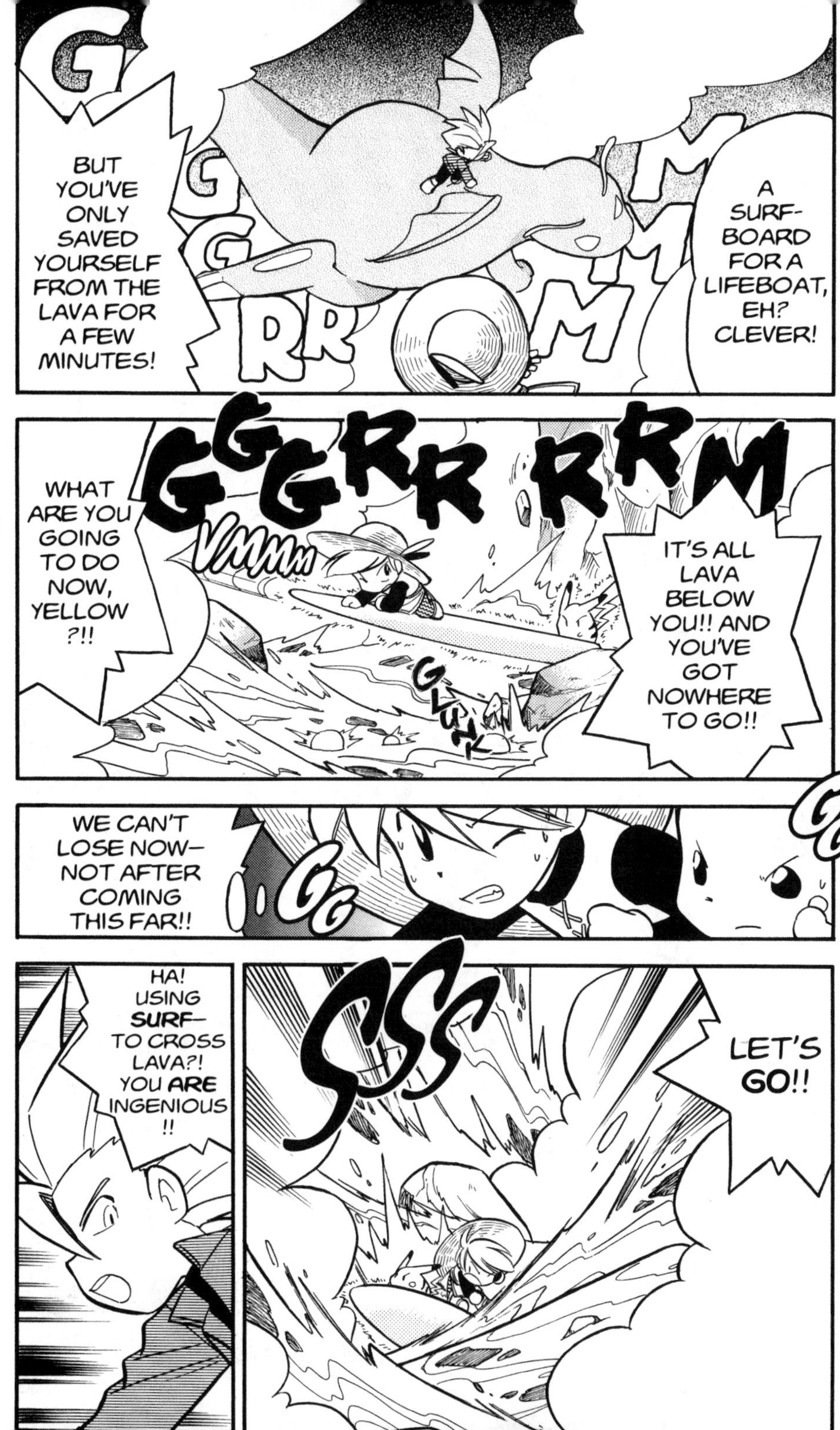
A SURF-BOARD FOR A LIFEBOAT, EH? CLEVER!
BUT YOU'VE ONLY SAVED YOURSELF FROM THE LAVA FOR A FEW MINUTES!
GGGRRRRRM
IT'S ALL LAVA BELOW YOU!! AND YOU'VE GOT NOWHERE TO GO!!
WHAT ARE YOU GOING TO DO NOW, YELLOW?!!
VMMMM
GLUNK
WE CAN'T LOSE NOW—NOT AFTER COMING THIS FAR!!
LET'S GO!!
SSSS
HA! USING SURF TO CROSS LAVA?! YOU ARE INGENIOUS!!

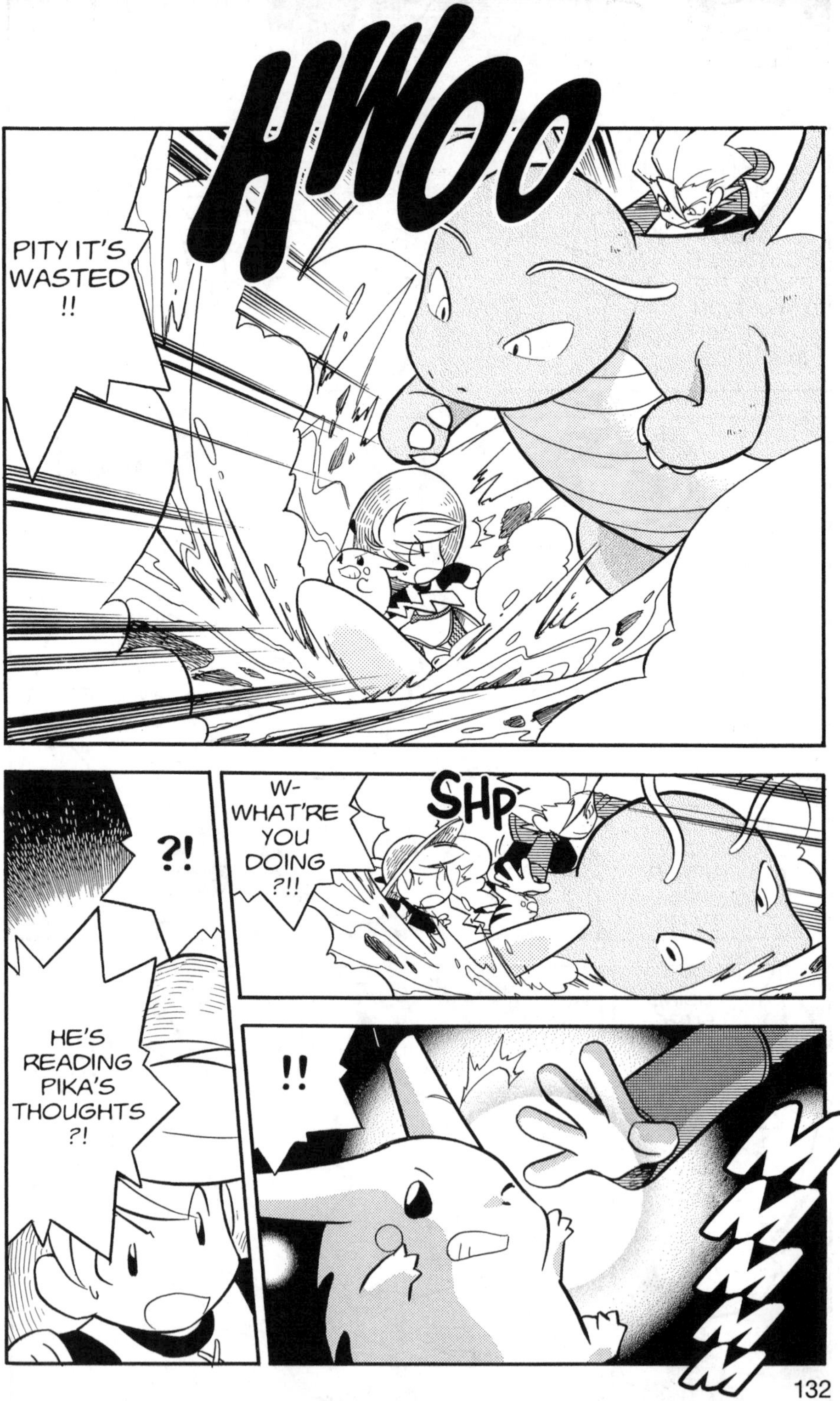

HWOO

PITY IT'S WASTED !!

?!

W- WHAT'RE YOU DOING ?!!

SHP

HE'S READING PIKA'S THOUGHTS ?!

!!

MMMMMMM

PIIIKAAAA!!
GRRR
YOU AND YELLOW BOTH GREW UP IN THE VIRIDIAN FOREST!!
SNORT
WRA HA HA HA! SO THAT'S IT!!
PIIKAAA!!
BZZT
BZZZZAK
BZZT
BZZT
WAAAGH!!
KRAK
SORRY, PIKA! HYPER BEAM!!
WHAT DID YOU SAY?!
JUST BECAUSE YOU CAME FROM THE SAME FOREST I DID...DOESN'T MEAN YOU CAN APPROACH MY POWER!
SSSSS
FRUS-TRATED, PIKACHU? SORRY!

YOU HEARD ME! I'M FROM THE VIRIDIAN FOREST TOO!!
AND I HAVE THE SAME EMPATHIC POWERS THAT YOU DO, YELLOW!!
I KNEW IT!!
GOOD FOR YOU!!
FIGHT BACK, PIKA!!
HYPER BEAM!!
ZAK
ZAK
ZAK
ZAK
THUNDERBOLT!!
I KNEW LANCE COULD READ POKÉMON'S FEELINGS!
HUF HUF
ZAK
ZAK
ZAK
BUT HOW CAN HE USE THOSE POWERS...THE POWERS GIFTED US BY THE VIRIDIAN FOREST...FOR DESTRUCTION?!

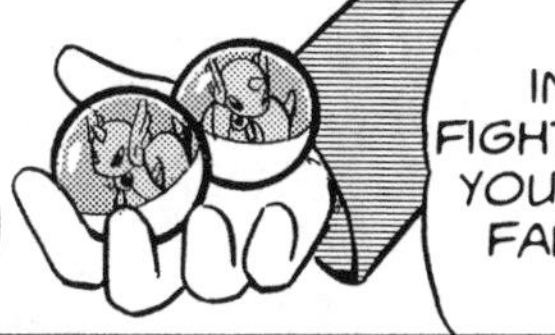

IN-DEED.
RRRRMMM
FIRST, TO GALLOP... NOT JUST ACROSS THE SEAS, BUT THROUGH THE AIR...
RKKKMMMB
SECOND, TO CHANGE THE DIRECTION OF ENERGY BLASTS ...
THIRD, TO CONTROL THE WEATHER ITSELF...
AND FINALLY, TO TOSS THEIR OPPONENTS AROUND BY COMBINING THEIR **ATTACK** MODES!

BZZT
BZT
...
IT'S RARE THAT I HAVE TO USE ALL FOUR.
BZT
IN MY EASIER BATTLES I USUALLY ONLY HAVE TO USE THE FIRST AND SECOND POWERS. I SAVE THE THIRD FOR MY STRONGER ENEMIES.
AND THEN ...
I'LL GIVE YOU A MOMENT TO TAKE PRIDE IN THAT DISTINCTION...
I'M AFRAID THAT'S A QUESTION YOU'LL NEVER ANSWER...
BZZZT
BZT
BZZT
... BECAUSE IT ALL ENDS HERE!!
HOW MANY POWERS DO YOU THINK I HAVE AT MY COMMAND AMONG ALL FIVE OF MY POKÉMON?!
I'LL POINT OUT THAT BOTH DRAGONAIR ADD UP TO ONLY A FRACTION OF MY POWER!
HWOOO
BZT
BZT
WHAT... CAN I DO...?
I CAN'T... HOLD OUT... MUCH LONGER!!
HUF
GYAAH !!

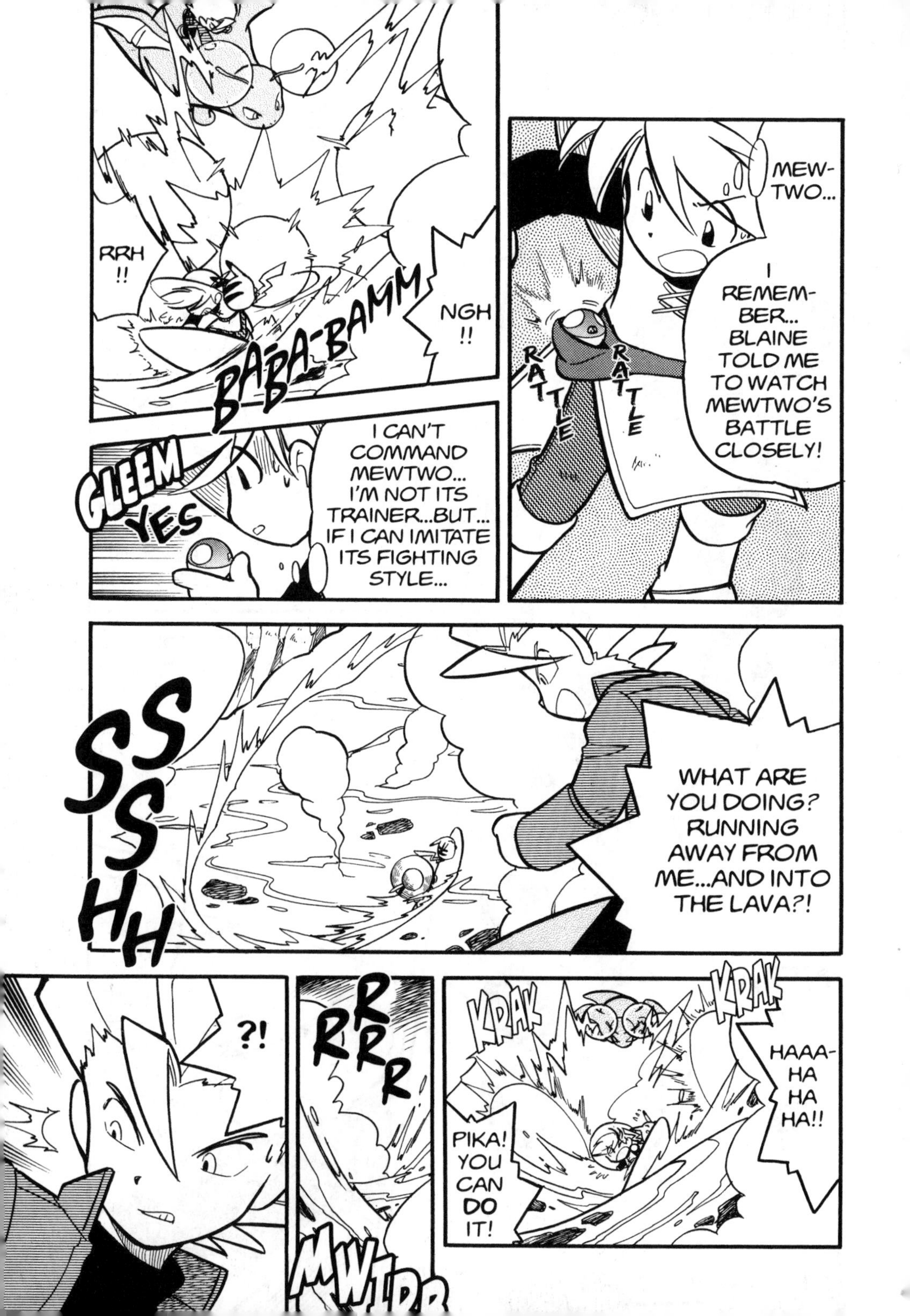

RRH !!
NGH !!
BA-BA-BAMM
MEW-TWO...
I REMEMBER... BLAINE TOLD ME TO WATCH MEWTWO'S BATTLE CLOSELY!
RATTLE RATTLE
GLEEM
YES
I CAN'T COMMAND MEWTWO... I'M NOT ITS TRAINER...BUT... IF I CAN IMITATE ITS FIGHTING STYLE...

GRROOO
W-WHAT—WHAT IS THIS?! THAT SPINNING...
IT'S STARTED A WHIRLPOOL IN THE LAVA!!
ROOOOOOOOOOO
THE CLEVER TRAP THAT MEWTWO MADE BEFORE...
...BUT THIS TIME WITH LAVA!!
NOW!!

N-NO!! I'M— I'M BEING SUCKED INTO IT—!!
NOT IF YOU SURRENDER NOW!
NOT IF YOU PLEDGE NEVER TO ATTACK ANYONE AGAIN!
SSSS
NGH... UHH...
DO YOU ACTUALLY... THINK YOU'VE... **WON**?! DO YOU IMAGINE... YOU'VE BEATEN...
HSSH!
... **LANCE** ?!!
!
RRRR
!
THEY'RE RIPPING THROUGH THE LAVA!! THEY'RE CHARGING !!

GZOO
!!

DOOM
MMRGH !!
SSSSSSSSS
NKH!

SKRIIIK
SSS
UHH!!
SSSS
BLOOSH
AAAAAGH!!

HUF
HUF HUF

GLUB
THERE'S... NO-WHERE TO HIDE...
GLP
AND IF HE DID SINK BENEATH THE LAVA...

87 Rhyhorn Rising

GGRRRR OOOOOO
HE CAN'T POSSIBLY... STILL BE ALIVE...
WE...CAN'T STAY HERE. IT'S DANGEROUS. WE HAVE TO FIND RATTY AND THE OTHERS...

IT'S THEM!

ZZZZIP
!

OKAY! LET'S GET BACK TO WHERE BLAINE IS.

HOORAY! IS EVERY-ONE ALL RIGHT?
OOF
OOOOOF
RATTY! DODY! OMNY! KITTY! GRAVVY!

?
STARE

PI?

GLUP

WHRRR
TMTMTM

FWOOF

EH?

WHAT'S WRONG, PIKA...?

TM TM TM

GLLLLRRR

LLLUUR

GL
LANCE!
VIP
BLUPBLUPBLUPBLUP

THE BUBBLES DISAP-PEARED—!

PF

PF

VIP

WHAK

!!

DMD

KRAK

AAAGH!! M-MY... **ARM**...!!

BWAAAAAAA
BLAP
BLAP
WHAT'S HAPPEN-ING?!
I CAN'T SEE HIS ATTACKS!
BOP
BIP
BOP
THE BUBBLE ATTACK... IT'S BEING LAUNCHED BY...THE TWO DRAGONAIR AND GYARADOS...?!
THEY'RE MAKING DIFFERENT COLORED BUBBLES EACH...RED, GREEN AND BLUE! THE PRIMARY COLORS OF PURE **LIGHT**!!
RED, GREEN, BLUE MIN-GLING
REFLEC-TION
SUNLIGHT
C- CAN IT BE...THAT WHEN THOSE THREE COME TOGETHER... THEY BECOME SIMPLE WHITE LIGHT...
...VANISHING INTO THE LIGHT OF THE SUN... AND BECOMING INVISIBLE?!
THAP
HUFF ... HUFF ...
DOPP
KLATTER
NHH ...!!
ZIP
YAH!

UUUUUU!

DGG

HUF HUF
HUF HUF
I'VE GOT TO COUNTER THOSE INVISIBLE BUBBLES...

EVERYONE...
GASP...
LISTEN
CLOSELY...
I HAVE A
PLAN...
HUF
HUF

WHILE
I WAS
RUNNING
TO ESCAPE...
I TOLD
KITTY...
SHLUUU

...TO SPIN
OUT SOME
THREAD...
CAN YOU
SEE IT?
IT'S JUST
THICK ENOUGH...
THAT LANCE
SHOULDN'T BE
ABLE TO SEE
IT...YET.

NOW,
RATTY...
AND
OMNY...
AND
PIKA...
YOU'LL...
PSS
PSS

GOT IT?
WE CAN'T
GO UP
AGAINST
THEM ONE
AT A TIME.
OUR TIMING
HAS TO BE
PERFECT!
RRRMMM

GO!
USH

VNN
PFF
PFF
VNN
VNN
YOU'RE NOT GETTING AWAY!
THE BUBBLES VAN-ISHED! THIS IS IT!!
TWIK
PING
RATAAAA !!
PIKAAA!
TNG
BZT BZT
BZT
POPP
NOD

POP
POP
POP
!
AND OMNY'S WATER DROPLETS WILL CONDUCT THAT ELECTRICITY ALONG KITTY'S THREAD!!
RATTY'S SENSITIVE WHISKERS WILL PICK UP THE VIBRATIONS WHEN THE BUBBLES HIT THE THREAD— SO PIKA KNOWS WHEN TO ZAP!
A TRAP! BUT...
NOW!
NNN NNN
VOOOM!
OUR COM-BINED ATTACK!

GNYOOOOOMG
DRILL PECK ...!!
IT DIDN'T WORK?! B-BUT WHY...?!!
THE PLAN WAS FINE...
HOW ...?
THE THREAD TRAP SLOWED ME DOWN, JUST AS YOU INTENDED.
UNFORTU-NATE THAT, IN THE END...
GYOOOO-
POP
...YOU JUST DIDN'T HAVE THE POWER TO BEAT ME!!
WAAAAAAAGH!!

B-BOOM
VSSSH

WHO... WHO ARE YOU...?

TAP

...

WOBBLE
IF... YOU'VE COME TO RESCUE ME... THANKS, BUT...
LANCE CAN ONLY BE DEFEATED... BY A TRAINER FROM VIRIDIAN...

HUF
...AND THAT MEANS... ME...

FOR I AM FROM THE VIRIDIAN FOREST TOO!

88 The Beedrill All and End All

KAAA
WWW

TOP
PIKA-
PII!

PIIPIKA!
PIIIIII!
P...PIKA...?!
W-WHAT'S...
WRONG...?!

HMPH
...

MMMMM
OH...!
PIKA'S...
MEMO-
RIES!

YOU...YOU
FOUGHT
AGAINST
THIS MAN
ONCE
BEFORE
...!
IN THE
VIRIDIAN
FOREST
!!

HSS
IS
HE AN
ENEMY?!
OR AN
ALLY?!

TWIK TWIK
WHAT IS THIS?! WHAT ARE YOU TRYING TO PULL ?!

I DON'T CARE WHO YOU ARE! NO ONE GETS IN LANCE'S WAY!
GYOOOOBBBBB
BUBBLE BEAM!!

THE...THE BUBBLES! HE'S ATTACKING AGAIN!!
PFF PFF
A BUBBLE ATTACK THAT BECOMES INVISIBLE WITH SUNLIGHT, HUH? HA HA!
RHY-HORN! HORN ATTACK!
RRRRRR
RRRMMMM
NOW... STOMP!

PFFFF

PIP
PIP
PIP
AND THE **SAND** MAKES THE BUBBLES VISIBLE!!

OH! THE BOULDER THAT WAS CRUSHED BY ITS HORN...! THE STOMP ATTACK IS THROWING IT UP...LIKE A SAND-STORM...

NOW THAT WE CAN SEE THE BUBBLES... THE BATTLE'S OURS!
CHK
RRRH!!
POP
NIDO-QUEEN, SCRATCH!
POP
POP

BOYOING
VMMM
?!
BURST THE MAIN BUBBLE!
MY TURN!
DOMP
THIS BUBBLE SHIELD WITH-STOOD THE HEAT OF LAVA! DO YOU THINK THAT CAN POP IT?!
KRAK
HYPER BEAM!

HOW'S THAT ?!
YAAAAAUGH!
KRKOOOM
OHH!

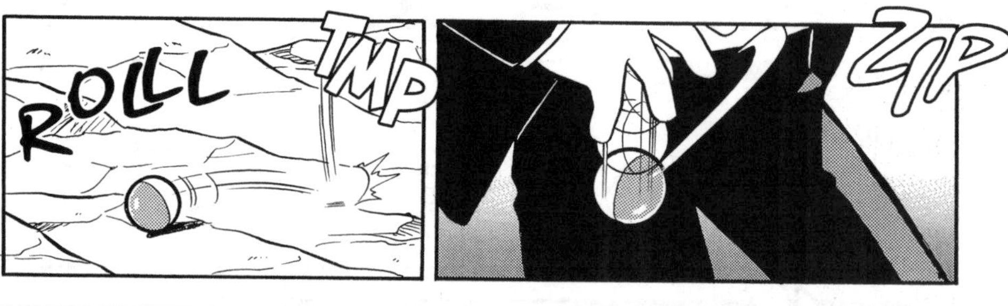

?!
KCH
ROLLLLLLLLLLL
YOU LEFT THE UNDER-SIDE OPEN!
VOOOM
BOM

TWINEEDLE!!
BOOOSH
GH!
!!
POP P

DMMM

Ss
TP
...
TNNNG
RRR... GH!

HE... HE DOWNED LANCE...!

GMMG
YOU'RE THE VIRIDIAN CITY GYM LEADER, AREN'T YOU...?

YES.

I ASSUME YOU KNOW THAT MY SPECIALTY IS **GROUND**-TYPE POKÉMON...

...AND THAT I RARELY VENTURE INTO OTHER TYPES. BUT THIS **BEEDRILL** IS SPECIAL.

THIS ONE EVOLVED IN OUR HOMELAND... THE VIRIDIAN FOREST.

FWP
SNAP

SNORT
AND NOW...?

SKRIK

SWF
?!

WOBBLE
M-MISTER GIOVANNI... PLEASE...

YOU THINK OUR ORGANIZATION TEETERS ON THE BRINK OF ANNIHILATION...
...BECAUSE OF YOUR ATTACKS... YOU OF THE CURSED "ELITE FOUR."
BUT WE ARE NOT SO EASILY DEFEATED. WHEN THE TIME COMES, WE WILL RISE AGAIN...

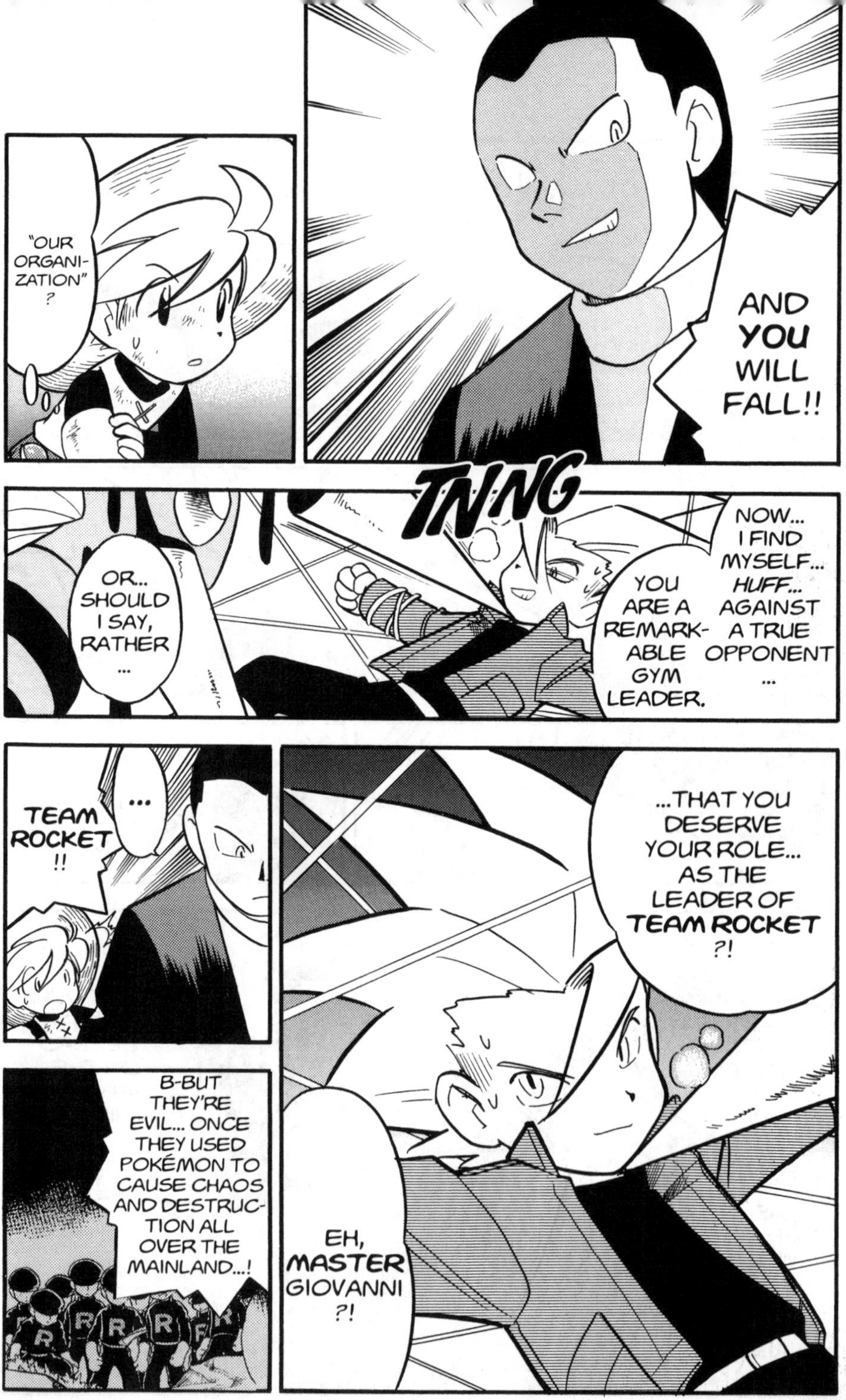

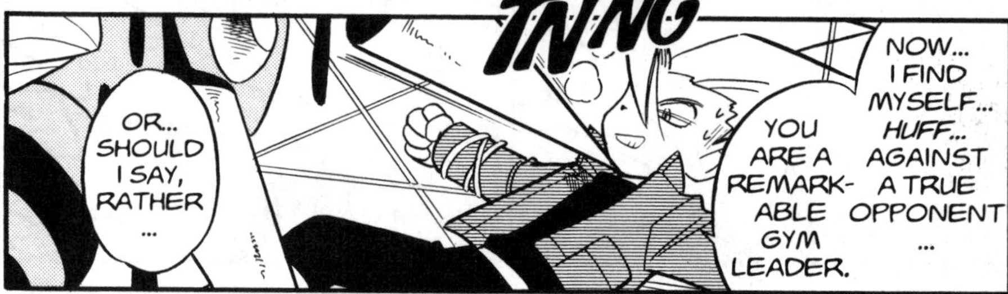

...THAT YOU DESERVE YOUR ROLE... AS THE LEADER OF **TEAM ROCKET** ?!

...

TEAM ROCKET !!

EH, **MASTER** GIOVANNI ?!

B-BUT THEY'RE EVIL... ONCE THEY USED POKÉMON TO CAUSE CHAOS AND DESTRUCTION ALL OVER THE MAINLAND...!

THIS MAN... USED MY HOME...

AND THIS MAN IS ITS LEADER ...?!

...USED THE BEAUTIFUL VIRIDIAN FOREST...TO PERFORM HIS EVIL DEEDS...

NNN
HUFF HUFF
HHHH

NNNN
ENOUGH.
THE GAME IS OVER.

HEH
GRRRRMMMMMM

RRRRMMMMMMMM

RRRRRU UUMMM

HA HA HA HA HA... WRA-HA-HAA!!!
?!
EH...? HEH... HEH-HEH...
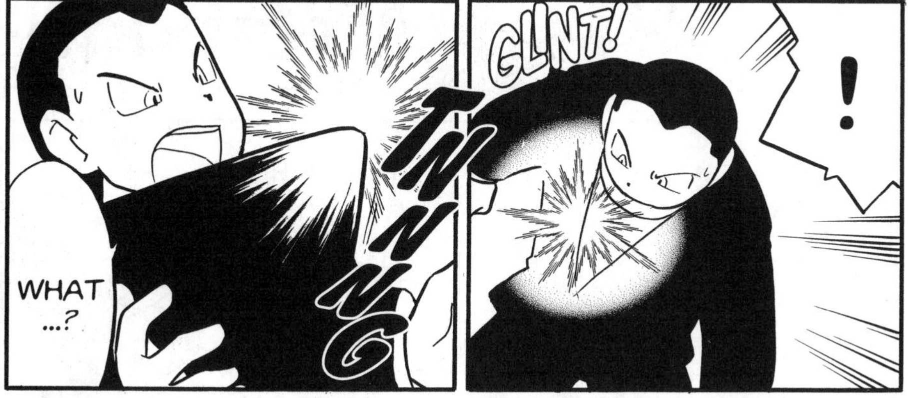
WHAT ...?
GLINT!
TINNNNG
!

GYUUUUM

89 The Might of… Metapod?!

GIOVANNI, I DON'T HAVE TO TELL YOU WHAT THIS MEANS. YOU'RE A GYM LEADER.

POK

THE MORE TRAINER BADGES YOU BRING TOGETHER, THE MORE POWER YOU HAVE TO CONTROL POKÉMON.

ZLOOP

THAT'S RIGHT!!

!

I ALREADY HAD SEVEN OF THE EIGHT BADGES IN HAND.

THEY'RE HIDDEN UNDER THE SEVEN STONE COLUMNS THAT JUT TOWARD THE SKY FROM THE PERIMETER OF THE ISLAND...

IT... IT CAN'T BE!!
FIRE, ROCK, GRASS, ELECTRIC, POISON, WATER, PSYCHE, GROUND...YOU REMEMBER THE ORDER, DON'T YOU?
ALL PLACED SO AS TO OPTIMIZE THE POWER I SIPHON FROM THEIR VIBRATIONS!

HEHNH

IT CAN. AND IT IS.

THIS ENTIRE ISLAND IS ONE GIGANTIC BADGE-ENERGY AMPLIFIER!!

THE ONE THAT JUST FLEW FROM YOUR CHEST AND STARTED TO GLOW WAS THE LAST ONE! THE ONE I'VE BEEN SEARCHING FOR!

THIS "AMPLIFIER" IS LAID OUT SO THAT MERELY BRINGING THE BADGE TO ITS MIDPOINT...
...WOULD AUTOMATICALLY RELEASE ITS ENERGY!

YOU THOUGHT THAT YOU WERE PUSHING ME TO THE EDGE?! HA!
I WAS IN COMMAND!
I LURED YOU TO THE CENTER OF THE ISLAND!

...

AND NOW...
GYO OOO

THE ENERGY OF THE EIGHT UNITED BADGES WILL RISE...
GLANCE
GYO OOO

OOOOOO OOOOOOOOO

...UNTIL IT REACHES MY SECRET WEAPON... THE OBJECT OF ALL MY DESIGNS!!
KRAK
THE LEGENDARY SPIRIT THAT APPEARS ABOVE THE ISLAND WITH THE BREAK OF DAY!

KIIIIIINNNN
SOME-THING WRONG, SABRI-NA?
OH ...!!

AND WE'VE DEFEATED LORELEI... MEANING THAT MOST OF OUR OBJECTIVES HERE HAVE BEEN COMPLETED... HEH...

I CAN FEEL IT. THE OTHER TWO BATTLES BEING FOUGHT ON THIS ISLAND... HAVE BEEN RESOLVED ...
KOGA, LT. SURGE AND THEIR PARTNERS MUST ALSO HAVE DEFEATED A MEMBER OF THE ELITE FOUR!

PFFF
!

SSSHHH
...AND OUR LITTLE ALLIANCE CAN BE DISSOLVED!

WELL, I'M GLAD SHE WAS ALONG FOR THE BATTLE WITH LORE-LEI.
EVEN SO, I HAD TO USE CLEFABLE, HORSEA, NIDORINA, BLAS-TOISE AND DITTO!!

H-HEY !!
SHEESH... JUST AS SELF-CENTERED AS ALWAYS...

GUESS YOU DIDN'T HAVE A CHANCE TO SHOW YOUR STUFF, EH, SNUBBULL?

EVERY-BODY BUT MY ACE IN THE HOLE... MY SEVENTH POKÉMON ...

HUH? WHAT WAS... OH!!

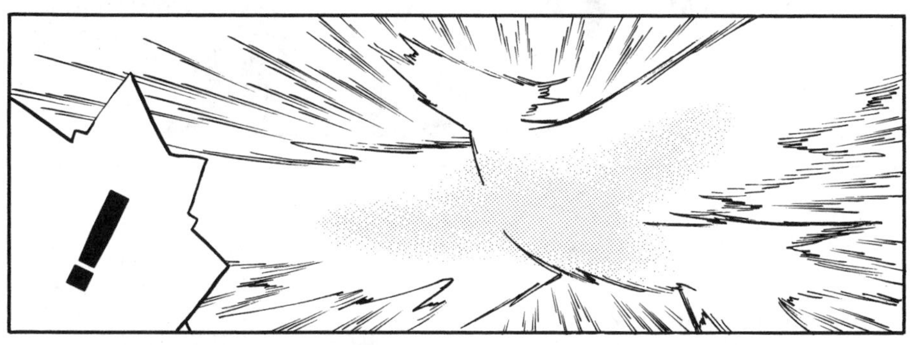
!

I HAVE TO GET TO IT--!
VSH

...

A... POKÉMON! A GIGANTIC POKÉMON !!

IS THAT... A POKÉ-MON?!
OH...!

GIO-VANNI—?!
VSSH

QUITE A SETUP YOU'VE CONTRIVED HERE, LANCE. WELL...

OUR ASSAULT ON VERMILION CITY... ALL THE TROOPS WE SENT TO THE MAINLAND...HAVE PAID OFF! WE HAVE THE POWER!!

WRA HA HA HA! THE GREAT GIOVANNI IS A COWARD! WELL, AT LEAST HE WAS BRAVE ENOUGH TO BE LURED HERE.

LANCE! WHAT ARE YOU DOING?!!
CAN'T YOU TELL?!
I'M GOING UP...TO WHERE THE LEGEND-ARY POKÉMON FLIES!

AERO-DACTYL! CARRY ME UP THERE!
TM

THIS WAS MY OBJECT FROM THE BEGINNING— TO TAKE CONTROL OF THIS POKÉMON! TO RIDE THE ONE THAT NO ONE HAS EVER BEEN ABLE TO TAME!
IF I CAN CONTROL IT... THEN NOT ONLY THE MAINLAND BUT THE ENTIRE WORLD...WILL BE FREED FROM HUMANS FOREVER!

TURN THAT POKÉMON AGAINST THE WORLD...?!
NO! YOU CAN'T!

LANCE, IT'S INSANE!!
DON'T YOU SEE HOW MUCH PAIN AND DESTRUCTION YOU'LL BRING?!!
NOD
DRAGONITE, I'LL BE WAITING FOR YOU UP THERE... SO FOLLOW ME UP!

GRRN
HWOOO
NKH!
VIIIIN

WOBBLE

WH... WHAT ...?

!

IT'S SO... EXHAUST-ED.

OF **COURSE**! IT WAS IN THAT LAVA ALL THIS TIME, WAITING FOR LANCE'S SIGNAL!

MMMM

WOBBLE

COULD LANCE REALLY NOT HAVE NOTICED HOW WEAK IT WAS...?

HWOOH

AH!

NO... THAT'S NOT IT! DRAGON-ITE WAS **HIDING** ITS CON-DITION SACRI-FICING ITSELF!

IT'S TRYING TO FOLLOW LANCE! BUT IT'S TOO EXHAUSTED...!

VSH

STOP!!
THE EFFORT WILL KILL YOU!!
HWOOH
GRAPP

WHY WOULD YOU DO ALL THIS FOR LANCE?

MY TRAINER FIGHTS FOR POKÉMON! WE WILL PUNISH THE HUMAN ENEMY!
I MUST DO ANYTHING FOR HIM!

!!
I'M READING... DRAGON-ITE'S FEEL-INGS!!

SO YOU THINK HUMANS ARE THE ENEMY? WELL, DRAGONITE... YOU'RE RIGHT! IT'S TRUE THAT HUMANS HAVE BEEN DESTROYING NATURE...
...TEARING DOWN FORESTS AND POLLUTING THE RIVERS... SLOWLY DESTROYING THE NATURAL HABITATS OF POKÉMON.
...ACTING AS THOUGH THE WORLD BELONGS TO THEM ALONE ...

OF COURSE YOU FEEL RAGE TOWARD HUMANS.
BUT LANCE IS JUST TAKING ADVANTAGE OF THOSE FEELINGS!
I UNDER-STAND WHY YOU THINK HE'S YOUR FRIEND!
BUT THINK—

HIS WAY ISN'T THE ANSWER! HUMANS DON'T DESERVE PUNISHMENT—ANY MORE THAN POKÉMON!
KLATTER
HUMANS AND POKÉMON **CAN** LIVE TOGETHER! I KNOW IT!
YOU KNOW IT TOO, PIKA... RATTY. BUT HOW DO I MAKE THEM BELIEVE?
KLATTER
OMNY, DODY, KITTY, GRAVVY... HOW DO I SHOW THEM?
GIVE ME THE POWER TO SHOW THEM!!

TP
KRAK
WHAT ARE YOU DOING HERE ?!
GWOOOM

TI NG
FSSSSSSS SHHHH

!

A METAPOD ?!

BUT WE'RE GOING TO STOP LANCE! ALL OF YOU, PLEASE...LEND ME YOUR POWER!

THE POWER... TO PROTECT THE WORLD!

MWEK MWEK

MWEK MWEK

MWEK MWEK

EVOLVING... TWO LEVELS ?!!
GLOWWW
KRAK
TMM
LANCE— I'M COMING !!
FSSH

HUMANS ARE THE ENEMY OF POKÉMON! IN ORDER TO PUNISH THEM...

YOU'RE WRONG! HUMANS AND POKÉMON ARE PARTNERS!!

I MUST HAVE THE POWER OF THAT POKÉMON!!

I WILL PROTECT **BOTH** OUR WORLDS!

DESTROY THEM!
HYOHHHH!!
90
The Legend

NO!!

WRAAAAAA!!

GOOWOOOM
RGH!
NKH!
VWIP
ICE BEAM!
HYPER BEAM!
KRAK
DE-FENSE CURL!
FALL! SLAM!
FOMP

UNTIL... YOU... SEE THE **TRUTH**!

GNNNNNG

HEH... HOW LONG CAN THIS BATTLE OF SHIELDS LAST?

GWOOP

IN MINUTES, THE LEGENDARY POKÉMON WILL HAVE DEVOURED ALL THIS ENERGY!

AND THEN... WITH A SINGLE FLAP OF ITS WINGS... IT WILL RENDER ALL THE TROOPS THAT WE'VE SENT INTO EVERY LAND UNDER ITS ABSOLUTE CONTROL! AND I WILL CONTROL **IT**!!

I CAN SEE IT NOW, DRAGON-ITE!!

NNOD

WE'RE ALMOST THERE!

KRAK
FREE FROM HUMANS!
HKK!
SHLUUU
SHLUU
PA-THET-IC!!
BZZZ
BWAP
BZZZZ
BM
PIKA!
RAGE!
BIDE!

VOOOOM
KEEEEN
PIKA!
GASP!

THESE ARE... PIKA'S MEMORIES!!
PIKA'S LOST MEMORIES ARE... COMING BACK...?!

PIKA SAW RED'S BATTLE WITH THE ELITE FOUR...
...SAW THE POWER GENERATED BY THE COMING TOGETHER OF THE BADGES...
...AND CAUGHT ON TO THEIR PLANS!

IT'S IMPOSSIBLE TO STOP THE FLOW OF THE ENERGY! THE ONLY WAY TO COUNTER IT—IS TO HIT IT WITH A POWER GREATER THAN THE ENERGY AND BLAST IT AWAY!
IF WE CAN BLAST THE ENERGY AWAY FROM THE BADGES, WE CAN STOP LANCE'S MADNESS!!

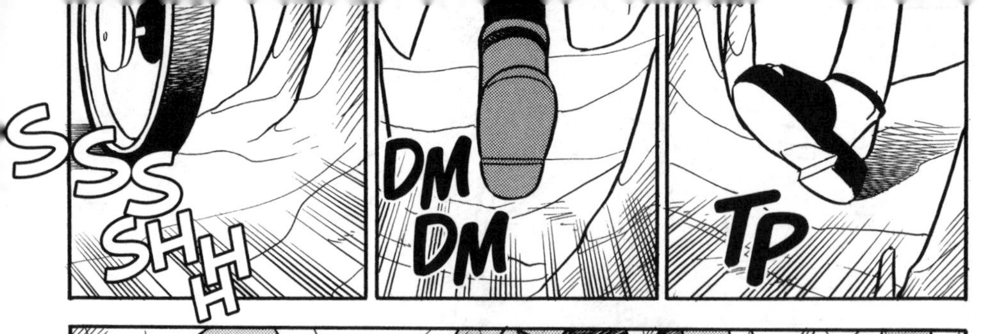
TP
DM
DM
SSSSHHHH

HEY!

RED!! SO YOU WERE SAFE!
LOOKS LIKE YOU GOT YOUR LIFE BACK, MM?
HA HA HA... I GUESS YOU COULD SAY THAT!
WE DON'T HAVE TIME TO TALK.
FIRST, WE'VE GOT TO GET OUT-SIDE.

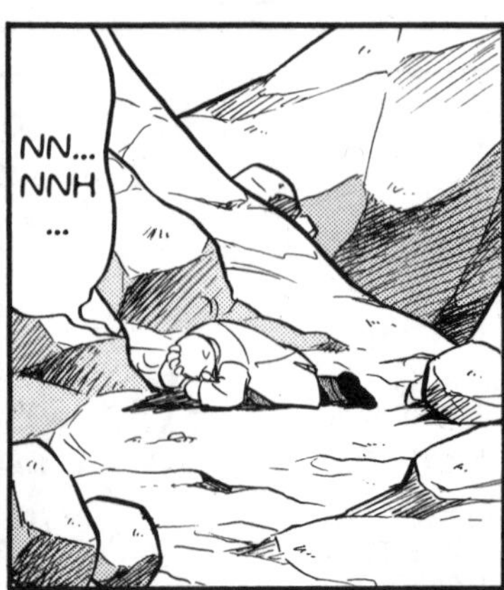
NN... NNH ...

FFFFF
THIS THREAD ...!

SHP
!

YUP. I DEFEATED BRUNO, THEN RAN HERE AS FAST AS I COULD.
YOU'RE SAFE !!
ALL OF YOU!
GREEN—BLUE—RED—!!
THERE'S A THREAD COMING DOWN FROM ABOVE... COULD THAT MEAN THAT YELLOW'S UP THERE TOO?!
OOOOOOOOO
BUT WHAT'S THAT THING UP THERE?
CHK
AND THAT HUGE POKÉMON IS LANCE'S ULTIMATE WEAPON!
NOD
WE'RE UP AGAINST LANCE... THE LEADER OF THE ELITE FOUR.
CHARRR
BOBOBOM
CHARI-ZARD!
BLAS-TOISE!
VENU-SAUR!

SEND ALL YOUR **POWER** UP THERE ALONG THIS THREAD!
UWOOO
OOOOOOOO
!!
...IT'S FROM THE OTHER POKÉ-MON!
THIS POWER ...
I CALL UPON THE POWER OF THE VIRIDIAN FOREST... GIVE US THE **POWER**!! THE POWER OF...
PIKA!
PI!

MEGA-
VOLT
!!

KRAK

TOO...
TOO
MUCH–!!
BWOOOOOOM

SSSHHHHH
NO GREAT SURPRISE. I DIDN'T THINK LANCE WOULD BE ANY MATCH...
...FOR THAT!
SSSSHHHHH
FLOW-ERS ?!
PWOP
YELLOW'S MYSTERIOUS POWERS SEEM TO HAVE TRANSFORMED THE DEFLECTED ENERGIES OF THE BADGES.
MWUP MWUP
MWUP MWUP
NOW THIS ISLAND TOO WILL BE LUSH WITH PLANT LIFE.
NOT THAT IT DOES ME ANY GOOD...
SHK

BOSS!! WAIT!!

I KNEW WE'D MEET AGAIN, BOSS!
AS YOU CAN SEE, WE'VE BEEN GETTING THINGS READY FOR THE ORGANIZATION TO RISE UP AGAIN! NOW'S THE TIME TO STRIKE BACK— TOGETHER!

LT. SURGE... AND SABRINA. I TAKE IT KOGA IS AFRAID TO SHOW HIS FACE.
AND DOES GETTING READY FOR THE RESURREC-TION MEAN SEEKING HELP IN DEFEATING THE ELITE FOUR...
...FROM **CHILDREN**?!
B-BUT BOSS—!!

I'M STILL IN THE MIDDLE OF A TRAINING JOURNEY, SEEKING TO BUILD UP MY OWN STRENGTH ENOUGH TO REALIZE MY PLANS.
I SUGGEST YOU GO HOME FOR NOW. TEND YOUR OWN GYMS!

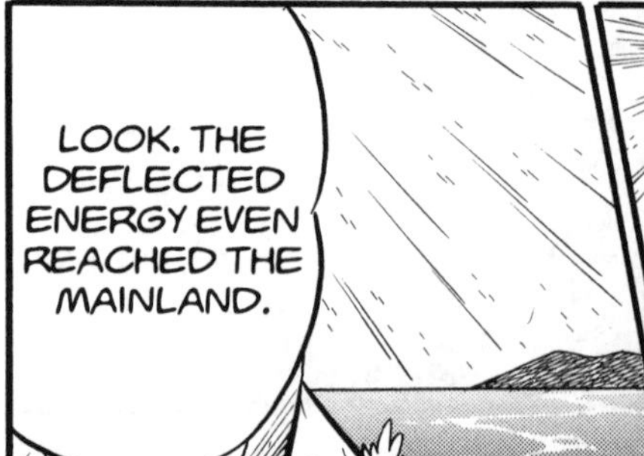
THE MEGA-VOLT... TEN TIMES MORE POWERFUL THAN THE THUNDER-BOLT.
IS THERE EVEN ONE AMONG US WHO CAN PRODUCE AS MUCH POWER AS RED OR YELLOW?
LOOK. THE DEFLECTED ENERGY EVEN REACHED THE MAINLAND.

POF

MWOK
MWOK

!
WHAT HAP- PENED ...?!

MWOK
MWOK
MWOK
IT... IT CAN'T BE...! THAT WHOLE RANGE FROM NORTHWEST CERULEAN TO THE ROCK MOUNTAINS HAD BEEN A WASTELAND FROM INDUSTRIAL RUINS...

SOMETHING MUST HAVE HAPPENED TO THE TRAINERS ...

PLUNG

PLUNG

PLUNG
THE FORCES OF THE ELITE FOUR ARE LOSING THEIR POWERS ...!

AS IF THEIR "POWERS OF DE-STRUCTION" HAD SOMEHOW...
...BEEN TRANS-FORMED INTO "POWERS OF LIFE"!

SSS
HHHH

HUFF ...
HUFF ...
SHOOOO
WAFT
OH ...
HUFF
FWOOOOOO

EH...?! WHERE AM I?! I THOUGHT I WAS HIGH ABOVE CERISE ISLAND...?
SHAKA
SHAKA
RATTY! DO YOU KNOW WHERE PIKA IS?
PIKA'S...GONE.
IS THAT YOU, PIKA?
RUSTLE
RUSTLE
PIKA! PIIIIKA! WHERE ARE YOU?

RUSH

RUSTLE RUSTLE
OMNY? GRAVVY?
NO... YOU'RE... DODY?

FLAP FLAP
YOU ALL LOOK SO DIFFERENT... OH. OF COURSE... YOU EVOLVED...
FLAP! FLAP!
AND...CAN IT BE? KITTY?!

COME ON, PIKA!
COME HERE!
PIKA!
WHRR
ZIP!
HEY!
CHUUUUU
ZZZZ
PIKA! WAIT!
ZZZIP

BOING!
GLINT
PIKA... THAT'S RIGHT! YOU'RE RED'S POKÉMON!
WE WERE TOGETHER FOR SO LONG I'D FORGOTTEN.
ZZZ
BUT LET'S...STAY LIKE WE WERE BEFORE... JUST FOR A LITTLE WHILE LONGER..

HEY THERE. YOU AWAKE?
GLOMP
WAUGH!!
...
HM?
BLINK

YOU BLASTED LANCE AWAY. AND THAT POKÉMON FLEW OFF TO THE WEST.

GASP!
WHAT ABOUT LANCE? AND THAT HUGE POKÉMON?!
OH NO! I FELL ASLEEP AGAIN...!

EVEN GOLEM, WHICH USUALLY ONLY EVOLVES WHEN TRADED...

ALL QUITE REMARKABLE. YELLOW HAD CANCELED HER POKÉMON'S EVOLUTIONS AGAIN AND AGAIN... ONCE THEY WERE FINALLY ALLOWED TO EVOLVE, THE RESULT WAS MIRACULOUS.

I JUST TALKED TO THE MAINLAND. APPARENTLY THE ELITE FOUR'S ARMY LOST ITS POWER AS SOON AS LANCE WAS OUT OF THE PICTURE!
PRRT

HEY, GREEN.
UH-HUH?
IT'S ABOUT... Y'KNOW... WHAT'S UNDER-NEATH YELLOW'S HAT.

YOU ALREADY KNOW... BLAINE SAYS HE'S SEEN IT ALREADY...
AND I'M SURE BLUE FIGURED IT OUT WHILE HE WAS TRAINING WITH HER. HE'S PRETTY SHARP.

SO THAT MEANS... ONLY RED DOESN'T KNOW?
YUP.

WELL? WHY DON'T YOU **TELL** HIM?!!

HMMM... I SUPPOSE BECAUSE ...

IT'S SO MUCH MORE FUN WAITING FOR HIM TO FIGURE IT OUT!! WA HA HA!!!
TEE HEE
...
WHAT AN OBNOX-IOUS GIRL.

PAP
THE BATTLE'S OVER.
GREAT JOB, YELLOW! THANKS FOR EVERY-THING!

SO WHAT TO DO, HUH, PIKA?
Oh!
I'D LOVE TO TRAVEL WITH PIKA AGAIN... BUT IT REALLY SEEMS TO LIKE YOU TOO!
...
HEY... MAYBE WE SHOULD JUST ALL LIVE TOGETHER!
Just kidding!
!

AND SO THE STORY OF AMARILLO DEL BOSQUE VERDE AND THE BATTLE WITH THE ELITE FOUR CAME TO A CLOSE.

YELLOW, RED, GREEN AND BLUE REUNITED WITH MISTY AND THE OTHERS ON THE MAINLAND, AND THEY ALL POURED THEIR ENERGIES INTO REBUILDING THE RAVAGED CITIES.

THE REST OF OUR CHARACTERS TURNED TO THEIR OWN SEPARATE PATHS, CHASING NEW GOALS.

LT. SURGE AND SABRINA FOLLOWED GIOVANNI'S ORDERS AND RETURNED TO THEIR RESPECTIVE GYMS.

OF WHAT HAPPENED TO KOGA AND GIOVANNI THEMSELVES, HOWEVER, NOTHING IS YET KNOWN.

SO TIME FLOWS, AND THE STORIES NEVER TRULY END...

HELLO ...
IT'S ME, GREEN. HAHA. YES, I'M DOING GREAT.
BY THE WAY... I HAVE A MISSION FOR YOU RIGHT NOW. YUP...

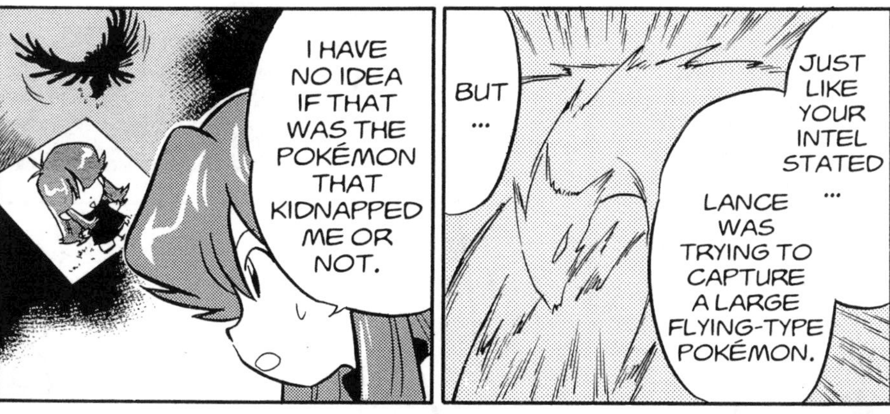
JUST LIKE YOUR INTEL STATED ...
LANCE WAS TRYING TO CAPTURE A LARGE FLYING-TYPE POKÉMON.
BUT ...
I HAVE NO IDEA IF THAT WAS THE POKÉMON THAT KIDNAPPED ME OR NOT.

AFTERWARDS, IT DISAPPEARED WEST, TOWARDS JOHTO.

SO I'D LIKE FOR YOU TO CONTINUE YOUR INVESTI-GATION.

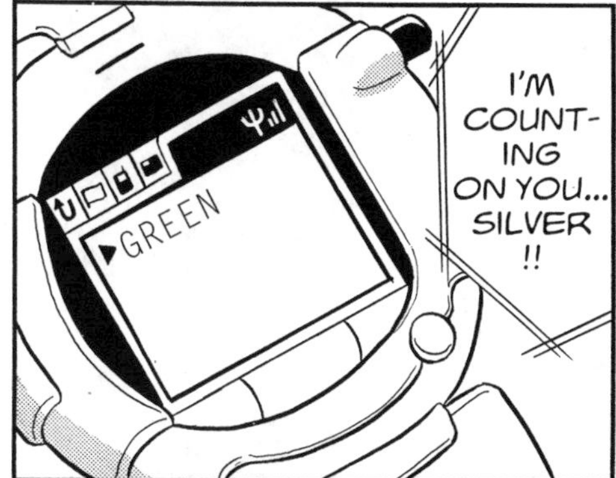
▶GREEN
I'M COUNT-ING ON YOU... SILVER !!

UNDER-
STOOD.
BE
BEEP

Cerise Island

Bird's-Eye View

"GOTTA CATCH 'EM ALL!!"

Route 7 Adventure Map

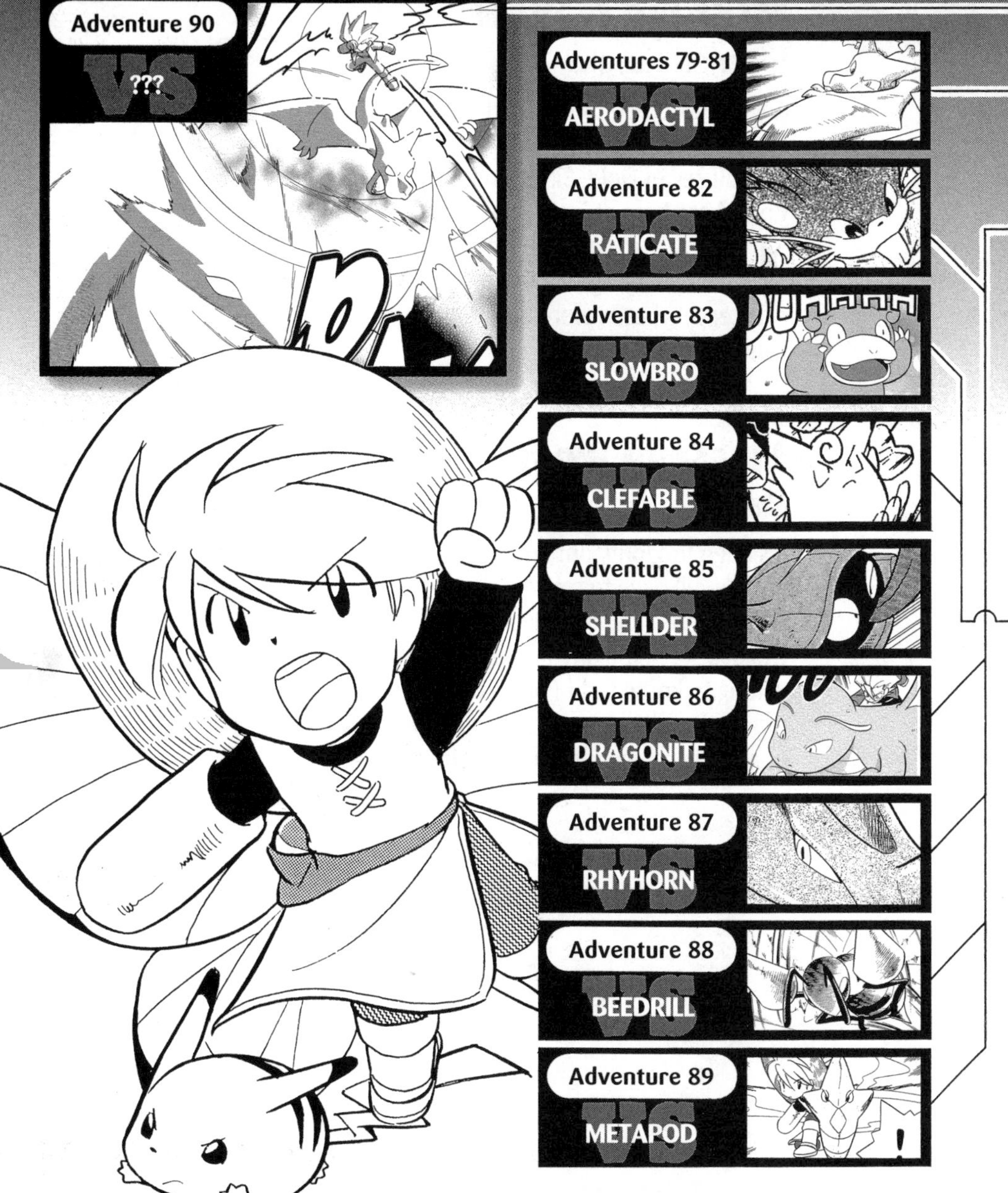

Message from
Hidenori Kusaka

A year has passed since the battle against the Elite Four—and the adventures of Gold, Silver and Crystal are here at last!! Whenever I start a new storyline, I feel sharp and focused all over again—wait'll you see chapter 3, where I went back to my original concept for the series!

—2001

Message from
Mato

It's been too long, but I'm glad to be back! We'll have to say goodbye to Red, Green, Blue and Yellow for a while, but I'm looking forward to getting to know Gold (who's a bit of a clown) and Silver (who's kind of a punk) and all the other new characters!

—2001

TNK TNK
OH... IT'S LATE. AIBO, GO WAKE UP THAT SLEEPYHEAD!
NOD
TATATA
KREEE...

91
Murkrow Row

AHH... AHH...
WSK
ACHOO !!
VOOP
TAP TAP
MMMG

SLURP
HA!! THAT TICKLES!! THANKS A LOT!!
HUH...? OH! THANKS FOR WAKING ME UP! NOW...
POP
GLEEM
MORN-ING, MOM.
NOM NOM
YOU WASHED YOUR FACE, I SEE.
I SURE DID.
YOUR HAIR EXPLOD-ED AGAIN.
I LIKE IT THIS WAY!
TNK
OKAY!
LET'S GO!!
ZSH

ELM RESEARCH CENTER
THIS WAY

JOHTO REGION
NEW BARK TOWN

A YEAR ALREADY SINCE THE BATTLE AT KANTO.

TIME FLIES ...

HEY, AIBO, IT'S DJ MARY!
♪
NEXT UP, "BOY AND HIS LAPRAS." IT'S BY ME—SO LISTEN!!
HOOT
HOOT

KAKI!
CAN YOU READ MY MIND?♪ CAN YOU EASE THE STRAIN?♪
TOK
RIPPLES IN THE WAVES♪ BATTLES ON THE BRAIN♪
NOT BAD, NOT BAD.

CARRY ME ACROSS THE SEA♪
GONK
CARRY ME TO SKZXXT—
VSH
!!

HUH?! THERE'S ...

HEY HEY HEY HEY!! WHAT'S UP WITH MY RADIO?!
I BETTER CHECK THE OUT-SIDE ANTEN ...

SOMEBODY SNEAKING INTO OUR YARD!

USH

HEY YOU !!

YOU GET UP THERE AND FIX THE ANTENNA YOU BROKE, OR...!
...!!

W-
WAIT!
MY
NAME'S
JOEY!
I DIDN'T
DO
ANYTHING
WRONG!!

ASIDE
FROM
SNEAKING
INTO
MY YARD
IN THE
MIDDLE
OF THE
NIGHT?!
AIBO-
SCRATCH
!!

ZZZ
KKK
GYAAA!

YOU'VE
GOT IT ALL
WRONG!
LOOK UP
THERE!!

THAT'S
...
A MURKROW!
I WAS
DELIVERING
A PIECE OF
LUGGAGE...
AND THAT
MURKROW JUST
STOLE IT!

WOMP
HEH
OH, YEAH. THIS HAPPENS ALL THE TIME.

WHEW! THEN YOU BELIEVE ME?!
IT MUST'VE TAKEN MY ANTENNA TOO.

NOT LIKE I CAN'T CLIMB UP THERE... BUT IT'S KIND OF A PAIN. HOW HEAVY'S YOUR BAG?
HUH?! UH... I DUNNO... KINDA HEAVY?

TOK

WSH
IN THAT CASE, WE'LL GO THIS ROUTE.

VIIIIIN

BUT WHAT'S THE POINT?!

THAT... WAS AN AWESOME SHOT...

WAP

BOOM

FWAAAA
HURRY !!
?!
TNG
WHOOP!
HE CAUGHT THE MURKROW, BUT NOW...
HE'S FALLING !!
BOOM
VSH

PONG
I CAN'T WATCH !!

ZOOM

AIBO'S AN AIPOM. ITS TAIL IS HANDIER THAN ITS HANDS... SO TO SPEAK!

C'MON, GUYS! DON'T WORRY! I'M FINE! C'MON!!

MY NAME'S GOLD. GOOD TO MEET YOU, JOEY. OH, AND GLAD YOU GOT YOUR BAG BACK!

TMM

WHEW
WHAT A RELIEF! IF I'D LOST THIS BAG THAT I'M SUPPOSED TO GET TO PROFESSOR ELM...

N- NICE TO MEET YOU TOO, GOLD!

ZZZIP
...WITH NOT ONLY ALL THESE POKÉMON BUT ALSO...

W-W- WHAT'S WRONG ?!

EEP
ARGH !!!

I MISSED THE REST OF DJ MARY'S POKÉMON SONG HOUR !!!
HEY, YOU WOULDN'T HAPPEN TO HAVE RECORDED IT, WOULD YOU...?
HOW IN THE HECK COULD I HAVE **RECORDED** IT?!

LET'S GO, JOEY !!

MOM! ME AND JOEY ARE HEADING OUT FOR A WHILE!!
HANG ON A SECOND!

I'VE NEVER SEEN YOU DRESSED SO EARLY! YOU SHOULD HAVE PEOPLE OVER MORE OFTEN!
THANKS FOR GOING WITH HIM, JOEY.
NO NO NO! THANK **YOU** FOR LETTING ME STAY OVER LAST NIGHT.
JOEY, C'MON !!

92 Who Gives a Hoothoot?

LET'S GO!!!

OUR LOCAL POKÉMON EXPERT? SURE I DO. NEVER MET HIM, THOUGH.
THEN I'M SURE YOU'VE HEARD OF THE PERSON WHO ASKED ME TO DELIVER IT TO PROFESSOR ELM.
GET THIS...
THE GREAT PROFESSOR OAK HIMSELF!!
WHAT?!! PROFESSOR OAK?!
HE'S STUNNED... OF COURSE! EVERY POKÉMON TRAINER IN THE WORLD HAS GROWN UP WITH THE LEGEND OF PROFESSOR OAK!
BRR BRR
BUT HE'S... HE'S THE GUY...
WHUMP
...WHO HELPS OUT DJ MARY WITH HER RADIO SHOW!
HE'S A LOT MORE THAN THAT, YOU KNOW!!

WELCOME TO THE POKÉMON HOUR. I'M PROFESSOR OAK, AND I'LL BE YOUR GUIDE TO THE SECRETS OF POKÉMON!
AND I'M HIS ASSISTANT, DJ MARY!!
HECK, NOBODY LISTENS TO THAT OLD GUY! BUT THAT VOICE OF MARY'S... *SIGH*
HEY!! I GOT IT!!
YOU GOT WHAT?
ARE YOU GOING BACK TO OAK'S PLACE AFTER YOU DELIVER THE BAG?
YEAH. THE PROFESSOR'S DOING RESEARCH IN CHERRYGROVE CITY, SO I'LL BE GOING...
AND I'M GOING WITH YOU!!
WHAT?!!
AS A POKÉMON TRAINER, I FEEL I HAVE AN OBLIGATION TO MEET THE GREAT PROFESSOR AT LEAST ONCE!
SURE. AND TO TRY TO SCAM YOUR WAY TO A DJ MARY AUTOGRAPH.

IS HE FOR REAL?
C'MON, MAN! WHAT'S UP?

TM TM TM TM

DOWN-TOWN NEW BARK TOWN

YO!

OH!

HEY !!

LONG TIME NO SEE!!
HOW YOU BEEN ?!
IT'S GOLD, FROM THE POKÉMON HOUSE!
MORN-ING, GOLD!
HEY!
HOWDY!

YAMA YAMA
NOW LET'S GET THIS BAG TO...
HUH ?!
WHAT'S GOING ON?

YOU'RE... SO POPU-LAR.
WELL, YEAH.

STEP RIGHT UP FOR THE...
...POKÉMON CAPTURE CHALLENGE !!
I WILL RELEASE ALL THESE POKÉMON— AND IF YOU CAN CAPTURE EVERY ONE OF THEM WITHIN ONE MINUTE, YOU'LL WIN A FABULOUS PRIZE! THIS HOOT-HOOT WILL TELL WHEN YOU'RE OUT OF TIME!
100 UNITS PER TRY!!
YAMMER YAMMER YAMMER

Hoothoot
Owl Pokémon
Height: 2'03"
Weight: 46.7 lbs
No. 163
It has a perfect pace of time. Whatever happens, it keeps rhythm by precisely tilting its head in time.
Cry
USING A HOOTHOOT IS SMART!
ITS INTERNAL CLOCK IS FAMOUS FOR ALWAYS BEING PERFECT!

JUST WATCH!
EXCEPT HE'S USING IT TO CHEAT!
WHAT ?!

SORRY! MINUTE'S UP!
TKTKTK DINNNG
HOOOOOT♪
NEXT!

HEY! STOP!
VVIP

THIS IS JUST TOO EASY...
...SINCE I TRAINED MY HOOTHOOT TO HOOT WHENEVER SOMEONE'S ABOUT TO WIN!

OOOOO
I ALMOST HAD IT...

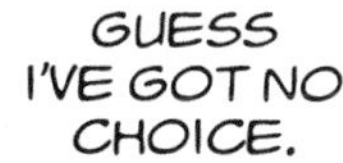
GUESS I'VE GOT NO CHOICE.
...

MISTER, MISTER, CAN I TRY?!
HEY, IT'S YOUR MONEY, KID. HEH HEH HEH.

I HOPE I CAN DO IT! I'M NOT SO GOOD WITH POKÉ-MON!

WHAT ARE YOU GOING TO DO?
I'M GOING TO CLEAN THAT GUY'S CLOCK!
WATCH MY BACK-PACK, JOEY!

EEE...
?
NEEE
NOD
OKAY, AIBO...
WOK
VSH
START!!
FWAP
GET 'EM—!!
COME ON, GOLD!!

THIS KID'S PRETTY GOOD...
HMM ...
BON
BON

OKAY, HOOT-HOOT!
TIME FOR A LITTLE PREMATURE HOOTING!

TWEET TWEET
DUHH
UHH
?!
FWAP
FWAP
H-HEY!! WHAT'RE YOU DOING ?!!
HEH

GRRR
SCAM, HUH?
NOW THAT YOU MENTION IT...
UH...

LOOKS LIKE HOOTHOOT'S TELLING YOU TIME'S UP... ON THIS **SCAM** YOU'RE PULLING!

I'M STARTING TO UNDER-STAND WHY HE'S SO POPULAR.

HOORAY
HOO-RAY FOR GOLD !!

TIME FOR ME TO GO HOME!
ZIP
ZIP

ZZHH

THANK YOU! THANK YOU!
SHLUUU...

CASE CLOSED! NOW LET'S GO GET DJ MARY'S AUTOGRAPH!
I THINK I PRE-FERRED IT...
...WHEN YOU AT LEAST PRETENDED TO CARE ABOUT THE PRO-FESSOR.

STILL, THAT WAS PRETTY AMAZING!

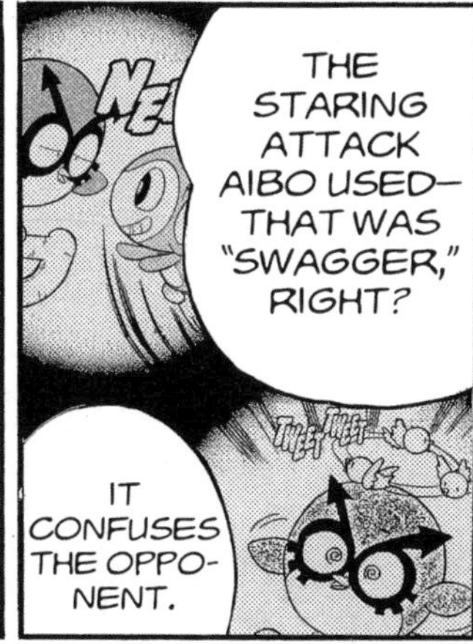
THE STARING ATTACK AIBO USED— THAT WAS "SWAGGER," RIGHT?
IT CONFUSES THE OPPO-NENT.

YOU REALLY HAVE TO KNOW YOUR POKÉMON WELL TO PULL THAT OFF!
I GUESS SO.
HEH HEH

GETTING INTO TROUBLE TOGETHER HAS ITS PERKS, HUH?
WOMP

OKAY... IT'S GOTTA BE AROUND HERE SOME-WHERE...
I... I... I DON'T ...

HUH?! HEY, JOEY... THE BACKPACK I LEFT RIGHT HERE... WHERE'D IT GO?!
WHAT ?!!

OH GEEZ... W-WAIT A MINUTE!

GOLD! YOUR BACKPACK WAS FULL OF POKÉMON IN POKÉ BALLS, RIGHT?!
JUST LIKE MY BAG!

SO MAYBE SOMEONE TRYING TO STEAL MY BAG TOOK YOURS BY MISTAKE!
WHO'D STEAL A BUNCH OF POKÉMON THEY DIDN'T KNOW?
BUT THERE ARE ALSO RESEARCH DOCUMENTS FROM PROFESSOR OAK IN THERE! VALUABLE DOCUMENTS!

THEN YOU MEAN...
...MY POKÉMON WERE STOLEN?
ALL OF THEM...

AND WHEN THE CROOK CATCHES ON TO HIS MISTAKE, WHERE DOES HE GO THEN?
TAK
TO PRO-FESSOR ELM'S PLACE!

...
WSH
GOLD ...?

THOSE POKÉMON HAVE BEEN MY FRIENDS SINCE I WAS BORN.

CHK
I WON'T REST UNTIL I'VE BROUGHT THEM ALL BACK.

I'M COMING, GANG!
ZSH

NEW BARK TOWN
EAST-ERN OUT-SKIRTS

SLAM
?!
JOEY, IS THAT YOU?!

I COULD HAVE SWORN I HEARD THE DOOR OPEN...
JOEY ...?
Huh?
KREEE
THAT WAS QUICK! WHAT DID PRO-FESSOR OAK SAY?
OH WELL...
SLAM

YOINK

93 Sneasel Sneak Attack

T-TOTO-DILE'S POKÉ BALL... IT'S GONE?!
WHAT?!
WSSH

SO THIS IS WHERE ELM DOES HIS STUFF, HUH?

YEAH! WE'VE GOT TO HURRY AND TELL HIM ABOUT YOUR STOLEN...

HANG ON, JOEY.

HF HF

ELM RESEARCH CENTER

THE THIEF MUST KNOW WE'RE COMING. WOULDN'T BE HARD TO SET UP A TRAP.

WE'RE GOING IN THE SECOND FLOOR WIN-DOW.

WHAT'S GOING ON?! HOW DOES A POKÉ BALL JUST DISAPPEAR ?!
PER-FECT.
TP

NOW I JUST HAVE TO SLIP OUT THE WIN-DOW.

BE CAREFUL, GOLD!
I'M FINE!

TM

READY, AIBO?

TOOM
!
HUH ...?
HEY, YOU !!
DOING

DID NOT !!

YOU STOLE MY TOTO-DILE!!

WHO ...?

WATCH OUT!

TP
YOU EXPECT ME TO BELIEVE—

SHEEEEE
ICY WIND.

SHLOO
SH SH SH SH SH SH SH
NO NO NO NO NO—
WHA ?!
TING!

PROFESSOR ELM!! ARE YOU OKAY ?!!

DUHHHH
GONK

WHAM
OOPH
JOEY !!

SHLOO

BAM
GOLD, WHERE ARE YOU?!!

AIBO! SCRATCH !!
LET'S GET 'EM!!
BUP
SNEASEL, PROTECT!
TA
SH
PAP
BON
FFFT

!
SHHHHH
TAK
IF WE CAN'T TAKE 'EM FROM THE FRONT—
WHAP
—COME FROM BEHIND!!
BOOM
GIVE ME MY BACK-PACK!!

WHAT BACK-PACK?
DON'T PLAY GAMES WITH ME!
I'M TAKING IT BACK!!

BIG WORDS... BUT THERE'S SOMETHING SCARY ABOUT THIS GUY...
...AND I'LL PROBABLY NEVER GET AWAY WITH ANOTHER SURPRISE ATTACK...
Aww, man.

SO WHAT DO I...
HUH?!
BMP
ONE MISS-ING?!

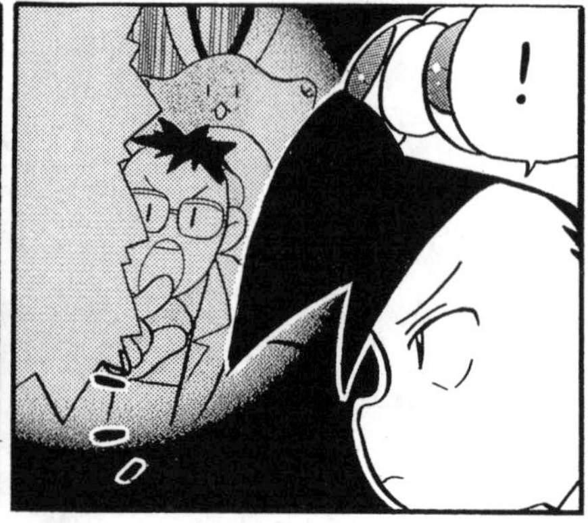
!

YOU'RE A KIDNAPPER TOO, EH?

SO YOU DON'T JUST SNATCH BACKPACKS.

IT'S ANGRY ...
...OF COURSE!
KATAKA

TAKATAKA

I KNOW WHAT IT'S LIKE TO HAVE ONE OF YOUR FRIENDS TAKEN.

WHAT DO YOU SAY TO COMBINING FORCES?
...THAT THIS CREEP STOLE.

LOOKS LIKE WE BOTH WANT SOME-THING...

BOOM
O-KAY !!

NOD

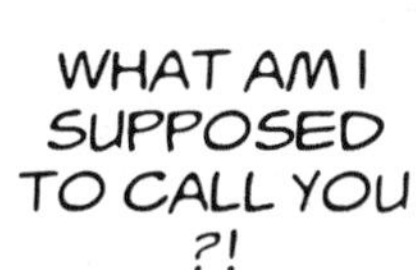
WHAT AM I SUPPOSED TO CALL YOU ?!

BUT I DON'T EVEN KNOW WHAT KIND OF POKÉMON YOU ARE...

HOW ABOUT IF I CALL YOU... EXBO? YEAH? OKAY...
YOUR BACK SIDE'S AS EXPLOSIVE AS MY HAIR...

POOM!
YEOW !!
WEIRD.

...
SHHH
LET'S DO THIS, EXBO!!

NYAHA HAHA HA!!

AND WHO'D HAVE THOUGHT THAT ALL WE HAD TO DO FOR IT WAS...
...GRAB A BACK-PACK OFF THE GROUND!
ZZHH

HEE HEE HEE!
ALL THE PRECIOUS RESEARCH THAT OAK AND ELM WANTED TO KEEP TO THEM-SELVES, AND NOW IT BELONGS TO...
...TEAM ROCKET!

NOW OPEN IT, AND LET'S...
?!
WHAT... WHAT ...?!
ZZZIP

THESE AREN'T THE POKÉMON THEY SAID WE'D FIND!!
IT CAN'T BE THE WRONG BAG!!

BUT IT IS! WE MESSED UP!
WE'VE GOT TO FIND THAT KID AGAIN!!
HEY! WHAT ABOUT THIS BAG?
JUST THROW IT AWAY!!

WHMP
ROLOLO

SPLSH

DMDM DM

GIVE ME MY BACKPACK !!

94 Elekid Incorporated

...

I'M NOT LETTING YOU GET AWAY...

GET BACK HERE!
WHOO

TP
HE'S TOO QUICK!

HEY!
SHP
SHP
SHP
EXBO, I DON'T KNOW WHAT KIND OF ATTACKS YOU CAN DO...
...BUT THAT FLAME ON YOUR BACK'S A WEAPON, RIGHT?
NOD
WELL, IF THERE'S EVER A TIME TO USE IT...
SSSZZZZ
USE IT...
ZOOOSH
...NOW!

OKAY !!
SHHH
!!
SSSSS
THAT HURTS ...
TUP
NH!!
THP
SNEASEL... YOU'VE GOT TO...
HFF... HFF...
TOO LATE.
FPP
TUG

HOOOSSH
?!

HEH HEH HEH.
TAKE A LOOK AROUND YOU.

I GOT TIRED OF CHASING YOU AROUND, SO I DECIDED TO CONTAIN YOU...
...WITHIN A RING OF FIRE.

HEY !!!
UP

JUST GIMME MY BACK-PACK...
AND GIVE TOTODILE BACK TO EXBO! RIGHT NOW!
SSS

WHAT ARE YOU UP TO BACK THERE?! NO TRICKS!!

ZAP

BZT
MUHA-HAAA! SORRY TO INTERRUPT YOUR FIGHT!
BZZT

WMM

OH, I'M SO GLAD YOU ASKED THAT! WE ARE TEAM ROCKET!!
AND WE'RE LAUNCHING OUR COME-BACK!

AND WHO ARE YOU?!
SHP

WE'RE AFTER A BAG CONTAINING SOMETHING PRECIOUS.
OAK
ELM
RESEARCH

YOUR FRIEND MENTIONED A BACK-PACK.
THAT ANSWERS ONE OF OUR QUES-TIONS.

SO THAT'S WHAT HE'S BEEN SAYING...

WE WEREN'T COUNTING ON OUR TARGET LINKING UP WITH ANOTHER KID WITH A BAG.

AND NOW, SINCE WE'VE COME ALL THIS WAY...
LET'S GO TAKE ELM'S POKÉMON TOO!
THOSE ARE THE SPECIAL ONES HE'S BEEN STUDYING...
CHIKORITA, CYNDAQUIL AND TOTODILE!!

TOUGH LUCK. I'VE ALREADY GOT TOTODILE. AND CYNDAQUIL ...
...IS THE ONE YOU JUST TOOK DOWN.

ZZZT
W... WHAT ?!!
THEN WE'RE GOING TO HAVE TO TAKE **YOU** DOWN TOO!!
VSH
ZZZT

WEEN
THAT'S ELEKID.
NOT TOO GOOD AGAINST THAT TYPE, BUT...
Status / Normal
Type / Electric
EXP Points
Level Up
Elekid
/Elekid
WEEN
BOOM
TOTO-DILE!!

NYAHAHAHA!! YOU'RE GOING TO USE A POKÉMON YOU JUST STOLE?!
THEY WON'T LISTEN TO YOU IF THEY'RE NOT USED TO YOU!!

BOPBOPBOPBOP
SOMETIMES IT'S BETTER WHEN THEY'RE NOT USED TO ME.
TOTODILE—FRUSTRATION!!
GAAAAH!!
EH?!
VSH
IMPOSSIBLE!!
VSH
THE... POKÉ B-BALLS! STOP THE...
HSSS
GULP
UH...

ZZZASH
FEINT ATTACK !!
THE LESS FAMILIAR THE POKÉMON IS WITH THE USER... THE MORE EFFECTIVE THE ATTACK IS!
Frustrati
Cut
Fly
Surf
Streng
s full-pow
grows more
less the
I TAUGHT IT THE ATTACK RIGHT AFTER I TOOK IT.
DM!
ELEKID !!
H-HE'S JUST... TOO STRONG...
WE'LL BE BACK !!
VOOM!

NN... UHH...

OWWW ...
BLINK

AWAKE AT LAST, ARE YOU?
HUH? WHO ARE YOU?

THE POLICE. DID YOU SET FIRE TO THIS LAWN?

SPT SPT
SPT SPT
P-POLICE?!! WHAT?! WHAT?!

BUT... BUT THERE WAS THIS THIEF! AND I WAS... I WAS...
I NEED YOU TO COME WITH ME SO I CAN TAKE YOUR STATEMENT. IF YOU RESIST, I'LL HAVE TO ARREST YOU.

STATE-MENT?! ARREST?!!

WAIT WAIT WAIT WAIT WAIT! NO! NO!
I'M THE VICTIM HERE!
J-J-JOEY!
TELL HIM I'M INNO-CENT, JOEY!
He's my friend.
Uh-huh.

ACCORDING TO PROFESSOR ELM, WHO-EVER STOLE TOTODILE ATTACKED HIM FROM BEHIND.
HE NEVER SAW THE PERPE-TRATOR'S FACE.

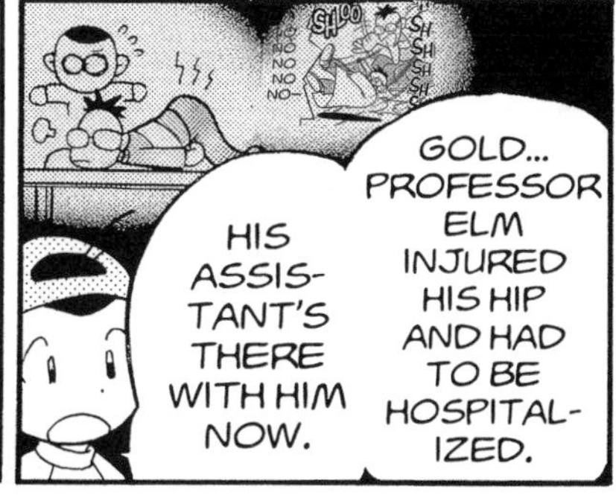
GOLD... PROFESSOR ELM INJURED HIS HIP AND HAD TO BE HOSPITAL-IZED.
HIS ASSIS-TANT'S THERE WITH HIM NOW.

HOW ABOUT YOU, JOEY?
I... UM... PASSED OUT AS SOON AS I STEPPED INTO THE RESEARCH CENTER.
SO... NO.
WHICH MEANS ...

YOU'RE THE ONLY ONE WHO SAW THE SUSPECT'S FACE.
WILL YOU COOPER-ATE?
...
UH... SURE.

THE BURNT GLOVE HE TOSSED!
FPP

HM?

ZIP

CHERRY-GROVE CITY
OH, I GET IT. THIS IS...
...ONE OF THOSE COMPOS-ITE DRAW-INGS...
TRANSIT
POLICE

ABOUT MY HEIGHT.
BLUE FLEECE TOP, BLACK BOOTS.
LONG RED HAIR...
YAWN
COMPOSIT
THE FACE IS WHAT REALLY MATTERS, SON.
WE'RE COUNTING ON YOU!!

...
BIG GOOGLY EYES...
AND A FLAT NOSE.
TK TK TK TK
THICK LIPS AND...
... CHUBBY CHEEKS.

TA-
DAA

THANKS FOR YOUR HELP. IT'S LATE. IF YOU'D LIKE TO SPEND THE NIGHT...
THANKS! BUT WE'VE GOT PLACES TO BE!
ZZZOOOM

WHY DIDN'T YOU WANT TO SLEEP THERE?
...

I MEAN, NOW THAT THEY'VE GOT THIS PICTURE, I'M SURE THEY'LL CATCH HIM RIGHT AWAY.
What a stupid face!

JOEY, THAT COMPOSITE PICTURE ...
...IT'S A FAKE.
He's nothing like that.
WHAT ?!!

I CAN'T LEAVE THIS UP TO THE POLICE.

I'M GOING TO CATCH HIM WITH MY OWN HANDS— AND GET MY BAG BACK TOO! RIGHT, EXBO?!

And add a Toto-dile!
YEAH, YEAH... MEAN LITTLE EYES...

GONG
SO WE'VE GOT TO MAKE A REAL COMPOSITE PICTURE FOR OUR OWN USE.
YOU HAVE A LAPTOP, RIGHT?

MMM
TK TK TK TK

GOLD. I WAS WONDER-ING...
WHAT'S UP, JOEY?
DOESN'T IT SEEM LIKE ALL THESE THINGS ARE HAPPENING SO FAST?
WHY DO YOU THINK THAT IS?
OH, I DON'T KNOW ...

TM
IT MEANS THAT FATE...
...IS MAKING ITS MOVE.
Y... YOU'RE... YOU'RE...

PRO-FESSOR OAK?!!

W-WHY ARE YOU HERE?!

HEY, I DON'T NEED YOUR HELP, OKAY?

G-GOLD!!

YOU MAY NOT HAVE A NEED...

BUT I NEED SOME-THING FROM YOU.

I CAME HERE ON A TIP FROM THE POLICE.
THE BOY YOU CONFRONTED. WAS HE CARRYING SOMETHING...
VP
!!

...LIKE THIS ?!!
WEEN
WEEN

A DEVICE TO RECORD DATA, ALL POSSIBLE POKÉMON DATA...

B-BUT WHAT IS IT...?

MY LATEST POKÉ-DEX!!

...

YOU'RE ASKING ME IF THAT GUY HAD ONE OF THOSE?

WELL, HE WAS HIDING SOME-THING...
...AND NOW THAT I THINK ABOUT IT... IT DID LOOK LIKE THAT.

MY POKÉDEX AND PROFESSOR ELM'S TOTODILE WERE PROBABLY STOLEN...

...BY THE SAME THIEF!

95 Stantler by Me

YOU'RE SURE IT WAS STOLEN ...?
YES. FROM THE VERY PLACE I GAVE YOU THIS ASSIGNMENT...
MY SECONDARY RESEARCH CENTER ON THE OUTSKIRTS OF CHERRYGROVE.
THE SAME PLACE WHERE I RECORD MY RADIO SHOW.
RESEARCH CENTER No. 2

THE PROFESSOR'S REAL HOME IS PALLET TOWN, IN KANTO, BUT HE COMES TO JOHTO FOR VARIOUS REASONS.
AND HIS GRANDDAUGHTER, DAISY, HOUSESITS...
UM...
I DON'T NEED TO KNOW HIS PERSONAL LIFE!!

LISTEN, OLD MAN, THIS POKÉDEX THING... DOES IT HAVE ANY FEATURES ...

...THAT WOULD MAKE IT USEFUL IN BATTLE?!

SURE IT DOES.
IT WILL INSTANTLY REVEAL YOUR OPPONENT'S LEVEL AND TYPES OF ATTACKS.
19/ 19
Status / Normal
Type / Electric
Elekid
/Elekid

IN ANY CASE, I APPRECIATE YOUR CONFIRMING THIS FOR ME.
I'LL GO TO THE POLICE AND...
HOLD ON!!

I KNEW IT!
HE WAS USING IT TO FIGURE OUT WHAT KINDS OF ATTACKS HIS POKÉMON SHOULD USE AGAINST EXBO.

DJ Mary
NOW THERE'S SOMETHING **YOU** HAVE TO CONFIRM FOR **ME**.
YOU WORK WITH DJ MARY, RIGHT?!

G... GOLD!
OKAY, OKAY, FORGET DJ MARY... FOR NOW. WHAT I REALLY WANT...

...IS THAT POKÉDEX! GIVE IT TO ME!
GLEEM

GIVE IT TO YOU ?!!

H-HOW COULD YOU ASK SUCH A THING?!
BOW
I AM **NOT** CRAZY!
I'M SO SORRY, PROFESSOR! HE'S BEEN THROUGH A LOT TODAY, AND HE'S NOT IN HIS RIGHT—

LISTEN... GOLD, IS IT? I ONLY HAVE TWO OF THESE LEFT.
AND I CREATED THEM SPECIFICALLY FOR MY OWN RESEARCH.
I CAN'T GIVE THIS TO YOU.

YEAH, YEAH, I GET THAT.
BUT I'M GOING AFTER THE GUY WHO STOLE YOUR OTHER GADGET...

...AND HOW DO I FIGHT HIM IF HE'S GOT ONE AND I DON'T?
THIS IS FOR YOU.
AND I DON'T THINK YOU WANT ME TO FAIL.

I ALREADY SAID NO!!
THEN CAN I JUST BORROW IT FOR A WHILE?
NO!!
YOU COULD JUST MAKE ANOTHER ONE!! YOU'RE A GENIUS, RIGHT?!
I CAN'T MAKE ONE THAT QUICKLY!!
PLEASE?!
NO!!

PANT PANT... TRY TO UNDERSTAND THIS...
I'VE ONLY GIVEN POKÉDEXES TO TRAINERS I TRUST TO GATHER THOROUGH AND ACCURATE DATA FOR MY RESEARCH...
...AND WHO HAVE THE CHARACTER AND SKILLS TO HELP OTHERS.
I DON'T GIVE THEM TO PEOPLE I DON'T KNOW.

SKILLS, HUH?
I'M FINE IF I'VE GOT SKILLS, HUH?!
OKAY THEN...
AIBO, SCRATCH!!
VAP
N-NO! THAT'S NOT WHAT I'M...
MMMG
STOP THAT!! STANTLER! LEDYBA!

THERE, AIBO!

IF THAT'S HOW IT'S GOT TO BE...

CHK

STANT-LER! **CONFUSE RAY**!

ZAK

!!

W-WHAT ...?!

WILL YOU LISTEN TO ME?! EVEN IF YOU SOMEHOW DEFEATED ME...
I STILL WOULDN'T GIVE YOU THE POKÉ-DEX.

BUT... BUT THAT'S STUPID!!
NOBODY COULD USE THAT THING BETTER THAN ME!
...
THANK YOU, SON.

BECAUSE YOU'VE JUST CONFIRMED MY OPINION... THAT YOU ARE NOT READY FOR A POKÉDEX.
WHAT?!

YOU'RE THE TYPE WHO FLINGS HIMSELF HEADLONG AFTER WHATEVER HE'S SET HIS HEART ON AND WON'T HEAR ANY ARGU-MENT.
THAT'S A FINE TRAIT... TO A POINT.
BUT WHEN YOU CAN NO LONGER CONSIDER ANY OF THE PEOPLE OR ISSUES AROUND YOU... YOU'VE LOST CONTROL!
TO SOME-ONE LIKE YOU ...

A WEAPON FOR DISCERNING **ATTACKS** AND **LEVELS.**
...THE POKÉDEX IS JUST A TOOL.

G... GOLD ...?
VIP
FINE. I DON'T WANT IT.

CHING!
I WON'T WASTE ONE ON YOU.

...
GOLD!
VMM
YOU JUST WATCH, OLD MAN!
I'LL BE BETTER WITHOUT IT!

ALTHOUGH THIS ISN'T THE KIND OF TRAINING THEY USUALLY MEAN IN THE POKÉMON COMMUNITY...
TM TM TM TM TM
SO TO SHOW UP THE PRO- FESSOR, HE'S TAKEN UP TRAINING.

SQUAT HOPS! ONE HUN- DRED LAPS!!

PANT PANT
HUFF HUFF

NOW THAT'S JUST CRUEL, GOLD!
THERE ARE GENTLER WAYS TO...
FORGET IT!
THAT OLD COOT WAS RIGHT— I'M NOT READY! I'VE GOTTA BE TOUGH!
RRM
BBBL
OH...
I DON'T LIKE THE LOOKS OF THAT SKY.
RRM
BBBL...

AND WHILE I'M TRAVELING!
I'VE GOT TO GET OUT OF...
WHAT A HORREN-DOUS STORM...
KRAK
PSSSH

WHAT?!! WHAT'S ALL THIS SLUDGE?!

H... HELP ME...
OH!
AND THAT TENT... IS IT...
... JOEY'S ...?

WHAT HAPPENED?! AND WHERE'S GOLD?!
HE... JUMPED ...
SSSH

JOEY!!

STANTLER, HURRY!
VM
HE JUMPED INTO THE RIVER TO SAVE MY RATTATA!
HE WHAT ?!
GOOD... JOEY'S RATTATA GOT TO THE OTHER SHORE.
PLP PLP PLP PLP
SSHHH...
IT'S TOO EXHAUSTED... BECAUSE OF THE TRAINING I PUT IT THROUGH...
...
NOW THE PROBLEM IS **US.** EXBO, CAN YOU FOLLOW RATTATA?
YOU **WILL** SEE TOTODILE AGAIN!
AND NOW I'M GONNA SAVE YOU!
BOOM
I'M SORRY, EXBO... I DID THIS.

TAK!
TOK
TOK
OKAY!
TUMP
ROLL
WATER-
FALL!
DOOOOM
SLIP-
PING...!
GLUG
AGH!
THAT
LEAVES
ONLY...
WUK
I'M
DOOMED
!!

YOU FOOL!!

AND DO YOU KNOW WHY THE GROUND WAS SO SLUDGY AND SLIPPERY IN THE FIRST PLACE?! BECAUSE OF **YOUR** EXCESSIVE TRAINING, THAT'S WHY!

WHAT DID YOU THINK YOU WERE DOING?!

CAN YOU IMAGINE WHAT COULD HAVE HAPPENED?!

YARH!

PR-PRO-FESSOR... I THINK THAT'S ENOUGH...

GET BACK ON YOUR FEET !!
I JUST WANT TO GET STRONGER! I WOULDN'T HAVE TO DO IT...IF YOU'D JUST GIVE ME THE POKÉDEX!!
NO! NOT TILL I GET THE POKÉ-DEX!
...
ONE QUES-TION.
YOU MEAN... YOU'RE ...?
HEY !!
TAK

WHAT DO POKÉMON MEAN TO YOU?

I'VE KNOWN TRAINERS WHO DESCRIBED THEIR POKÉMON AS COMRADES AND FRIENDS.
COMRADES
FRIENDS
CAN YOU HONESTLY SAY THE SAME?

...
I'M WAITING.

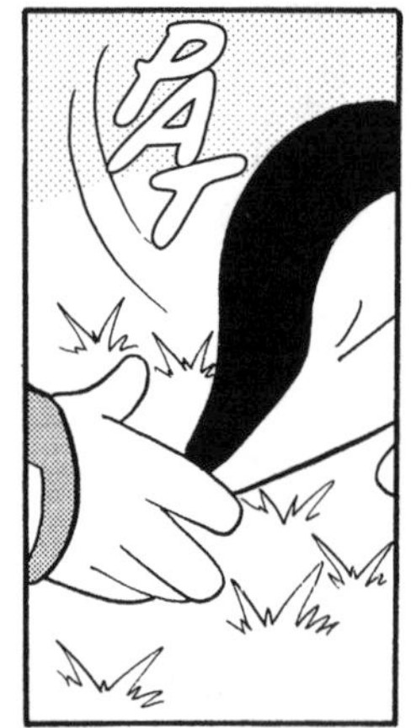
PAT

HONESTLY... I CAN'T SAY THAT "FRIEND" OR "COMRADE" IS RIGHT...

AIBO'S LIVED WITH ME FOREVER... SO AIBO'S LIKE FAMILY.
BUT EXBO I JUST MET...
...AT ELM'S RE-SEARCH CENTER.

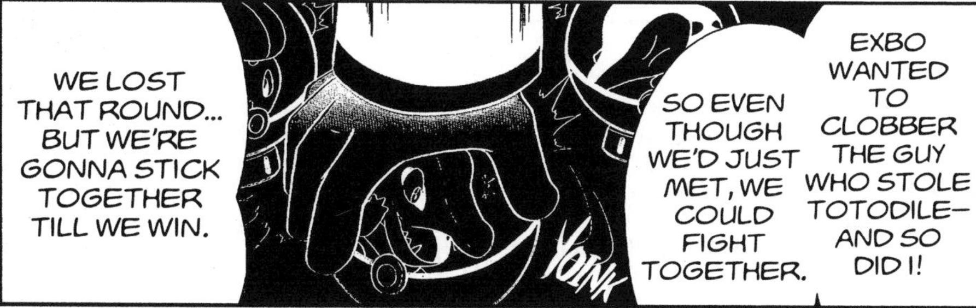
EXBO WANTED TO CLOBBER THE GUY WHO STOLE TOTODILE— AND SO DID I!
SO EVEN THOUGH WE'D JUST MET, WE COULD FIGHT TOGETHER.
YOINK
WE LOST THAT ROUND... BUT WE'RE GONNA STICK TOGETHER TILL WE WIN.

I WANT IT TO BE THAT WAY WITH EVERY POKÉMON I MEET FROM NOW ON...
NOT JUST FRIENDS OR COMRADES ...
PARTNERS
...BUT PARTNERS !!
UNITED BY THE SAME GOAL!!

TRAINER AND POKÉMON...
... PARTNERS ...

HEH
GOOD ANSWER. SO TAKE THIS AND BE GRATEFUL!

NOTHING'S GOING TO STOP ME FROM GETTING TOTODILE AND MY BACKPACK!
THEN I GUESS IT'S SO LONG, JOEY!

SO LET'S GO!!
I HAVE TO CHECK UP ON PROFESSOR ELM IN NEW BARK TOWN.

BACK-PACK ?!
YOU CAN'T MEAN **THIS** ?!
MY BACK-PACK!! BUT WHERE... WHERE?

I SAW IT BY THE RIVER, AS IF IT HAD JUST BEEN TOSSED ASIDE.
AND SINCE I WAS GOING TO THE POLICE ANYWAY...

SIGH
JOEY, CAN I ASK YOU A FAVOR?

IT'S THEM!! ALL OF THEM!! THEY'RE OKAY!!

THEY'RE HOUSE POKÉMON. THEY SHOULDN'T BE GONE THIS LONG. AND... MY MOM WILL BE WORRIED!

ON YOUR WAY TO SEE ELM... CAN YOU TAKE THEM HOME FOR ME?
BUT... BUT...

PILILILI
MY POKÉ-GEAR! IT'S STILL CHARGED?!

PEEEP
DIG DIG
PROB-ABLY MY MOM SINCE WE WERE JUST TALKING ABOUT HER...

OKAY, MY CLUES TO THIS GUY...
A PICTURE AND A GLOVE...

BINGO!
YES, MOM, I KNOW I HAVEN'T CALLED. IT LOOKS LIKE I'LL BE GONE A WHILE LONG ...
MOM!
I'LL BE FINE! JUST ONE LITTLE MATTER TO SETTLE!
OKAY! FINE! I KNOW!
SIGH

SILVER
!

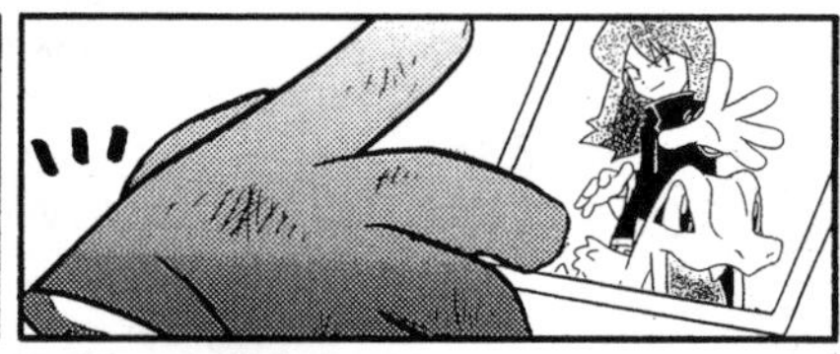

WHY WOULD HE HAVE "SILVER" STITCHED INTO THE INSIDE OF HIS GLOVE...
...UNLESS THAT'S HIS NAME!!

OKAY, THEN! I'M OFF!!
SEE YOU, JOEY! AND YOU TOO, OAK!

HE'S CHANGING ALREADY.
HEH
SUDDENLY I'M "OAK"...INSTEAD OF JUST "OLD MAN."

WE KNOW OUR MISSION.
SHK
FSH
VIP
KLAK
ZSH
SO...
LET'S GO...
... PARTNER !!

NEW BARK TOWN GENERAL HOSPITAL
QUIET ZONE

OW! OW! OW! OW! OW!
PRO-PRO-FESSOR!

ARE YOU OKAY?!

I CAN'T BELIEVE THIS HAPPENED TO ME! OW! OW!
WHAT I CAN'T BELIEVE IS THAT SOME-BODY BROKE INTO THE RESEARCH CENTER AND YOU DIDN'T EVEN SEE HIM!
BUT I WAS CON-CEN-TRAT-ING ON MY RE-SEARCH...

WELL, THERE'S ONE GOOD THING...
IT WASN'T THIS **EGG** THAT GOT STOLEN!
YEAH... THERE'S THAT, I GUESS...

AWP!
VOON

THE NAME'S GOLD. SORRY I DIDN'T HAVE TIME TO INTRODUCE MYSELF BEFORE. HOW'S YOUR BACK?!

EEP
HIYA, PRO-FESSOR ELM!!
Y-Y-YOU!!

I'M SURE YOU HEARD THIS FROM THE COPS, BUT...
...THEY STILL HAVEN'T FOUND YOUR TOTO-DILE!

GAPE
WAIT, I DON'T HAVE TIME TO WASTE ON SMALL TALK.

WOMP
THE GOOD NEWS IS THIS FRIEND OF YOURS IS GONNA BE HELPING ME!

WE'LL CATCH THAT CROOK AND BRING BACK YOUR POKÉMON... AND YOU JUST KEEP OUT OF IT!!
OVER!!

96 Number One Donphan

FWUMP
WHAT... WAS THAT ALL ABOUT?!
I HAVE NO IDEA... EXCEPT NOW IT LOOKS LIKE I'VE LOST TOTODILE... AND CYNDAQUIL...!

SIGH.

I THOUGHT I SHOULD RETURN THESE POKÉMON TO GOLD'S MOTHER BEFORE I WENT TO SEE THE PROFESSOR, BUT...
FIDGET
FIDGET
THIS ISN'T EASY.

HE'S BEEN GONE A REALLY LONG TIME, HE DIDN'T CALL, HE WON'T TELL HER WHERE HE'S GOING OR WHEN HE'LL GET BACK...
SHE'S GOING TO BE REALLY FURIOUS ...
DID YOU PUT HIM UP TO THIS?!

WHO IS IT?
KRIII
AAGH!!
JOEY!! WHERE IS MY SON?!!
UM... WELL... HE...

I FINALLY KNOW WHAT THEY MEAN...
... ABOUT SHARED FAMILY TRAITS.

WRR
WHAT-EVER. HE'LL COME BACK EVENTU-ALLY.
GOMP

UM... THESE ARE POKÉMON THAT GOLD ASKED ME TO BRING HOME. HE SAID THEY'RE HOUSE POKÉMON.
OH, THAT'S SO SWEET!

THERE'S ONE MISSING.
POLIBO, THE POLI-WAG!

THAT'S ODD...
WHAT IS IT?!

HM ...?

POLIBO ?!

RATS! I WAS SO HAPPY TO GET THEM BACK...
...THAT I DIDN'T COUNT TO MAKE SURE!
IT'S THEM!! ALL OF THEM!! THEY'RE OKAY!!
I'M SO SORRY, POLIBO!

YOU'RE SURE, JOEY ?!

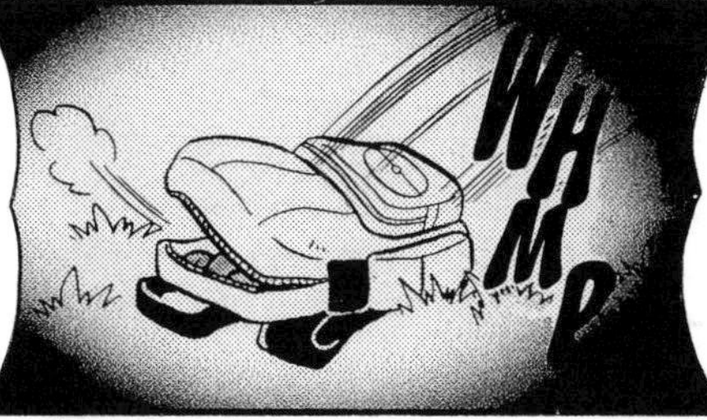
OAK SAID SOMEBODY TOSSED THE PACK ASIDE BY THE RIVER. PROBABLY WITH THE ZIPPER OPEN...
WHMP
SO POLIBO'S POKÉ BALL COULD'VE ROLLED INTO THE WATER!

I'VE GOT TO HUNT THIS SILVER DOWN...
TM
...BUT POLIBO COMES FIRST!

JUST HANG ON, PARTNER! I'M COMING!

SHHH
ROUTE 31

GLUBGLUB
WHERE ARE YOU, POLIBO?!
IT'S NO USE! POLIBO'S NOWHERE AROUND HERE! DOES THAT MEAN...
...POLIBO GOT CARRIED FARTHER DOWN-STREAM?
SO MANY FALSE LEADS... DEAD ENDS...
RRG!
SPLISH

BUT I'M NOT GIVING UP!
I'VE GOT TO STAY ON SILVER'S TRAIL NOW... BUT I'LL COME BACK FOR YOU, POLIBO!

MEAN-WHILE ...

WANTED
BURGLARY

ELM
BURGLARY
GONG

...

JOHTO REGION

VIOLET CITY

RRRGGL

MAN, AM I HUNGRY ...

HEHEH. TOO EASY.

THIEF!! STOP HIM!!

PFF PFF
DMDMDMDM
ACK !!
DIRT!
KOFKOF
HEY! GIMME A NEW RICE CRACK-ER!
I'M NOT THE ONE WHO GOT DIRT ALL OVER IT!

SO THAT GUY THINKS HE CAN MESS UP MY RICE CRACKER AND GET AWAY WITH IT, DOES HE?!

TMM
FAT CHANCE !!

GET BACK HERE!!

DM DM DM DM

PUFF PUFF

AH, YOUNG MAN! ARE YOU GOING TO GET MY POUCH BACK FOR ME? I'D BE SO GRATEFUL!

GET YOUR POUCH BACK?!

I WASN'T PLANNING ON IT!

WMP

I JUST WANT HIM TO PAY FOR MY RICE CRACKER!

DM DM DM DM DM

HEY, YOU!

YOU KNOW, ALL YOU HAVE TO DO TO AVOID A FIGHT IS BUY ME A NEW RICE CRACKER.

WHO ARE YOU?!

OKAY, NOW YOU'VE MADE ME MAD!!
AIBO— **SCRATCH** !!

WOP
OWW!
DON'T WASTE MY TIME WITH YOUR GIBBERISH !!

TING

NUISANCE! DONPHAN, **HORN ATTACK**!
WAGH!

WEEEN
SO IT'S CALLED DONPHAN, HUH?
VIP
KWRL
KWRL

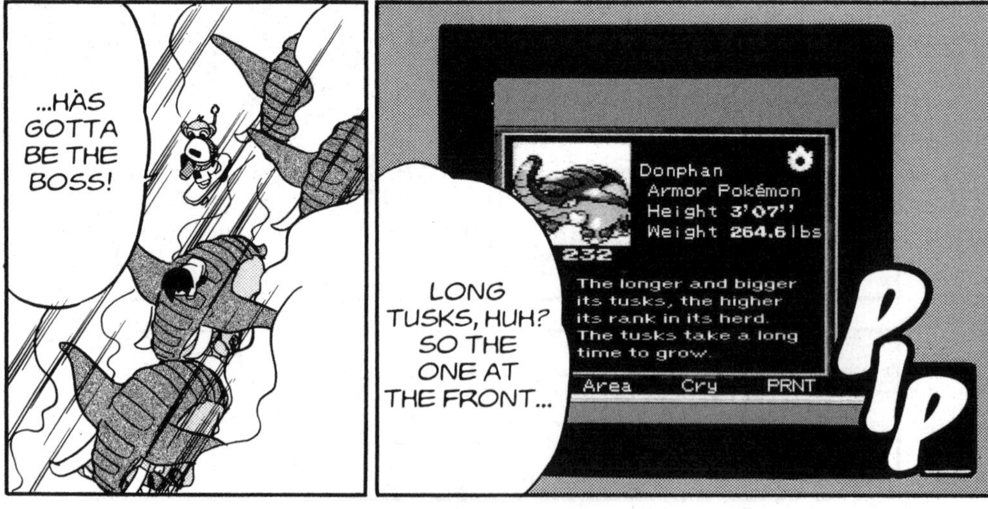
Donphan
Armor Pokémon
Height 3'07''
Weight 264.6lbs
232
The longer and bigger its tusks, the higher its rank in its herd. The tusks take a long time to grow.
Area Cry PRNT
PIP
LONG TUSKS, HUH? SO THE ONE AT THE FRONT...
...HAS GOTTA BE THE BOSS!

OKAY, AIBO. I'M COUNTING ON YOU.
NOD
READY ... SET ...
VP

FLING

HOOOOO

RRRRAH!!

COME ON BACK, AIBO!

TUG

BYON BYON

HE PULLED AIBO BACK BY ITS TAIL!!

KROOM
JAB
WRL
HEH
THAT'S WHY I NEVER FOLLOW THE HERD! ♪
CHK
HYUUU

AH AH AHA!
NOMNOM NOMNOM

YOU'RE TOO GENER-OUS!
NOMNOM
I REALLY DON'T DESERVE THIS!

IT'S REWARD ENOUGH JUST KNOWING THAT I DID THE RIGHT THING AND BROUGHT A CRIMINAL TO JUSTICE! HO HO HO...
LIAR.
LIAR.

STILL... I'M PLEASED THAT THIS POUCH IS SAFE.
MY NAME IS EARL, AND I RUN A POKÉMON ACADEMY HERE IN VIOLET CITY.

I'M SUPPOSED TO GIVE THE DOCUMENTS IN THIS POUCH TO SOMEONE TODAY... PROFESSOR ELM'S ASSISTANT.
PUH.
PRO-FESSOR ELM'S ASSISTANT IS GONNA BE HERE ?!
WHAT-WHAT-WHAT?!
WRRRRL

NEW BARK TOWN

BEFORE I LEFT THE HOSPITAL I HEARD FROM THIS BOY GOLD...

YES. HE WORRIES ME TOO, ELM.

MY ASSISTANT HEADED TO VIOLET CITY TODAY.
I TOLD HIM TO KEEP HIS EARS OPEN FOR NEWS ABOUT GOLD.

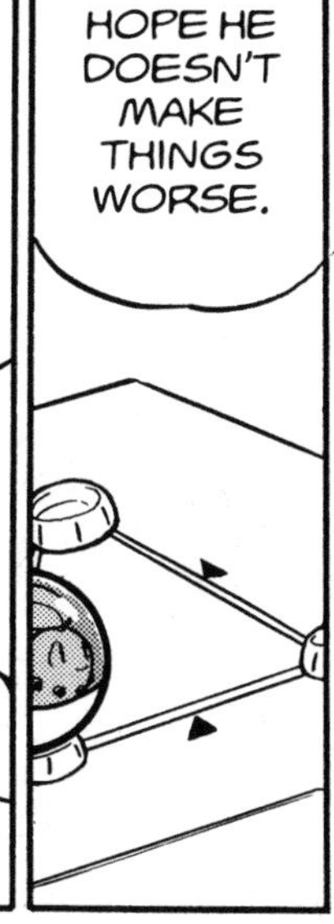
I JUST HOPE HE DOESN'T MAKE THINGS WORSE.

WE THOUGHT **RED** WAS TOO RASH, BUT THIS KID...
...MAKES HIS KIND OF RASH LOOK LIKE A PIMPLE.

HEY!
RICE
CRACKER
WRECKER!
?
EEK!
OH FINE!
YOU JUST **KNOW** THIS
ASSISTANT GUY IS
GONNA YELL AT ME
FOR TAKING EXBO!
I GOTTA SHOW SOME
RESULTS...
MY NAME'S
GOLD. I'M
FROM
NEW BARK
TOWN.
FP
I'M LOOKING
FOR ONE OF
YOUR FELLOW
THIEVES. TAKE
A LOOK!
HE'S GOT
RED HAIR
AND A
TOTODILE.
HE
STOLE A
POKÉMON
FROM
PROFESSOR
ELM'S
RESEARCH
CENTER.
FLIP

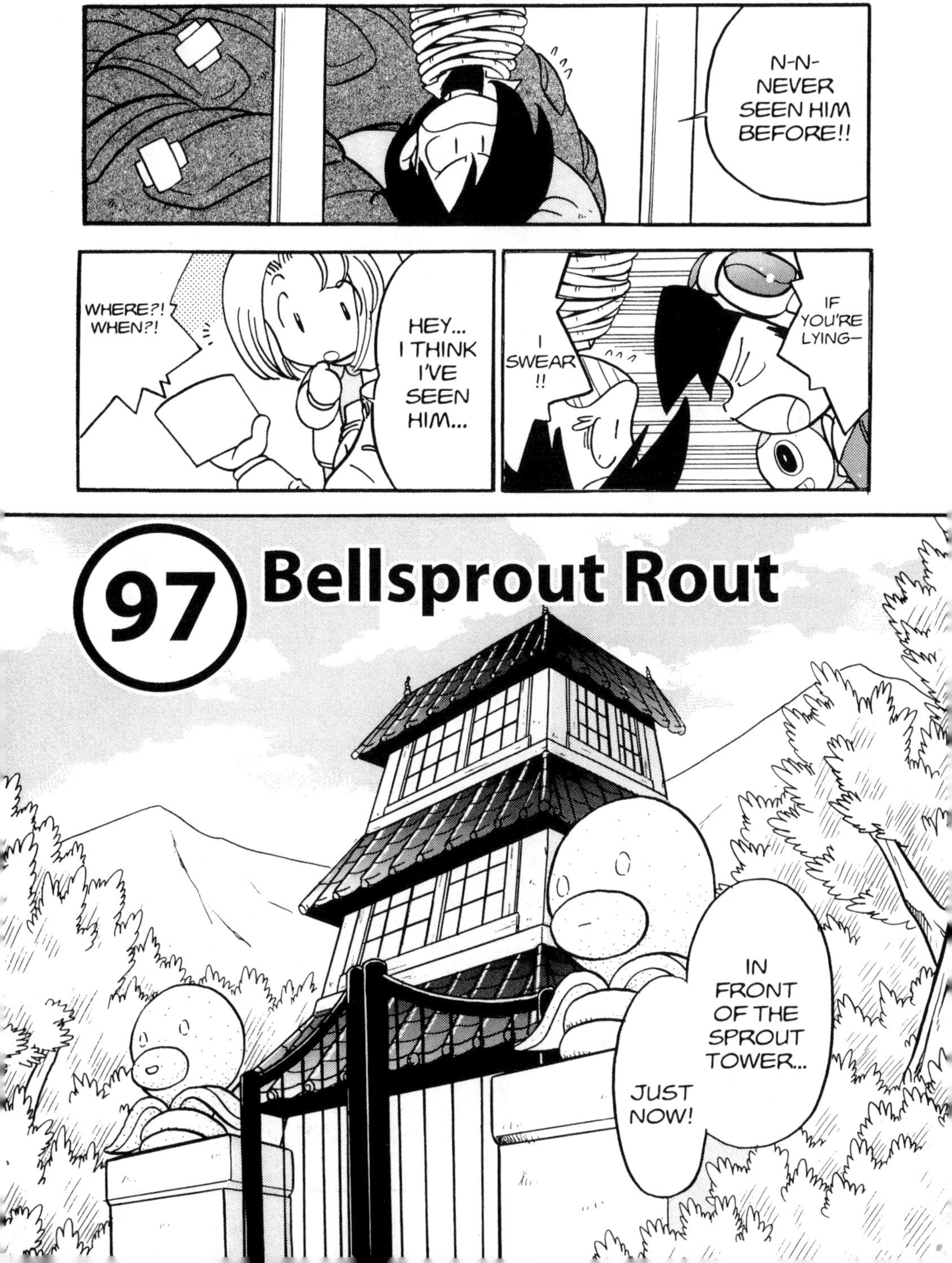

97 Bellsprout Rout

IN FRONT OF THE SPROUT TOWER...

JUST NOW!

SO IT IS IN YOUR HANDS.
GWOM
GWOM

WHETHER OR NOT IT CAN EVOLVE...
...IS ENTIRELY UP TO YOUR SKILLS.

UNDER-STOOD, SILVER?

SNAP

UNDER-STOOD.

WEIRD.
WHY DO THEY CALL IT SPROUT TOWER?

"LEGEND HOLDS THAT THE TOWER WAS BUILT AROUND A 100-FOOT BELLSPROUT." THAT'S... INSANE.
SPROUT TOWER
VIOLET

KRIII
GWOM
GWOM

GWOM
GWOM
WHAT'S ALL THIS MACHINERY, I WONDER...?

VIP VIP
OKAY... WHERE IS HE?

DUCK
WHOA.
GRRNG

YOU HAVE COME TO TRAIN IN POKÉMON COMBAT?
SHAKE SHAKE

TOOM
WAAAA!

TROY.
NEAL.

JIN.
ED-MOND.

NICO.
WE WELCOME YOU. I AM CHOW.

BALD !!!

SHING!
YOU'LL HAVE A NEW NAME AS WELL.
FIRST WE MUST SHAVE YOUR HEAD...

WHOA WHOA WHOA WHOA!! I HAPPEN TO LIKE MY HAIR!!
AND I DON'T NEED A NEW NAME!
THE NAME GOLD'S BEEN GOOD ENOUGH SO FAR, AND IT'LL STAY GOOD ENOUGH!!

GASP
AND WHY WOULD I WANT TO JOIN YOU ANYWAY?!
I'M JUST TRYING TO CATCH A BURGLAR!!
YOU MEAN... YOU DID NOT COME TO TRAIN?!
YES! EXACTLY! PRECISELY THAT!
BUT THE SPROUT TOWER IS DEVOTED TO OUR ORDER!
NONE BUT TRAINEES MAY STEP INSIDE!

SO YOU'RE GOING TO JOIN US WHETHER YOU WANT TO OR NOT!!
WOMP

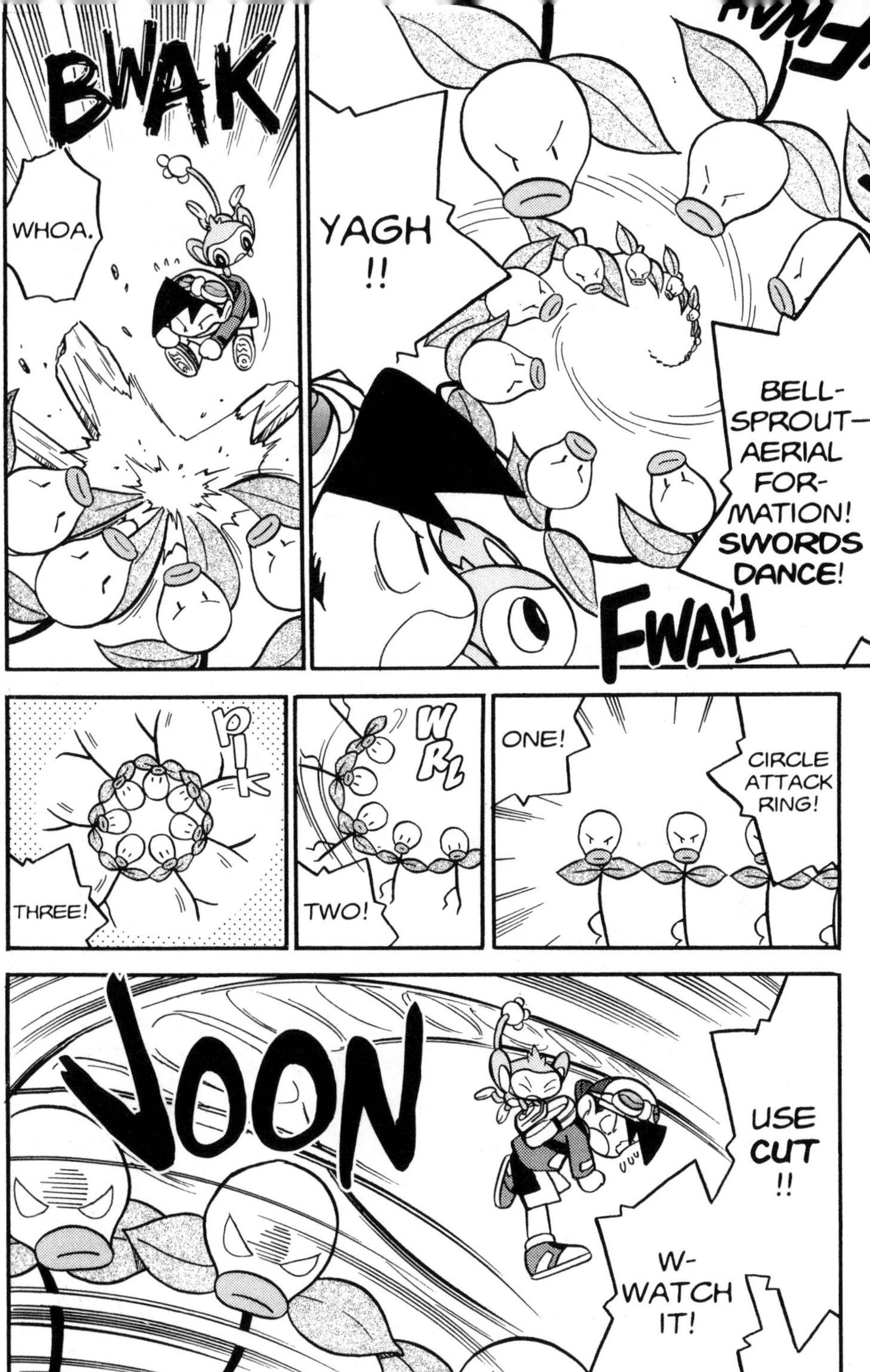

BELL-SPROUT-AERIAL FORMATION! SWORDS DANCE!
FWAH
YAGH!!
BWAK
WHOA.
ONE!
CIRCLE ATTACK RING!
WRL
TWO!
PIK
THREE!
USE CUT!!
W-WATCH IT!
VOON

YEEEEG!
PING
PING
ROOLOLO
SHVV
ACK!
HSSS
THESE ARE THE REWARDS OF OUR TRAINING. YOU TOO CAN...
YOU KNOW, I WAS HOLDING BACK 'CAUSE I FELT BAD FOR BARGING IN...
TWIK
BUT YOU HAD TO GO AND MAKE ME MAD!
FORGET TRAINING— I'M READY TO FIGHT! AIBO!!

AIBO !!

GONG

REFLECT!

VIP

OF COURSE THEY CAN! THEY CAN ATTACK FROM ANY FORMATION!

THAT IS SERIOUSLY AMAZING. I COULD NEVER DO THAT!

TOO BAD FOR YOU, I JUST WON.

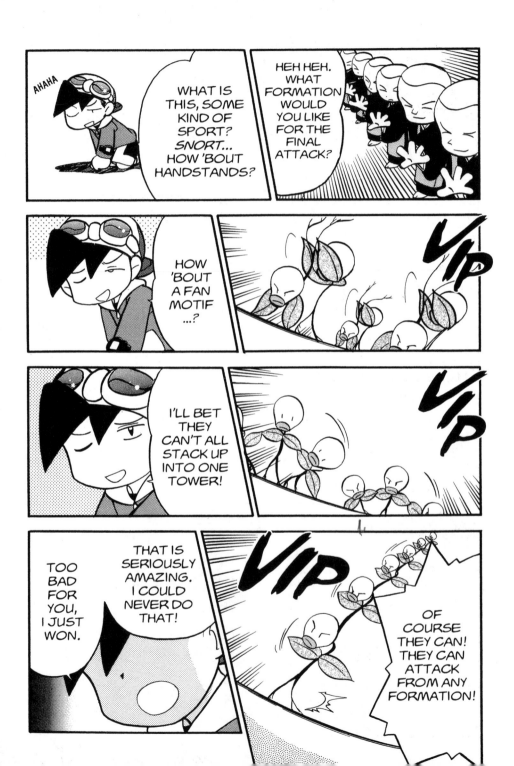

!
MWK
WSSH
FIRE !!
WHAT ?!
I KNEW I'D NEVER WIN ON SPEED OR SHEER NUMBER.
BUT IF I COULD ATTACK THEM ALL FROM BELOW...
...BY PLANTING EXBO UNDER THEM ...!
MY CYNDAQUIL'S NAME IS EXBO 'CAUSE ITS BACK EXPLODES.

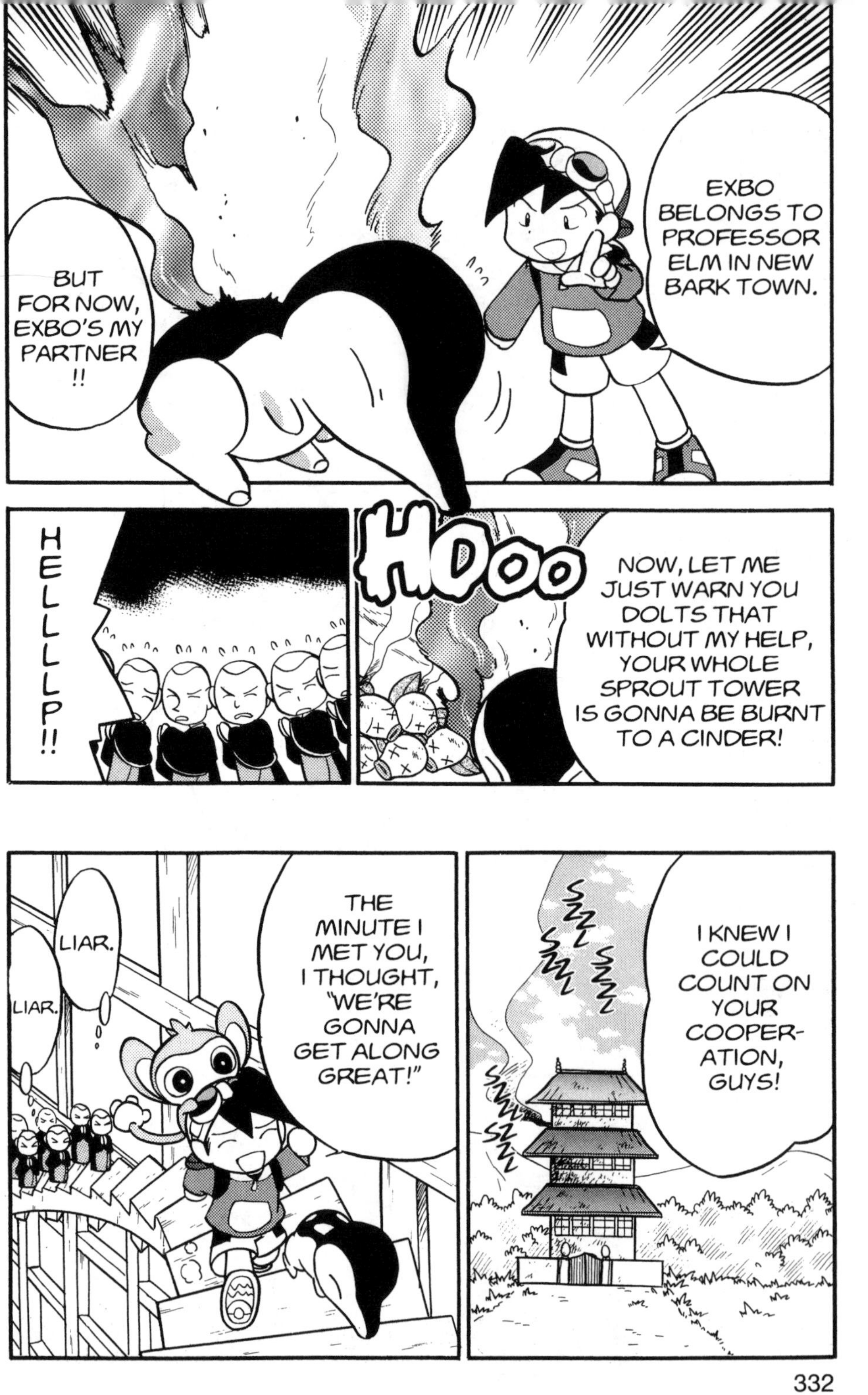

EXBO BELONGS TO PROFESSOR ELM IN NEW BARK TOWN.

BUT FOR NOW, EXBO'S MY PARTNER !!

NOW, LET ME JUST WARN YOU DOLTS THAT WITHOUT MY HELP, YOUR WHOLE SPROUT TOWER IS GONNA BE BURNT TO A CINDER!

HOOO

HELLLLLP!!

I KNEW I COULD COUNT ON YOUR COOPER-ATION, GUYS!
SZZZ
THE MINUTE I MET YOU, I THOUGHT, "WE'RE GONNA GET ALONG GREAT!"
LIAR.
LIAR.

VSH
NOW!
HANG ON.
SKRK
WHY'S THAT GUY HERE ANYWAY ?!

HEY, SAGE! THERE TREASURE UP THERE OR SOMETHING?
IT IS THE SAME AS HERE, A TRAINING FLOOR.
THERE BETTER NOT BE A BUNCH OF WEEPINBELL LYING IN WAIT...
LOOM
ABSOLUTELY NOT.

WE TOLD YOU, THIS ENTIRE TOWER IS A TRAINING PAGODA.
SKILLED YOUTH COME FROM ACROSS THE LAND TO TRAIN.
FLOOR 3
?
FLOOR 2
FLOOR 1
FIRST IS A HALL OF STUDY, DEDICATED TO KNOWLEDGE.
NEXT IS A BATTLE ARENA FOR HONING THE SKILLS OF TRAINERS.

WHILE THE TOP FLOOR IS DEDICATED TO THE HONING OF ONESELF.
HOOHOO...
ARE YOU SERIOUS ABOUT LEAVING US?

THREE—
A
TOTO-
DILE!
YES,
YES.

TWO—
MEAN
LITTLE
EYES.
YES,
YES.

YES I'M SERIOUS! I'M GONNA DESCRIBE THE GUY I'M LOOKING FOR ONE MORE TIME— SO LISTEN! ONE— LONG RED HAIR.

SOME-THING LIKE HIM?
YES! EXACTLY LIKE HIM!

GONG!

HUH?

IT'S HIM !!!
STOP !!
TM
...
TOTO-DILE-SLASH !!
FWSH

WWOOOOO
AIBO!
WHOA!
NKH!
KLATATA
KSSH
I AM **NOT** LETTING YOU GET AWAY!!
HF HF

GOM

98 Totodile Rock

G
GGGGG...

TOTO-
DILE!
SCRATCH
!!

FWIP

FSH

EXBO!
TACKLE
!!

BM
FSH

GOM

NOW GIVE BACK THE TOTO-DILE YOU STOLE FROM PROFESSOR ELM!!

...
WHY?

SIGH. I GUESS IF YOU'D GIVE IT BACK AFTER BEING ASKED POLITELY...
YOINK
...YOU WOULDN'T HAVE STOLEN IT IN THE FIRST PLACE, HUH?

BUT Y'KNOW, I'VE GOTTA GET IT BACK TO FULFILL MY PROMISE TO THE PROF.
SO ONE WAY OR ANOTHER, I'M JUST GONNA HAVE TO—
—TAKE IT!!

GWOB

WATER GUN!

OOSH

WSH

PTPTPTPT

EMBER!!

THAT'S GOTTA MATTER!
EXBO'S JUST GOTTA KEEP FIGHTING!
WOMP
SS
SS
SS

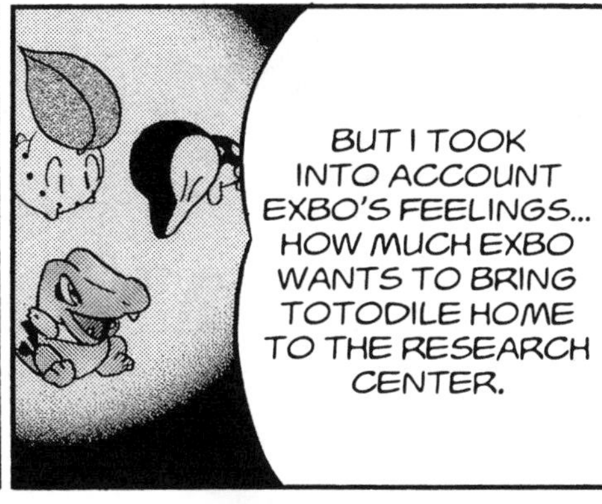
BUT I TOOK INTO ACCOUNT EXBO'S FEELINGS... HOW MUCH EXBO WANTS TO BRING TOTODILE HOME TO THE RESEARCH CENTER.
I DON'T DOUBT THAT EXBO HAS STRONG FEELINGS. BUT THERE ARE... YOU KNOW... PHYSICAL REALITIES HERE...
FIRE
WATER
GRASS

...
...

FWOOSH
IT'S REAL !!
WHAT ?!

THE POWER OF EMOTION ISN'T SOMETHING YOU CAN FIND IN TEXT-BOOKS... BUT...
SPT
SPT
SPT

JUST LIKE I PLANNED!
VP
FILL-ING UP THE ROOM!!
SS SS
ALL THIS SMOKE ...!

SMOKESCREEN!!

WATER'S STRONG AGAINST FIRE. FIRE'S STRONG AGAINST GRASS. AND GRASS IS STRONG AGAINST WATER!
I'VE HEARD IT ALL BEFORE!
BUT IF EXBO WANTS TO FIGHT, THEN WE HAVE TO WIN, NO MATTER WHAT!

THANKS FOR TELLING ME! NOW...
I'VE GOT TO FIND THAT...

KOFF KOFF!! C...CAN'T SEE...!

TOTO-DILE!
COME WITH US! YOU DON'T HAVE TO OBEY HIM ANY-MORE!
YOU MUST'VE HATED BEING WITH A THIEF LIKE THAT!
LEMME TAKE YOU BACK TO PROFES—
ZP

GOMP

YEEEOW!!

DON'T TELL ME YOU WANT TO BE WITH THIS CREEP INSTEAD OF ELM?!!

HEY HEY HEY HEY HEY HEY! WHAT'S THE BIG IDEA?!
PFF PFF

HUH ?
WSH
FINE. TOTO-DILE WON'T TELL YOU.

HEH
WEEZ

WRRRL
I CAN SEE AGAIN, THANKS.
BAP BAP

FSH FSH
THAT IS ONE LAME POKÉ-MON.
I MEAN, COME ON! A CAM-OUFLAGE ATTACK?

YOU'RE WRONG !!
IT'S ELM'S FAULT.
THAT'S WHY TOTODILE WANTS TO STAY WITH ME. I'LL TEACH TOTODILE HOW TO USE ITS POWER!
I WON'T WASTE TOTO-DILE'S TIME WITH SILLY TRICKS.
FHOOOO
TOTO-DILE, IS THAT TRUE?!
WITH THAT PERPETUAL GRIN OF YOURS, I CAN'T FIGURE OUT WHAT...
RRRR
EH ?!
IS SOME-THING... RUM-BLING?
RRR
SHOK
AGH!! SPIKES FROM THE WALLS !!
GAAAAAAA!
VOP
HMF!
SHK

ZZ...Z

FAP

WHAT'S GOING ON IN HERE ANYWAY?!!

IT'S A MECHANISM IN THE SPROUT TOWER TO TEST THE TRAINEES! THAT STUPID SMOKE OF YOURS MUST'VE TRIGGERED IT!

RRRAAGH!!

YOU'RE NOT GONNA BLAME THIS ON ME !!

KRRUNK
KII

WHATEVER! IT'S A POKÉMON TRAINING EXERCISE, RIGHT?!
SO, TOTO-DILE-SAVE US!!

YOU'RE THE ONE WHO SMASHED THE STAIRS ...
SO WE DON'T HAVE A WAY OUT!!
GGGG

NOD
NOD

EXBO?! WHAT CAN YOU DO?!
CREEP CREEP CREEP

PF
FWOO

...?!
EXBO IS SIGNAL-ING... TOTO-DILE...?!

EXBO'S FLAME IS BACK!! BUT... WHAT'S THAT GONNA DO?!
FOOOOSH
MMMMMM...
EXBO CAN'T MELT THE BALL WITHOUT MELTING US FIRST! OW! OW!

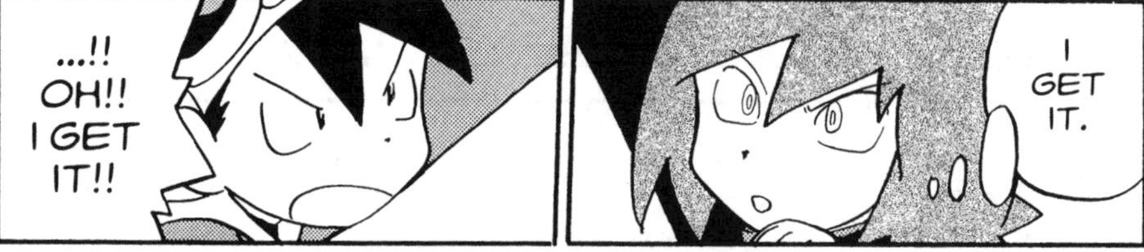
I GET IT.
...!! OH!! I GET IT!!

KEEP IT UP, EXBO!! DON'T MIND US!! USE YOUR FLAME!!
MEEEE
THAT'S IT, TOTODILE! BUILD UP YOUR COLD... BUILD IT... AND...

ICE PUNCH !!
WOK
KKKKK
KKKK

YOU DID IT!
EXBO!

IT LOOKS LIKE I OWE YOU ONE, TOTO...

I CAN TELL YOU TWO WERE RAISED BY A SCIENTIST. HA HA!
YOU KNEW THAT SUDDEN CHANGES OF TEMPER-ATURE CAN CRACK SOLID METAL!

G-GONE?!
WHAT?!

FLIP

WE RAN INTO A LITTLE TROUBLE, BUT...

BING!

FLIP

MISSION ACCOMPLISHED.

TOTODILE HAS EVOLVED INTO CROCONAW!

VOOP!!

99 Sunkern Treasure

ALL RIGHT... THE NEXT TOPIC OF DISCUSSION IS...
GOLDENROD CITY

JOHTO POKÉMON SOCIETY HQ
...REVIEW OF THE GYM LEADER ORGANIZATION...
...FOR BOTH JOHTO AND KANTO REGIONS.

VP
IF I MAY DEMONSTRATE.

IT SEEMS CLEAR TO ME THAT WE NEED TO BE A LOT STRICTER WITH OUR REQUIREMENTS FOR THE OFFICE OF GYM LEADER.

THESE ARE THE GYM LEADERS FOR VERMILION CITY AND SAFFRON CITY.

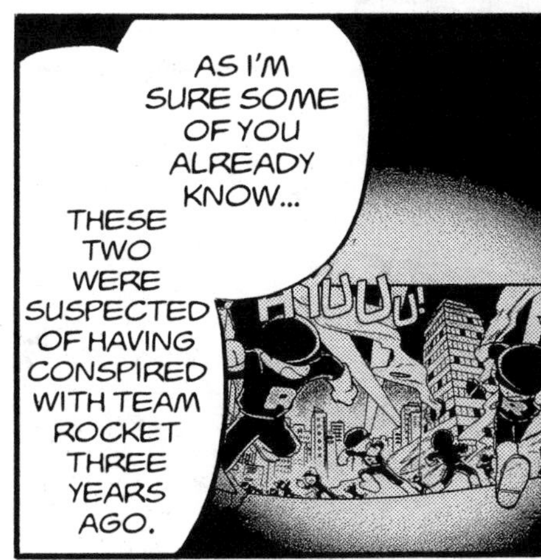

AS I'M SURE SOME OF YOU ALREADY KNOW...
THESE TWO WERE SUSPECTED OF HAVING CONSPIRED WITH TEAM ROCKET THREE YEARS AGO.

THESE GYMS CONTINUE TO BE RUN WITHOUT A LEADER.
MEANWHILE, THE WHERE-ABOUTS OF THEIR FELLOW SUSPECTS, THE FUCHSIA AND VIRIDIAN CITY GYM LEADERS, REMAIN UNKNOWN.

THEY WERE ONLY **SUSPECTED** OF COOPER-ATION WITH TEAM ROCKET. THERE WAS NO PROOF.

EXCUSE ME!
THESE PEOPLE WERE SUPPOSED TO LEND THEIR ABILITIES TO BRINGIN' UP THE LEVEL OF ALL THE TRAINERS IN THE REGION! WELL, TO MAKE SURE NOTHING LIKE THIS HAPPENS IN JOHTO...

IN MY VIEW, ALL WE NEED TO DO IS FIND NEW LEADERS FOR FUCHSIA AND VIRIDIAN.
AND IN ANY CASE, TEAM ROCKET HAS DISSOLVED... AND THE NEW VERMILION AND SAFFRON GYM LEADERS ARE FILLING THEIR DUTIES ADMIRABLY.

AM I RIGHT, BILL?

INSTEAD OF WORRYING ABOUT ISSUES BEYOND YOUR PURVIEW, I SUGGEST YOU FOCUS ON WHAT YOU ALONE CAN DO... RESTORING THE POKÉMON STORAGE SYSTEM!

MAN.
THOSE GUYS WERE TOUGH!
AND HERE WE ARE CHASING 'EM AGAIN...
SIGH
PLOD PLOD...
Y'KNOW...
HMM.
I HATE TO ADMIT IT... BUT WE DON'T CLICK LIKE THEY DO. MAYBE IT'S BECAUSE...
I KEEP QUESTIONING WHETHER I'M REALLY DOING THE RIGHT THING.
HEY, EXBO.

... THIS ISN'T YOUR FIGHT.
I'M STILL SWORN TO BRING THAT THIEF IN. BUT MAYBE ...

WRRRL
TOTODILE REALLY SEEMS TO WANT TO BE WITH THAT JERK.

YOU WANT TO STOP TRYING TO GET TOTODILE BACK?

IF YOU STAY WITH ME, YOU'LL KEEP FINDING YOURSELF IN SITUATIONS WHERE YOU'LL HAVE TO FIGHT YOUR OLD FRIEND.

THINK ABOUT IT, EXBO.

IT'S JUST... YOU DON'T HAVE TO GO THROUGH THIS.
SORRY. I'M NOT TRYING TO GIVE YOU A HEAD-ACHE OR ANYTHING.

...

I CAN STILL TAKE YOU BACK TO PROFESSOR ELM'S PLACE.

WELL... I DON'T NEED AN ANSWER ANYTIME SOON...
WUMP
ANY-WAY, I'M BEAT!
LET'S BOTH SLEEP ON IT, OKAY?

SHH...
SHH...

HOOO
WHOA!!
WHAT'S WITH THE WIND?!
VSH VSH VSH VSH VSH
AAAGH!

?
DO THEY TRAVEL IN PACKS?

PIP
Sunkern
No. 191
It may drop out of the sky suddenly. If attacked by a Spearow, it will violently shake its leaves.
Area
Cry
SUN-KERN...

WHAT WAS THAT?!
POING

FLAPFLAP...
WUMP
THEY KNOW HOW TO RUIN A GOOD NAP ANYWAY.

PIDGEOTTO! NOCTOWL! RETURN!
FLAPFLAP
W... WAIT A MINUTE...

YARG!! ANOTHER POKÉMON NOW?!
FLAP FLAP FLAP FLAP

YOU! YOU'RE ...
EH...?
AREN'T YOU...?
GONG
I FOR-GET.

I DIDN'T RECOG-NIZE YOU WITHOUT YOUR UNIFORM.
WHAT-CHA DOING OUT HERE ANYWAY ...?

RE-MEMBER CREATING THE COM-POSITE PICTURE OF THAT THIEF?
YEAH! YOU'RE THAT COP!
YAWN

THIS IS PURELY MY OWN DREAM.
DREAM ...?

I GUESS I HAVEN'T INTRO-DUCED MYSELF.
NAME'S FALKNER. I'M OFF DUTY TODAY. CAME OUT TO TRAIN.
WHOA. I DIDN'T KNOW POLICE DID POKÉMON TRAINING TOO!

I WANT TO BE THE ONE TO CARRY ON MY FATHER'S WORK.
SO FAR NO ONE'S BEEN ABLE TO REPLACE HIM.

VIOLET
GYM
VIOLET
HAVE YOU BEEN TO VIOLET CITY?
DID YOU SEE THE GYM?

MY FATHER WAS THE GYM LEADER THERE. RIGHT NOW HE'S IN A... SITUATION... WHERE HE'S HAD TO GO INTO HIDING.

THAT'S WHY I KEEP TRAINING LIKE THIS! SO I CAN PASS THE POKÉMON LEAGUE'S QUALIFYING EXAM!
THAT'S MY ONLY GOAL!

GOAL ...

OCCURS TO ME... THAT SILVER ISN'T ACTING LIKE HE STOLE THAT TOTODILE JUST SO HE COULD SELL IT...

HAS HE GOT SOME BIGGER GOAL TOO...?
HOOOO
HM?

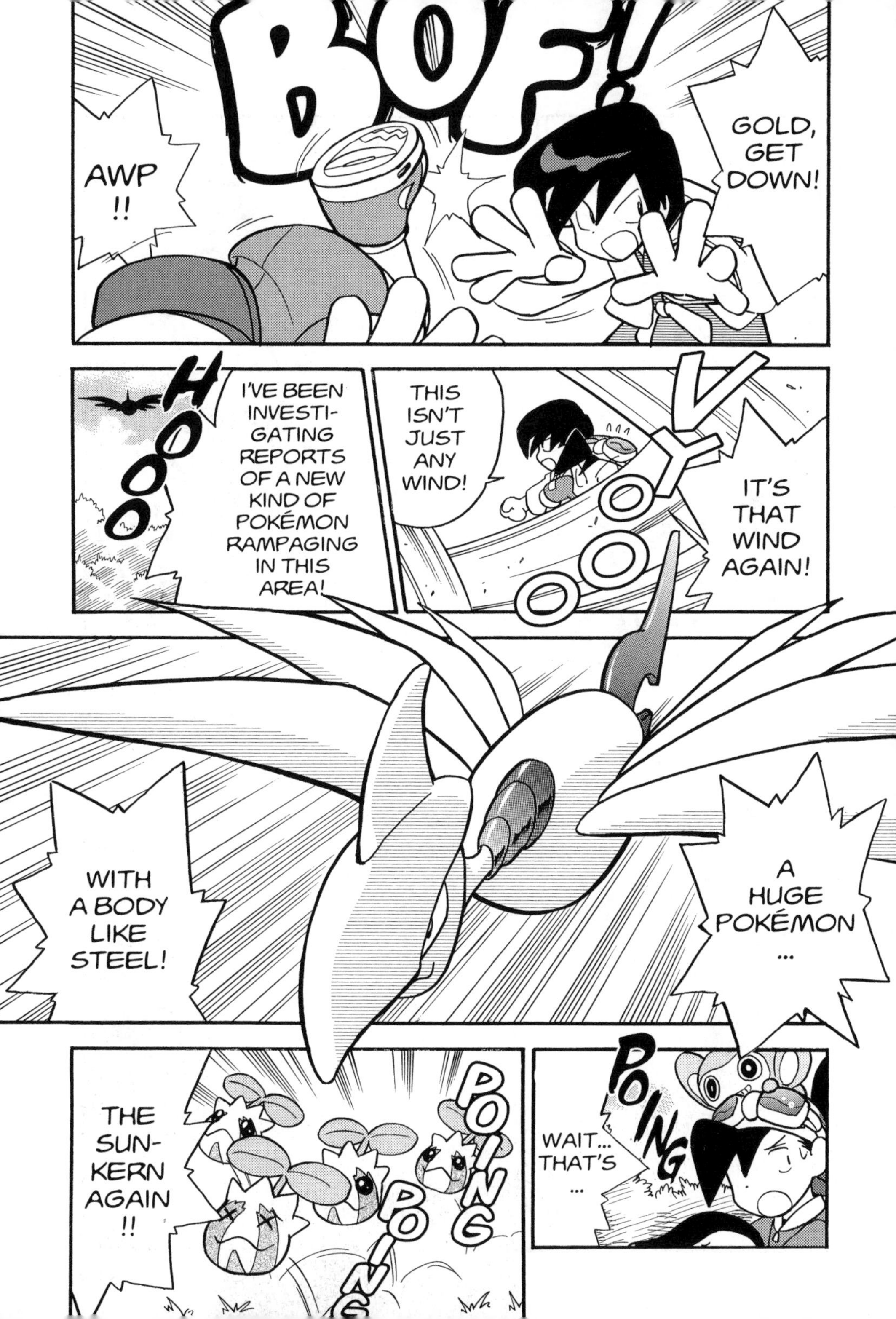
BOF!!
GOLD, GET DOWN!
AWP !!
VYOOOO
IT'S THAT WIND AGAIN!
THIS ISN'T JUST ANY WIND!
I'VE BEEN INVESTI-GATING REPORTS OF A NEW KIND OF POKÉMON RAMPAGING IN THIS AREA!
HOOOO
A HUGE POKÉMON ...
WITH A BODY LIKE STEEL!
POING
WAIT... THAT'S ...
POING
POING
THE SUN-KERN AGAIN !!

THEY MUST BE RUNNING AWAY FROM THAT HUGE POKÉMON.
WHICH WOULD EXPLAIN WHY THEY KEEP RUNNING BACK AND FORTH.
OR... BOUNCING, I MEAN.
PIDGE-OTTO! NOCT-TOWL !!
LET'S GO!
KANG
KANG
KING
KING
AN AERIAL BATTLE!
YOUR POKÉMON ARE REALLY PRESSING THAT THING!
BUT THEY CAN'T DEAL THE DECIDING BLOW.

WE'VE FOUGHT AGAINST THAT POKÉMON ONCE BEFORE.
THAT METAL SHELL DEFIED US!
BUT ...
WHOK
NO !!

PIDGEOTTO! KEEP BACK!
BUT IT'S GOTTA ...
...HAVE A WEAK SPOT, RIGHT ?!

YOU'D THINK... BUT WHAT WEAKENS METAL? MAGNETISM... RUST... INTENSE HEAT...
HEAT ?!

BING!
SOUNDS TO ME LIKE A JOB FOR...

... EXBO !!

BUT NOT EVEN A JUMP SHOT WITH A POOL CUE WOULD GET YOU WAY UP THERE.
POING
HUH?
PAP
AIBO, GRAB IT!
BON
HYAH!!
YOU WANT TO HELP ME STOP THAT POKÉ-MON?
RATTLE
RATTLE
HO! CAN'T WAIT TO GET 'IM, EH?
YOU'RE A POKÉMON AFTER MY OWN HEART, SUNKERN!
SO LET'S GO!!
BOOM
WHAT ARE YOU PLANNING, GOLD?
JUST YOU WATCH!
I'M COUNT-ING ON YOU!
BOOM

TAKING ADVANTAGE OF THAT JUMPING SKILL...
POING POING POIIIING
POING
AHA!!
A DELIVERY METHOD FOR CYNDAQUIL!
VOOOO
EXBO, NOW!
BOM
YOU WANTED HEAT?!!
HOO
CHK
YOU DID IT! NOW LEAVE THE REST TO ME!

GOT IT!!
BOOM
NOTHIN' SPECIAL FOR ME!
THAT WAS QUICK THINKING, GOLD.
THANK YOU.
TO-GETHER, HUH...?
WHADDYA THINK, EXBO?
OBVIOUSLY I HAVE A LOT MORE TRAINING TO DO.
MAYBE GETTING TOTODILE BACK JUST MEANS ...
...MORE TRAINING TOGETHER.
WE CAN DO IT TO-GETHER... CAN'T WE, TEAM?

NOD

YOU WANT TO TRY AGAIN... TOGETHER?

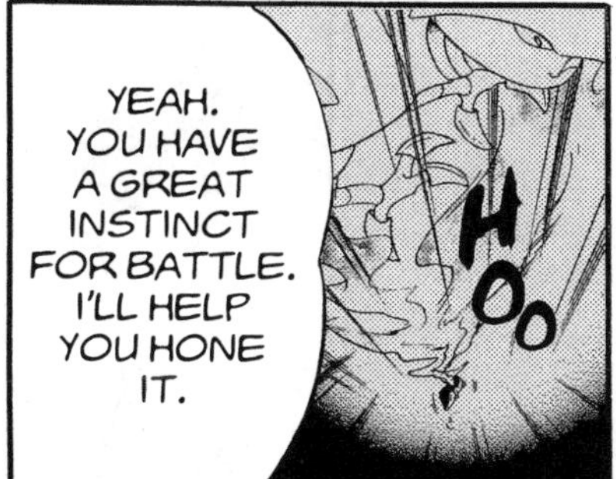
YEAH. YOU HAVE A GREAT INSTINCT FOR BATTLE. I'LL HELP YOU HONE IT.
HOO

HEY, GOLD. DO YOU WANT TO TRAIN WITH ME AWHILE?
T-TRAIN?

IT PROBABLY...
...WOULD BE GREAT TO GET STRONGER.

EXCEPT...

I'VE GOT A COUPLE OF JOBS TO FINISH THAT CAN'T WAIT.
FOR NOW... I'VE GOT TO KEEP MOVING.

YEAH ... I KNOW ALL ABOUT MISSIONS THAT CAN'T WAIT.
IT'S UP TO YOU WHETHER YOU SUCCEED OR FAIL. GIVE IT ALL YOU'VE GOT!
YOU TOO!
SEE YOU AGAIN, FALKNER!

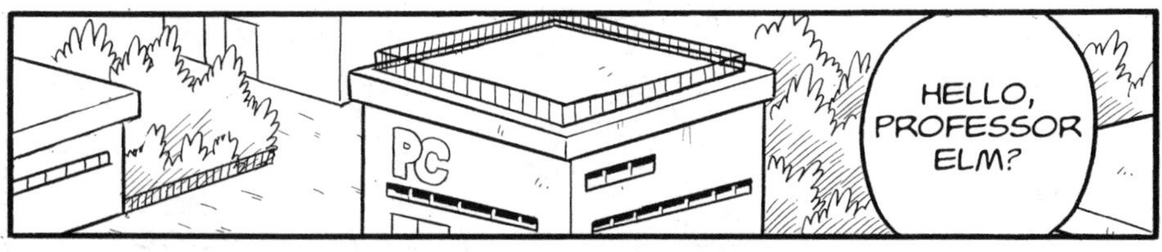
HELLO, PROFESSOR ELM?

I'VE ARRIVED IN VIOLET CITY...
...BUT I CAN'T FIND ANY SIGN OF GOLD.
I SEE.
HE HASN'T COME UP ON THE POKÉ-GEAR EITHER.
IF ONLY THE STORAGE SYSTEM WERE BACK UP.

UM, PRO-FESSOR, I KNOW IT'S A BIT LATE TO BRING THIS UP... BUT...
WHY DO YOU WANT TO GIVE SUCH AN IMPOR-TANT ITEM TO A RECKLESS KID LIKE THAT?
WELL...
THE BEST WAY TO HATCH IT...

...IS TO BE NEAR HIGH-ENERGY POKÉ-MON.
AND SINCE IT WASN'T REACTING HERE AT THE CENTER...

YOU THOUGHT GOLD AND HIS CRAZY POKÉMON MIGHT DO IT...
IN ANY CASE, I WANT YOU TO GIVE HIM...
...THAT MYSTERY EGG!

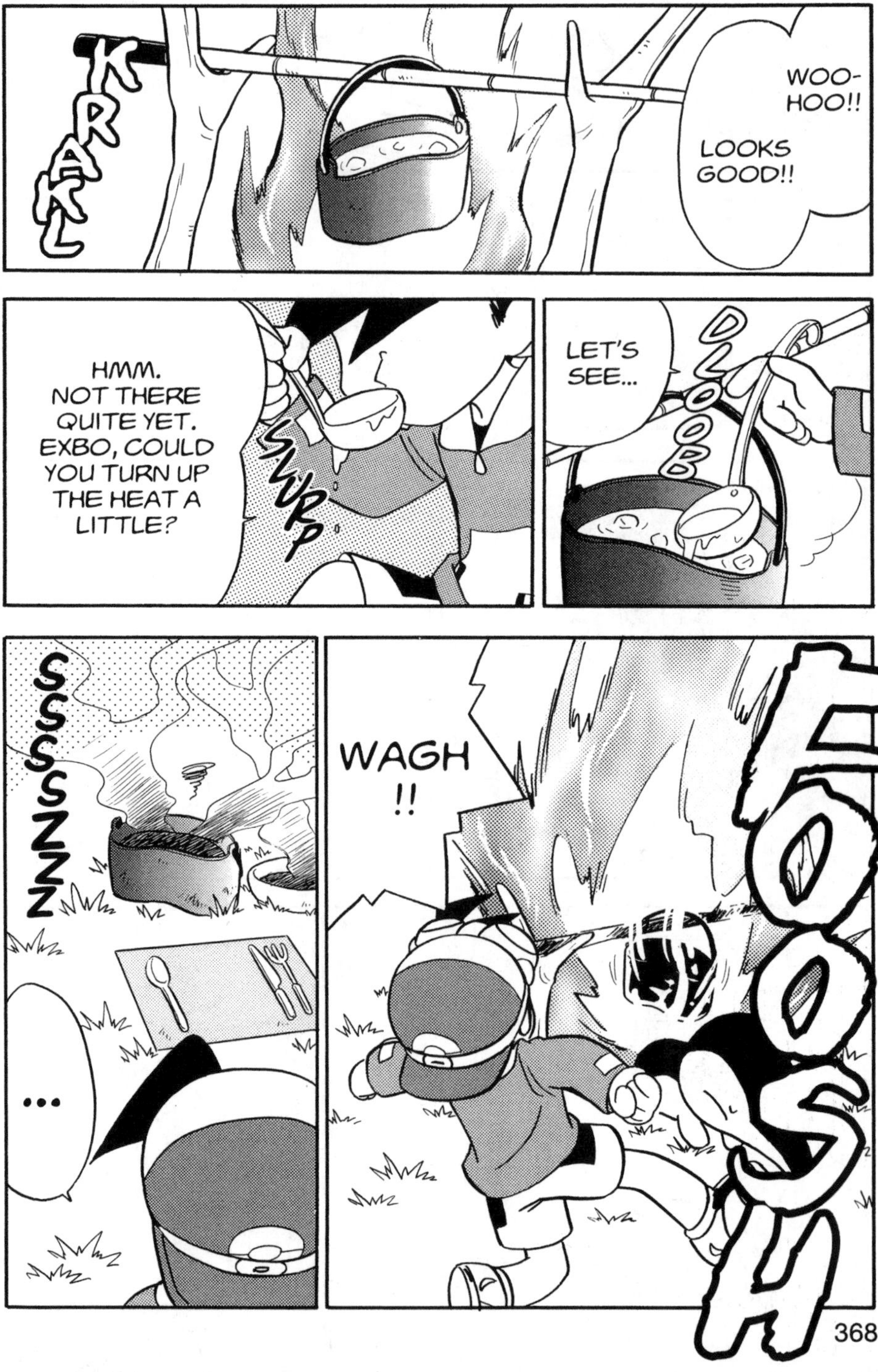

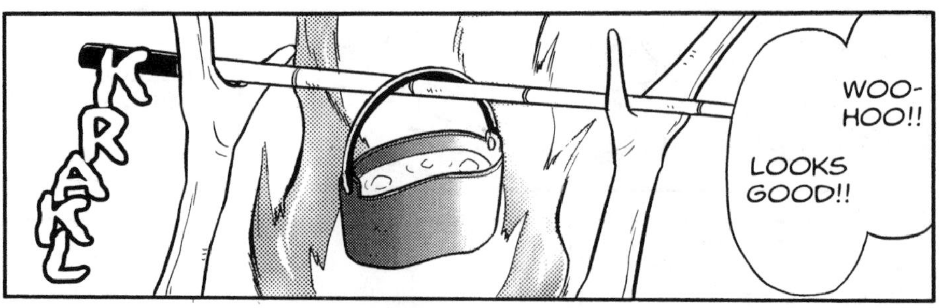

WOO-HOO!!
LOOKS GOOD!!
KRAKL

LET'S SEE...
DLOOOB

HMM. NOT THERE QUITE YET. EXBO, COULD YOU TURN UP THE HEAT A LITTLE?
SLURP

FOOOSH
WAGH !!
SSSSZZZZ
...

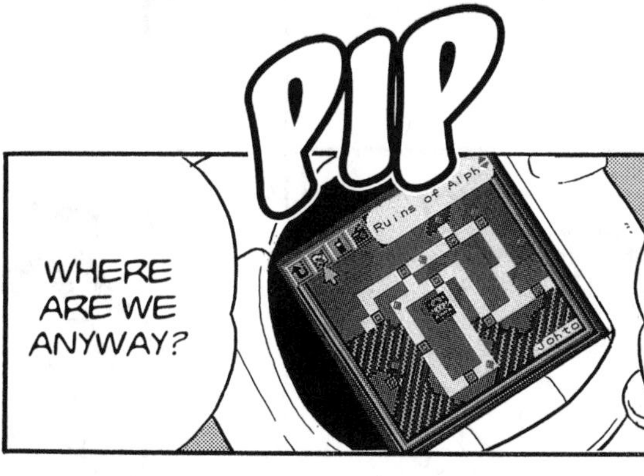

LOOKS LIKE YOU STILL NEED TO WORK ON THAT **FINESSE.**

WHATEVER. WE'VE STILL GOT TO FIND POLIBO...

100 Into the Unown

RUINS, HUH? THAT MIGHT EXPLAIN ALL THESE PILES OF ROCKS...

HUH?

VIP VIP

YOW! SHE'S CUTE!

WELL HELLO, MISS.
TP
HUH ...?

MUST BE BORING, TOURING THESE RUINS ALONE.
GLEEM

YOU WANNA GO GET SOME TEA OR SOME-THING?
UM...
OH! THE NAME'S GOLD. I'M FROM NEW BARK TOWN.

I'M BUGSY. FROM AZALEA TOWN. AND YOU DO KNOW...
... DON'T YOU... THAT I'M A **GUY**?
FOMP

D-DUH! OF C-COURSE I KNEW!
HMF
AND ONE MORE THING.

I'M NOT TOURING THE RUINS. I'M LOOKING FOR MY FRIENDS WHO'VE GONE MISSING.
YOUR FRIENDS ARE MISSING ?!

WE'RE ALL IN THIS RUINS EXPLORATION CLUB. THEY WERE POKING AROUND HERE YESTERDAY...
...WHEN SUDDENLY ALL COMMUNI-CATION STOPPED!

WHY ARE YOU HERE?
WELL, IT'S ONE OF MY POKÉMON.
IT'S GONE MISSING, AND I'M TRYING TO TRACK IT DOWN.
PING!
MISSING?!

MAYBE IT WAS CAPTURED BY WHOEVER KIDNAPPED MY FRIENDS!
ACTUALLY... I DON'T REALLY EVEN KNOW WHEN OR WHERE POLIBO WENT MISSING...

REALLY...?
SOUNDS LIKE WHAT I'VE HEARD...
...ABOUT THE FISHING HOLE...
TP
TP

FAP
HUH? WHAT'S UP, AIBO?

YOU HEAR SOMETHING FROM INSIDE THERE? VOICES?
NOD NOD

OKAY, EXBO...
WHAT?! N-NO... WAIT...!

HWSH

THIS ...

...JUST ISN'T RIGHT.

LET'S GO!!

WAIT'LL MY EYES ADJUST AND...

WHERE ...?

HUH ?

WHAT'S THAT?! IS IT SOME KIND OF CODE?

MY GOODNESS ...
I NEVER IMAGINED I'D FIND... THIS!
HEY HEY HEY! TRY TALKING TO ME INSTEAD OF YOURSELF!
FLIP FLIP
THIS STRUCTURE HAS STOOD HERE FOR OVER 1,500 YEARS.

THERE IS A THEORY THAT THE MYSTERIOUS SYMBOL POKÉMON ONCE LIVED HERE...
BUT NO ONE'S FOUND ANY PROOF... UNTIL NOW!
SYMBOL POKÉ-MON ?!!

IF WE CAN DECODE THESE CHARAC-TERS...
...WE MAY FIND THEY TELL US ALL ABOUT THOSE ANCIENT CREATURES.
WOW ...
SO THIS WAS WRITTEN 1,500 YEARS AGO?

SOME LEGENDS SAY THAT HUMANS AND POKÉMON LIVED TOGETHER EVEN THEN.
TO SEE EVIDENCE OF THOSE LEGENDS WITH MY OWN EYES ...
Y'KNOW, THIS IS REALLY EXCITING ...
BUT WEREN'T YOU TRYING TO FIND YOUR FRIENDS ...?
OH... R-RIGHT. SORRY. HA HA HA...

TM
THIS HALL KEEPS GOING DEEPER IN.
THE VOICES PROBABLY CAME FROM IN THERE...

SHULULU

VRP
HEY !!
WHAT ... WHAT ...?!

THANKS SO MUCH FOR SMASHING OPEN THE SECRET CHAMBER.
WHO ARE YOU ?!

WE THOUGHT THE ONLY WAY IN...
...WAS SOLVING THIS PUZZLE IN THE STONES.
ohto

BUT NOW WE CAN JUST WALK IN AND GRAB THOSE SYMBOL POKÉMON!
TA-DAA

TEAM ROCKET?! BUT THEY SAID YOU WERE DESTROYED!!
EXBO— GET 'EM!

SORRY. CYNDAQUIL'S TOO CONSTRICTED TO IGNITE.
GRRNNNN

ELEKID!!
ZZZZAK
VM

NOW WE COLLECT THE POKÉMON ESSENTIAL TO RESURRECTING OUR ORGANIZATION!

ZZZK
NNK
AND YOU GET TO WATCH!
BZZAK

ZZZZZ
OKAY... OKAY... I GUESS YOU'RE RIGHT. THERE'S NOTHING... WE CAN DO...
HF
HF

WP
ZZZZZZ
KCH
'CEPT THIS!!
FSH

BOM
KWEEEEEE
SUNBO-
FLASH!!
POF

SWP
MEET SUNBO THE SUNKERN... MY NEW BEST FRIEND!

AIIIEEEE!!!
MY EYES !!

SUNBO LOOKS EXTRA BRIGHT IF YOU'VE BEEN IN THE DARK AWHILE!

VOOP
Move it, Bugsy!

TH- TH-THE SYMBOLS! THEY'RE... THEY'RE...
POK POK

MWOOON
POK
HUH ?

UN- OWN ...

Unown
Symbol Pokémon
Height ???
Weight ???
No.201
Area Cry PRNT
PIP

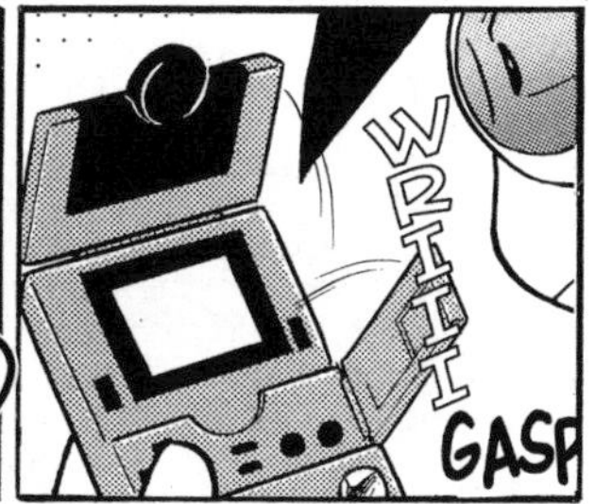
WRIIII
GASP

THOSE LETTERS AREN'T **ABOUT** THE SYMBOL POKÉMON...
MWOO... OON...
BUGSY, IT LOOKS LIKE BOTH YOU **AND** THE BAD GUYS GOT IT WRONG.

...THEY ARE THE SYMBOL POKÉMON!
VWRR
THAT FLASH MUST'VE WOKEN THEM UP!
ROROO
I THINK WE OUGHTA ...
RUN !!
OOOMMMM

LITTLE CREEP... DIDN'T HAVE TO MAKE IT SO BRIGHT ...
SPOTS IN FRONT OF MY EYES...

STILL, WE'VE LEARNED SOMETHING VITAL TODAY. NOW WE KNOW...
... EXACTLY WHAT WE'RE SUPPOSED TO BE HUNTING FOR!

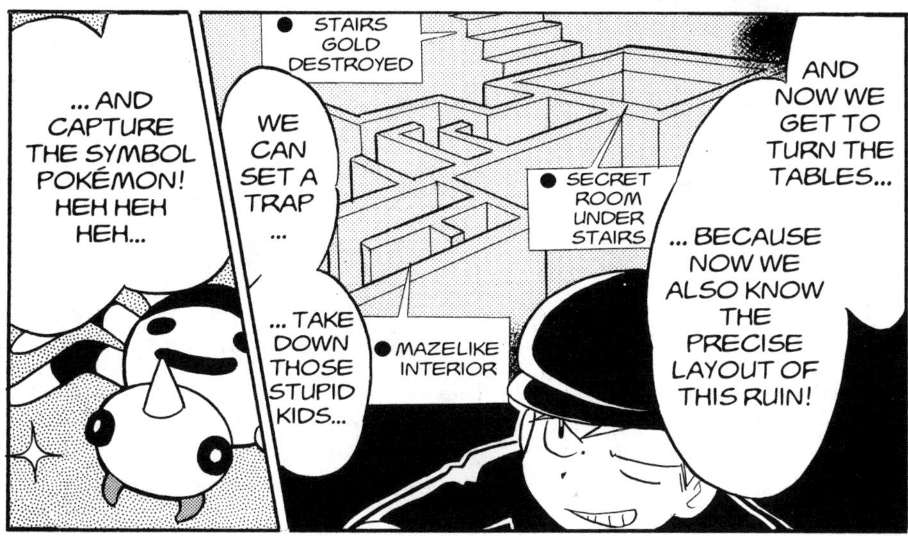

AND NOW WE GET TO TURN THE TABLES...
... BECAUSE NOW WE ALSO KNOW THE PRECISE LAYOUT OF THIS RUIN!
STAIRS GOLD DESTROYED
SECRET ROOM UNDER STAIRS
MAZELIKE INTERIOR
WE CAN SET A TRAP ...
... TAKE DOWN THOSE STUPID KIDS...
... AND CAPTURE THE SYMBOL POKÉMON! HEH HEH HEH...

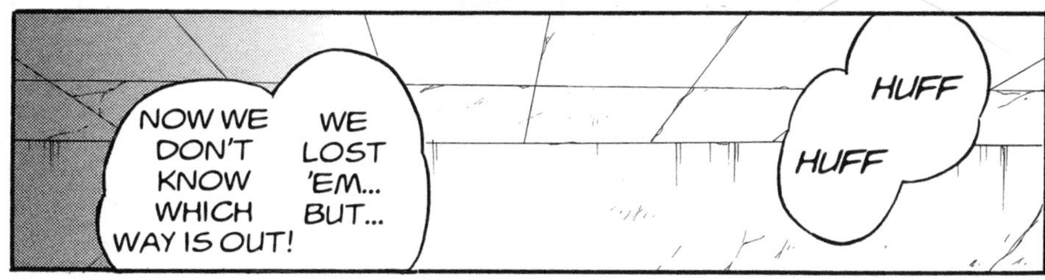

HUFF
HUFF
WE LOST 'EM... BUT...
NOW WE DON'T KNOW WHICH WAY IS OUT!

WE'VE GOTTA ...
HUH ?!
DO YOU HEAR SOME-THING FROM BEHIND THAT WALL?
COULD IT BE ...?
HELLLP! PLEEASE!
IT IS! MY MISSING FRIENDS!

NOW WE'VE JUST GOTTA GET 'EM OUT OF THERE!
VSH
A WEB?!
IT'S SPINARAK'S SPIDER WEB.

BUT DIFFERENT FROM THE THREAD THEY USED BEFORE... STICKIER!
HE !!
RP
AS A BUG-TYPE POKÉMON SPECIALIST, I KNOW!
WE'VE GOT TO GO A DIFFER-ENT WAY!

WAIT!! IT'S HERE TOO!!!
AND BEHIND US NOW!! WE'RE TRAPPED !!
THERE'S NO WAY OUT!
YOUR ONLY HOPE IS TO SURREN-DER!
RG!

AND I HEAR THE UNOWN COMING FROM THE OTHER WAY!! WHAT CAN WE DO?!
VOOO
FOOT-STEPS!
THEY'RE COMING FOR US, BUGSY!
TM TM TM TM
...ALL WE'VE GOT TO DO IS BLOCK THE EXIT... AND WE'VE GOT EVERYBODY!!
OOOOO
HEH HEH... WHEN THE SYMBOL POKÉMON COME AFTER THEM...

OOMMM
WHAT?! THE POKÉ-MON ARE IN THE WEB?!
AND WHERE ARE THOSE KIDS?!
!
W-WHAT'S ALL THIS SMOKE?!
SSSS
KOK

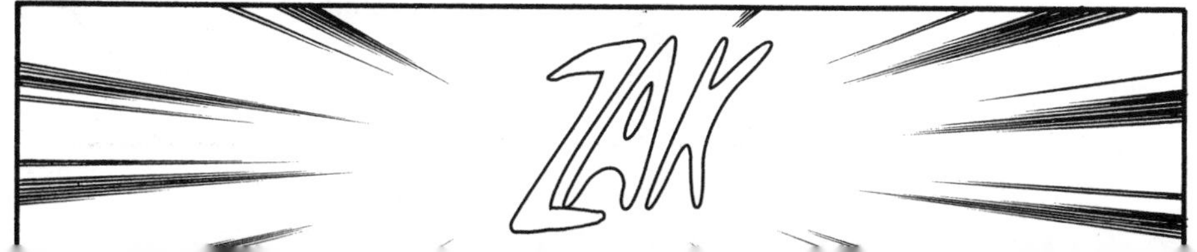
ZAK

GLNK
W-WAIT... WE'RE NOT THE ONES...
LNK
...WHO BROKE INTO... YOUR...
WMP
PWIP
PWIP
KZZZZZ
AIEEE!!!

THANKS, GOLD. I COULDN'T HAVE SAVED THEM WITHOUT YOU.
NO SWEAT!

OKAY, THAT'S EVERY-ONE!

AND WE FOUND THE UNOWN!
AN EPIC DISCOVERY!!

WHAT WAS ONCE JUST A RUIN CAN BECOME A PLACE OF STUDY, OF...
OKAY, BUGSY! I GET IT, I GET IT!

THAT MUST HAVE BEEN THEIR ANCIENT ATTACK, THE "HIDDEN POWER."
...BUT OUR STUDY OF THEM HAS JUST BEGUN!
WE STILL DON'T KNOW ITS EXACT NATURE...

NOW, I'VE GOT TO GET BACK TO MY MISSIONS!
KLNK
SO I'LL SEE YA!

TAKE CARE, GOLD!
YOU TOO!

HOOOO
HERE'S THE HINT... A POKÉMON CRAWLING ON THE FLOOR OF THE ANCIENT OCEAN...

WAIT A MINUTE. DIDN'T WE ALREADY DO THIS ONE?
FORGET THE STUPID PUZZLE!
IT'S GONNA TAKE FOR-EVER!

NOT AS LONG AS IT'LL TAKE TO DIG OUR WAY THROUGH ALL THAT ROCK!
PIP
EH ?!
A TRANS-MIS-SION ?!

YOU SCREWED UP AGAIN ?!!
BZZ
EEEK!! BOSS ?!

DID I MAKE A MISTAKE GATHERING YOU CLOWNS BACK TOGETHER?!
WELL ?!

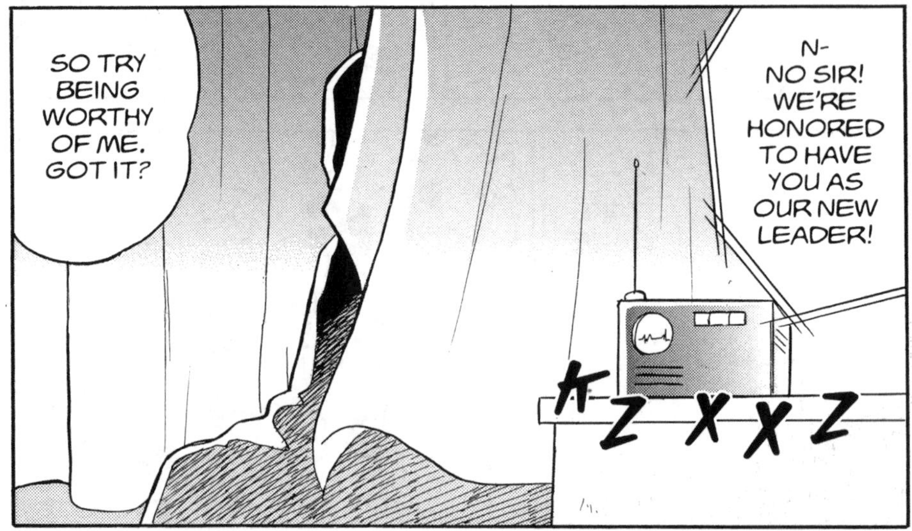
N- NO SIR! WE'RE HONORED TO HAVE YOU AS OUR NEW LEADER!
SO TRY BEING WORTHY OF ME. GOT IT?
KZZXXZ

ROUTE 32

BUGSY SAID IT WAS AROUND HERE...

101 Teddiursa's Picnic

...THE PLACE WHERE POKÉMON KEEP GOING MISSING...

Route 32

...THE FISHING HOLE.

PIP

GUESS I'D BETTER ASK... NOT THAT THERE'RE MANY PEOPLE AROUND ...

A POKÉ BALL WITH A POLIWAG IN IT?

ANOTHER VICTIM OF THE POKÉMON SNATCHER, HUH?

THEN HE'S HERE?!

WHERE CAN I FIND THIS CREEP?!
DON'T KNOW. HE'S TOO QUICK.

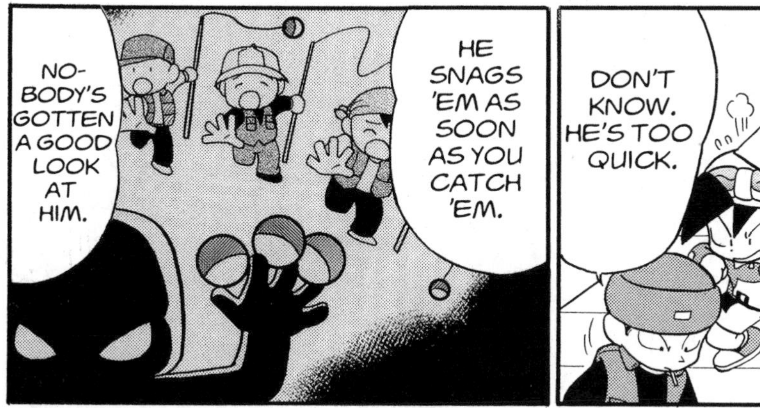

HE SNAGS 'EM AS SOON AS YOU CATCH 'EM.
NO-BODY'S GOTTEN A GOOD LOOK AT HIM.

COULD IT BE TEAM ROCKET AGAIN?
ARE THEY USING POLIWAG FOR SOME EVIL PLOT?

YOU GOTTA BE ALERT! THAT'S WHY I'M HANGING ON TO MY...
VIP
HUH ?!
WSSH
MY OCTI-LLERY !
CHK
HE'S FAST, ALL RIGHT ...

TAK
BUT NOT FAST ENOUGH!!
VYOOO
WHOA !!

!!
GONK
HUH?! THE POKÉMON THIEF...IS A POKÉMON?!

I GUESS IT'S HARD JUST TO WALK UP TO PEOPLE AND ASK FOR HELP WITH A SCARY MUG LIKE THAT.
OKAY. I'LL TAKE YOU TO THE POKÉMON CENTER TO GET THAT JAW LOOKED AT. BUT FIRST...

NOD NOD
...GIVE BACK ALL THE POKÉMON YOU STOLE!

GOLOGOLO
THAT'S A TON !!

OH ...!
BOM
P-POLIBO !!
IT'S REALLY YOU!!
THE RIVER CARRIED YOU ALL THE WAY HERE!

YOU MUST HAVE BEEN SO SCARED!
WAG WAG

I'M HAPPY FOR YOU, KID.
THANKS! NOW I GOTTA GET BACK TO...
HANG ON, KID. HERE'S MY PHONE NUMBER.
LET'S STAY IN TOUCH. WE CAN TALK POKÉMON SOMETIME.

YOU SERIOUS?
I MEAN, WE JUST MET...
HEH
WHAT? YOU DON'T LIKE MAKING NEW FRIENDS?
IT'S NOT THAT! I'M JUST IN A HURRY! SEE YA!
YEAH... SURE...

HE HANDLES POKÉ BALLS ALMOST AS WELL AS **YELLOW** DOES.
SOMETHING TELLS ME I SHOULD TALK TO YELLOW ABOUT THIS...

I WONDER WHAT THAT WAS ALL ABOUT?
HUH? WHAT'S WRONG, POLIBO?
WHINE
WHINE
OH YEAH! I'M SORRY!

MEET EXBO, AND THIS HERE IS SUNBO. THEY ARE COOL!
SO YOU'VE GOT NOTHING TO WORRY ABOUT!
AND THIS... IS POLIBO.
POLIBO'S STILL LITTLE, SO LOOK AFTER POLIBO, OKAY?

REALLY? THAT'S GREAT!
ELM RESEARCH CENTER
I CAN'T BELIEVE YOU FOUND POLIBO!
HEY, COULD YOU SAY HI TO MY MOM TOO?

SURE, BUT... WHAT ARE YOU GOING TO DO WITH POLIBO?
OH YEAH ...
THE TRANSFER SYSTEM'S DOWN IN ALL OF JOHTO, HUH? I GUESS I'LL HAVE TO TAKE POLIBO WITH ME.
POKéMON CENTER
BOX 1
I WISH THEY'D GET THAT SYSTEM BACK UP.

NO KIDDING. IF I COULD'VE JUST DONE A TRANSFER...
STAGGER
?
?
WHAT IS IT?

HELLO, GOLD? THAT'S MY ASSISTANT! I'M SO GLAD YOU TWO WERE FINALLY ABLE TO MEET!

SOB
WHO THE HECK ARE YOU?!
ARE YOU CALLING PROFESSOR ELM? CAN YOU PUT HIM ON?

GOLD, I WANT YOU TO KEEP EXBO TO HELP YOU RECOVER TOTODILE.
IN EXCHANGE, CAN YOU DO ME A FAVOR?
I WANT YOU TO TAKE SOME-THING WITH YOU.

THIS POKÉMON EGG!
A POKÉMON EGG?!

BUT WE'VE NEVER SEEN ONE IN AN EGG STATE BEFORE.
ONLY NEW-BORN... OR NEW-HATCHED?

WELL, WE'RE ASSUMING IT'S FROM A POKÉMON AT ANY RATE...

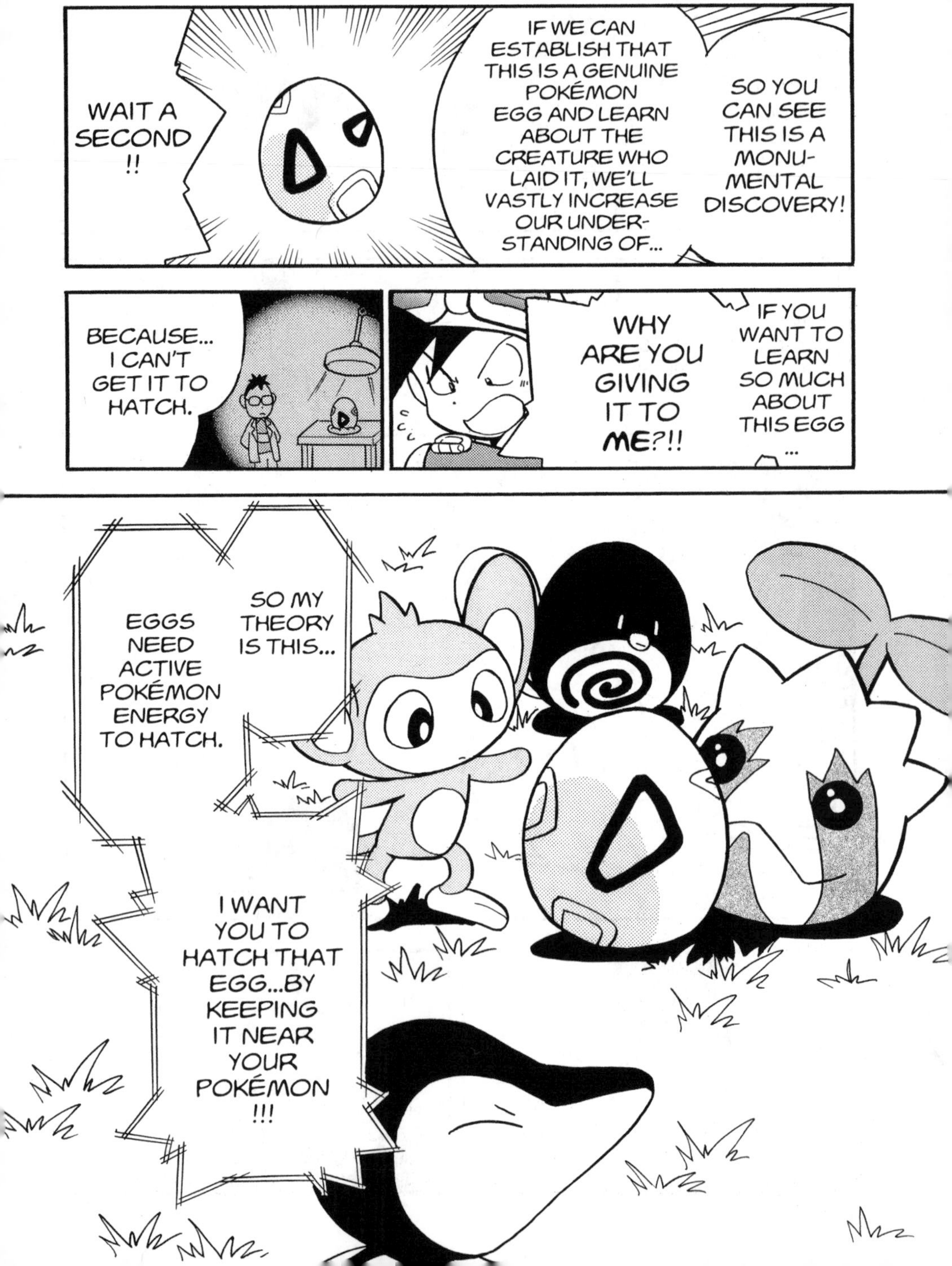

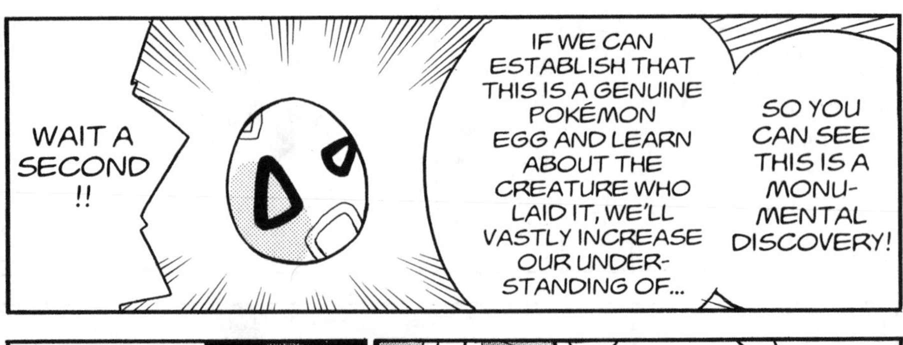

SO MY THEORY IS THIS...

EGGS NEED ACTIVE POKÉMON ENERGY TO HATCH.

I WANT YOU TO HATCH THAT EGG...BY KEEPING IT NEAR YOUR POKÉMON!!!

AZALEA TOWN
KLANG KLANG
BY THE WAY...

WHAT ARE YOU PLANNING ON DOING WITH THIS POKÉ BALL YOU'RE HAVING ME MAKE?
SOME SPECIAL POKÉMON YOU'RE AFTER?

POWERFUL POKÉMON ARE THE ONLY ONES I REALLY WANT.

KLANG
HA HA HA... SUCH INTENSITY YOU HAVE!

WELL, I DON'T CARE.
AS LONG AS I KNOW THE GREAT POKÉ BALLS I FORGE...
...GO TO TRAINERS WHO TRULY KNOW HOW TO USE THEM.
THERE, THE POKÉ BALL MADE FROM THE BLACK APRICORN YOU BROUGHT.
TNG
SS
THE FAMOUS "HEAVY BALL."

SO... HUNGRY...
WOBBLE
OHHH ...

FRUIT! AND NOT JUST FRUIT... FREE FRUIT!!
HUH ?!
I RAN OUT OF MONEY FROM ALL THE TAKE-OUT I ATE...

...
GOMP
CHOW TIME!!

THAT'S APRI-CORN FRUIT.
I'VE NEVER SEEN ANYBODY TRY TO EAT THAT BEFORE.
AGH!! PEH!! PEH!! PEH!!
TEE HEE
YOU'RE FUNNY, MISTER!

HERE YOU GO!
RICE BALLS !!

THANKS! I OWE YOU ONE, LITTLE GIRL!!
GMP GMP
YOU AND YOUR POKÉMON! TEE HEE!

MY GRAMPA MAKES POKÉ BALLS FROM THOSE APRICORNS.
HE MAKES A WHOLE BUNCH OF DIFFERENT KINDS TOO...
WHOA WHOA WHOA! HE MAKES POKÉ BALLS OUT OF FRUIT?!

UH-HUH. I WANT POKÉMON TO LIKE ME, SO I ASKED HIM...
...TO MAKE ME A "FRIEND BALL."

BUT HE SAYS HE ONLY MAKES POKÉ BALLS FOR PEOPLE WHO CAN REALLY USE THEM.
BALLS MADE OUTTA FRUIT, HUH?

HEH
HA! I'D LOVE TO SEE WHAT KIND OF TRASHY POKÉ BALLS THOSE ARE!

WHAT ARE YOU CALLING TRASHY, BOY?!!

W-W-WHAT...? WHO...?
MY NAME IS KURT!
REMEM-BER THE GRAMPA I WAS TELLING YOU ABOUT?

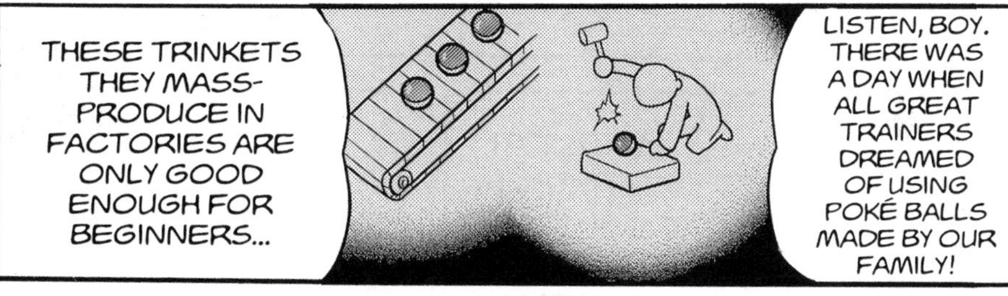
LISTEN, BOY. THERE WAS A DAY WHEN ALL GREAT TRAINERS DREAMED OF USING POKÉ BALLS MADE BY OUR FAMILY!
THESE TRINKETS THEY MASS-PRODUCE IN FACTORIES ARE ONLY GOOD ENOUGH FOR BEGINNERS...

...AND TALENTLESS TRAINERS... LIKE YOU.
Let's go, girl.
ZING

HEY, YOU WANNA TALK SMACK?
YOU BETTER SEE WHAT I GOT FIRST.

I'LL MASTER THAT POKÉ BALL OF YOURS IN NO TIME!
TRY ME!
HM.
YOU DO HAVE SPIRIT.

AND IF YOU CAN'T MASTER IT?
THEN I'LL WORK AS YOUR ASSISTANT FOR THE REST OF MY LIFE.
THOSE ARE BIG WORDS!

ALL RIGHT THEN. I'LL MAKE ONE JUST FOR YOU.
TUG
CHOOSE THE TYPE OF POKÉ BALL YOU WANT... AND BRING ME AN APRI-CORN.

WHAT?! I HAVE TO SUPPLY THE MATERIALS?!
BETTER GET IT BEFORE THE SUN SETS!
BRRR BRRR

A FRIEND BALL...
ACTUALLY MADE OUT OF GREEN APRICORN...

I GUESS THIS ISN'T A JOKE AFTER ALL.
WEIRD.
WHY'D YOU DECIDE ON A FRIEND BALL?
THEY'RE SUPPOSED TO LIKE YOU IF YOU CATCH 'EM WITH THIS, RIGHT? I'M GONNA GIVE ONE TO YOU.
REALLY?!

OH, THANK YOU SO MUCH!
IT'S ALL GOOD. SO WHICH POKÉMON DO YOU WANT?
UM... IT LIVES UP THERE... BUT...
...GRAMPA SAID NOT TO GET CLOSE TO IT...

I'LL BE WITH YOU, SO YOU'RE FINE.
LET'S GO!
O... OKAY!

TM TM

YOU DON'T LIKE DOING THINGS THE EASY WAY, DO YOU?
CLOSE! WE BETTER BE CAREFUL ...

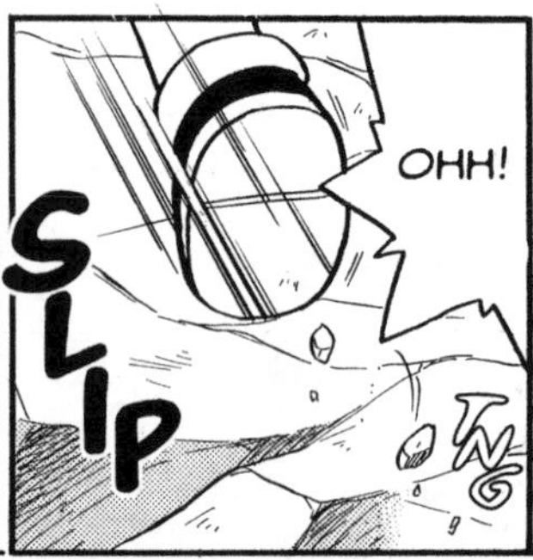
OHH!
SLIP
TNG

PAP
IT'D BETTER BE WORTH ALL THIS.

WELL, IT'S LITTLE... AND ROUND... AND CUTE!
PIP
Teddiursa
Little Bear Pokémon
Height ???
Weight ???
No. 216
Area
Cry
PRNT
TELL ME MORE ABOUT THIS TEDDI-URSA.

BE VERY QUIET.
BING
EH?

THERE IT IS! THAT'S TEDDI-URSA!
OKAY. HERE GOES.

OH!!
TUP
TUP TUP

YAAAA!

W...
WHA...?
URSARING! TEDDI-URSA'S EVOLVED FORM!

BMM
RUN !!

YOU DIDN'T TELL ME ABOUT THE EVOLVED FORM!!

ACK! TIME-OUT!! TIME-OUT!!
TMP TMP TMP

TM
MOVE. YOU'RE BLOCKING MY CAPTURE.
!

SILVER!!
YOU AGAIN.

HEY!!
THAT'S GRAMPA'S POKÉ BALL!

STEAL-ING AGAIN, EH?
NO! GRAMPA GAVE IT TO HIM 'CAUSE HE'S SO GOOD!

Y'MEAN... THE GUY WHO MADE FUN OF ME...
TWITCH

...GAVE **THAT** CHUMP A FREE POKÉ BALL?! WHAT A JOKE!

AND YOU'RE GONNA CATCH URSA-RING?
CHK
THAT'LL TAKE REAL SKILL.
Hibernator Pokémon
No. 217
Height ???
Weight ???
Area Cry PRNT

...
HEH

FOR-GET TEDDI-URSA!
I'M BRING-ING IN URSA-RING!!

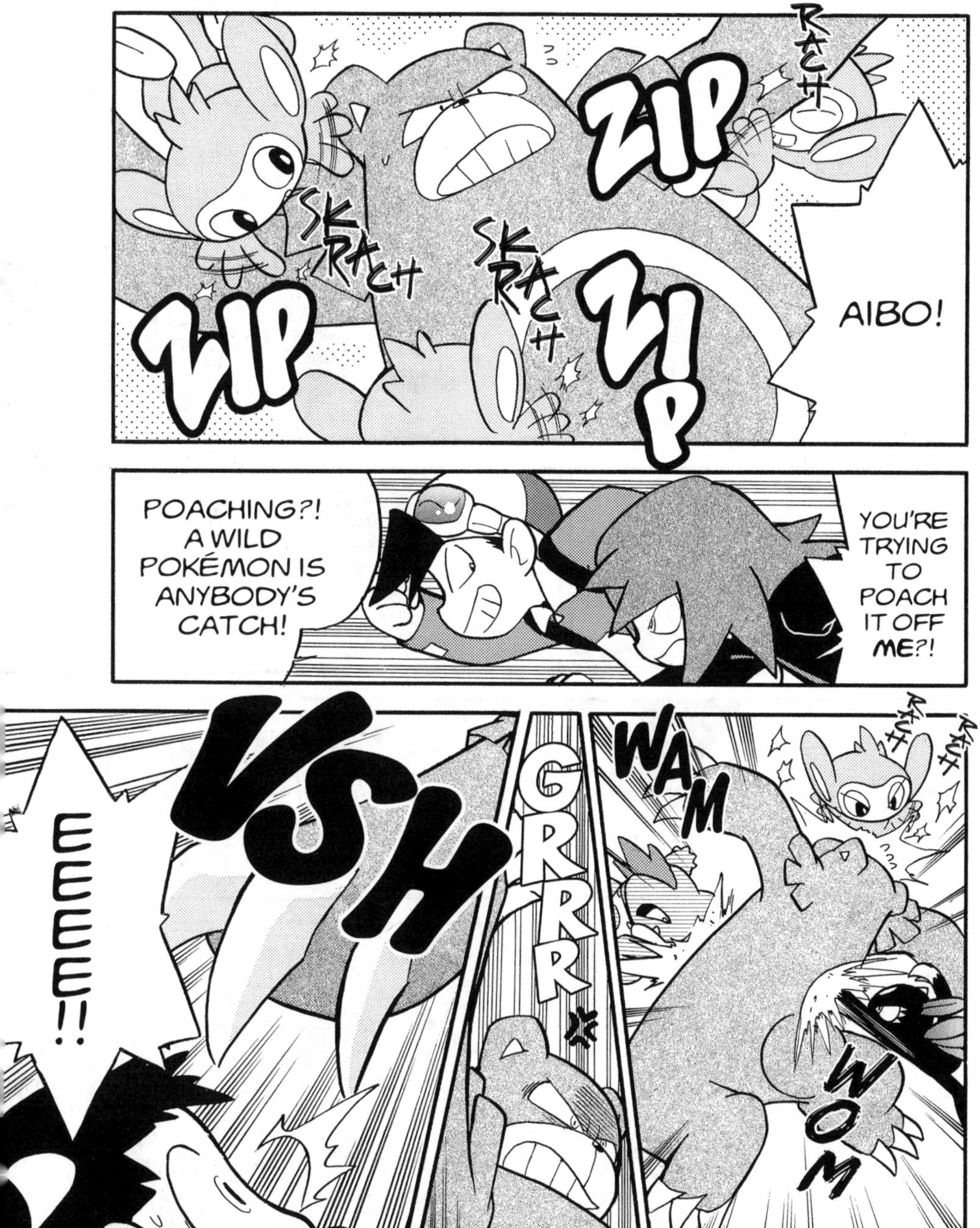

RACH
ZIP
SKRACH
SKRACH
ZIP
ZIP
ZIP
AIBO!

YOU'RE TRYING TO POACH IT OFF ME?!

POACHING?! A WILD POKÉMON IS ANYBODY'S CATCH!
RACH
RACH
WAM
WOM
GRRR
VSH
EEEEE!!

BOOOM
WHOA.
VIP
WILD ATTACKS ...
AMA-TEUR-ISH AS ALWAYS.
QUICK FOR A BRUISER!
WHAT—?!
VSH
TNG
WAGH!
!!
BOOOM!

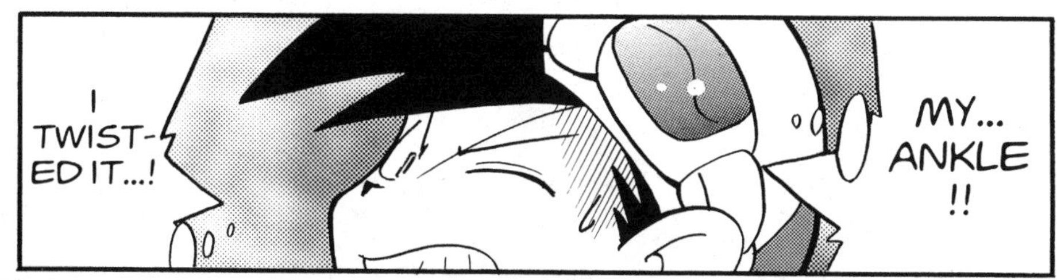

NGH...

UM... MISTER ...?

DOOM

102 Ursaring Major

SHWANNG
S... SNEASEL?!
!!

YOU... YOU... YOU...
THAT'S WHAT HAPPENS WHEN YOU POACH.

TINK
!!

...PROTECTING THE GIRL...?

WAS HE...
MELTING IT WITH FIRE PUNCH, MM?

HSSH
DRIP...

FSH
ACK!
DON'T LET THE CUTE FACE FOOL YOU!!
BM
BM
BM
HWN
I'LL TAKE CARE OF TEDDI-URSA FIRST!!

KONG
HUH ?!

W-WHAT'S GOING ON?
I'M SURE IT MADE CONTACT ...
GRP
KOLOLO

ONE MORE TIME!
PWAP
AGAIN!

I KNEW HE MADE TRASHY POKÉ BALLS!
DON'T BLAME THIS ON SOME-ONE ELSE.

WHAT DID YOU SAY?!
YOUR INABILITY TO USE THIS POKÉ BALL SHOWS YOUR LACK OF SKILL.

CHK
THERE'S A TRICK TO USING A POKÉ BALL THIS SUBTLE.

ZHP
SORRY, BUT I'M TAKING URSARING.

BOMP
?!
FP
KOLO...

HSS
TH-TH-THAT WAS AN ACCI-DENT !!

GRAAA
RUN !!

CHK
N-NO! IT'S A CLIFF!

THROB

NG!
GOLD ...?

SNIF

GR...

GRAM-PA...
...TOLD ME IT WAS TOO DANGEROUS IN THE MOUNTAINS ...

I'M SORRY, GRAM-PA!
I'VE PUT US ALL IN A LOT OF DANGER!

EASY, KID. IT'S NOT TIME TO GIVE UP YET.
PAT
I'LL CATCH TEDDI-URSA...
AND I'LL GET YOU HOME SAFELY.

TRUST ME!

...
SNIF...

OKAY, THIS FRIEND BALL WE'VE GOT...
IT'LL HAVE TO DO.

SILVER, YOU SAID THERE WAS A TRICK TO THESE POKÉ BALLS.
YOU'D BETTER TELL ME WHAT IT IS.

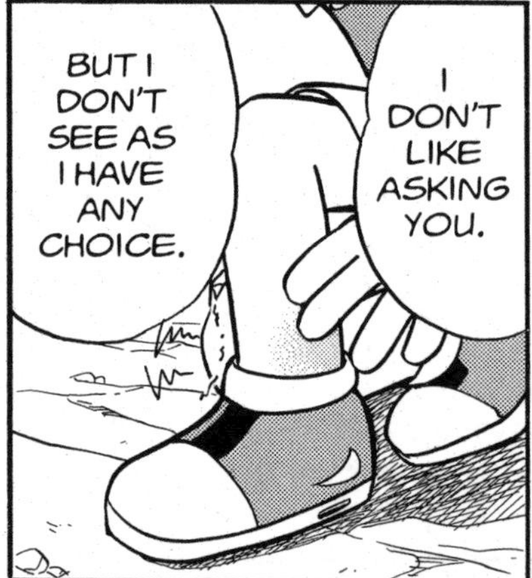
I DON'T LIKE ASKING YOU.
BUT I DON'T SEE AS I HAVE ANY CHOICE.

...

OKAY?

TMM

FINE. IT'S ALL ABOUT HITTING THE ENERGY POINT.
EVERY LIVING THING HAS A SPOT IN WHICH ITS LIFE FORCE IS CONCEN-TRATED. ONLY WHEN YOU HIT THAT SPOT ...
...WILL THESE POKÉ BALLS REVEAL THEIR TRUE POWERS!

AND THE ENERGY POINTS FOR THESE TWO ARE...
URSARING—THE CENTER OF ITS CHEST CIRCLE.
TEDDI-URSA—THE CRESCENT ON ITS HEAD.

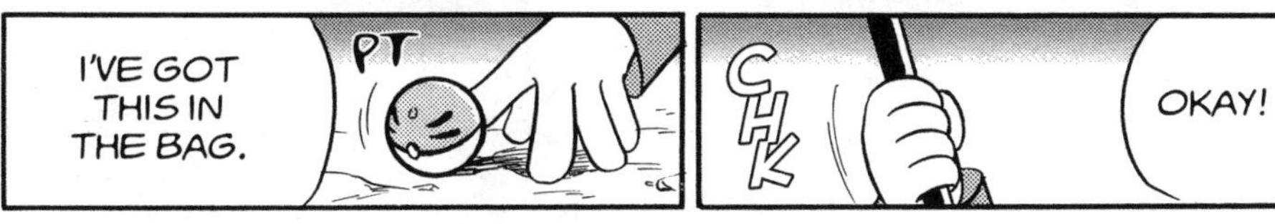
OKAY!
CHK
PT
I'VE GOT THIS IN THE BAG.

I DON'T HAVE THE HEAVY BALL ANY-MORE.
WHICH ONE WILL YOU TARGET WITH THAT ONE?
HOW ABOUT... NEITHER ?

WATCH THIS!!
TA
TK
TK
TK
TK
TK
TK
PAK
FP
WHAT ?!
NICE CATCH!
FP
NOW LET'S GET 'EM!!

WHKK
BOTH OF THEM !!
BONBON
LISTEN, GOLD. THIS IS MY LAST WARN-ING.
STAY OUT OF MY WAY FROM NOW ON.
NOW, SILVER... I'D CALL US EVEN!
WSH
I JUST DON'T GET THAT GUY.
VSH
HEY ...!

VP
HERE'S YOUR TEDDI-URSA.

TP
TP

BOOM!
I THINK YOU TWO WILL GET ALONG GREAT.

WILL YOU BE MY FRIEND?
GRIN

NOW... LET'S GET OFF THIS MOUNTAIN!

SLOWPOKE WELL
WELL, THAT WAS A GOOD CATCH.

THIS IS SOME BIG MONEY.
THERE'S A GOOD MARKET FOR SWEET SLOWPOKE TAILS.

?!

WHO ARE YOU?!

HEH

IT'S ALREADY DARK.
HOOTHOOT
GRAND-PA'S GONNA BE WORRIED! WE'VE GOTTA HURRY!
GTNK
WELL, WE GOT YOU HOME.
I BETTER RUN AND TELL HIM!
GRAM-PA!
GRAM-PA...?
GRAMPA'S NOT HERE?
AND NO WATER ...? MAYBE SOMETHING HAPPENED AT THE WELL...?
PLIP...
TM
WHAT ...?

GRAMPA!!
!!
WELL...
IT'S ALL RIGHT.
HOW MANY TIMES HAVE I TOLD YOU TO STAY OFF THAT MOUNTAIN?!!
BAD GIRL!!!
I'M S... SORRY...
I'M JUST GLAD YOU'RE SAFE.
YOU'RE GOING TO TAKE GOOD CARE OF YOUR NEW POKÉMON, AREN'T YOU?
POKÉMON HAVE SCARY SIDES... BUT IF YOU TREAT THEM WELL, THEY'RE VERY LOYAL.

DID YOU PILE UP THE TEAM ROCKET THUGS?
NO. THEY WERE LIKE THAT WHEN I GOT HERE.
TMP
WHO'S THERE ?!
IT'S ME... BUGSY!
BUGSY !!
I'VE BEEN FOLLOWING REPORTS OF TEAM ROCKET SIGHTINGS IN THE AZALEA TOWN AREA...
BUT I DIDN'T EXPECT THIS!
DID YOU DO THIS, GOLD?
WASN'T ME!
THEN WHO...?

LET'S TEST IT OUT, AIBO!
WHAP!
THAT'S RIGHT! THERE'S A LEGEND AROUND THESE PARTS...
"THE YAWN OF A SLOWPOKE WILL CALL FORTH WATER."
WRIIIIN
POOR SLOWPOKE... GETTING THEIR TAILS CUT OFF.
MAYBE THAT'S WHAT HAP-PENED TO THE WELL...

GOLD! WHAT ARE YOU DOING?!
TUG TUG
THE BEST WAY I KNOW...

...TO GET A SLOWPOKE TO **YAWN**...
YAAAAAAAW
THEN IT USES YAWN TO **REST**!
HEH HEH
...IS TO WEAR IT OUT IN BATTLE.
SPLOOSH

SO WAS IT SILVER WHO BEAT UP TEAM ROCKET?
...WAS AN URSARING CLAW MARK.

THAT...

IS THAT WHY HE WANTED THAT HEAVY BALL? TO STOP THIS TEAM ROCKET GROUP?
THAT WOULD MEAN HE KNEW THEIR MOVEMENTS BEFORE BUGSY.

HE'S DEFINITELY FOLLOWING SOME PLAN.
BUT WHAT IS IT?!

VSH
SUDDENLY I DON'T WANT TO CATCH HIM...
I JUST WANT TO FIND OUT WHO HE REALLY IS!

SLICE!

CUT!

WHDD

GREAT JOB, FAR-FETCH'D!

HEH

I'LL BE ABLE TO MAKE LOTS OF CHAR-COAL REAL SOON!

HEH HEH

Ssooo

THE MIST AGAIN...

IT COMES IN SO OFTEN THESE DAYS.

BETTER GET HOME BEFORE ...

...

LEAVE... THIS... FOREST...

SHHOOOO

HSHH

103 You Ain't Nothin' but a Houndour

LOOKS LIKE SILVER'S LEADING US RIGHT THROUGH IT.

Ilex Forest

PIP

ILEX FOR

SO THIS IS ILEX FOREST.

BUT MAN, IS THAT CREEPY LOOKING...

NO... IT CAN'T MEAN...

SKRIK
...
HUH?

?
NO DATA
...

AHAHAHA
GONG
W-WHAT DO YOU KNOW? NO MAP!

STARE
HEHHEH HEH
GUESS WE BETTER JUST KEEP GOIN' STRAIGHT...

I'VE NEVER KNOWN THAT THING TO LOSE RECEPTION.
CAN'T HELP FEELING... THERE'S SOMETHING WEIRD ABOUT THIS FOREST...

FWOMP

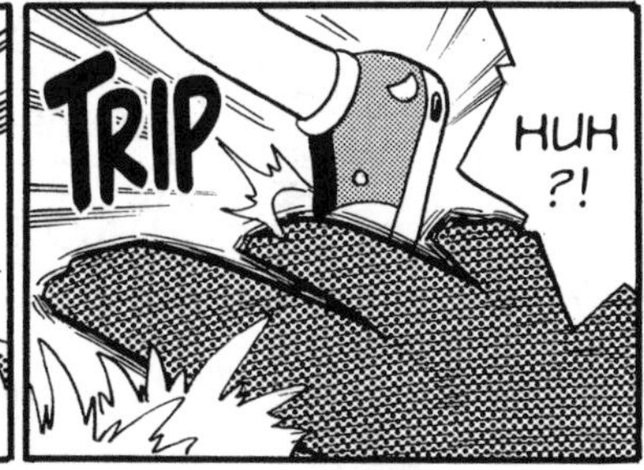
TRIP
HUH ?!

A FAR-FETCH'D ?!

FWOMP

TRIP TRIP TRIP
!!

HEY, WHAT'S WRONG ?!
YOU OKAY ?!
...I GUESS NOT.

A PER-SON ?!

HOW DO WE GET OUTTA HERE?!!
WHAT A LOUSY TIME TO GET LOST!!
GRATTA
THOSE WOUNDS ARE BOTHERING ME...
WHAT KIND OF BATTLE WAS IT IN?

JUST... GET OUT OF THIS FOREST... QUICK.
GTNK
FOR-GET IT...

HE'S GET-TING... HEAVIER ?
RR RK
...
RNK...
JUST... GET...

NO-BODY'S THIS HEAVY!!
FMP...
FMP...
NO !!

WOBBLE...
NNN...
?!

VMP
WHAT ARE YOU?!

GASTLY ?!

HOOO

GASTLY MADE THEM HEAVY ?!

BOP

AIBO!

HEY!

WAP

SH

GET OUT!

VSH

WE CAN'T FIGHT THEM NOW!!

ZZIP

GREAT. NOW WE'RE EVEN...
... DEEPER IN THE FOREST!
HF
HF

NOW WHAT ?
I'M UP FOR ANY POKÉMON BATTLE...
BUT NOT IF THEY'RE BEING MANIPULATED BY GASTLY!
GASP
?!
TPTP
POLIBO ?!

WHEN DID WE GET SEP-ARATED?!
VUM
POLIBO! OVER HERE!!

NGH!
Whoa
GRAB

UP
UP
!!
UP

...
KRIIII
CHK
NEW-COMERS!

DELIBIRD, GASTLY, ARIADOS, HOUNDOUR...
PIPI PIPI
Ice
Bug
Flying
Poison
Ghost
Dark
ALL DIFFERENT TYPES. THIS IS GONNA BE TOUGH.

VSH
YAAAA!
ROAR!!
PIP
HOUN-DOUR'S BITE, HUH?!
THEN HOW ABOUT...
WOOSH
EXBO-SMOKE-SCREEN!!
WOK
OH NO! EXBO!
POLIBO! WATCH OUT!!
GASP
SHH
FMP

COME ON, SUNBO!
GROWTH ...!

HSH
WHAT ?!

WAK
SUNBO ?!

MY COMMANDS... AREN'T FAST ENOUGH ?!

HOOO
IT'S THE SAME, FOUR AGAINST FOUR...
BUT I'M SO MUCH SLOWER WITH MY COMMANDS.
DRIP
THIS IS MY FIRST GROUP BATTLE... I JUST HAVEN'T...
... GOTTEN INTO THE GROOVE.
SSS...
!
ANOTHER ONE?!
FFF
GOTTA HIT FIRST!! EXBO— EMBER!!
FWOOOO
SHP
FLAME-THROWER!!
!!

SSSS...

!!

EXBO!

WDD

STAY... AWAY ...

STAY AWAY... FROM THIS FOREST.

Johto region—the arena in which Gold's battle with Silver plays out!

"GOTTA CATCH 'EM ALL" ROUTE 8 ADVENTURE MAP

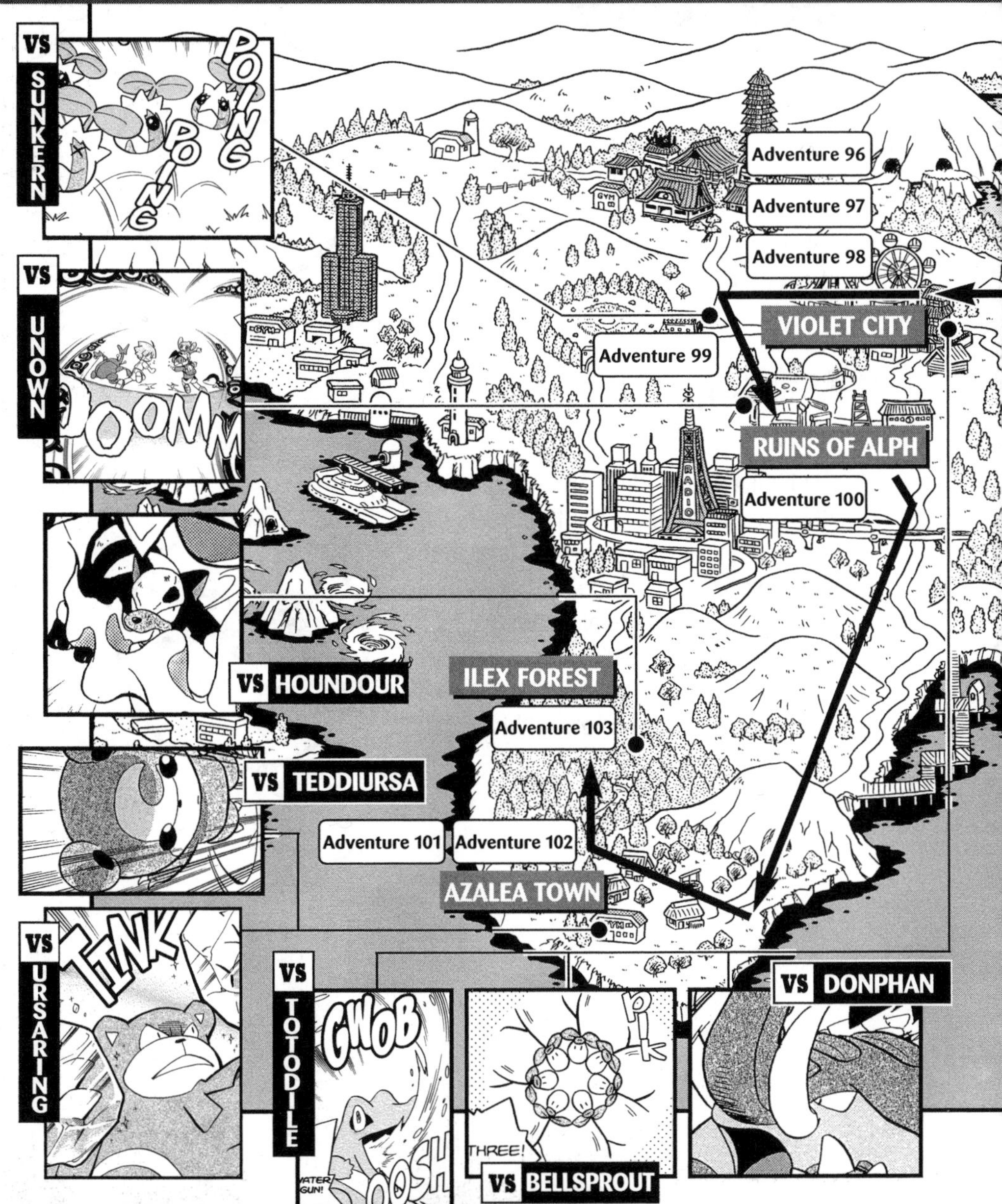

Message from
Hidenori Kusaka

For me the 21st century began when I got my first Game Boy Advance... a Pokémon Center limited edition! I was totally excited! Suicune blue! (Of course, I get excited easily.) I still play it to get in the right creative mood...Azurill♪♪

–2001

Message from
Mato

Gold, Silver, Red, Blue, Green, Yellow and all those Pokémon... The four years I've spent with them have seemed long, but it also feels like just yesterday that we first met. It's an amazing feeling. We've been able to have this great run because of the enthusiasm of you, our fans. And so, with deep gratitude, we bring you this book!

–2001

THIS MUST BE THE GUY WHO JUMPED US...
WHAT DOES HE MEAN, "STAY AWAY FROM THIS FOREST"?

THE ONLY THING I KNOW FOR SURE IS...
HE'S ONE HIGH-LEVEL TRAINER!

SERIOUSLY CREEPY MASK TOO.
I COULD JUST SKIP OUT NOW...

BUT I'D HAVE TO LEAVE THEM BEHIND.

I'VE GOT NO CHOICE...
GG

I'LL NEVER BEAT HIM.
DMM
ALL I CAN DO NOW IS... SAVE MYSELF.

104 The Ariados up There

I GOT 'EM, AIBO!!
NOW LET'S GET OUTTA—

ZSHH
AGH!

HE-HE-HEH...
SHALL WE GET TO WORK THEN?
WHAT?!
YOU'LL DO WHAT HE DID...
...KEEP INTRUDERS OUT OF THIS FOREST.

SO I WAS RIGHT! YOU USED GASTLY TO CONTROL THIS GUY AND HIS FARFETCH'D!
OF COURSE!

I DON'T KNOW WHAT YOU'RE UP TO HERE– BUT I DON'T LIKE IT!
WHO ARE YOU TO DECIDE WHO COMES INTO THIS FOREST AND WHO DOESN'T ?!

WHAT GIVES YOU THE RIGHT TO TAKE CONTROL OF ANOTHER TRAINER'S POKÉMON?!
NOT TO MENTION TAKING CONTROL OF THEIR BRAIN!!

...
...

VP
TO SHOW MY RE- SPECT ...

HA HAHAHA! BRAVE KID, AREN'T YOU?
MOST PEOPLE JUST RUN AS FAST AS THEY CAN.

FMP
... HERE'S A LITTLE GIFT.
HUH ?!

BOOM!
YAAAG!
JERK !!
HAK KOF

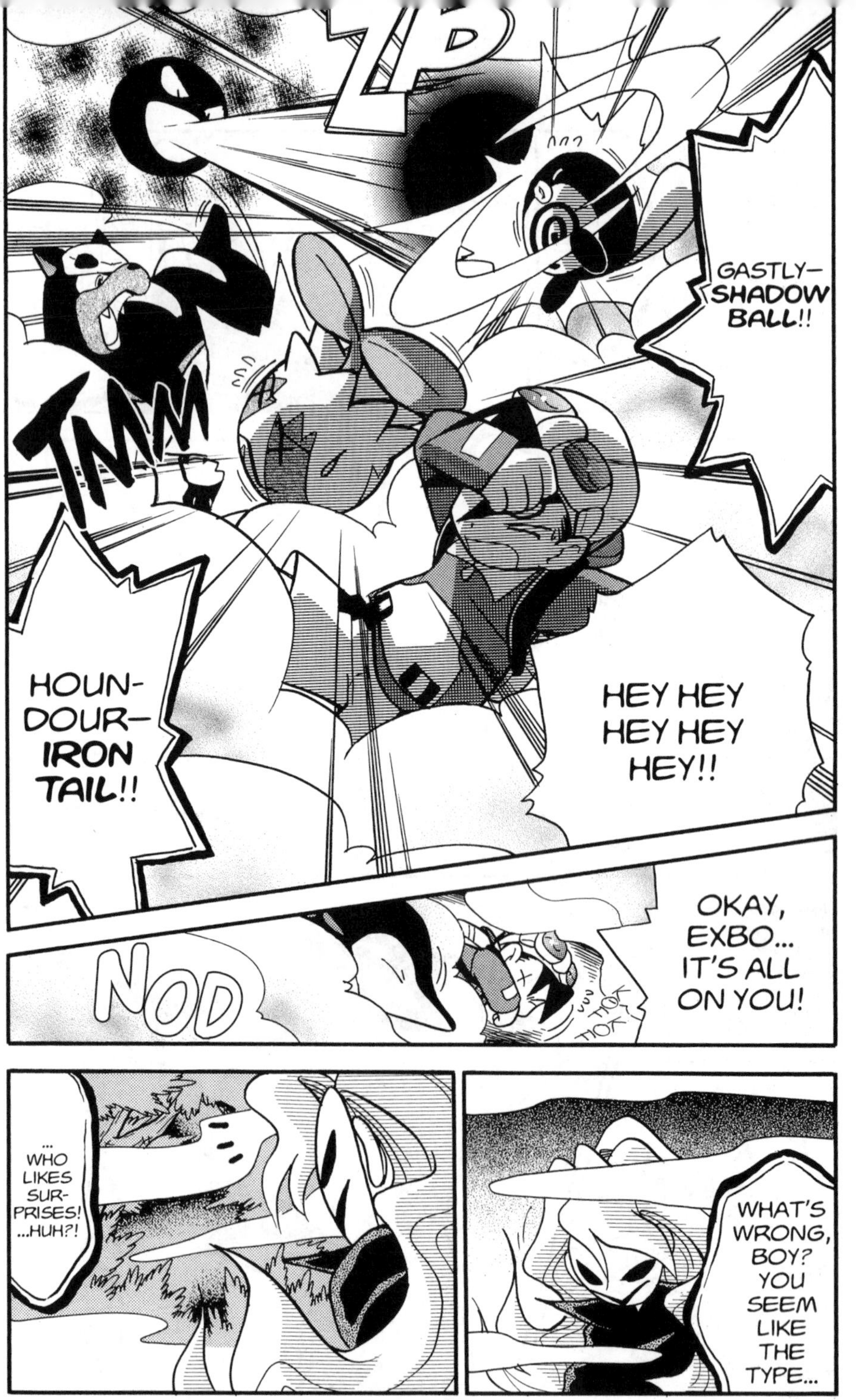

ZP
GASTLY—SHADOW BALL!!
HEY HEY HEY HEY HEY!!
HOUN-DOUR—IRON TAIL!!
OKAY, EXBO... IT'S ALL ON YOU!
NOD

CLEVER, USING CYNDAQUIL'S SMOKESCREEN TO BLEND IN TO THE SMOKE FROM THE BLAST.
WHAT ?!

HEH
BUT SINCE MY SERVANT IS PRO-GRAMMED TO FOLLOW HIM...
... AND HE HASN'T REACTED ...

FSH...
... THE BOY MUST STILL BE CLOSE.
WHICH MEANS HE MUST BE...
... HIDING IN A TREE!

VLULULU

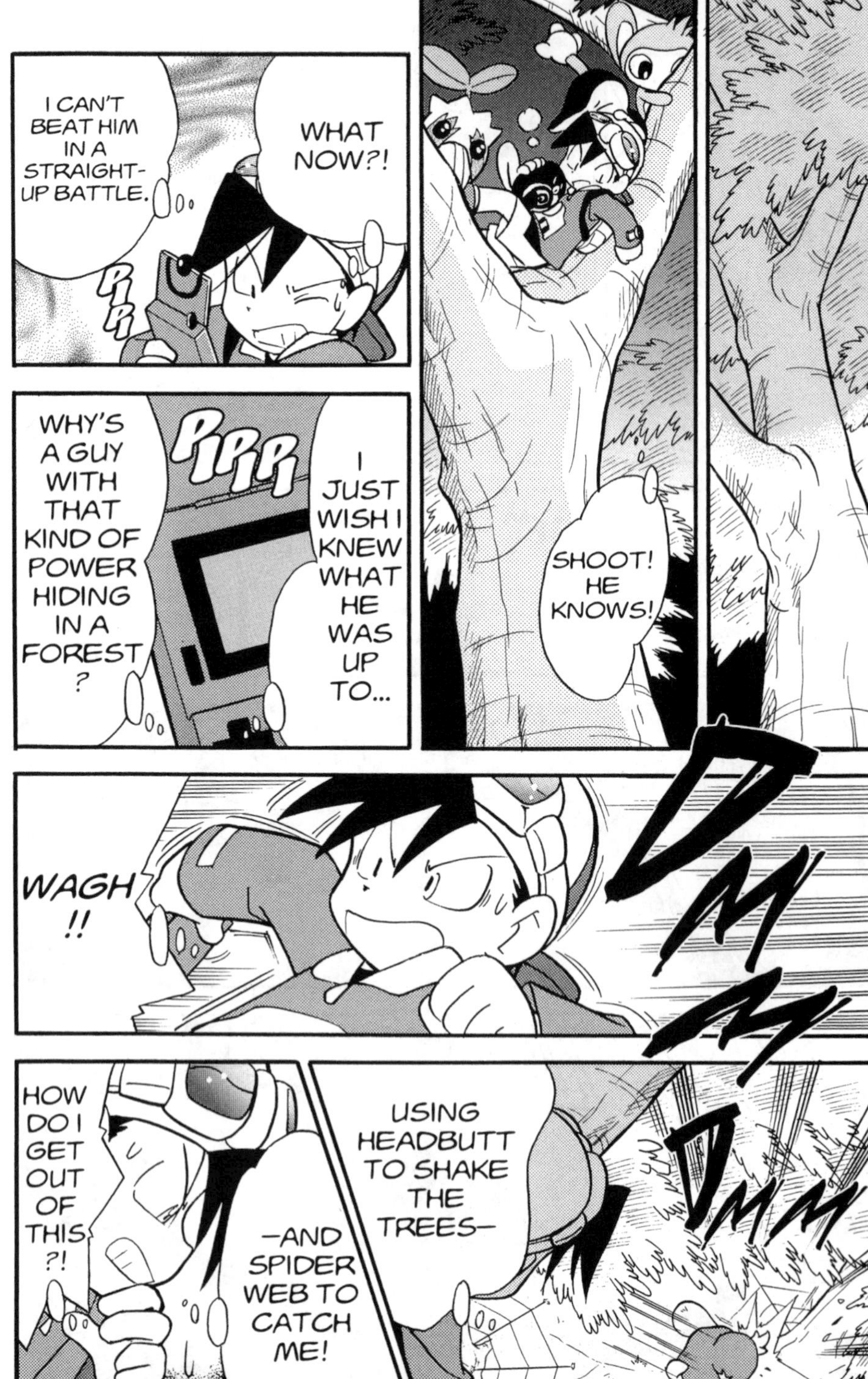
WHAT NOW?!
I CAN'T BEAT HIM IN A STRAIGHT-UP BATTLE.
PIPI
SHOOT! HE KNOWS!
I JUST WISH I KNEW WHAT HE WAS UP TO...
PIPIPI
WHY'S A GUY WITH THAT KIND OF POWER HIDING IN A FOREST?
DMM
WAGH!!
DMM
USING HEADBUTT TO SHAKE THE TREES—
—AND SPIDER WEB TO CATCH ME!
HOW DO I GET OUT OF THIS?!

SHAKA
SHAKA
EEH.
DMMM

SLIP
VSH
YAAA!

KIIII
SSSS
!!
LIGHT... FROM THE SHRINE?!

FOR-GET THE BOY FOR NOW.
KRAKA
WE CAN'T LET THIS CHANCE SLIP AWAY.

YULULU

NOT NOW!

?!

VMM

HOLD HIM!

ARIA-DOS!

FSH

HE FELL FOR IT!!

GOT HIM WITH MY TRAP!

WHAT ?!

GIVE 'IM A TASTE OF MEGA DR—

ACK! STRING FROM THERE TOO?!
FOOL !!
?!
NOW LEAVE HIM!
TING
WM
...
AGH ...
SHHHHH
THE SHRINE IS... DARK AGAIN.

SQUIRM
NG... NGHH !!

VSH
ANOTHER CHANCE LOST... BECAUSE OF THAT FOOL.
ONCE AGAIN... WE WAIT.

WHAT'S THE BIG IDEA?!

YOU CAN'T JUST BAIL IN THE MIDDLE OF A BATTLE!
I DEMAND YOU COME BACK!
LOOK ...
I DON'T MIND FIGHT-ING KIDS...

BUT YOU'RE NOT NEARLY AS GOOD AS THAT LAST PUNK I FOUGHT.
THE ONE WITH THE CROCO-NAW.
OH YEAH ?!

VOOP

ANYWAY, WE'VE GOT TO HURRY UP AND GET THESE GUYS OUT OF THIS CREEPY...

THANKS, AIBO.
THAT CREEP REALLY KNOWS HOW TO PUSH MY BUTTONS.

GLOOOM
WHAT'S WITH ALL THE LONG FACES?
HUH?

HEY. THIS FIGHT ISN'T OVER.

NOD
NOD
DON'T TELL ME IT'S BECAUSE HE KNOCKED US AROUND?

WE'RE GONNA GET A REMATCH! AND NEXT TIME—
EVERY ONE OF US IS GONNA BE STRONGER!

...

WE'LL BEAT 'EM NEXT TIME EVEN IF THEY OUTNUMBER US TEN TO ONE!

TP

I PROMISE YOU.

HOW ARE THE POKÉMON AND THE TRAINER YOU RESCUED?
ALIVE, BUT BARELY.
ARE YOU ALL RIGHT, GOLD ?!
DEPENDS ON YOUR DEFINITION OF "ALL RIGHT."
PoKé
RIP
RIP
THAT STUFF WAS ALL OVER AIBO'S TAIL.
I THINK IT WAS UNDER THE GUY'S CAPE.
IT MAY BE IMPOR-TANT.
MEANWHILE, I'M ANALYZING THE GOLD POWDER YOU SCANNED AND SENT TO ME.
I'LL LET YOU KNOW AS SOON AS MY CHEMICAL ANALYSIS IS COMPLETE. IN THE MEANTIME...
...I WANT YOU TO BE CAREFUL FROM HERE ON OUT!

PIRIRIRI

SILVER. NEW DATA.

THE KID CAME INTO CONTACT WITH THE MASKED MAN.

IT WAS IN THE FOREST IN QUES-TION. AFTERWARD LIGHT WAS SEEN EMANATING FROM THE SHRINE... BUT THE MASKED MAN FAILED TO OBTAIN THE LIGHT.

I WANT YOU TO KEEP UP WITH YOUR SURVEIL-LANCE OF THE MASKED MAN.

I'M ON IT.

CHAK
RESERVED FOR CEREMONY
KRIIIII
VIOLET GYM
VIOLET
TMM
105
Smeargle Smudge
FALKNER, WE NOW DESIGNATE YOU...
...THE NEW LEADER OF VIOLET GYM!!

W-
WAIT!
PLEASE!
BUT
IF I
CAN'T
EVEN
FIGURE
OUT WHY
IT
BROKE—

I TOLD
YOU! I'M
TRYIN'
TO FIX
THE DANG
POKÉMON
STORAGE
SYSTEM!
ALL RIGHT,
BILL. WE
APPOINTED
THIS
FALKNER
FELLOW AS
YOU ASKED.
NOW YOU
OWE US...

I'M
HONORED
TO HAVE
BEEN
GIVEN
THIS
POST.
BUT I'D HATE
TO THINK THAT
MY APPOINTMENT
HAS CAUSED
TROUBLE WITHIN
THE POKÉMON
ASSOCIATION.
IF
THERE'S
ANYTHING
I CAN
DO TO
HELP...

WELL, WE
SURE DO
APPRECIATE
THAT, SON!
BUT NONE
O' THIS IS
YOUR FAULT!
NONE-
THE-
LESS
...

RIGHT
NOW
WE'RE
IN THE
MIDDLE
O' YOUR
INSTAL-
LATION
CERE-
MONY!
...AND
BETWEEN
THE
TWO
OF YOU...
WELL,
WE'LL
TALK.

WE'LL
BE FINE.
YOU JUST
THINK ABOUT
BEIN' A GOOD
GYM LEADER.
ANOTHER
FRIEND O'
MINE'S ABOUT
TO TAKE
THE EXAM
TOO...

FALKNER.
FSH
ONE OF THE SACRED RESPONSIBILITIES OF THE GYM LEADER IS TO GUARD THIS...

...THE ZEPHYR BADGE.

TRAINERS WILL SOON BE COMING FROM ALL OVER TO CHALLENGE YOU IN YOUR GYM... YOU MUST TEST THEIR ABILITIES.
YOU ARE TO BESTOW THIS BADGE ONLY ON THOSE WHOM YOU DEEM TRULY WORTHY.

FURTHERMORE...
BLAH BLAH
WELL, GOLD...
I PASSED... USING THE SKARMORY WE CAPTURED TOGETHER.
HOO
YOU WANTED HEAT?!!

I WISH I KNEW HOW TO FIND YOU NOW... OR KNEW HOW YOU'RE DOING, AT LEAST...

GOLDEN-
ROD
CITY
THAT CITY... IS REALLY...

...HUGE!!

AND ALL THOSE LIGHTS! UP HERE IT'S MIDNIGHT... AND DOWN THERE IT'S AS BRIGHT AS NOON!

IT'S SUPPOSED TO BE FULL OF STORES AND GAME CORNERS AND EVERY-THING!
PIPI

TOO BAD I'VE GOT NO MONEY.
SHKSHK

OH WELL. GUESS WE CAN WORRY ABOUT THAT TOMORROW. G'NIGHT, GANG.
YAWN

SNEAK
ZZZZZZ

TP TP TP

ZZZ

SME-HE-HE

FSH
FSH
FSH
FSH

ARRRH!

W... WHA ...?
BLLP

WHAT'D YOU DO THAT FOR?!
I'M SUPPOSED TO GO INTO GOLDEN-ROD CITY LOOKING LIKE THIS?!

BING

IT'S HEADING FOR THE CITY !!
RUBRUB
VMM

BOING
NYAA

DOMP
YOU GOTTA BE FASTER THAN THAT TO GET AWAY FROM US!
HEEHEE

AAAAAGH!
BLAP
I CAN'T SEE!! WHERE'D IT GO ?!!

SAY. ARE YOU OKAY, KID?
DMM...
THAT STUPID THING TRICKED ME!
NOW WE'LL NEVER CATCH IT!!

LISTEN, KID! YOU HAD A TOUGH OPPONENT, BUT I SAW SOME IMPRESSIVE TEAMWORK AMONGST YOUR POKÉMON!
R-REALLY ?!
I PRODUCE A RADIO SHOW—*POKÉMON TALENT ROUND-UP!*
I HAPPEN TO BE ON MY WAY TO BROADCAST THE NEXT EPISODE RIGHT NOW. HOW WOULD YOU LIKE TO BE ON IT?!

NOT ONLY AM I GONNA MAKE SOME MONEY...
I CAN'T BELIEVE MY LUCK!!

THIS IS OUR BROAD-CAST HEAD-QUARTERS...

BUT I DO BELIEVE THIS IS THE SAME RADIO STATION WHERE DJ MARY DOES HER SHOW WITH THAT OAK GUY! WHICH MEANS...
...I MIGHT ACTUALLY GET TO MEET HER!!

THE STUDIO IS IN HERE.
I'M THERE!

HUH ?!

BAM
BAM
BAM
YOU'RE GONNA BE SORRY YOU EVER PAINTED MY FACE !!
H- HEY!! CUT THAT OUT !!
YOU AGAIN !!
WHAM
EEEEEE!!
BAMBAM
I'M DJ MARY, AND I'LL BE YOUR HOST. MY GUEST TODAY IS WHITNEY, GYM LEADER FOR GOLDENROD... HUH?!
WHAT'S GOING ON OUT...
WHAT DO YOU THINK YOU'RE DOING?!
YOU KNOW THIS GOOF, MARY?!
NEVER SEEN HIM BEFORE.
NO, NO!! IT CAN'T BE!!
THAT FACE-PAINTING PEST CAN'T BELONG TO DJ MARY!

NEW BARK TOWN
MIND IF I PLAY THE RADIO, PROFESSOR? IT'S DJ MARY'S SHOW!
SNAP
NO, IT'S GOTTA BE THIS OTHER CHICK'S!! TELL ME IT'S HERS!!
FOMP

IT S-SOUNDS LIKE HIM... BUT SURELY IT CAN'T...
DRIP

LISTEN, YOU MORON—
MY NAME HAPPENS TO BE **GOLD**, LADY!
WMP
IT CAN.
SOMEHOW I DON'T THINK HE'S BEING VERY CAREFUL...

BING
ON AIR
OFF AIR
WHAT DO YOU PEOPLE THINK YOU'RE DOING?!

S-SIR!! LISTENERS ARE CALLING IN BY THE HUN-DREDS!!
YOU SEE?! COM-PLAINTS !!

ARE YOU TRYING TO DESTROY THIS SHOW?!
I DON'T CARE !!
YOU STARTED IT!
SIGH

ACTUALLY... MOST OF THEM WERE ALONG THE LINES OF "THIS LINEUP IS HOT" AND "WHY DON'T YOU LET THEM BATTLE FOR REAL?"
FOMP
WELL, IF THAT'S WHAT THEY WANT...
I'M MORE THAN HAPPY TO GIVE IT TO THEM.

I GAVE SMEA-SMEA TO DJ MARY. IF YOU HAVE A PROBLEM WITH THAT... WE'LL SETTLE IT ON THE AIR!!
HEY, THE BIGGER THE STAGE, THE BETTER I FIGHT !!

STOP IT, BOTH OF YOU!!
SIR! HOW DO WE MAKE THEM STOP THIS?!
HMM ...

I THINK WHAT THIS NEEDS IS A TWO-HOUR SPECIAL!!
FOMP

POP
POP
SHOO
SHOO

I CAN'T BELIEVE THIS...
GOLD THE MYSTERY BOY VS. OUR LOCAL GYM LEADER... WHITNEY!!
YOU DEMANDED IT... YOU'VE GOT IT!

AND OF COURSE—BATTLING ALL THE WAY!!

THEY'LL FOLLOW POKÉMON BATTLE RACE RULES FROM GOLDENROD CITY THROUGH THE NATIONAL PARK TO THE GOAL—THE ROUTE 37 ROAD SIGN!!

THIS PROGRAM IS BROUGHT TO YOU BY **THE BIKE SHOP** TO CELEBRATE THEIR NEW GOLDENROD CITY HEAD-QUARTERS!
WE'LL PROVIDE COMPLETE LIVE COVERAGE THROUGH OUR MOBILE BROADCAST-ING VANS!

I'LL FIGHT ANY-BODY!!
BUT WHY DO I HAVE TO RIDE A BIKE?!

AND I'M BORROWING SMEA-SMEA—RIGHT, MARY?
OKAY. I'M READY WHEN YOU ARE.
THIS IS SMEA-SMEA'S FIGHT TOO!
MIRACLE

IT'S NOT FAIR!!
I SHOULD BE PUSHING A BOARD, NOT PEDALS!

THEIR LOGO...
!!

AND THEY WANT TO HEAR US TALK ABOUT THEIR PRODUCT!
SORRY. OUR SPONSOR MAKES BIKES.
MIRACLE

THEN HOW 'BOUT THIS?!
ZIP ZIP
ZIP
ZIP
WHOA WHOA!! WHAT ARE YOU DOING?!

MIRACLE

IT'S STILL GOT TWO WHEELS, RIGHT?
...MY OWN WHEELS!!

WELL... I GUESS THAT COUNTS...
SO LET'S GET THIS GOING!!
OKAY... ON YOUR MARKS... GET SET...
DMM
MIRACLE
MIRACLE

GO!!

WRRRL

MILMIL!! ROLL-OUT!!

GONK

TM

KLAK

... JUST GOT YOU ...!!

I...

HAKHAK

TH-THIS IS TOO SOON !!

VAN 3! HEAD UP ROUTE 37 AND WAIT!

VAN 2! STAY WITH THEM!
GOT 'EM!

WE'RE AT ROUTE 37... BUT WE CAN'T GET THROUGH!
WHY NOT ?!

ACTUALLY, SIR... WE HAVE A PROBLEM ...

THERE'S AN ODD **TREE** IN THE MIDDLE OF THE ROAD!!
AND I **SWEAR** IT WASN'T HERE YESTERDAY !!

WAIT!!!

HAS THAT LINE EVER ACTUALLY WORKED FOR YOU?!

106 How Do You Do, Sudowoodo?

WHO PUT THAT STUPID TREE THERE?!
SKRIIII
THEY'RE ABOUT TO ENTER... WHAT?!
WHAT'S THE BIG IDEA?!

NOT MINE, NOT MINE!
WHOSE FAULT IS THIS?!
I HAD THIS RACE WON!!

YOU SEE?! HE CAUGHT UP!!
SKCH
IS THAT A TREE?!
?!!
WHAT THE—?!
SSSH

DM
ROLL-OUT!!
WRRRR
I'LL JUST HAVE TO TAKE CARE OF IT MYSELF!!
NO ONE IS LISTENING TO ME!!

W-W-WHAT KIND OF TREE **IS** THIS?!

THUD

FOOM
EXBO—EMBER!!

I'LL SHOW YOU HOW IT'S DONE!!
ZM

HOW AM I SUPPOSED TO WIN WITH THAT THING IN THE WAY?!

THAT'S MY LINE!!

LIKE YOU SAID...

W-W-WHAT KIND OF TREE **IS** THIS?!

FWOOSH

BRR R BRR
SPYU
WAK WAK
TIME TO GO ALL OUT! AIBO! SUNBO! POLIBO!

ARE THOSE... FOOT-STEPS?!!
!!
TMM TMM TMM
NOW WHAT ?!
WEIRD.
THE ONLY THING IT REACTED TO WAS POLIBO'S WATER ATTACK...

EEEEYAAAA!!!

FIRST AN INDESTRUC-TIBLE TREE BLOCKING THE ROUTE ...
NOW A WILD POKÉ-MON!!

VIP VIP

TOOM

IT'LL CRUSH YOU WITHOUT BATTING AN EYE!!
WE HAVE TO STRIKE FIRST!!
VSH

IS IT LOOKING FOR SOME-THING?
DON'T JUST STAND THERE, IDIOT!! THAT'S RHYDON !!

WOOM

MILMIL !!
GGGG
GASP
GLARE

WK
!

WHIT-NEY!!

OUR GYM LEADER'S BEEN KIDNAPPED BY A WILD RHYDON!!
...!!
TOOM TOOM

KOFF!
BOOR
SAVE HER!!
THE RACE IS OFF!! ALL VANS—GET RHYDON !!
BRRROOM

WHERE DO YOU THINK YOU'RE GOIN' WITHOUT...
HUH ?!

IT'S SHAKING AGAIN... SAME AS BEFORE!
BRR
BRR
BRRR

HEY!! POLIBO !!
DO THAT SAME WATER ATTACK AGAIN!!
SSSH
SPYUU

WAIT A MINUTE... YOU MEAN...

YOU'RE A POKÉ-MON ?!!

!

VOOP VOOP

VOOP VOOP

NOD

THAT CRAZY RHYDON— ARE YOU WHAT IT WAS AFTER ?!

NOD

Sudowoodo
Imitation Pokémon
Height: 3' 11"
Weight: 83.8 lbs
No. 185
It disguises itself as a tree to avoid attack. It hates water, so it will disappear if it starts raining.
Cry Area

MAN, THAT WAS THE BEST TREE IMITATION I'VE EVER SEEN!

BUT WHAT'S THE BIG IDEA ?!

YOU HIDING FROM SOME-TH...

OH!!

GEEZ. NOW I FEEL BAD.
I MEAN, IF WE'D JUST LEFT YOU ALONE AND WAITED...
WE COULDA SAVED YOU A LOT OF STRESS!
WAK
WAK

SO WHAT HAPPENS WHEN THAT RHYDON COMES AFTER YOU AGAIN?
SOONER OR LATER YOU'RE GONNA HAVE TO STAND UP TO IT!

BRR BRR
WHAT ARE YOU AFRAID OF?! YOU BRUSHED OFF ALL OUR ATTACKS!
YOU'RE A TOTAL HERO!!

OKAY.
!!
I GUESS I'M GONNA HAVE TO SAVE YOU FROM YOURSELF!
YOU'RE GONNA LEARN—
—HOW TO FIGHT !!
VSH

NOW GET THIS THROUGH YOUR HEAD. YOU'RE STRONG ENOUGH TO BRUSH OFF MILTANK'S BEST ATTACK. YOU'VE GOT NOTHING TO FEAR!
NOD

THERE !!

I'M GONNA SHOOT YOUR POKÉ BALL AS CLOSE TO IT AS I CAN. THE INSTANT YOU HIT THE GROUND, POP OUT–

KLAK
–AND HIT RHYDON BEFORE IT REALIZES IT'S YOU!!

YOU CAN ONLY DO THIS ONCE, SO–
HOOO

CHK

DO IT!!
VOOP

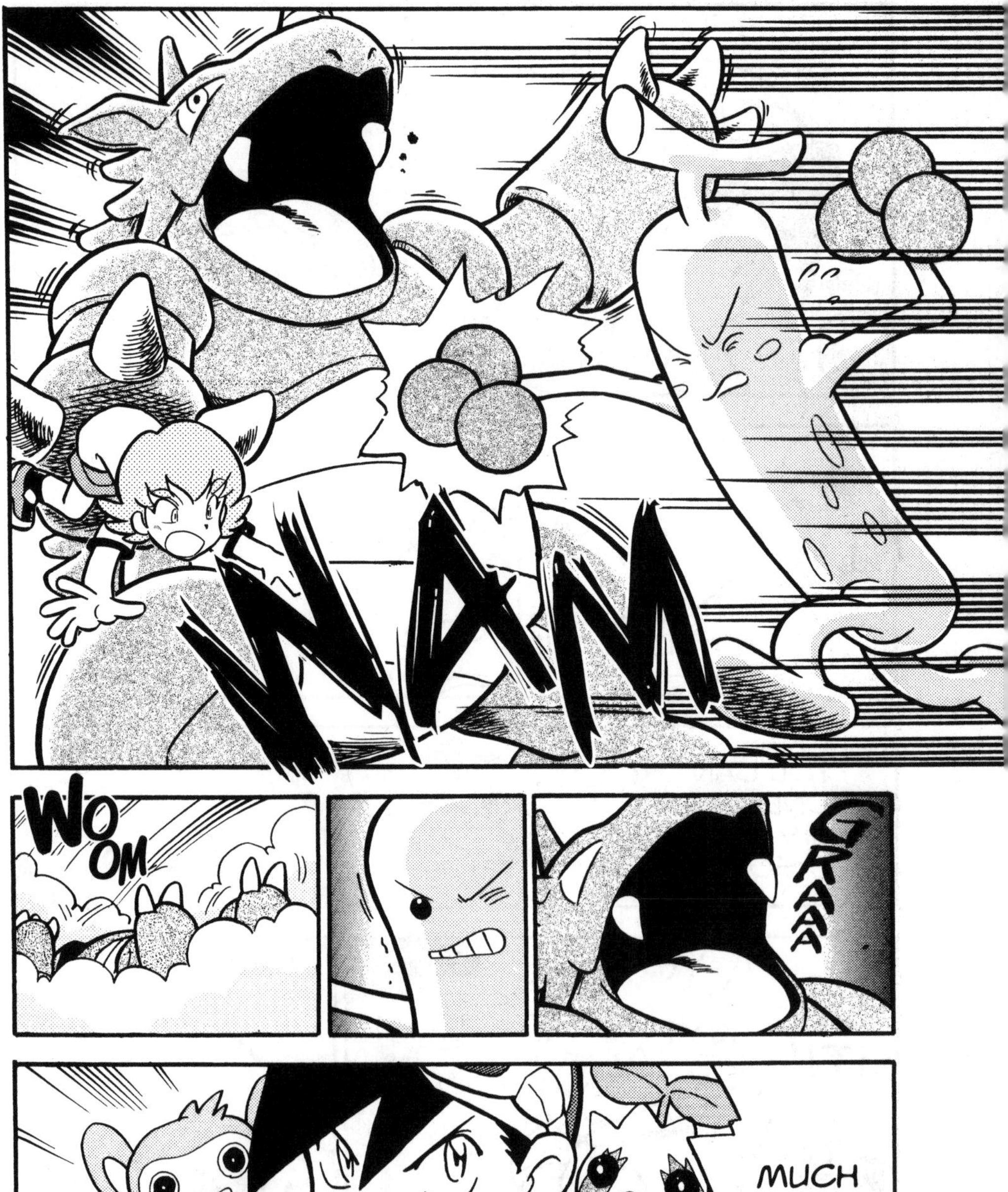

WAM

STUDIO
THE RACE MAY BE CANCELED, BUT THE WINNER'S CLEAR!

NEH HEH HEH HEH HEH!!

I MEAN, WHO MOVED THE IMMOVABLE TREE, HUH?
AND WHO HAD TO RESCUE HIS OPPONENT?! WAHAHA!
You got lucky!

SPCH
HEY!

I GUESS I DESERVE A LITTLE RESPECT, EH, SMEARGLE?
HONK

NEXT TIME, PUNK... WE'RE GONNA HAVE A **REAL** MATCH!!

WHY, YOU CHEESY LITTLE—
UM, GOLD? HOW MANY AUTOGRAPHS DID YOU SAY?
WAM WOOD
DJ Mary
DJ Mary

HUH
?!
DM DM
DM
O-KAY
!!
NOW THAT
I'VE GOT
SOME CASH,
I'M GOING TO
THE GAME
CORNER!
YOU
WANT TO
COME WITH
US, HUH?
WELL, OKAY...
SUDOBO!
...
GLEAM

GOLDEN-
ROD
CITY
GOLDEN-
ROD
GAME
CORNER
GAME
SHP

TK
KLAK
107
Gligar Glide

WHOA!
THAT KID'S INCRED-IBLE!!

KONK

KONK

AWW... IT'S NOTHIN'!

?!
IN FACT... ISN'T IT A LITTLE TOO UNREAL?!

TOMP
LOOK AT THAT!!
SHULULU
SKRIK
HOW DOES A BALL CURVE LIKE THAT?! IT'S UNREAL!!
KWRRR

PLIP PLIP
RRRIP
OH... NO!

FOMP
PLIP

YOU DISGUISED A POKÉ BALL AS A POOL BALL?!
ALL THOSE MOVES— WERE FROM THAT THING?!
Heh heh. Clever, huh?!

GET OUTTA HERE!!
GAME
FYOOOOOO

HMPH.
SOME PEOPLE CAN'T TAKE A JOKE.

PRRRRRT
....

A CALL ON MY POKÉ-GEAR! MAYBE IT'S THAT PICNICKER GIRL!
She totally dug me.
PIP

Professor Elm
WELL, GOLD.
!!

I HEARD YOU ON THE RADIO THE OTHER DAY.
HAVING FUN?!
YEEPS! PROFESSOR?!

WHAT'S THE STATUS OF YOUR POKÉMON TEAM AT PRESENT?

EXBO... THAT'S YOUR CYNDAQUIL... IS DOING GREAT!

SO ARE AIBO THE AIPOM, POLIBO THE POLIWAG...

...SUNBO THE SUNKERN... AND A NEW ONE...

...SUDOBO THE SUDOWOODO.

OH, AND THE EGG!!

IT'S... WELL... STILL AN EGG!

Exbo
Polibo
Aibo
Egg

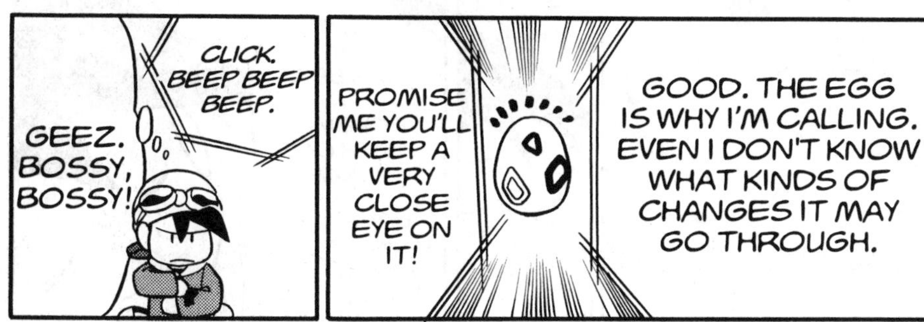

GOOD. THE EGG IS WHY I'M CALLING. EVEN I DON'T KNOW WHAT KINDS OF CHANGES IT MAY GO THROUGH.
PROMISE ME YOU'LL KEEP A VERY CLOSE EYE ON IT!
CLICK. BEEP BEEP BEEP.
GEEZ. BOSSY, BOSSY!

AN EGG, HUH ...?

HOOT
HOOT

YAWN
WISH I KNEW WHAT POKÉMON IT WAS FROM.

MAYBE SOMETHING REALLY STRONG...
ONE THAT CAN BEAT ANY POKÉMON WITH ONE PUNCH...
YEAH, RIGHT. HEH HEH...
ZZZ ZZZ.
TNK

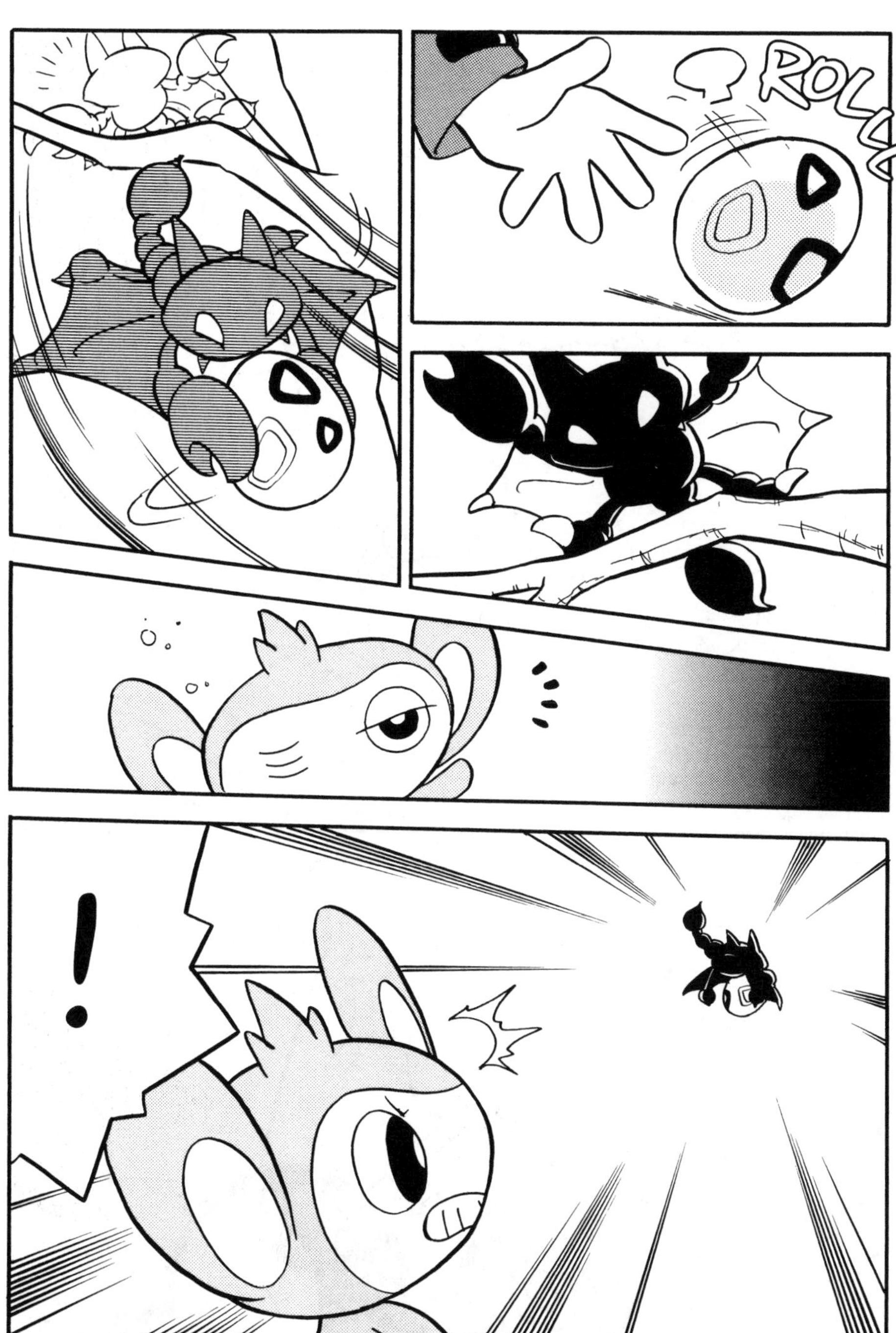
ROLL
!

FWAP

SHNORR
FOMP
NOT HUNGRY ...

SHAKA
SHAKA
NNN... NO...

WIIIN

SLIP

BOING

Gligar
Fly Scorpion
Pokémon
Height
Weight
No. 207

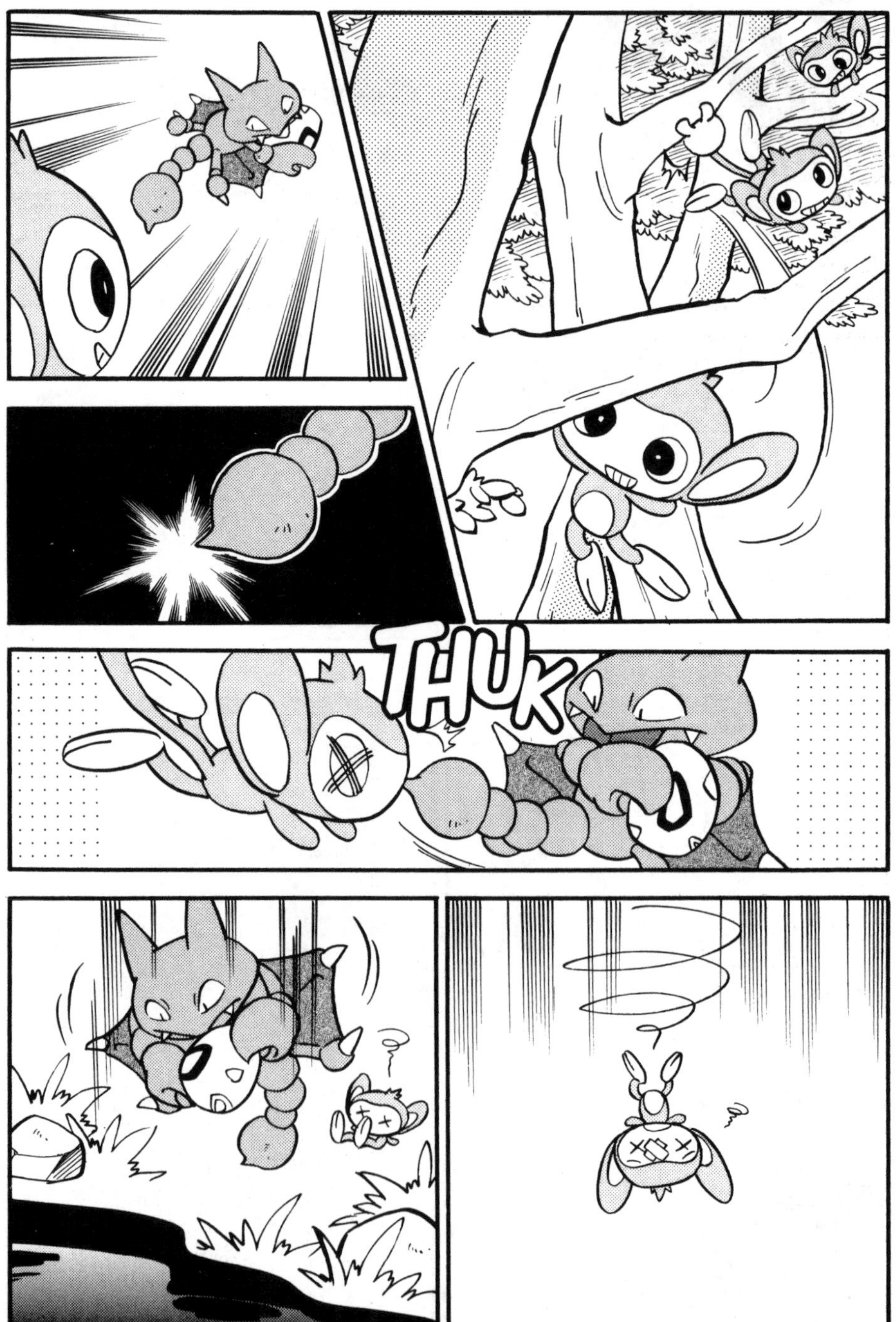
THUK

BLOOOSH

PLIP

TP

NNNN...

SHOOOO

NWUK!
WHEEE!
DM
FOOSH

KRIK
BRR
BRR
BRR BRR
KRIIII
KRIK...
KRIK

HYAH!

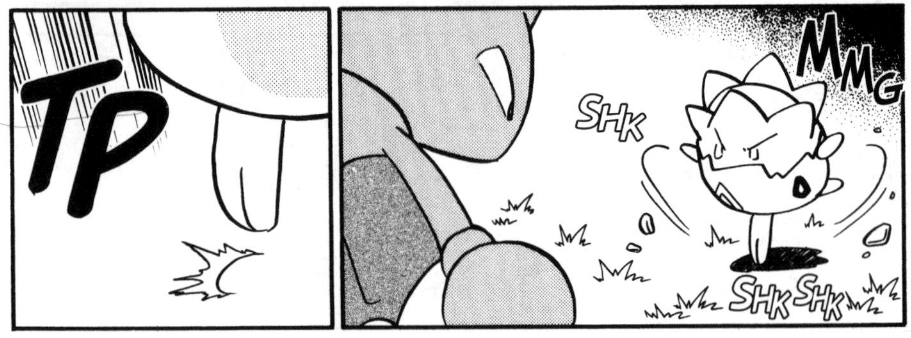

GUUUH
WMP
MMM?
FOOO
WHOUD
NNN
NOP

HYAH!

TK TK TK TK TK

HWEEEEN

WOP
GYOOOO
BONK
FWCH
?!
VIP

GOLDEN-ROD CITY POKÉ-MON CENTER
AW, IT WAS NOTHING!! SERIOUSLY... NOTHING!!
NOTHING?! RAISING THE EGG'S LEVEL UNTIL IT HATCHED ?!
HA HA HA
MAY AS WELL TAKE CREDIT.
SO SHOW ME WHAT THIS NEWLY HATCHED POKÉMON CAN DO!!
SURE THING !!
SHAKE SHAKE
TINK TINK TINK
HUH ?
SHUFFLE!
VIP
WSH
TAK

YOU'VE TURNED THIS POKÉMON INTO A...A...A DELINQUENT !!

UGH.

AS IF IT'S NOT BAD ENOUGH BEING YELLED AT...
NOW I'VE GOTTA GO THROUGH THIS TOO.

YOU WILL TAKE IT TO THE OLD COUPLE AT THE POKÉMON DAY CARE!
I GUESS WHERE THEY DISCOVERED IT IN THE FIRST PLACE...
OH WELL! IF WE GOTTA, WE GOTTA!

SHF
SHF
HUH?

POINT
WAGH!

JUST TOO BAD WE GOTTA BACK-TRACK... SOUTH OF GOLDEN-ROD, HE SAID...

POING

POING

WHO **ARE** ALL THESE LITTLE ONES?!

AND AN OLD LADY ?!
THIS MUST BE THE POKÉ-MON DAY CARE!
SHF
OHHH, WAIT! WAIT! WAIT!

WHAT ELSE ARE YOU?!
...DARE YOU CALL ME AN OLD LADY, YOU YOUNG RUFFIAN?!

HOW ...
GLARE

AWP.
SHOVE
TO MAKE UP FOR YOUR RUDENESS, HELP ME CATCH THEM!
AND HURRY !!

IF THIS LAD HADN'T COME AROUND, WE'D'VE LOST THEM ALL!
GOOD THING FOR US, EH, SWEETIE?

WHEW.

THOSE THINGS ARE... HUFF... HUFF... FAST!
THE FENCE BROKE DOWN, AND THEY WERE RUNNING ALL OVER. WE'RE GLAD YOU WERE PASSING BY!

OH, ARE YOU THAT GOLD BOY? WELL, WE'RE THE DAY CARE COUPLE YOU'RE LOOKING FOR!
PRO-FESSOR ELM TOLD US YOU'D BE COMING.

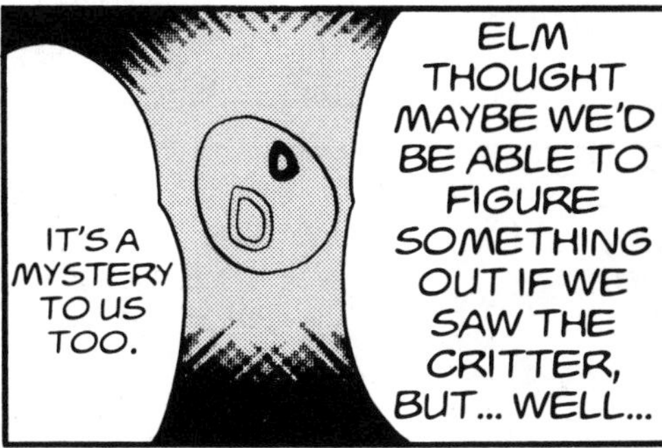
ELM THOUGHT MAYBE WE'D BE ABLE TO FIGURE SOMETHING OUT IF WE SAW THE CRITTER, BUT... WELL...
IT'S A MYSTERY TO US TOO.

I HEAR YOU HATCHED THAT EGG WE FOUND, EH?
GOOD JOB!

WE WERE TAKING CARE OF TWO POKÉMON... DON'T EVEN KNOW WHAT THEY WERE.
SUDDENLY THEY WERE GONE... AND THERE WAS AN EGG!
WHAT ?!!

GEEZ... SO NOTHING TO REPORT TO ELM... AGAIN.

WE'RE KEEPING AN EYE OUT FOR ANY FURTHER EGGS, BUT NO LUCK.

YOU'RE AT THE FAMOUS POKÉMON DAY CARE!
NO BETTER PLACE FOR TIPS ON RAIS-ING THEM RIGHT!

WELL, GUESS I'LL BE GOING!
BYE!
WAIT !!!

YOU COULD MAKE THOSE POKÉMON OF YOURS MIGHTY STRONG!
REALLY ?!

YOU DON'T HAVE TO ASK ME TWICE!!
I DIDN'T THINK SO.

THIS IS MY CHANCE TO SHRINK THE GAP BETWEEN ME AND SILVER—FAST!!
I'M NOT GETTING ANY YOUNGER. I NEED ALL THE HELP I CAN GET TO KEEP UP WITH THESE ZANIES!

SO... ANOTHER ONE CAUGHT IN GRANDMA'S WEB, EH?
AH, WELL.

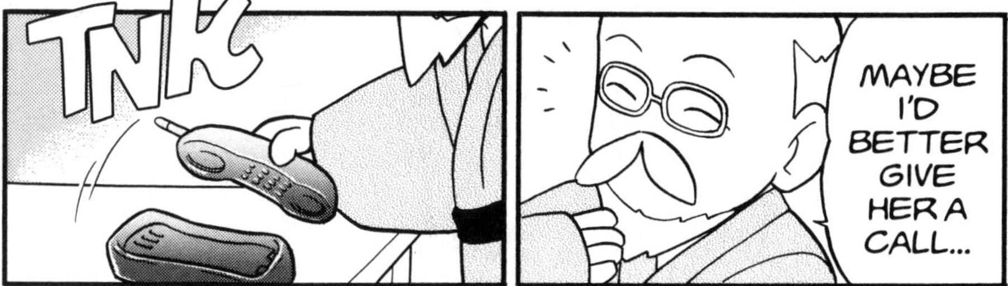
MAYBE I'D BETTER GIVE HER A CALL...
TNK

PRRRT
CHK ...
HELLO?
IT'S ME, THE OLD FELLER... FROM THE DAY CARE.
REMEMBER THAT MYSTERIOUS EGG WE FOUND? WELL, IT HATCHED.
I'M LOOKING AT THE LITTLE CRITTER RIGHT NOW.
WANT TO SEE IT?
ARE YOU KIDDING?!
COME ANYTIME, JASMINE.
COOL, I'M ON MY WAY NOW!!

BACK DOOR OF THE BREEDING CENTER.
HUH?

C'MON, C'MON! PICK UP YOUR FEET!
WHERE ARE WE GOING?

FLIP
"POKÉMON LEAGUE PAST WINNERS"?

WOW! THAT'S A LOT OF BOOKS!
GRANDPA'S RESEARCH LIBRARY.

POLIWRATH, HUH...
WINNER
RED
WHOA!

POLIBO, ARE YOU GONNA LOOK LIKE THIS WHEN YOU GROW UP?!
WHEE WHEE
TAKE GOOD CARE OF POLIBO AND IT WILL!
KRIIII

108 Quilava Quandary

RAAA

HEY HEY HEY! WAIT A SECOND!

GRAND-MA!!

DMDMDM

WHAT?

WHO ARE THESE POKÉ-MON?!

THEY'RE OUR ELITE FIGHTERS. PERFECT FOR TOUGHENING YOU UP. SO START!

NOT EXACTLY WHAT I HAD IN MIND...

TAK

BUT I'LL SHOW YOU!!

DOOM
YOU'RE NOT TELLING ME YOU CAN'T FIGHT WITHOUT THOSE GIMMICKS?
UM... OF COURSE NOT.
BLAH BLAH
THIS IS POKÉ-MON TRAIN-ING!
YOU SHOULDN'T RELY ON ANYTHING BUT THEIR POWERS AND YOUR KNOWL-EDGE!
OKAY, I GOT IT! POWERS AND KNOWL-EDGE!
FINE THEN.
LET'S GET IN THE ZONE...
...AND GO!!
VSH
OH DEAR.
I DON'T THINK THIS'LL BE FINISHED TODAY.
GYAAA

WOM
ACK!
THESE POKÉMON ARE ALL VETERAN FIGHTERS!
YEEE!
WAP

ROLLLL
PFF
AGH! IT'S NOT WORKING!!
FWOOSH
WE'VE JUST GOTTA FIGHT BACK!
EXBO! **EMBER**!
HUH?! O-OKAY! EXBO, BACK!!
THAT'S A GROUND TYPE! BRING YOUR FIRE TYPE BACK AND USE A WATER TYPE!
NOW... HIT 'EM WITH **WATER GUN**!!
IF THEY TRY TO MOVE IN CLOSE, HIT 'EM WITH A LONG-RANGE ATTACK BEFORE THEY'RE IN POSITION!
PSHUUU
ARE YOU FIGURING OUT HOW TO DO THIS?
HMPH
STRENGTH DOESN'T MATTER IF YOUR TIMING'S RIGHT.
WHOA! IT WORKED!!

ECRU-
TEAK
CITY
SIGH
I WISH OLIVINE AND GOLDEN-ROD WEREN'T SO FAR APART.

I WONDER WHAT KIND OF POKÉMON CAME OUT OF THAT EGG?
GIGGLE
I CAN'T WAIT TO SEE IT!

DMM
!
WHAT?!
EARTH-QUAKE?!

OH...
KRAAAK
YAAAA!

I DON'T HAVE ANYBODY STRONG AGAINST FIGHTING TYPES...
RRG...
SUDO-BO—MIMIC!!
WAP
HERE IT COMES!! PRIMEAPE'S CROSS CHOP!!
AND NONE OF THIS SMOKE-SCREEN NON-SENSE!
I KNOW!!
REMEM-BER... SLOW AND STEADY!!
I KNOW!!
IF THERE WAS SOME WAY TO BOOST OUR POWER...
PI PI
PI PI
YES! AN ATTACK THAT BOOSTS FIRE ATTACKS!
GLEEM
SUNBO! SUNNY DAY!!
BOOF!
NOW, EXBO—EMBER!!

WHOOSH
I GUESS THAT'S WHAT OAK SAW IN HIM WHEN HE GAVE HIM THE POKÉDEX.

HOW IS IT GOING, SWEET-IE?
COULD BE WORSE. BOY'S GOT POTEN-TIAL.
GRIN
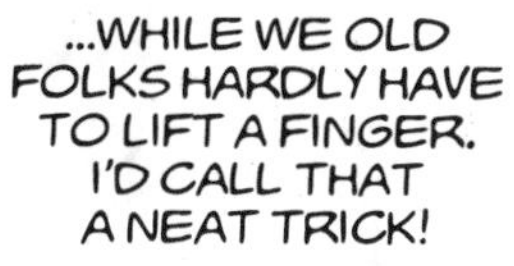

HE'S GIVING HIS POKÉ-MON SOME USEFUL PRACTICE ...
...AND LETTING OURS BLOW OFF SOME STEAM...
HEH
...WHILE WE OLD FOLKS HARDLY HAVE TO LIFT A FINGER. I'D CALL THAT A NEAT TRICK!

HEY, GRAND-MA!
YOU'RE NOT GIVING UP ALREADY?
NO WAY! BUT...ISN'T THIS KINDA ROUGH ON MY POKÉ-MON...?

THIS IS WHAT THEY'VE GOT TO GO THROUGH IF THEY'RE GONNA GET STRONGER! YOU **DO** WANT 'EM TO GET STRONGER?
SURE I DO! BUT I JUST DON'T KNOW IF...

PING

EXBO, WHAT'S WRONG?!
BRRR BRRR

LOOKS LIKE IT EVOLVED INTO QUILAVA.
NOW, ARE YOU GONNA LISTEN TO ME OR NOT?
!
POOOOM
FOMP
YOU DO THAT.
GRAND-MA... I'LL FOLLOW YOU TO THE ENDS OF THE WORLD!!
OH WELL ...
THAT'S THE TICKET!
VN VN
NOW, LET'S TAKE CARE OF THE REST!!

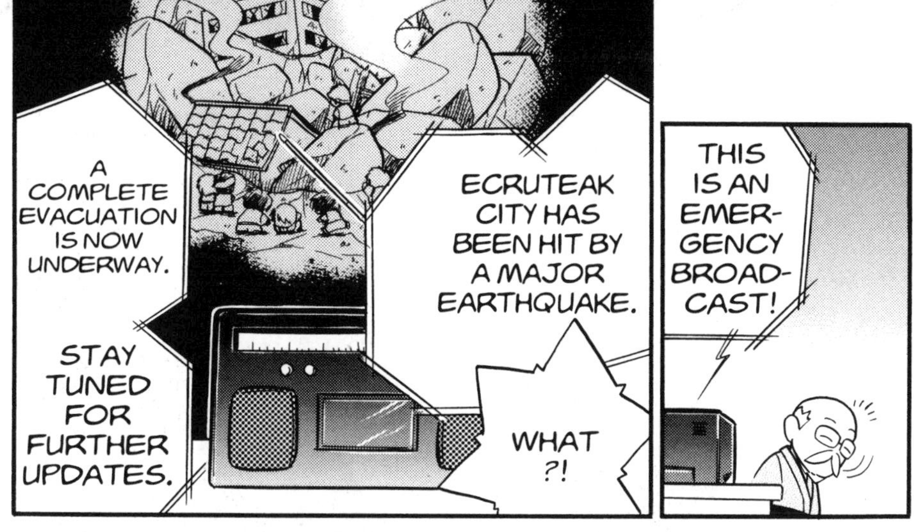

HMM ...
OH!
YOU'RE RIGHT!
WE HAVE SOMEONE HERE WHO CAN HELP!
PHEW!

MAN...

TNK...

ECRU-TEAK CITY

THIS IS REALLY BAD.

I JUST HOPE I CAN FIND THIS GIRL IN THE MIDST OF ALL THIS...

I'D LIKE TO TELL YOU THAT YOU'VE MASTERED YOUR TRAINING.

BUT HONESTLY, THESE ARE JUST THE BASICS. FROM HERE ON OUT...

...YOU'LL HAVE TO HONE YOUR SKILLS ON YOUR OWN.
HERE.

A REWARD FOR YOUR HARD WORK.

KING'S ROCK.

IT MAY COME IN HANDY.

RRM
!
AFTER-SHOCKS!

WE GOTTA HURRY!!
NOD

COME ON, EXBO!
VSH

FWUP
TAK
...
THE EARTH'S BEEN... COM-PLETELY SHAT-TERED.
VSSH
LET'S GO!

HUH...? THAT LIGHT FROM THE TOWER...

GLEEM

GLEEM

109 Ampharos Amore

SO MAYBE ...
TM

THIS GIRL, JASMINE, WASN'T AT THE EVACU-ATION SITE.
AND THIS AREA SHOULD BE BLACKED OUT...

IS SOME-ONE THERE ?
GLEEM

RRRM
!!
RRR

MORE AFTER-SHOCKS !!
KRIIII...
WAAGH !!
RRRRK
THE TOWER LOOKS LIKE IT'S...
... ABOUT TO GO DOWN!!

NH...
RRRM
WHO... ARE YOU...?
SHMP

WE GOTTA GET TO THE TOP! WHERE THE LIGHT WAS!
YO!! ANY-BODY HERE ?!!

TM TM TM
WELL THEN, WE BETTER BE QUICK !!

GLEEM
HEY! I SEE IT!!

!

SILVER?! WHAT ARE YOU DOING HERE?!

WHAT ARE YOU GONNA DO WITH HER?!
I HAP-PENED TO FIND HER... AND THOUGHT I'D HELP.

TSK
YOU AGAIN ...

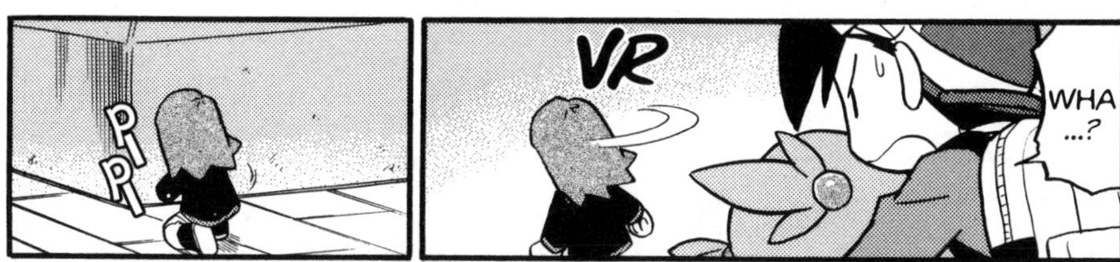

?

WHAT'S HE UP TO...?

A SCULPTURE OF A POKÉMON?!

RRRM...

WHOA! CAN'T STAND AROUND HERE!

KREEEE

THAT SOUNDS ...

UH-OH.

KOOM

GYAAAAA!

KOOM
OKAY, OKAY!
CARRY HER OUT!
DON'T JUST STAND THERE! GET HER OUT!
THE EXIT ...!!
SHM
SHE MADE IT!
NNG
BOM
BUT NOW... WE'RE TRAPPED!
PAF
...
KOOM
YAGH !!

K
K
KRIII...
WE'RE JUST GONNA HAVE TO FIND IT FAST, THAT'S ALL!
THERE'S GOTTA BE ANOTHER WAY OUT!

IT'S SINKING EVEN FASTER THAN I THOUGHT ...

WISH IT WASN'T SO DARK...
BRRR

OH! EXBO! LIGHT!!
FSH
!!

IDIOT!!
WE'RE IN A SEALED SPACE!!
FIRE WILL EAT UP ALL OUR OXYGEN!!
WHY DO YOU KEEP GETTING IN MY WAY?!
I JUST CAME TO RESCUE THE GIRL!
I DIDN'T WANT TO SEE YOU!

!!
K
K
RRRR
K
K
N-NOW WHAT?!

KRŌOOM
LAND-SLIDE! WE'LL BE CRUSHED!
NO !!
THE WALLS !!
HOOOM
EXBO! BLAST THROUGH THE CEILING!!
SKWISH
SILVER, DO SOME-THING!!
OH GREAT ...
WMM
NO LUCK!
WHAT GOOD IS WATER GONNA DO AT A TIME LIKE THIS?!
GET OUT YOUR WATER-TYPE POKÉ-MON!!
!
ICE ?!
WMM...

...ARE TIED TO THE POWERS OF NATURE! SO...
RIGHT! POKÉ-MON POWERS ...
IT CAN PULL UP UNDER-GROUND WATER— AND WE'LL USE THAT FORCE TO ESCAPE!
CHK
BOM
CROCO-NAW!
POLIBO !!
BOM

WHAT'S WRONG WITH YOU?
YOU MAY AS WELL USE A SQUIRT GUN!
...
SPYUU
ALL THE WATER YOU CAN!!

BRRR
BRRR
WE NEED A SOURCE OF REAL POWER! WE...
HUH ?

WOOHOO! HE EVOLVED !!

SKWEEZ

BOMP

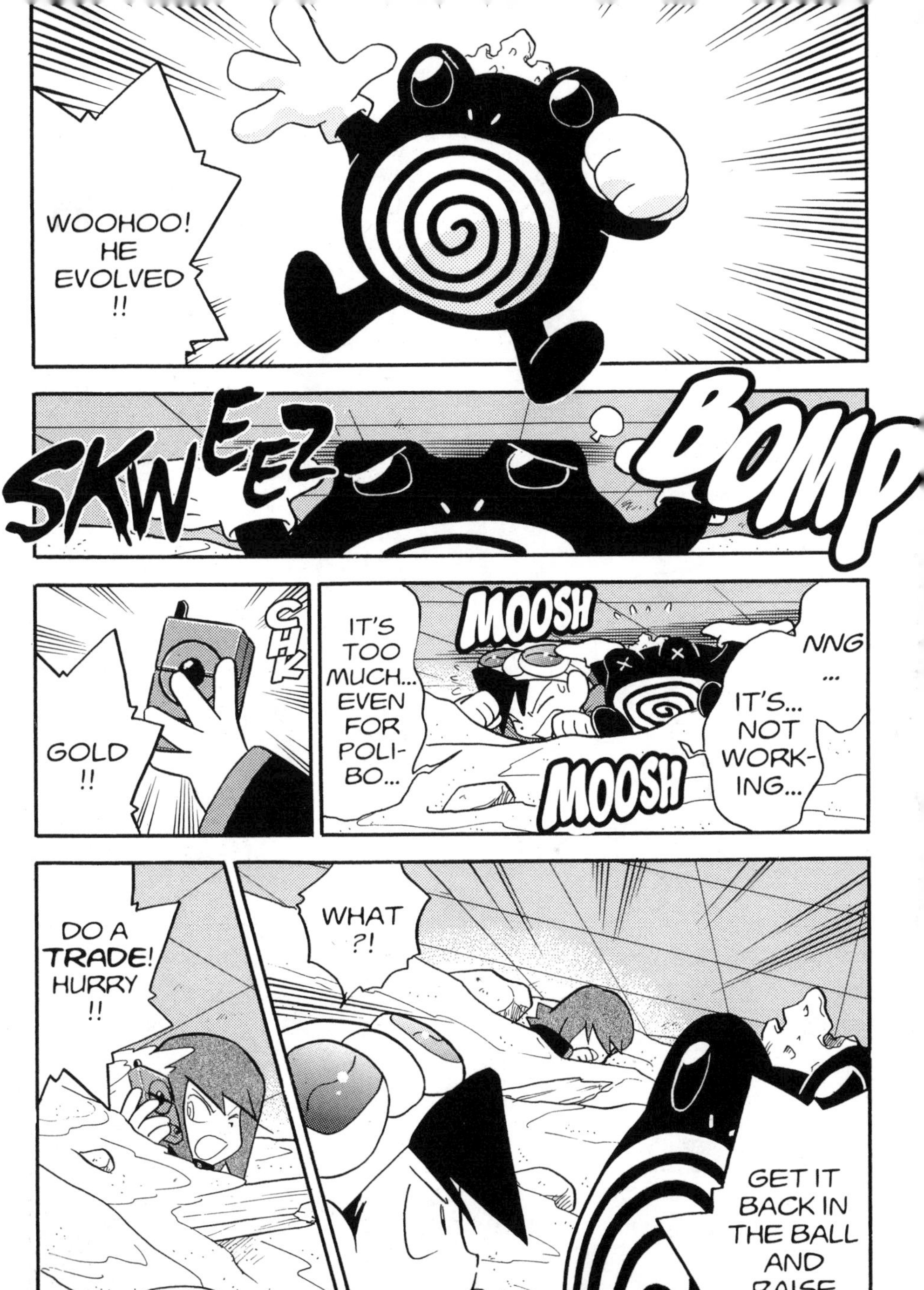

CHK
GOLD !!
MOOSH
IT'S TOO MUCH... EVEN FOR POLI-BO...
NNG ...
IT'S... NOT WORK-ING...
MOOSH

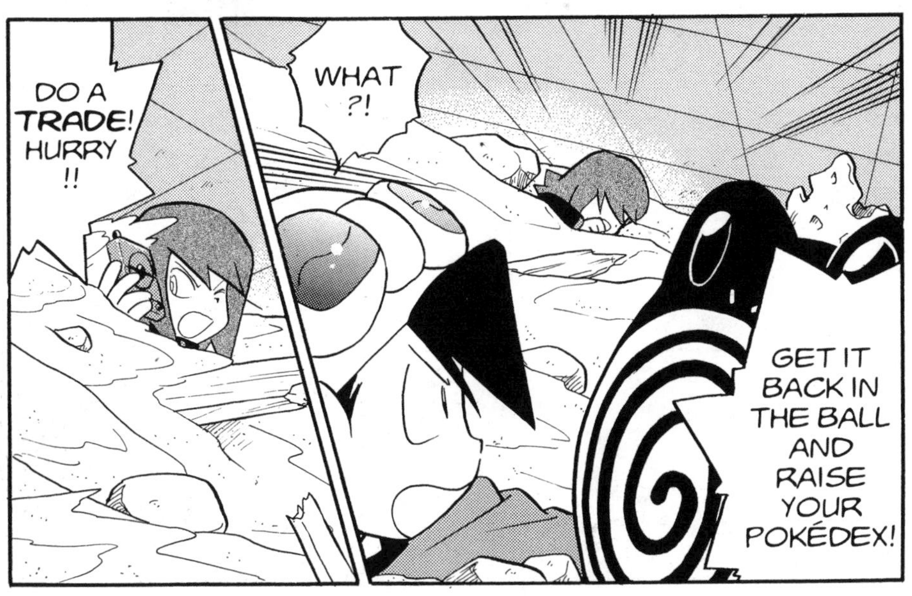

DO A **TRADE**! HURRY !!
WHAT ?!
GET IT BACK IN THE BALL AND RAISE YOUR POKÉDEX!

WHAT-EVER YOU'RE PLAN-NING...

... HAD BETTER BE... AGH!

DMM

KROOMMMM

MMMM...

POLIBO EVOLVED AGAIN ?!

BUT... IT'S NOT POLI-WRATH ?!

WHIRL-POOL!!

BOOOSH

WD
WHAT DID YOU JUST DO?!
OWW!
TM
WHAT ?!
IT'S A TRADE EVO-LUTION.
THIS POKÉMON HAS **TWO** FINAL FORMS.
FOR WATER POWER, POLITOED IS BEST.

TP
GET BACK HERE!

WMP
H... HEY!
I DON'T HAVE TIME TO GIVE YOU A POKÉMON LESSON.
HAVEN'T I TOLD YOU NOT TO GET INVOLVED?

A DROP IN GROUND LEVEL THIS HUGE CAN'T BE NATURAL.
IT'S GOT TO BE THE WORK OF A POKÉMON... AND NOT A WILD ONE EITHER.

AND THOSE ICE COLUMNS IN THERE...
ICE COMING OUT OF THE GROUND... GROUND AND ICE...

DOOOM...
!
WH-WHO IN THE...?

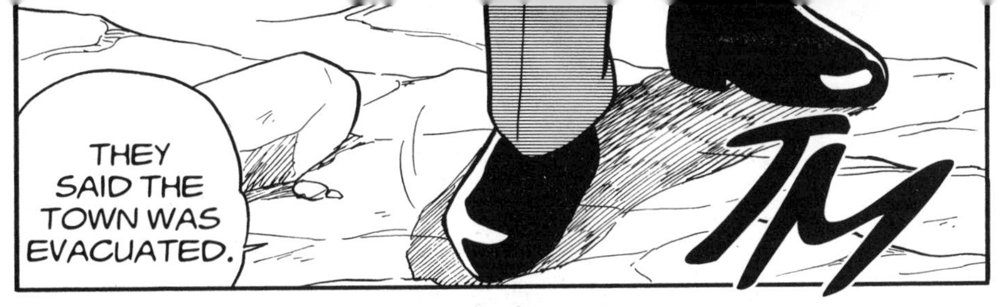

THEY SAID THE TOWN WAS EVACUATED.
TM

SO WHAT ARE THESE KIDS DOING IN THE BELL TOWER?

TEAM ROCKET ?!

110 Piloswine Whine

SNEER
SO THEY KNOW US.
I'VE BEEN WANTING ANOTHER SHOT AT YOU!

WE CAN'T LET THEM WALK AWAY AND TELL, CAN WE?
SINCE THEY'VE SEEN US HERE, WHAT MUST WE DO?

TM
TM
ASSUME BATTLE POSITIONS!
!
BMBM BMBMBM
AGH!
BMBM...BM
HEY, SILVER!!
WE'RE SITTING TARGETS OUT HERE!!
HEY!
STUPID.

THERE'S GOTTA BE THIRTY OF 'EM!
WHAT ARE THEY GONNA DO WITH A FORCE LIKE THIS?

!!
THEY'VE ALREADY DONE IT.

THE DESTRUCTION OF ECRUTEAK...
...WAS A GIFT FROM THESE TEAM ROCKET THUGS.

WHAT?!

SO YOU KNOW THAT TOO, EH?
WHO ARE YOU?

WAIT...

I'VE HEARD ABOUT A KID WITH RED HAIR...
YOU'RE THE ONE WHO MEDDLED WITH US IN NEW BARK TOWN—AND AT THAT SLOWPOKE WELL IN AZALEA!
BOP BOP BOP BOP

VSH
DM
DON'T UNDER-ESTIMATE THIS PUNK!
TAKE HIM OUT—NOW!!

WK
WK
WK
?!

Y'KNOW, I THOUGHT SOMEBODY MIGHT'VE INTERFERED IN MY BATTLE WITH SILVER BACK IN NEW BARK TOWN!

SO IT WAS YOU GUYS!

EVEN MORE REASON NOT TO LIKE YOU! LET'S TAKE 'EM, SILVER!!

WILL YOU JUST STAY OUT OF MY FIGHTS?

THIS IS **MY** FIGHT!!

R RR...
SNEER
OR MAYBE YOU'RE FORGET-TING WHAT WE CAN DO?
SNAP
WE'LL JUST DESTROY YOU BOTH...
...AT THE SAME TIME.
PRMMMBL
OH MAN...
ANOTHER QUAKE!

IT'S HERE! WHATEVER CAUSED THE EARTH MOVE-MENT!
KOOM
WHOA!
KOOM

KRRK
TM TM TM
LOOK OUT!!

BWOOM

IT'S... HUGE!!

YOU'RE SAYING THIS THING CAUSED THE EARTHQUAKE?!
I AM.
ICE AND GROUND... TWO TYPES UNITED IN THE PILOSWINE.
BUT EVEN I DIDN'T REALIZE HOW BIG THE THINGS CAN GET.

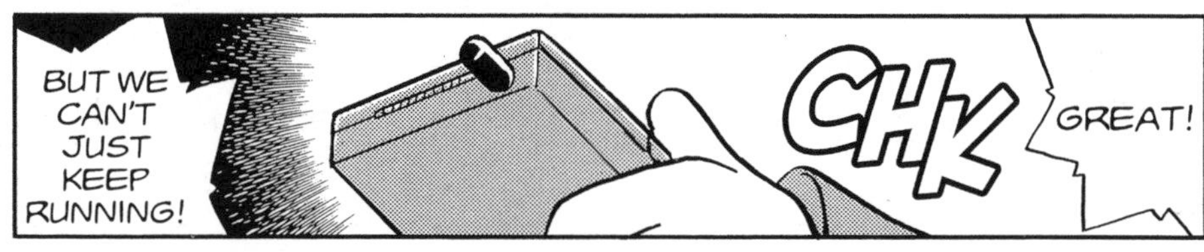
GREAT!
CHK
BUT WE CAN'T JUST KEEP RUNNING!

POLIBO! WATER GUN!!
...
HUH ...?
HOP HOP
W-WHAT'S THE MATTER, POLIBO?!

WRA HAHAHA!
TMM
THIS KID'S EVEN LAMER THAN THE REDHEAD!
I'LL LEAVE THESE GUYS TO YOU.
YOU'LL WHAT?!
VSH

DM DM DM DM
DM DM
DM DM DM

TAKE DOWN!! ROCK SMASH!!
IT HAS THE POWER TO SHATTER THE EARTH UNDER A WHOLE CITY!!
AND IT'S GOING TO KEEP CRUSHING THE GROUND—UNTIL YOU'VE GOT NOWHERE TO STAND! THEN WE'LL SEE HOW LONG YOUR POKÉMON CAN CARRY YOU!

...
THINK SO?

DM DM DM DM DM DM
BUT YOU KNOW WHAT HAP-PENS, DON'T YOU...
...WHEN THE GROUND GETS SHAKEN BADLY ENOUGH?

IT'S CALLED... LIQUE-FACTION!

VUSH
WHIRL-POOL !!
H-HEY !!
NO WAY !!
WHEN SHOCK WAVES MAKE SOLIDS ...
TM
... BEHAVE LIKE LIQUIDS!
ALL FORCES!
LEAVE THE OTHER KID! WE'VE GOT TO...
DMDMMDM

!!
SORRY. I KINDA BEAT 'EM ALL.
W-WHAT?!
SNEER
HEY, SILVER SAID HE WAS LEAVING 'EM TO ME.

WE'VE ATTACKED THE BELL TOWER AS PLANNED.
IF WE'RE RIGHT ABOUT THE INSTINCTS OF HO-OH... THEN OUR MISSION HAS ALREADY BEEN COM-PLETED.
NO. WE CAN'T GET IN ANY DEEPER.
!

HO-OH ?!

VSH
ALL FORCES... RETREAT !!
RRRGH.

I'M GETTIN' SICK OF THIS!
HEY, WAIT !!
TM
TM
TM
TM

WHY WOULD TEAM ROCKET ATTACK ECRU-TEAK CITY?

GIVE ME BACK MY POLI-BO.
THAT WAS A LOAN, NOT A GIFT.
NO WONDER IT WOULDN'T LISTEN TO ME...

HEY.
VP

PSSSH
HEHEH! YOU COULD TELL, HUH?
I GUESS THAT DAY CARE TRAINING WAS WORTH IT!

...
LOOKS LIKE YOU'VE GOTTEN BETTER.
PIP

HOP
WHEW
WEL-COME BACK, POLIBO!

BOM

BY THE WAY, SILVER.

PING
WHO'S "HO-OH" ?

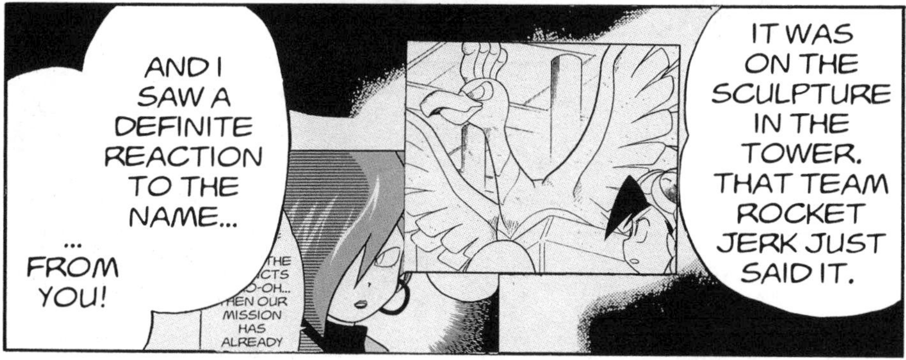
IT WAS ON THE SCULPTURE IN THE TOWER. THAT TEAM ROCKET JERK JUST SAID IT.
AND I SAW A DEFINITE REACTION TO THE NAME...
...FROM YOU!

WHAT'S THIS ALL ABOUT?
...

YOU CAME HERE FOR A REASON. I KNOW IT.
HMF
WELL, I DON'T NEED TO KNOW THAT.

TM
BUT AT LEAST ANSWER ME THIS.

HAVE YOU EVER REALLY **ENJOYED** A POKÉMON BATTLE?

WHAT?

CHK

YOU HEARD ME.

WE'VE BOTH GOT A POKÉDEX AND A POKÉMON FROM PRO-FESSOR ELM.

THAT'S ABOUT AS FAIR A PLAYING FIELD AS YOU'RE EVER GONNA FIND.

WHAT DO YOU SAY?

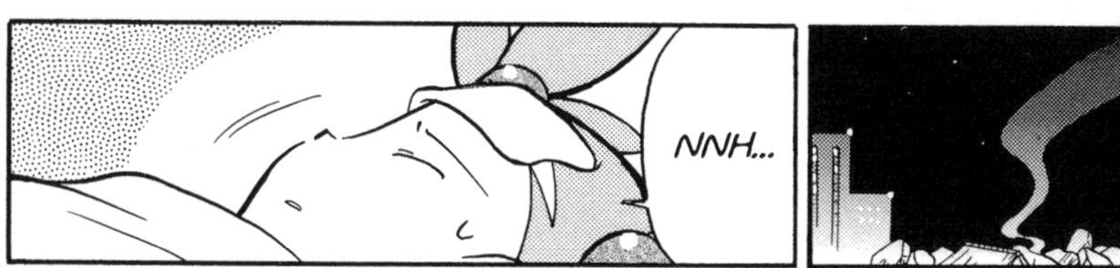
NNH...

WHERE AM I...?
DON'T WORRY. YOU'RE AT THE EVAC-UATION SHELTER.

AMPHY ...
SIGH
THIS MEANS PEOPLE ARE STILL ALIVE OUT THERE!
WE'LL WAIT FOR DAYLIGHT AND SEND OUT A RESCUE PARTY.

VOOP
WHAT ABOUT THE PEOPLE WHO RESCUED ME FROM INSIDE THE TOWER...?
N-NO! YOU SHOULDN'T GET UP YET!
THE PEOPLE WHO SAVED YOU...? THIS AMPHAROS IS THE ONE WHO CARRIED YOU HERE.
THEN... WAS IT A DREAM ...?

UM... WHAT ABOUT THE AREA AROUND THE TIN TOWER ...?

IT'S BEEN CLOSED OFF UNTIL MORNING. NO ONE SHOULD BE THERE NOW.

OH... I SEE...

THIS LOOKS GOOD.

ALREADY TOTALLY DESTROYED ANYWAY.

POP

POPOPOP

OKAY THEN.

WE CAN DO TAG TEAM MODE.
LET'S USE SIX POKÉ-MON EACH.
ROLL ROLL

THE EMERGENCY POWER IS STILL WORKING! FIRST, WE BETTER HEAL OUR POKÉ-MON...
WEEEN
WE'RE IN LUCK!

I'M GIVING YOU A ONE-POKÉ-MON HANDI-CAP.
VNN
HUH? HOW COME YOU'VE ONLY GOT FIVE?

YOU TALK BIG.
GRRRR
CHK
ALTHOUGH I COULD PROBABLY GIVE YOU FOUR AND STILL WIN.

WELL, IT'S TIME TO STOP TALKING...
CHK

...AND FIGHT!!

BBOM

111 Tyranitar War

WATER GUN!

PSSH

EMBER!!

I'M ALREADY IN A HOLE!

AGH!!

MMF

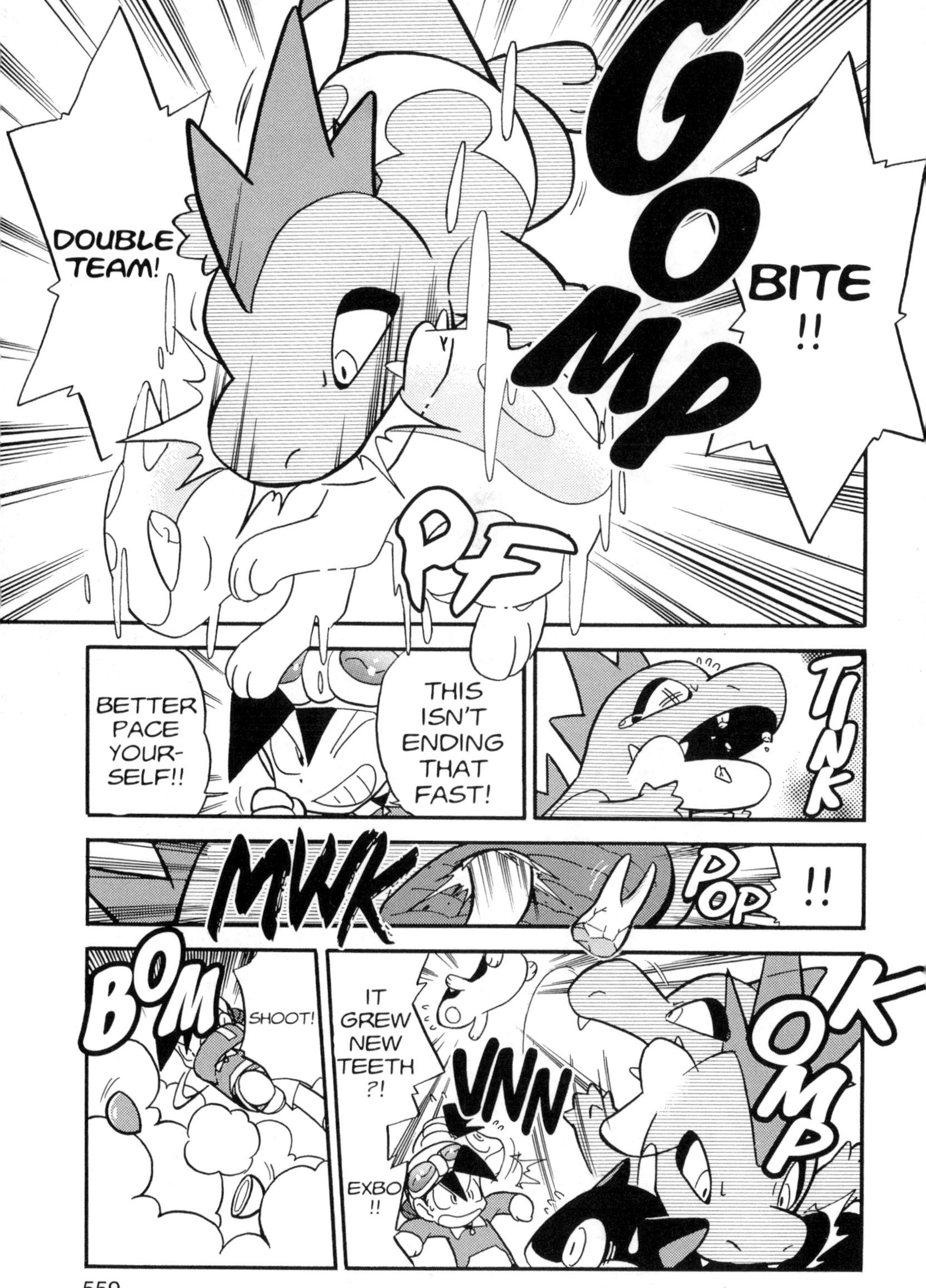
GOMP
BITE !!
DOUBLE TEAM!
PF
THIS ISN'T ENDING THAT FAST!
BETTER PACE YOURSELF!!
TINK
MWK
POP !!
KOMP
IT GREW NEW TEETH ?!
BOM
SHOOT!
VNN
EXBO !!

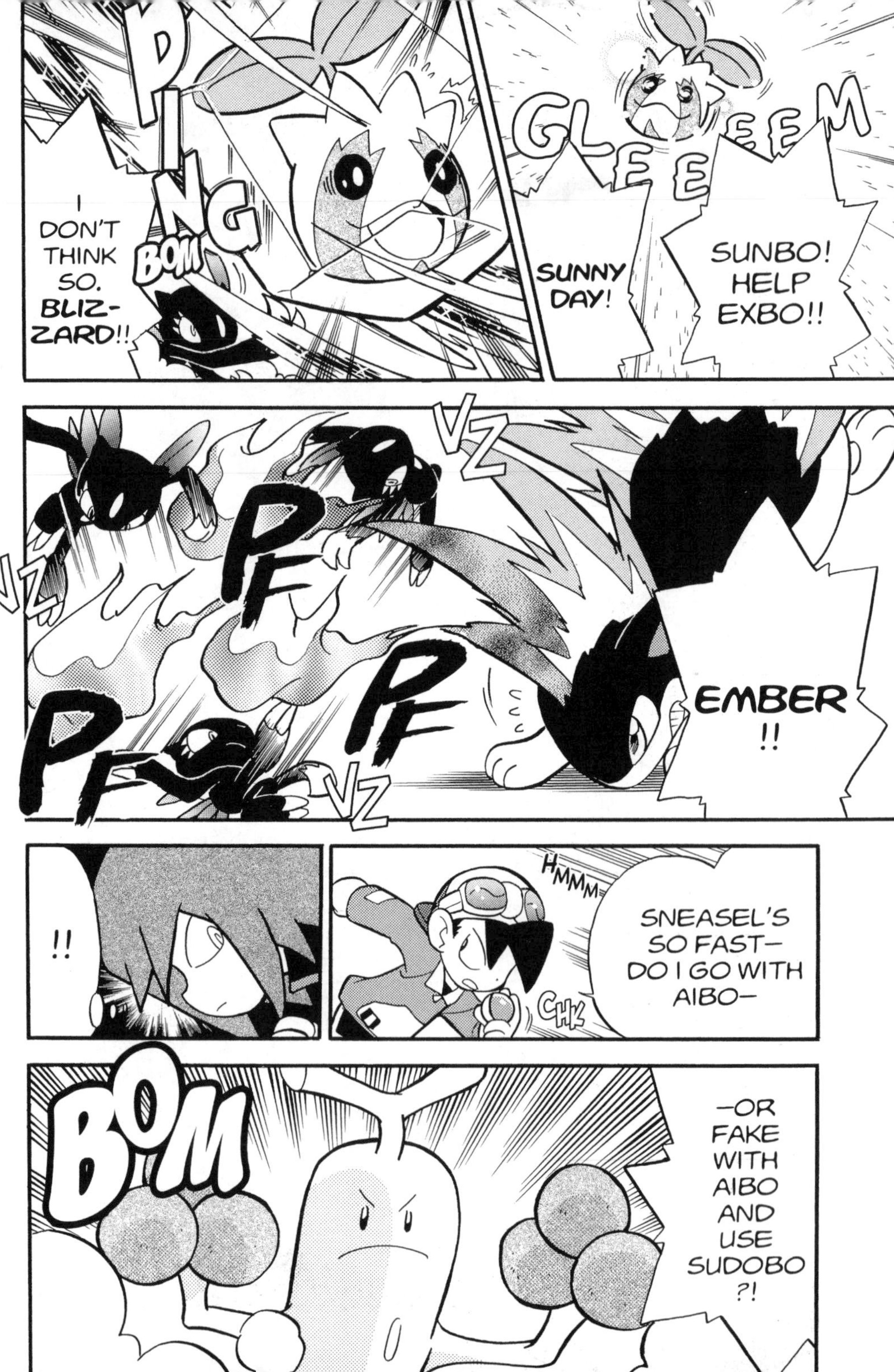
PING
BOM
I DON'T THINK SO. BLIZZARD!!
GLEEEEEM
SUNNY DAY!
SUNBO! HELP EXBO!!
VZ
PF
PF
PF
VZ
VZ
EMBER!!
!!
HMMM
SNEASEL'S SO FAST—DO I GO WITH AIBO—
CHK
BOM
—OR FAKE WITH AIBO AND USE SUDOBO?!

LOW KICK!
SNOOOO
GG...
NOW GO!!
GOTCHA!
WHAT ?!

DYNAMIC PUNCH!!
NKH!
TNK
DGGG

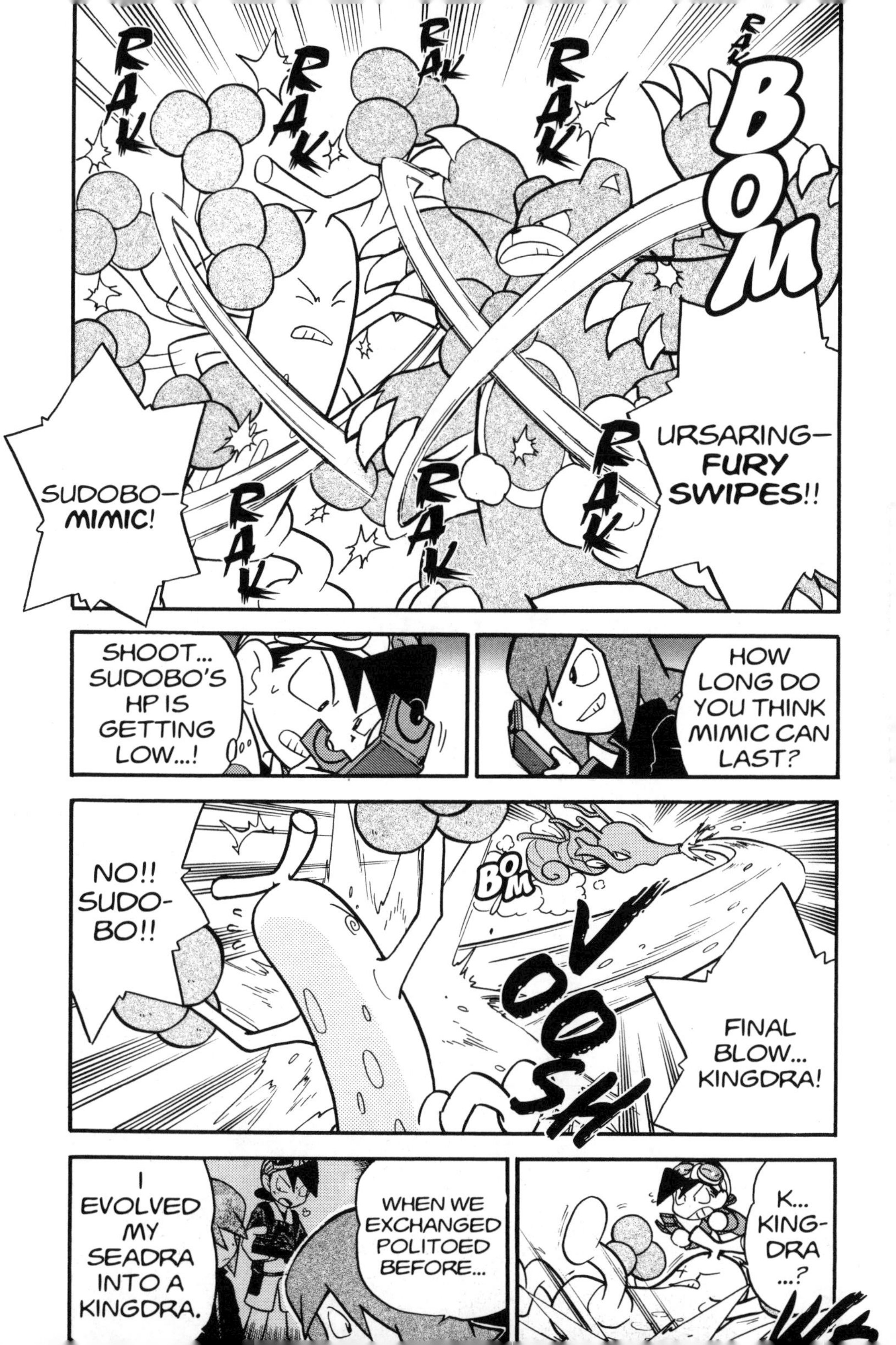

RAK RAK RAK RAK RAK

BOOM

SUDOBO—MIMIC!

URSARING—FURY SWIPES!!

RAK RAK RAK

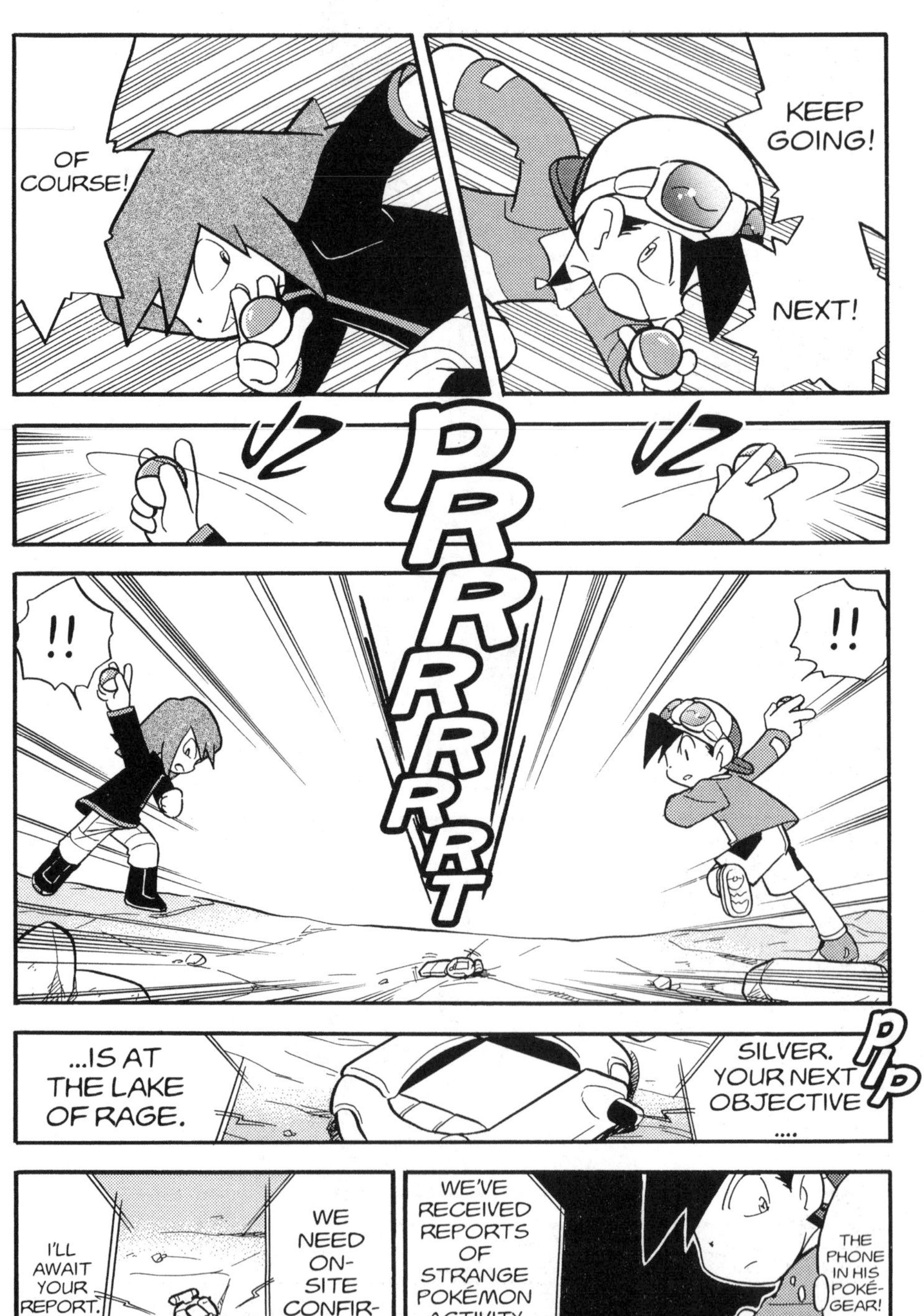
KEEP GOING!
NEXT!
OF COURSE!
PRRRRRRT
!!
!!
SILVER. YOUR NEXT OBJECTIVE ....
PIP
...IS AT THE LAKE OF RAGE.
THE PHONE IN HIS POKÉGEAR!
WE'VE RECEIVED REPORTS OF STRANGE POKÉMON ACTIVITY IN THE VICINITY.
WE NEED ON-SITE CONFIRMATION.
I'LL AWAIT YOUR REPORT.
KLIK

SHHHH

WHAT WAS THAT?!
AND WHO ARE YOU?!
CHK

...
SHF

SORRY, GOLD. BUT I HAVE TO END THIS BATTLE RIGHT NOW.
VSH!

BOOM!!

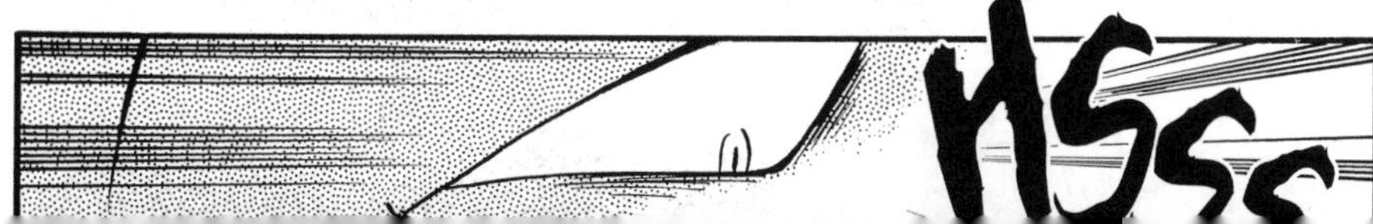
HSSS

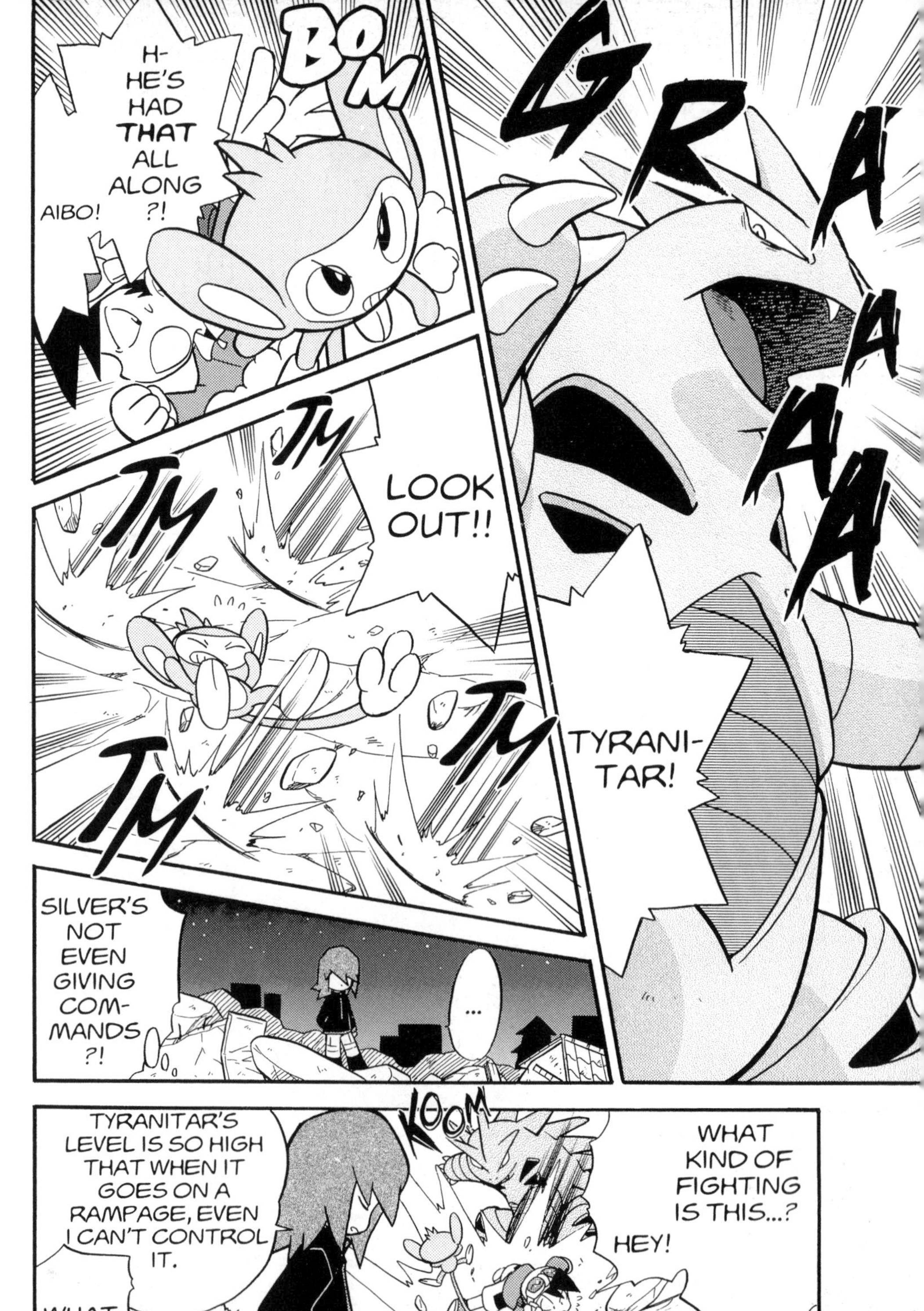
BOM
GRAAAAAA
H-HE'S HAD **THAT** ALL ALONG?!
AIBO!
TM
TM
LOOK OUT!!
TM
TM
TYRANI-TAR!
SILVER'S NOT EVEN GIVING COM-MANDS?!
...
KOOM
WHAT KIND OF FIGHTING IS THIS...?
HEY!
TYRANITAR'S LEVEL IS SO HIGH THAT WHEN IT GOES ON A RAMPAGE, EVEN I CAN'T CONTROL IT.
WHAT?!

...FOR IT TO BRING OUT...
...ITS SPECIAL ATTACK.
VP
SIGH
BUT IT'S ABOUT TIME...
HOOOOO
SAND-STORM!
WAAAGH!
SHOO
EXBO! SUNBO! SUDO-BO!
AIBO!
HSS

SPYUU
POLI-BO...
W-WATER GUN!
PSSSH
IT'S NO USE.
VZZ
HWP
HWP
HWP
WHAT?!
RRK
FUMP
POLI-BO!
?!

...
SH
HHHH

... WHAT ?!

DID IT WORK ...?

WOBBLE...

?!
TYRANITAR?! IMPOSSIBLE!!
WHAT HAPPENED ?!

TOGEPI ?!
BUT WHEN ...?!

POLI-TOED WAS A DECOY...
...SO TOGEPI COULD SLIP IN WITH DOUBLE-EDGE!

PLOP
NOW... ACK!!
TOGE-BO!
GET OUTTA THE WAY!

DOOOM!
OUCH.

...

TYRANI-TAR, DEFEAT-ED...?

EXBO, SUNBO, SUDOBO.
AIBO, POLIBO... AND TOGEBO ...
ALL DOWN FOR THE COUNT.

WELL, SILVER ...
FOMP
...IT LOOKS LIKE I LOSE!

BUT I MADE YOU RESORT TO YOUR SIXTH POKÉMON! SO MUCH FOR YOUR HANDICAP!

HMPH ...

FSH
PAP
!
THERE YOU GO.

JAB
AND NEXT TIME... I'M GONNA WIN!!

COULD HE REALLY ...
HEY!!

...HAVE PICKED THIS UP IN THE MIDDLE OF THE SAND-STORM?

UP
LET'S GO, SNEASEL.
IF HE'D USED THAT TIME TO GIVE A COMMAND INSTEAD...
...THIS BATTLE COULD ACTUALLY HAVE GONE HIS WAY...

GOLD. YOU'VE PROVEN YOUR-SELF.
YOU SHOULD BE SATIS-FIED NOW...
...AND STOP FOLLOW-ING ME AROUND.
B-B-BON
TM

VNNN
...FOR YOUR EFFORTS, I'LL ANSWER YOUR QUESTION.
WSH
...

YOU MEAN ...?

PAP
TEAM ROCKET ATTACKED ECRUTEAK IN ORDER TO CALL FORTH HO-OH.

"CALL FORTH" ?!

IT'S SAID THAT THE BELL TOWER IS WHERE THE LEGENDARY POKÉMON HO-OH NESTS.

TEAM ROCKET HOPES THAT DESTROYING THE BELL TOWER WILL TRIGGER HO-OH'S HOMING INSTINCTS.
YOU MEAN THEY DESTROYED THE CITY... JUST TO BRING SOME POKÉMON BACK TO ITS NEST?!

AS FOR MY MISSION... IT'S TO CRUSH THEM.

AND ALSO TO FOLLOW HO-OH.
IN ORDER TO ACHIEVE THOSE ENDS...
...I CAN'T BE CHOOSY ABOUT THE MEANS.
NOT EVEN IF I HAVE TO BREAK THE LAW.

GLANCE

...
MMG...

SNEASEL. CROCO-NAW.
VSH
LET'S GO!

NOD
PLUS TOTODILE... I MEAN, CROCO-NAW... ISN'T BACK HOME YET, IS IT, EXBO?

I DON'T CARE WHO HE'S GOING UP AGAINST ...
...I STILL DON'T SEE WHY HE HAS TO FIGHT ALONE.

WAIT UP!
I'M COMING WITH YOU!!
VSH

MEAN-WHILE, IN VIRIDIAN CITY...
HM.
SHK
I HOPE SHE'S DOING WELL...
IT'S BEEN A WHILE SINCE I'VE BEEN IN KANTO ...
DINGDONG

AND DIDN'T I GIVE YOU... DODUO?

HOW IS DODUO ANYWAY?

WOOM

FISHERMAN!

IT'S SO GOOD TO SEE YOU!!
WAHAHAHA! I'VE MISSED YOU, YELLOW!

I HEAR YOU WENT THROUGH A LOT LAST YEAR, HUH?!
HA HA.

HOW'VE THINGS BEEN SINCE THEN?
IT'S BEEN OKAY. THE CITIES OF KANTO ARE MOSTLY REBUILT...

AND PEOPLE SEEM A LOT MORE RELAXED LATELY.

HUH?! WHO'S THIS ONE?!

I FOUND CHUCHU INJURED IN THE VIRIDIAN FOREST AND BROUGHT IT BACK WITH ME.

POING
CHUCHU, MY PIKACHU.

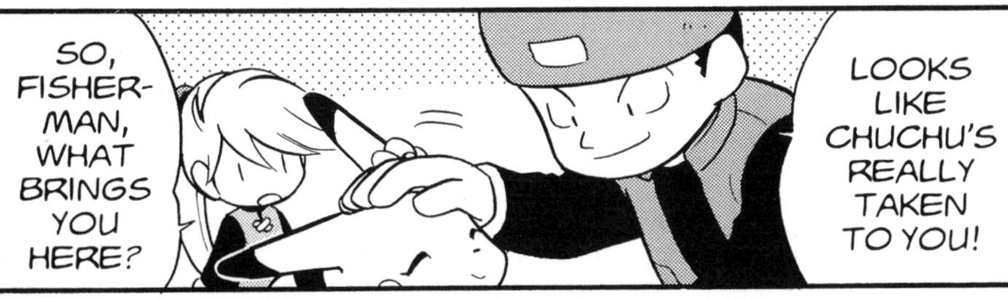
LOOKS LIKE CHUCHU'S REALLY TAKEN TO YOU!
SO, FISHER-MAN, WHAT BRINGS YOU HERE?

I'VE MISSED YOU!
AND... WELL. I HAVE A FAVOR TO ASK.
A FAVOR?

YEAH. CAN YOU COME TO JOHTO WITH ME?
WHY JOHTO?

FWOOOOO
I LOOKED INTO WHAT YOU ASKED ME ABOUT BEFORE...
THE BIG FLYING-TYPE POKÉMON THAT DISAPPEARED A YEAR AGO IN JOHTO.

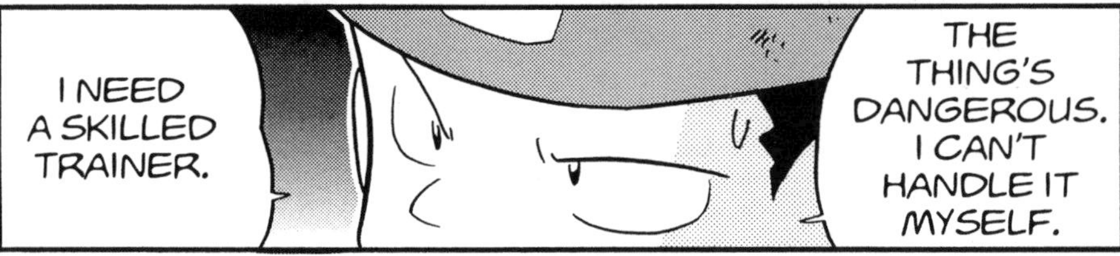
THE THING'S DANGEROUS. I CAN'T HANDLE IT MYSELF.
I NEED A SKILLED TRAINER.

IN THAT CASE, I'M HARDLY THE ONE TO ASK!
THE ONLY REASON I WAS ABLE TO WIN A YEAR AGO WAS BECAUSE OF EVERYONE ELSE'S HELP!
BUT... WHO ELSE CAN I TURN TO?
...
HM

HOW ABOUT RED?
THAT RED?

VOOP
HOW MANY REDS DO YOU KNOW?

FSH

GO, VENUSAUR!!

WHIPP

VINE WHIP!!

HWRRR
BON
VENUSAUR, RETURN!
AMAZING!

ZF
UH...

DO YOUR HANDS STILL GET WEAK, RED?
HAHAHA
VP
SHAK SHAK
ROLL ROLL
OH WELL...

?!

ONLY SOMETIMES... BUT...
...WHEN THEY DO, THEY GO TOTALLY NUMB.
MY ANKLES TOO... WHERE LORELEI'S ICE RINGS GOT ME.
GRIP...

LAKE OF RAGE
...

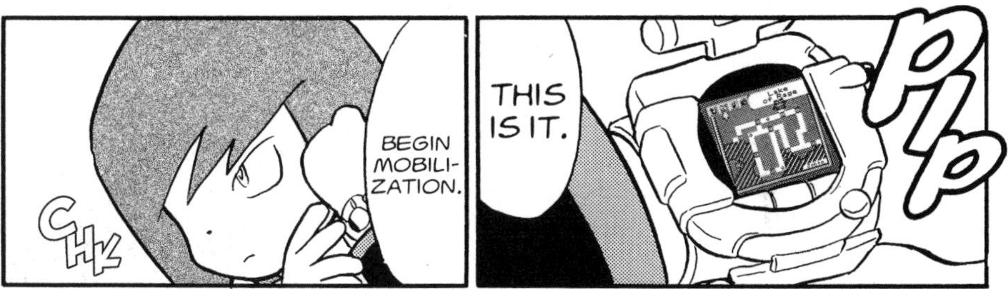
PIP
THIS IS IT.
BEGIN MOBILI-ZATION.
CHK

HFF
BUT WHERE'D HE GO ?!
WEIRD, I KNOW I SAW HIM AROUND HERE...
LET'S... REST AWHILE ...
HOO
HF HF

PLIP...
HUH ...?

ZWOOSH

EEYOW!!

112 Raise the Red Gyarados

SILVER !!

AAAAAA
VZ
HUH ?

GOTCHA!! LET'S GO, EXBO!!
TM

OKAY.
CHK

VSH

WHAT'S THIS THING YOU HAVE ABOUT GOING IT ALONE?!
I CAN HELP!

WP
WHOA.

BOOM
WAGH?!
SHOVE
HEY!
IF YOU KNOW WHAT'S GOING ON IN THIS...

HUH?
IF YOU WANT TO FOLLOW, TAKE A LOOK AROUND YOU.

PLASH
SENSE?
CAN'T YOU SENSE IT?

POP
WHAT'S GOING ON?!
?
ZZZZD

... AND FORCING POKÉMON EVOLUTIONS. HENCE THE MASS GYARADOS OUTBREAK.
KVZZZT
ELECTRO-MAGNETIC WAVES FILLING THE AIR...

FORC-ING ...?!

BUT WHERE ARE THE WAVES COMING FROM?!
VWAH
GET BACK HERE!

YOU KEEP THEM CONFINED THERE!

YOU'RE NOT THE BOSS OF ME!!

DOOM
YAAA!

PAPAPAPAP
SHOOT!
POLIBO! DOUBLE SLAP!!

MWK
POP
MORE ?!
PAPAPAPAP
PLOSH
PLISH
THERE'S NO END IN SIGHT.

HOW DID I LET MYSELF GET STUCK WITH THIS?!
IDIOT !!

CAN'T WASTE MY RESOURCES FIGHTING ALL OF THEM. GOT TO HIT THE SOURCE.
BUT WHERE'S THE TRANS-MITTER ?

...
PLISH
PLASH

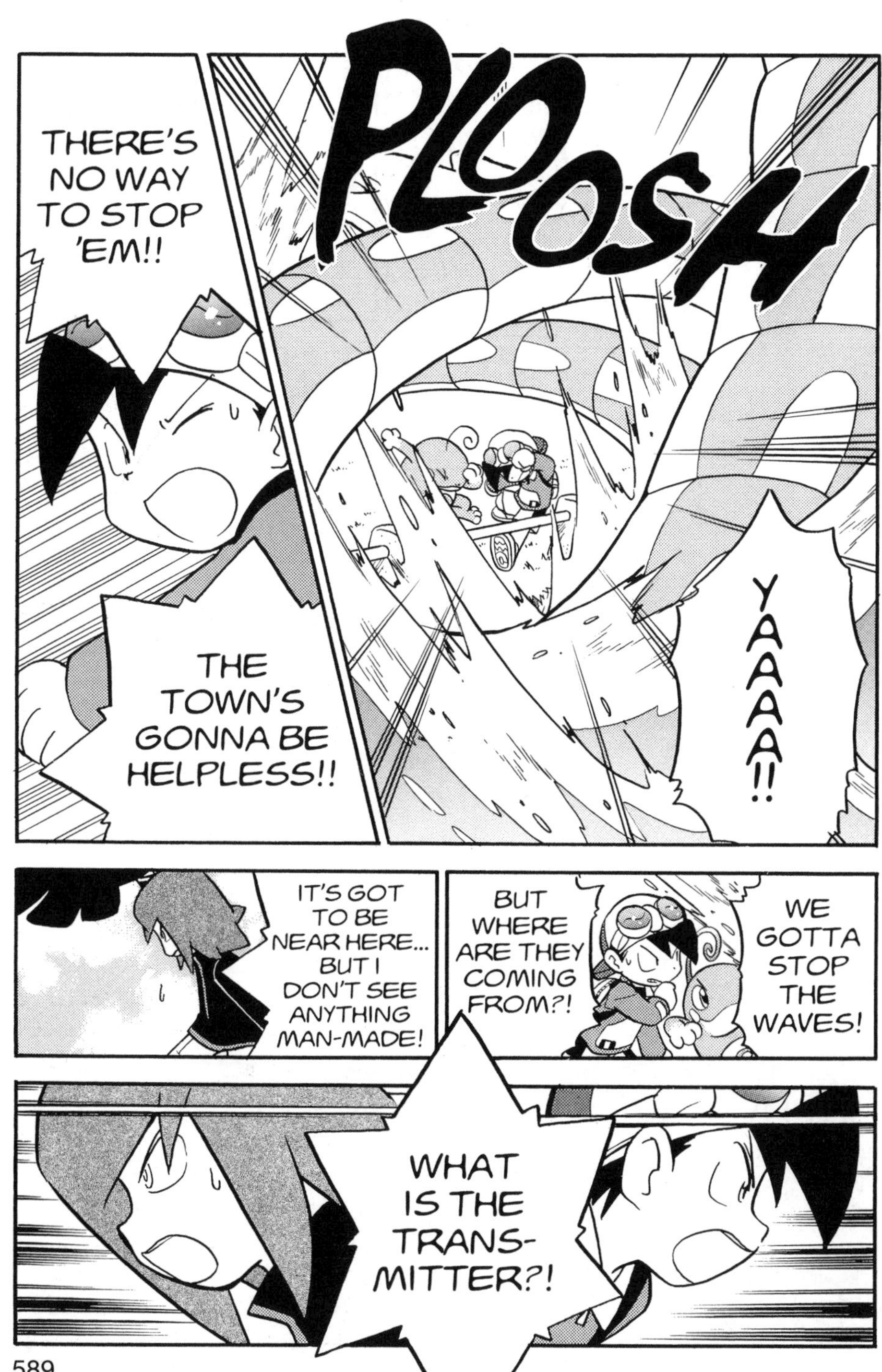
PLOOSH
THERE'S NO WAY TO STOP 'EM!!
THE TOWN'S GONNA BE HELPLESS!!
YAAAAA!!
WE GOTTA STOP THE WAVES!
BUT WHERE ARE THEY COMING FROM?!
IT'S GOT TO BE NEAR HERE... BUT I DON'T SEE ANYTHING MAN-MADE!
WHAT IS THE TRANS-MITTER?!

WHAT'S UP, PRO-FESSOR?
I DON'T LIKE THIS...

ELM RESI-DENCE

OH... ACTU-ALLY...
CAN YOU GET IN TOUCH WITH GOLD RIGHT NOW?

NOT BROKEN. SOME SORT OF ELECTRO-MAGNETIC INTERFER-ENCE.
IS IT BRO-KEN?

NOTH-ING BUT STATIC.
THE CONNEC-TION'S DOWN.
KXXZ
ZXXZZZ

I JUST HOPE GOLD ISN'T CAUGHT UP IN ANYTHING DANGEROUS...

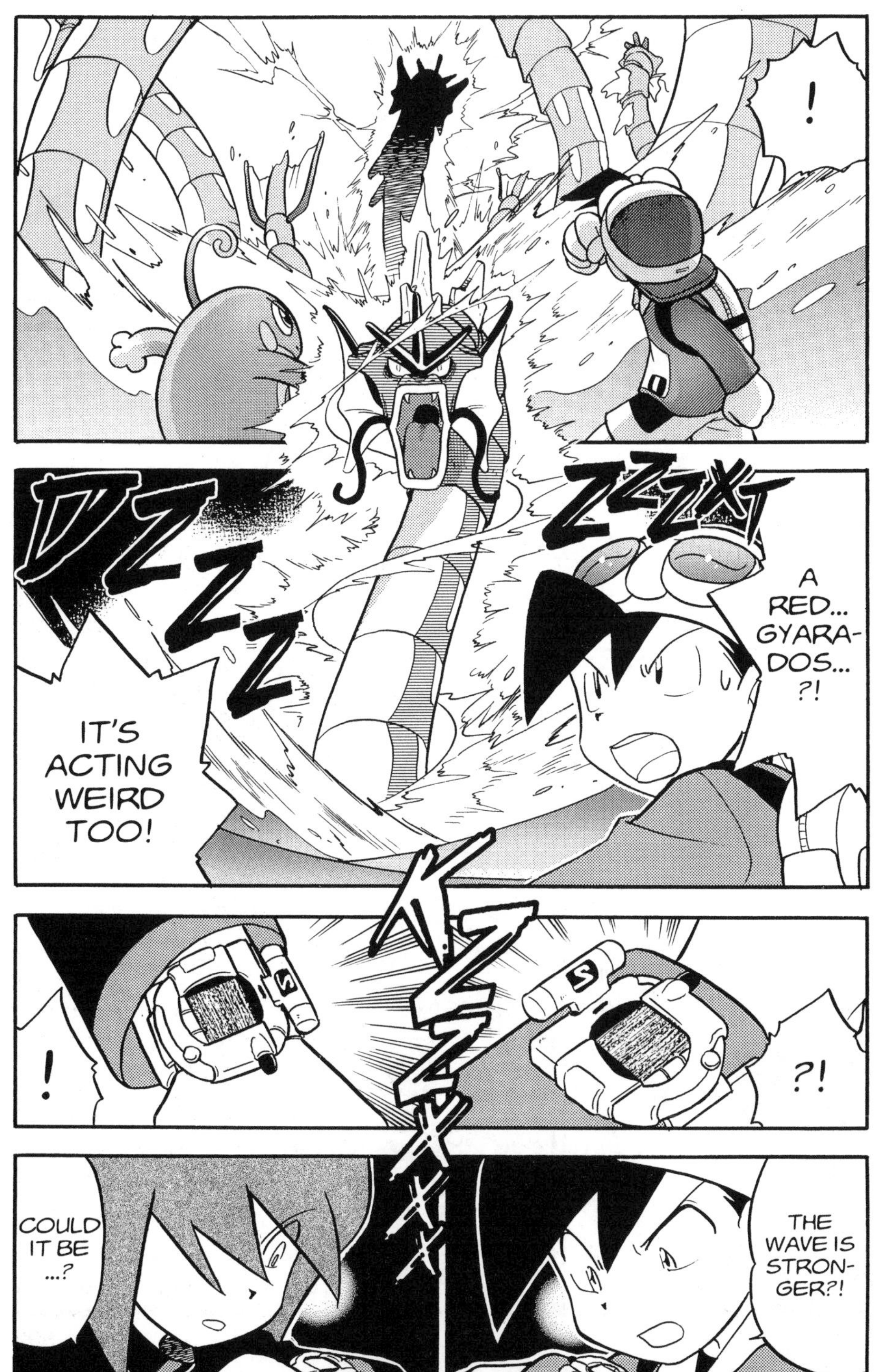
!
A RED... GYARADOS...?!
IT'S ACTING WEIRD TOO!
?!
!
THE WAVE IS STRONGER?!
COULD IT BE ...?

THE TRANSMITTER IS...THIS POKÉMON?!

CAN'T REACH IT FROM HERE! YOU GOTTA CAPTURE IT!
HWOO
I'VE JUST GOTTA STOP IT! **WHIRL-POOL**!!
POKÉ BALL!
OKAY! **PURSUIT**!
YES !!
!
BOOM

PLSH
PLOOSH
THEY'RE ALL GOING BACK TO THE LAKE.
PIPIPI
...
I GUESS WE ACTUALLY PULLED IT OFF...

WHAT'RE YOU DOING?
ANA-LYZING THE WAVE'S FRE-QUENCY.

SO I CAN TRACK DOWN THE ULTI-MATE SOURCE... AND DESTROY IT!
PIP
GOOD THINK-ING!

BUT WHY WOULD ANYBODY DO THIS...
ARTIFI-CIALLY FORCING POKÉMON TO EVOLVE?
SHHHHH

IS IT LIKE THE EARTH-QUAKE ...?
HMPH

...

GOLD, THIS IS MY LAST WARNING.
DON'T GET INVOLVED WITH ME.

THE OPPONENT I'M PURSUING NOW IS FAR STRONGER THAN THOSE TEAM ROCKET STOOGES WE FOUGHT IN ECRUTEAK.
AN AMATEUR TRAINER LIKE YOU CAN ONLY GET IN MY WAY.
I'M ALREADY IN-VOLVED!
WHAT?

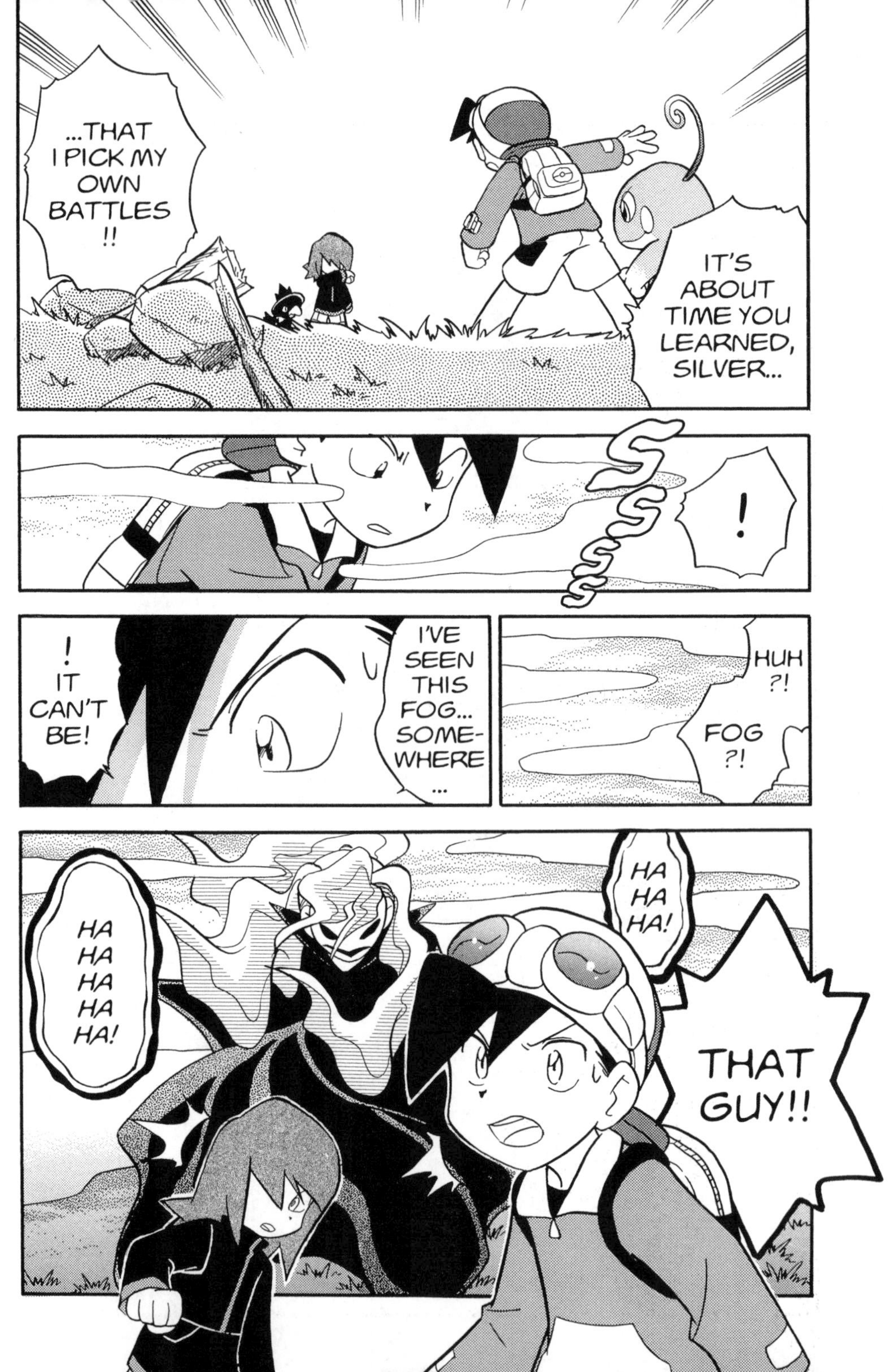

...THAT I PICK MY OWN BATTLES !!
IT'S ABOUT TIME YOU LEARNED, SILVER...
SSSSS
!
HUH ?!
FOG ?!
I'VE SEEN THIS FOG... SOME-WHERE ...
! IT CAN'T BE!
HA HA HA!
HA HA HA HA HA!
THAT GUY!!

LOOK WHO'S TALKING!
I THOUGHT YOU STAYED IN YOUR FOREST!

YOU TWO AGAIN...

I OWE YOU NO EXPLANATIONS.
WHH

YOU'RE RIGHT! LET'S JUST SETTLE THIS FIGHT!
GOLD! STOP MOVING AROUND OR YOU'LL PLAY RIGHT INTO HIS HANDS!

SSS...
...

WHAT AM I SUPPOSED TO DO, STAND STILL?!

DYNAMIC PUNCH!
CHOK
113
Delibird Delivery, Part 2
YES! IT CONNECT-ED!!
WE REALLY ARE STRONGER !!
THIS TIME I'M NOT GONNA ...
SH
HUH ?
TING
YOUR HAND'S FROZEN ?!

WOOOO
HAHAHA... THAT'S WHAT YOU CALL STRONGER?
!
SHOOT...
MMG
VSH
YOU'LL REGRET THAT!!
KINGDRA!
TM
WMP
TWISTER!!
!
HWAAH
BUTT OUTTA THIS!
I OWE THIS CREEP BIG-TIME AND I'M GONNA—
SHUT UP! LOOK AROUND YOU!

!
ICE THORNS?! BUT HOW–?!

...
GULP
IF YOU'D CHARGED, YOU'D BE HASH NOW.

OH, I GET IT... HIDDEN BY THE FOG.

PRRRRT
...! PRO-FESSOR ELM?!

PEEP
Professor Elm
GOLD, IS THAT YOU?!
I'M SO GLAD I CAUGHT YOU!

I'VE COMPLETED MY ANALYSIS OF THAT GOLD POWDER.
I ALMOST CAN'T BRING MYSELF TO BELIEVE IT...

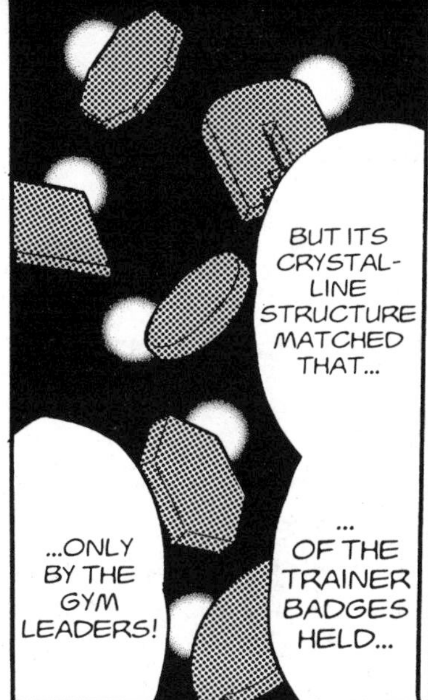
BUT ITS CRYSTAL-LINE STRUCTURE MATCHED THAT...
... OF THE TRAINER BADGES HELD...
...ONLY BY THE GYM LEADERS!

THE MASKED MAN YOU FOUGHT IN ILEX FOREST MAY BE A FORMER GYM LEADER! BUT WE DON'T KNOW WHICH ONE!
IT'S HARD TO IMAGINE A MORE DANGEROUS OPPONENT THAN A GYM LEADER!

BUT KNOWING YOU, YOU'LL RUSH RIGHT INTO COMBAT WITH HIM!
NO MATTER WHAT... DON'T FIGHT HIM!

DO YOU UNDER-STAND, GOLD?
PIP!
BZZ
BZZ
...

THANKS FOR THE WARNING, PROFES-SOR....
HMF

...BUT IT CAME A LITTLE TOO LATE.
HOOO...

LOOKS LIKE WE'VE GOT A REAL FIGHT ON OUR HANDS.

I THINK I SAID THAT AL-READY.
OH, SHUT UP!

I'M TIRED OF YOU PESTS ...
S...
... BUZZING ME!

BLIZZARD !!
HOO
!!

!!
JAB
... SILVER.
YOU CAN'T RUN AWAY LIKE LAST TIME ...
HSH
SNEASEL !!

SILVER?!

WHAT'S GOING ON?!

WAFT

VRR
WKWKWK
THAT'S THE TARGET!
!!
GAH!
WHAT ...?!
SILVER !!
UGH!
WOK
WD
FOOLED YOU!
NN...
FMP

IT'S BEEN FIVE YEARS, SILVER.
HOW PERFECT THAT YOU'D BE THE ONE FOLLOWING ME.

NNG...
THEY... KNOW EACH OTHER ...?

WHAT ARE YOU THINKING OF?
RE-VENGE?

PER-HAPS ...

HEY, HEY! WHAT'S ALL THIS ABOUT?

NINE YEARS AGO, I SEARCHED THE LAND FOR CHILDREN WITH HIGH TRAINER POTENTIAL ...
...AND KID-NAPPED THEM.

YOU WERE KIDNAPPING KIDS?! FOR WHAT?!
WHAT ELSE? TO USE AS MY SLAVES.

WHY WAS THE ONCE POWERFUL TEAM ROCKET DE-STROYED?
BECAUSE OF DISSENSION WITHIN ITS RANKS.
POWER REQUIRES OBEDIENCE! SERVANTS AS UN-THINKING AS THOSE GYARADOS!

CHILDREN CAN BE MOLDED INTO PERFECT SLAVES IF YOU TEACH THEM EARLY ENOUGH.
WOO...
JUST LIKE A GYARA-DOS, TRAINED FROM WHEN IT'S A MAGI-KARP.
WAHA-HAHA HAHA-HA!

KRG
YOU... ARE GONNA PAY...

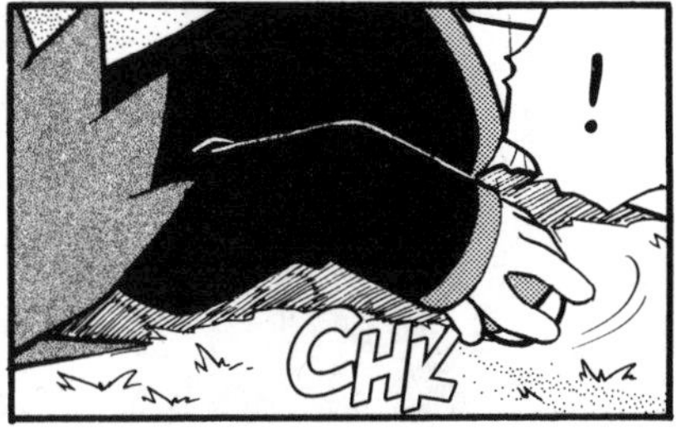
!
CHK

GLINT
DON'T DO ANY-THING RASH, SILVER!

HMF

NOT UNLESS YOU WANT SOMETHING TO HAPPEN TO HIM.

HEHEHEH... AS I THOUGHT.
YOU'VE GONE WEAK, SILVER.
IF YOU'D STAYED UNDER ME...
YOU'D HAVE BECOME THE PERFECT TRAINER, FREE OF ALL WEAKNESSES... INCLUDING COMPASSION.
NNG...

YOU'RE WRONG !!
WHAT?

OH?

YOU THINK SILVER'S WEAK?
THEN YOU DON'T KNOW WHAT STRENGTH IS!

VWSH
ZZZKASH
I'VE SEEN HIS STRENGTH OVER AND OVER AGAIN!
AND IT'S A STRENGTH THAT GOES DEEP IN HIS SOUL!
EXACTLY THE STRENGTH A GREAT TRAINER NEEDS!
...
YOU'RE THE WEAK ONE... LEANING ON THOSE TEAM ROCKET MORONS!
RRK
YOU'RE A MOUTHY LITTLE ...
WATCH YOUR FEET, BUDDY!
WOK!!
SNEASEL !!
VSH
WHAT ?!

YOU'RE SMARTER THAN I THOUGHT.

I'M FINALLY PUTTING SOME PIECES TOGETHER!
LIKE HOW THIS CHUMP IS PULLING ALL THE STRINGS...

...AND HOW I'M GONNA HELP YOU BEAT HIM!
!

SAVE THE ARGU-MENTS.

... WHAT-EVER.

THIS GUY USES POKÉMON AND PEOPLE LIKE THINGS!
HE'S A DISGRACE TO EVERY TRAINER!!

LET'S SHUT HIM DOWN!!

EXBO!
SNEASEL!
HE-HEHEH...
I WARNED YOU AGAINST THIS...
...BUT I'M GLAD YOU DIDN'T LISTEN!
VWAH
!!
ZSH

114 Delibird Delivery, Part 2
FLAME WHEEL! ICY WIND!
A DARING COMBINATION. TOO BAD...
HEH
YEAH?
TP
INTER-ESTING.
HMM...
TP

...! THEY DISAP-PEARED?!
PF
...IT CAN'T LAST.
PF
HEY!
WK
I'M GONNA—
WK
UNGH!

VSH

QUICK ATTACK !!

KINNG

DG DG

GDDG

ROCK SMASH !!

OUT OF MY WAY, GOLD!!
WOM
NGH!
HEY!! WHAT—? ICE?!
FWAH
TINK

WSH

STOP!!

HEH. SO FEARLESS.

VM

MURKROW!! KNOCK THEM DOWN!!

TM

YOU'RE FILLED WITH SO MUCH COURAGE...

VK VK VK VK VK VK

...YOU'VE GOT NO ROOM FOR BRAINS!

AFTER ALL THIS TIME, STILL SO NAIVE...

I KNEW EXACTLY WHAT YOU WERE DOING.

...THAT YOU'D FALL FOR A TRICK LIKE THAT!

VP VP VP VP

WAM
!
YOU WANTED TO SEPARATE ME FROM GOLD.
VWOP
...I'LL FIGHT ANY-TIME... ANY-WHERE.
PEK PEK PEK
BUT AGAINST YOUR WICKED-NESS...
INCLUDING THE MIDDLE OF THIS LAKE...
...WHERE I JUST LED YOU !!
CHK

VOOOSH
!
THE GYARA-DOS—THAT I EVOLVED!!
HOOO
LOOKS LIKE I LEARNED SOME-THING FROM YOU AFTER ALL.
SNEER
AGH!!

YOU ...
I CAUGHT THE ONE YOU WERE USING AS A TRANS-MITTER.
THAT MEANS THEY'VE ALL BEEN FREED FROM YOUR CONTROL...
AND THEY'RE ANGRY!! **HYPER BEAM!!**
FSH

ZSSHSHHH
DMDMDM
OKAY! THAT MELTED THE ICE ON MY SHOES—BUT WE GOTTA DO SOMETHING ABOUT THESE TWO!
ZIP
AIBO, DO YOUR STUFF!
ZIP
ZIP
GRRRR
NOW—
GONK
DOUBLE TEAM!!
WUD
WE DID IT, AIBO!
SILVER!!
VZ
WHERE ARE YOU?!

!

HUH?! THE LAKE'S FROZEN ?!

WHERE'S SILVER ?!

AND WHERE'S THE MASKED GUY?!

!

C-FOOOM
!!
WHERE ARE YOU?!
SILVER !!
DM
YOUR TURN !!
DM
DM
DM
DM
DM
IF YOU'VE HURT HIM—!
AIBO !!
ZNK
NG ...
ZK
ZK
ZK

YOU...
HEH HEH. QUITE A LETDOWN AFTER ALL YOUR TALK.

HEH
NOT EVEN AS GOOD AS MY OLD SLAVE.

YOU DIDN'T HAVE TO DO THAT!
YOU'D ALREADY WON THAT BATTLE.
GRP
YOU... SCUM...

BE-SIDES...
BUT LIFE WILL BE SIMPLER WITHOUT HIM.
WAFT
PER-HAPS NOT.

HE RAN AWAY FROM ME.
FOR THAT, HE DESERVES TO BE PUNISHED.
"DESERVES" ?!
WHO ARE **YOU** TO SAY WHAT ANYBODY DESERVES ?!

HUH?
TPTPTP
CHU!
CHU!
PIKA!

WHAT'S THIS, PIKA?
PAT PAT
YOU FEELING SHY?
HEY, RED.
YO! YELLOW! LONG TIME NO SEE!

HAVE YOU TOLD HIM ABOUT WHAT'S IN YOUR HAT?
PSS PSS
NOT YET ...

UM... RED? WHAT HAPPENED WITH YOUR HAND ...?
OH. YOU SAW?
JUST THE GHOST OF AN OLD INJURY.
IT'S NOTHING.
SERIOUSLY! DON'T WORRY!

BUT IN THAT CONDITION... TOMORROW...
SHE'S RIGHT, RED. YOU SHOULD BE RESTING.

LOOK, GUYS. I APPRECIATE YOUR CONCERN, BUT...
THERE'S NO WAY.

BECAUSE TOMORROW'S EXAM DAY... FOR THE VIRIDIAN GYM LEADER.

115 Forretress of Solitude

NOW... LET'S KEEP TRAINING!!

HONESTLY, RED, I THINK YOU CAN EASE OFF.
RED

THIS'LL BE A PIECE O' CAKE IF THERE EVER WAS ONE.
THE POKÉMON ASSOCIATION KNOWS YOU INSIDE OUT.

YOU KNOW SOMETHING I DON'T?
I'VE JUST GOT FAITH IN YOU, IS ALL!
DINGDONG
MORE VISITORS?

YEAH ...?
HOW YOU DOIN', RED?
KRIII

MISTY! BROCK!
HERE'S THE VIDEO I PROMISED OF MY GYM LEADER EXAM! PLUS NOTES!
AND HERE'S MINE!

THANK YOU! THESE'LL HELP A TON!!
TO-MORROW, HUH? FINALLY!
DO YOU HAVE A PLAN OF ATTACK?

YOU'RE A SHOO-IN NO MATTER WHAT.
GOOD LUCK ANY-HOW!

... VERY FUNNY.
GUTS &
WILL!

MY POKÉ-MON ARE READY ...
AND I'VE MEMO-RIZED EVERY ATTACK.
IT'D BE A SURE THING ...

Charizard.
I CAN'T HELP BEING NERVOUS ...

I NEED A PLAN OF ATTACK.
BUT ALSO... A BACKUP PLAN IF I GO NUMB DURING THE FIGHT.

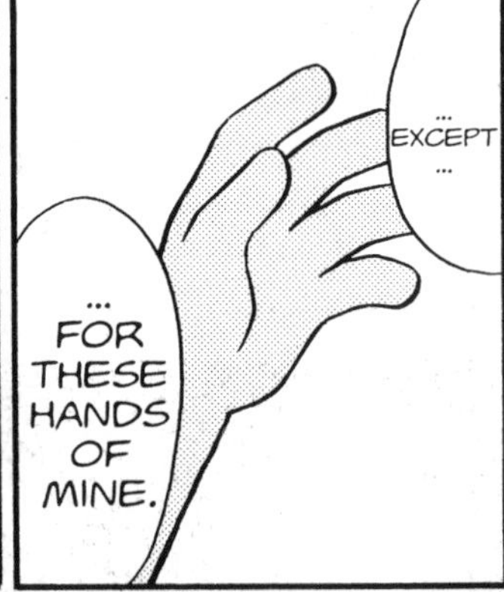
... EXCEPT ...
... FOR THESE HANDS OF MINE.

VIRIDIAN GYM
DAY OF BATTLE

I SHALL READ THE RULES OF THE EXAM.
THE CANDIDATE MUST DEFEAT SIX POKÉMON. THOSE POKÉMON WILL HAVE NO TRAINERS.
YADA
YADA
YADA
THEY WILL BATTLE ON THEIR OWN INITIATIVE.
THE CANDIDATE IS ALLOWED SIX POKÉMON OF HIS OWN. BUT...

...IF EVEN ONE OF THEM IS INCAPACI-TATED, THE CANDIDATE IS DIS-QUALIFIED.
B-BOM
BOMB
OM
PLACE YOUR POKÉMON IN THE POKÉ BALLS, PLEASE.

GG
...

THE EXAM WILL NOW...
... BEGIN !!
VSH
BOOM
LEADING WITH A PINECO, EH?
OKAY ...
BOOM
IT'S ALL YOURS, VENU-SAUR!

BOOM
NOW A FORRE-TRESS!
WHPP
VINE WHIP!
WHPP
AGAIN !!
OOO
OR... MAKE THAT THREE...
HE'S ALREADY THROUGH TWO!!
HERE COMES NUMBER FOUR.
KEEP UP THE PACE!
GOMP

ANOTHER FORRETRESS—AND IT'S UNLEASHED SPIKES!!
BOM
SHM
SHM
SHM
!!
NOW RETURN!
SNOR! **BELLY DRUM**!!
BOM
FUAAA
SAUR—SWEET SCENT!
SNORLAX IS NO BETTER AGAINST SPIKES THAN VENUSAUR!
WHAT'S HE PLAN-NING?
BIDDYBOM
BIDDYBOM
WHAT'S HE UP TO?

VOP VIP
YELLOW! DOESN'T BELLY DRUM TURN PHYSICAL STRENGTH INTO ATTACK STRENGTH? SO...
BM

YES! IT POUND-ED THE GROUND ...
VSH
HWRRR
...AND SENT THE SPIKES FLYING STRAIGHT AT ITS OPPONENT!!

NOW—MEGA PUNCH!!
POW!

SO THAT'S WHY HE SLOWED IT DOWN WITH SWEET SCENT!
OOOO
AMAZING! FOUR OPPONENTS ARE DOWN!!

BOOM
NOW IT'S AZUMARILL... WITH ITS WHIRLPOOL!!
WOOOO
WOOOO
SHOOT... CAN'T SWAP OUT WHILE I'M CAUGHT IN THIS!

MEGA KICK!!
SO QUICK!!
GOOD JOB, SNOR!!
BON
FAP
RETURN!!
BOM
OKAY, VEE... IT'S DOWN TO YOU!
BOM
FINAL OPPO-NENT... PORY-GON2!
SNAP
?!

THEY'VE LOCKED ON!

AND HERE COMES THE ZAP CANNON!

STORE POWER—
GLEEM
WITH MORNING SUN!!
NOW—
ZING
PSYCHIC!
FINISH IT!!
PORY-GON2 IS DOWN!!
PHEW
THE EXAM'S OVER!
BRRRR
...
GRIP

CONGRAT-ULATIONS, RED. FROM THIS DAY FORWARD ...
...YOU ARE THE LEADER OF THE VIRIDIAN GYM!
THANK YOU... BUT I'M SORRY. I'LL HAVE TO DECLINE.

WHAT ?!
IT TOOK ME LONGER TO WIN THAN I EXPECT-ED...
...AND RIGHT NOW, TO BE HONEST, I'M BARELY STAND-ING.
I'VE WANTED TO BE A GYM LEADER FOR SO LONG THAT I IGNORED ALL MY OWN DOUBTS.
BUT TO TAKE THE JOB IN MY CONDI-TION WOULD BE... IRRE-SPON-SIBLE.

SO WHO'S GONNA PROTECT THE GYM?
GRUMBLE GRUMBLE
WE STILL HAVE A LEADERLESS GYM?!
I'LL TAKE THE JOB.

I'LL EVEN TAKE THE EXAM... IF YOU INSIST.

YOU'RE BACK?!

BLUE!!

BLUE?!

TM TM TM

WHO ARE YOU?!

ARGH!

THROB

GRAB

...

!

DOMM

116 Rock, Paper... Scizor

D-D...DM
WHAT WAS THAT?!
EARTH-QUAKE!!

HEY! YOU!!
VM

!!

EVERY-ONE, REMAIN CALM!!
CALM !!

STOP RED! HE'S IN NO CONDI-TION TO FIGHT!
VM
O-OKAY!

D-D-M..M

!
WILD POKÉ-MON?!
BUT WHY?!
HERE THEY COME!
NO TIME TO EVACUATE THE GYM! RED—PROTECT THE ENTRANCE!!
GOT IT!
RRAR
POOM
SCIZOR! METAL CLAW!!
VTTIN

GO!
WOK
FAST— AS USUAL!!
!
EXEGGUTOR'S OLD TRICK— INTIMIDATING THE ENEMY WITH ITS THREE HEADS!!
OKAY, THEN!
HMF

EEP
VWM
EXEGGUTOR'S AFRAID! BUT OF WHAT?!

WOK
FALSE SWIPE!
GOOD!
THWAP
YEAH !!
BON
B-B-BON

LIKE NO ONE BUT PROFESSOR OAK'S GRANDSON COULD!!

YOU DID IT, BLUE!!

UM... NOT TO MENTION ...

THE PRO-FESSOR'S... GRAND-SON?!

THAT WAS THE "POKÉMON MARCH."
WHOSE CAR IS THIS?
IT'S TH-TH-THE COMMITTEE CAR. IS SOME-THING...?

YOU FOOL! WILD POKÉMON LOVE THAT SONG! NO WONDER THEY WERE SWARMING!
YOUR STUPID SONG COULD HAVE BEEN A CATAS-TROPHE!
I-I'M SO SORRY... I...I DIDN'T REALIZE...

MR. DIREC-TOR.
WHAT?! WHAT?! WHAT?!
IF YOU DECIDE I'M NOT QUALIFIED, FINE.
BUT IF YOU WANT PEOPLE TO KEEP TRUSTING YOU...
YOU'D BETTER FIND SOMEBODY AS GOOD AS RED. AND QUICK.

Y...YOU THINK...?

I FOUND THAT INFO YOU WERE LOOKING FOR.
!

FWA
RED!

BLUE ...

ASK MY SISTER FOR MORE DETAILS.

MAKE THE ANNOUNCE-MENT! WE HAVE FOUND A NEW LEADER FOR THE VIRIDIAN CITY GYM!
WHAT?! BUT WHAT ABOUT THE COMMITTEE'S APPROVAL?! AND THE EXAM?!

IT'LL BE FINE.
HE ALREADY FIXED ONE OF OUR MISTAKES.
LET'S NOT ADD ANOTHER ONE.

WHAT WILL AN EXAM SHOW? WE KNOW HE HAS SKILL, LEADER-SHIP ABILITY ...
...AND MOST IMPORTANT OF ALL... PLENTY OF LOCAL RESPECT!
GO!
B-BUT...

TUG
OKAY.
RED!
RED?
RED
YOU'RE HEADING OUT ALREADY?
YEAH. I CAN'T WAIT.
I FINALLY HAVE THE INFO I NEEDED...
...ON HOW TO HEAL MYSELF!
YOU MEAN... HIS HANDS AND FEET CAN BE FIXED?!
SOUNDS LIKE IT!

THERE'S THIS SECRET HOT SPRING ON MT. SILVER...
...WHERE POKÉMON GO TO HEAL THEIR WOUNDS.
SEEMS SABRINA'S UP THERE. SIMILAR SYMPTOMS ...
... AFTER SUFFERING THE SAME ATTACK.
I CAN'T BELIEVE IT! AFTER A WHOLE YEAR OF TRYING TO GET WELL!
EX-CEPT ...
?
THERE ARE A LOT OF POWERFUL POKÉMON ON THAT MOUNTAIN.
TO GET THIS CURE... HE'S REALLY GOING TO HAVE TO WANT IT.
OKAY, CHARIZARD! LET'S GO!
BOOM

PIKA, YOU WAIT FOR ME AT YELLOW AND CHUCHU'S PLACE.
!
LOOK AFTER PIKA, YELLOW!
YOU'RE SURE ...?
SORRY, PIKA. I DON'T WANT TO BE BLAMING MYSELF FOR ANYTHING HAPPENING TO YOU.
GUIDE HIM SAFELY, CHARI-ZARD.
WE'RE OFF—TO MT. SILVER!!
WWWSH
...

DO YOU WANT TO COME WITH ME?
I WANT TO INVESTIGATE THAT HUGE POKÉMON THAT VANISHED TO THE WEST.
HEY, PIKA.
I'VE DECIDED TO GO WITH THE FISHERMAN TO JOHTO.
SOUNDS LIKE YES!
CHU!
PIKA!
WE'RE OFF TO JOHTO!!
SO COME ON, YOU TWO!!
TO BE CONTINUED

ROUTE ADVENTURE MAP 9

FROM ILEX FOREST TO MAHOGANY AND THE LAKE OF RAGE! (WITH A LOOK AT THE VETERAN TRAINERS' MOVEMENTS TOO!)

"GOTTA CATCH 'EM ALL!!"

ROUTE 9 ADVENTURE MAP

POKÉMON -YELLOW-

POKÉDEX	
008	------------
009	------------
010	**CATERPIE**
011	**METAPOD**
▶ 012	**BUTTERFREE**
013	------------
014	------------
015	**BEEDRILL**
016	------------
017	------------
018	**PIDGEOT**
019	**RATTATA**

TRAINER: YELLOW
BADGES: 0
POKÉDEX: 14 POKÉMON

NUMBER SEEN
81
NUMBER CAUGHT
14

YELLOW'S POKÉDEX

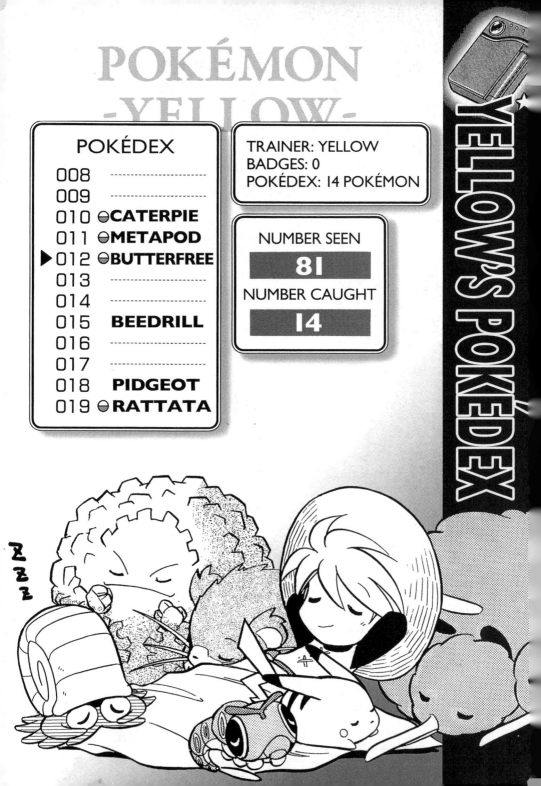

PIKACHU: L71
Type 1 / Electric
Trainer / Red
NO. 025

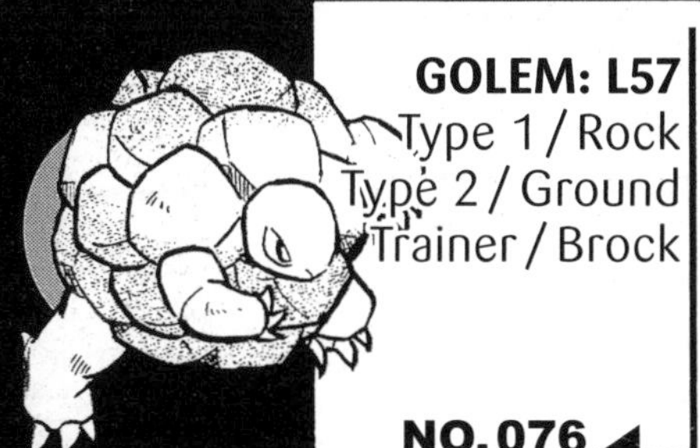

GOLEM: L57
Type 1 / Rock
Type 2 / Ground
Trainer / Brock
NO. 076

RATICATE: L64
Type 1 / Normal
Trainer / Yellow
NO. 020

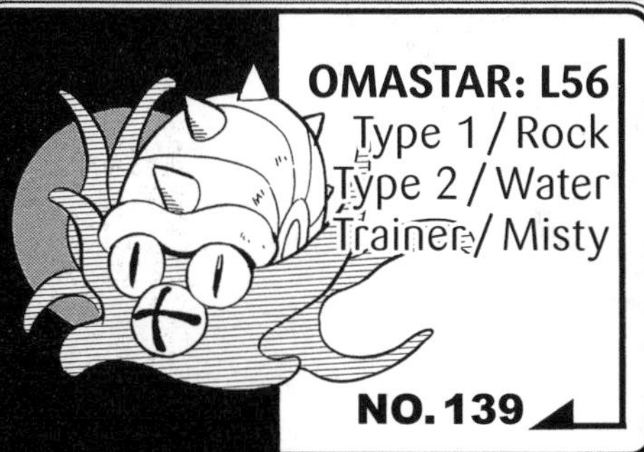

OMASTAR: L56
Type 1 / Rock
Type 2 / Water
Trainer / Misty
NO. 139

DODRIO: L62
Type 1 / Normal
Type 2 / Flying
Trainer / Yellow
NO. 085

BUTTERFREE:
L60
Type 1 / Bug
Type 2 / Flying
Trainer / Yellow
NO. 012

▶ SEE DATA

CRY

SEE ASSIGNMENT

QUIT

POKEMON
-YELLOW-

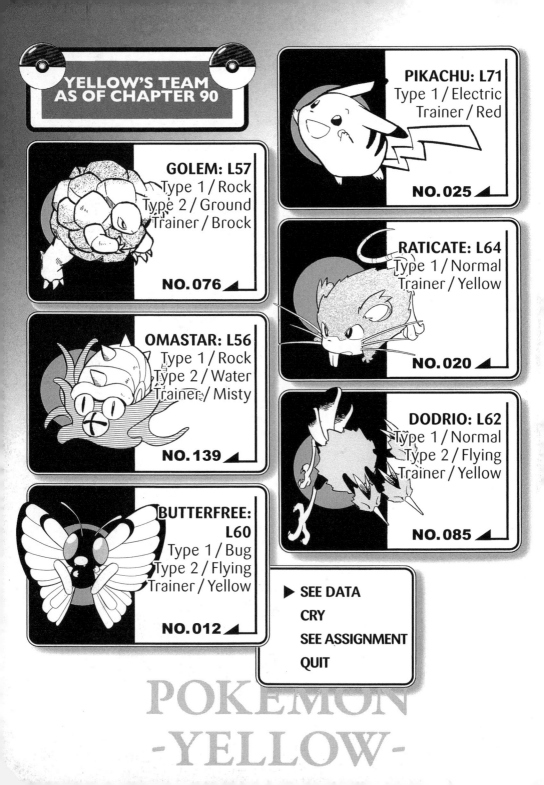

POKÉDEX SECRETS

○ GOLD TEAM ○

POKÉDEX

▶155	CYNDAQUIL
156	-------------
157	-------------
158	TOTODILE
159	CROCONAW
160	-------------
016	PIDGEY
017	PIDGEOTTO
018	PIDGEOT

TRAINER: GOLD
BADGES: 0
POKÉDEX: 6 POKÉMON

NUMBER SEEN
35

NUMBER CAUGHT
6

Uses Pokédex mainly during battle. Catch number has not increased.

Gold's Team

Although all his Pokémon are at low levels, they've kept going on brains and determination.

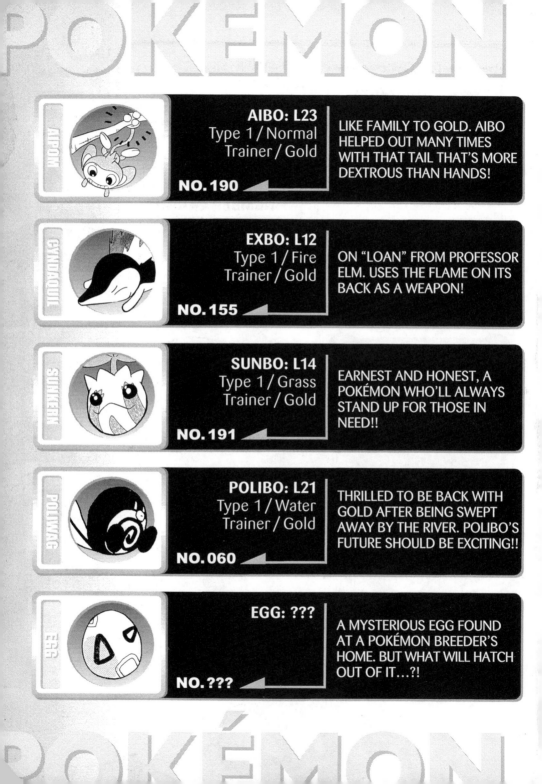

POKEMON

AIBO: L23
Type 1 / Normal
Trainer / Gold

NO. 190

LIKE FAMILY TO GOLD. AIBO HELPED OUT MANY TIMES WITH THAT TAIL THAT'S MORE DEXTROUS THAN HANDS!

EXBO: L12
Type 1 / Fire
Trainer / Gold

NO. 155

ON "LOAN" FROM PROFESSOR ELM. USES THE FLAME ON ITS BACK AS A WEAPON!

SUNBO: L14
Type 1 / Grass
Trainer / Gold

NO. 191

EARNEST AND HONEST, A POKÉMON WHO'LL ALWAYS STAND UP FOR THOSE IN NEED!!

POLIBO: L21
Type 1 / Water
Trainer / Gold

NO. 060

THRILLED TO BE BACK WITH GOLD AFTER BEING SWEPT AWAY BY THE RIVER. POLIBO'S FUTURE SHOULD BE EXCITING!!

EGG: ???

NO. ???

A MYSTERIOUS EGG FOUND AT A POKÉMON BREEDER'S HOME. BUT WHAT WILL HATCH OUT OF IT...?!

POKÉMON

SILVER'S SECRETS!
POKÉDEX
152 CHIKORITA
153 -------------
154 -------------
155 CYNDAQUIL
156 QUILAVA
157 -------------
158 TOTODILE
159 CROCONAW
160 -------------
TRAINER: SILVER
BADGES: 4
POKÉDEX: 10 POKÉMON
NUMBER SEEN
54
NUMBER CAUGHT
10
Silver is always seeking Pokémon who'll help him fulfill his objective!
The Team Thus Far:
Seems to favor Dark types. An attack-oriented team.
TEAM SILVER

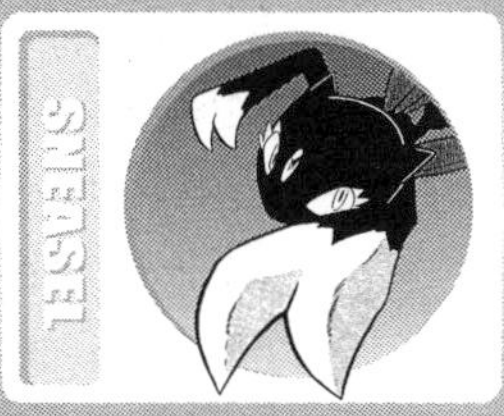

SNEASEL: L36
Type 1 / Dark
Type 2 / Ice
Trainer / Silver
NO. 215

THE TEAM LEADER! BEATS OPPONENTS WITH SHARP CLAWS, SHARP WITS AND FAST MOVES!

MURKROW: L29
Type 1 / Dark
Type 2 / Flying
Trainer / Silver
NO. 198

LOOKS LIKE THE WINGS OF DARKNESS AS IT CARRIES SILVER—AND GIVES HIM A BIG ADVANTAGE IN NIGHT BATTLES!

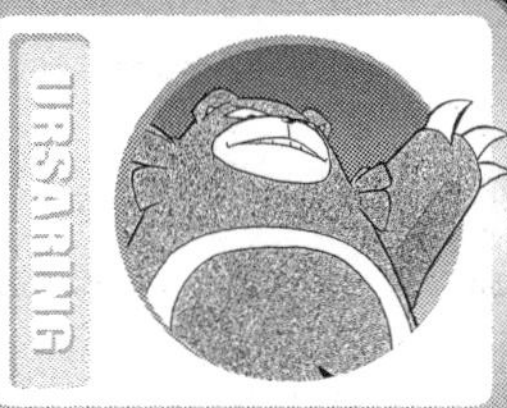

URSARING: L35
Type 1 / Normal
Trainer / Silver
NO. 217

THE HEAVIEST MEMBER OF THE TEAM, CAUGHT USING A HEAVY BALL—AND A HEAVY-DUTY FIGHTER!

CROCONAW: L29
Type 1 / Water
Trainer / Silver
NO. 159

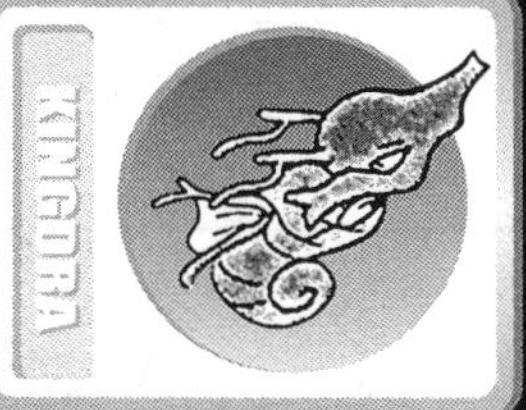

KINGDRA: L33
Type 1 / Water
Type 2 / Dragon
Trainer / Silver
NO. 230

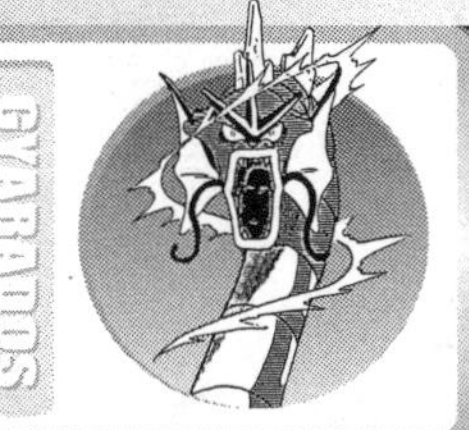

GYARADOS: L30
Type 1 / Water
Type 2 / Flying
Trainer / Silver
NO. 130

Croconaw evolved from the Totodile that Silver stole from Professor Elm's lab. Kingdra evolved during a trade with Gold. A rare red Gyarados appears. Why does he want three Water types? And who did he borrow Tyranitar from? There's a hint in the Poké Ball it came out of...

TYRANITAR NO. 248

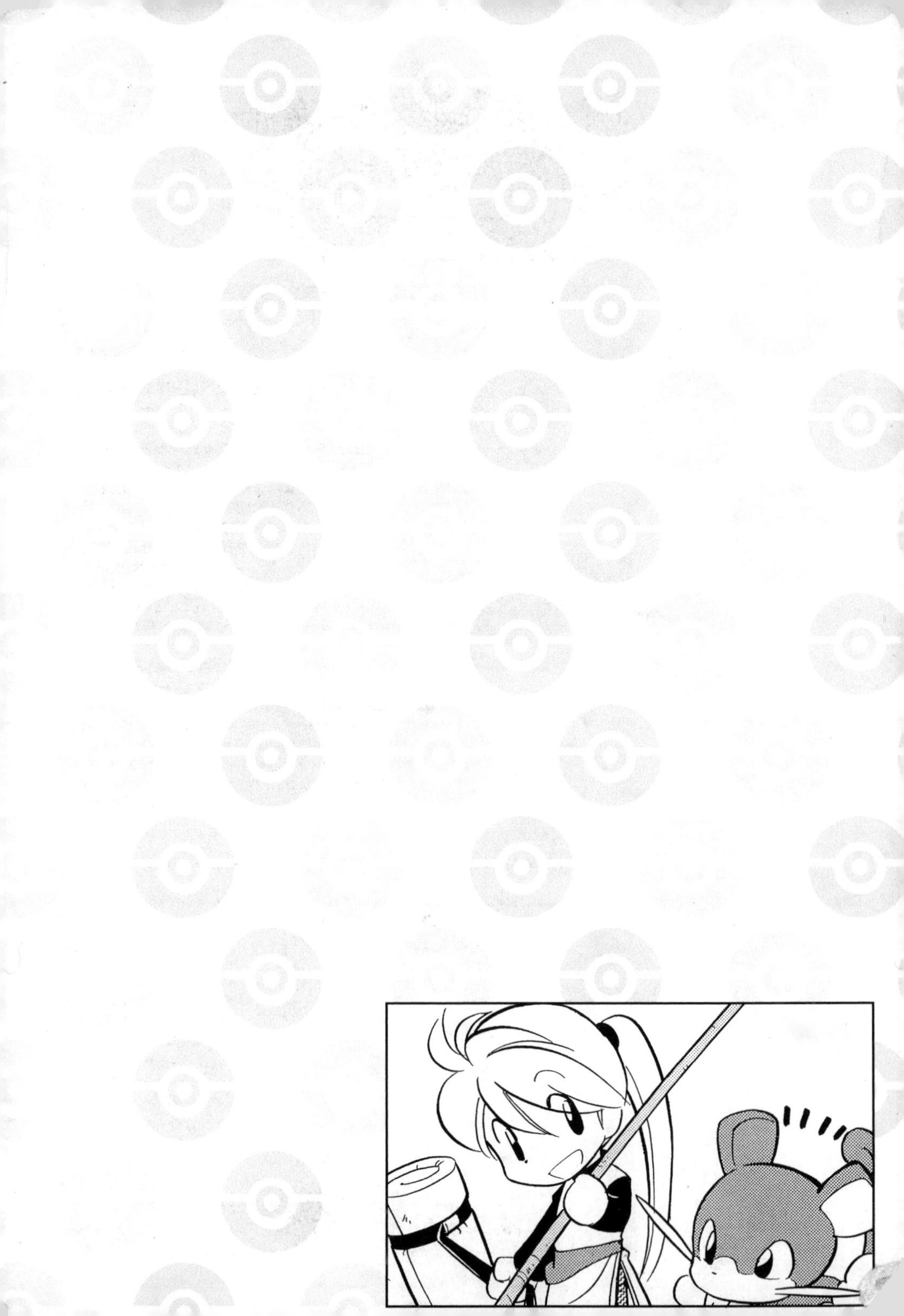